E. D. Michael

Shadow of the Alleghenies

Shadow of the Alleghenies

The Wilderness Adventures of a Frontiersman and his Wolf Pup

Edwin Daryl Michael

quarrier press

Charleston, West Virginia

Quarrier Press
Charleston, WV

First Edition

10 9 8 7 6 5 4 3 2 1

Printed in the United States of America

Library of Congress Control Number: 2009933037

ISBN-13: 978-1891852-65-7
ISBN: 1-891852-65-5

Book and cover design: Mark S. Phillips
Front cover : Erin Turner

Distributed by:

West Virginia Book Company
1125 Central Avenue
Charleston, WV 25302
www.wvbookco.com

CONTENTS

DEDICATION

THIS BOOK IS DEDICATED to my brother, Roger Gerald Michael (1943-2009), who enjoyed and appreciated the great out-of-doors as much as I do. He would have been an ideal partner for anyone attempting to survive the challenges presented by the Appalachian frontier and experiencing the adventures described herein. May his spirit ever roam the West Virginia hills. I will forever miss him and sadly regret he was never able to read this novel.

ACKNOWLEDGMENTS

THE AUTHOR IS INDEBTED to many individuals who made this book possible. Frank Jernejcic provided maps of the Monongahela River and offered ideas regarding its character as a free-flowing, undammed river in the 1700s. Numerous persons graciously reviewed early drafts and provided constructive comments, including: Julie Dzaack, Erin Dzaack, Ann Hutchison, Norm Julian, Martha Michael, Charles Segelquist, and Scott Shalaway.

I will forever be indebted to my wife, Jane, who painstakingly edited every word and every sentence of the preliminary manuscript, often at the expense of her own personal projects. Without her advice, assistance, and encouragement the book would never have come to fruition. I would be remiss not to acknowledge the many Scotsmen and Scotswomen, including my wife's Callander ancestors, who roamed the Scottish Highlands and settled the Appalachian Mountains.

FOREWORD

ANYONE CAN WRITE ABOUT nature, and many people do. Many keep personal journals that describe their observations and experiences afield. But only a field biologist with a keen sense of man's role in the natural world can write a natural history that uses an historical narrative to tell a nature story. Ed Michael is one such man.

When I read Ed's first book, a historical novel entitled *A Valley Called Canaan: 1885-2002*, I knew I'd learn about the history of one of West Virginia's most beautiful places, but I wasn't prepared for a story whose central characters were snapping turtles. Only a biologist would attempt such as tale, and Ed Michael is one of the few who could pull it off.

When I received a manuscript of *Shadow of the Alleghenies*, I knew it would be a both a natural and cultural history of man and beast. The cast of characters includes Native Americans, pioneers, explorers, soldiers, wolves, deer, trout, and passenger pigeons. Again, only a biologist with an understanding of the history and culture of the region could pull this off. In fact, I doubt anyone else would dare try. This is a book that deserves to be in libraries throughout Appalachia.

It's funny how lives can converge, diverge, and later intersect. I first came to know Dr. Michael as I was finishing my undergraduate degree at the University of Delaware. I was looking for a graduate program in wildlife ecology, and Dr. Michael's research at West Virginia University tempted me. Instead, I succumbed to wanderlust and headed west to Northern Arizona University in Flagstaff.

Years later, after a stint in academia at Oklahoma State University and the University of Oklahoma Biological Station, I moved to

PROLOGUE

THE EARLY 1700s WERE an exciting time in the American Colonies. The coasts were alive with endless activity as ships arrived weekly from Europe. Seaports grew rapidly as ocean-going ships demanded bigger and better facilities for handling the cargoes moving between England and the colonies.

The entire Atlantic seaboard was bustling with commerce as new settlers arrived with their families and high expectations. Word of the great opportunities awaiting those who braved the dangerous Atlantic crossing had spread throughout the British Isles and Western Europe. Awaiting them were rich farmlands, immense forests, coastal bays with great quantities of seafood, and wildlife in unlimited numbers. The sea and the land would provide boundless sources of food to those who were not afraid to work.

As the seaboard cities became firmly entrenched, the eighteenth century saw settlers pushing westward. The Potomac River provided a major travel route for explorers, traders, and trappers to move into the great valleys of western Virginia. When word of the riches along the Potomac and Shenandoah Rivers, and later the Ohio River, reached the seaboard cities, settlers began the western migration that would eventually be stopped only by the Pacific Ocean. Once the attractive flatlands of central Pennsylvania and the rich bottomlands of the major valleys were settled, further settlement west was delayed by the long chain of mountains that extended from New York to Virginia. But the Alleghenies, a part of the larger Appalachian Mountains, posed only a minor barrier for the real frontiersmen, who were always eager to discover what lay on the other side of every mountain they faced. In a short time, travel routes through the mountains were discovered and settlers pushed on into western Pennsylvania and what is now West Virginia. Some crossed the mountains of southern Virginia and reached the headwaters of the Kanawha and New Rivers, while others crossed the mountains of Pennsylvania and reached the Monongahela River. All three rivers flowed into the Ohio, the major water route that would eventually carry tens of thousands of travelers to the Mississippi River.

The wilderness served as the master architect of the settlement of Appalachian. The harsh, unforgiving environment produced strong individuals and even stronger societies. It eliminated, often ruthlessly, many who could not adapt. Those who possessed the skills, senses, and physical attributes essential to survival became the individuals succeeding on the frontier.

One of the explorers who reached the headwaters of the Monongahela River, in what was then western Virginia, was a Scotsman named Angus McCallander (a fictional composite of several individuals, including Meshach Browning, George Croghan, Christopher Gist, John and Samuel Pringle, Lewis Wetzel, and Jonathan and Silas Zane). In the rugged Appalachians, the Shawnee, Iroquois, and Cherokee welcomed those first traders bearing goods that the Indians thought they needed. Items made of iron were in great demand by the Indians, from awls to needles, kettles to skillets, knives to axes, but most especially firearms. Deer hides and beaver pelts were prized in European cities, and the Appalachian wilderness yielded countless numbers of these and other furs.

Angus McCallander was a husky, young Scotsman who spent several years trapping and trading in the Appalachian Mountains; most of that time was spent in and around the watershed of the river named "Monongahela" by the Indians. McCallander lived with the Shawnee for several winters, providing them with European goods in return for piles of animal hides and furs. Tales of the tall red-haired Scotsman and the large gray wolf that was his constant companion were carried from campfire to campfire. The exploits of man and wolf were so embellished that fact and fiction melded smoothly into folklore. All the tales centered around the man's extraordinary ability to communicate with animals, especially his huge wolf. Word-of-mouth tales, passed throughout the mountains, grew with a life of their own. How much was truth and how much was frontier exaggeration will never be known. The adventures that follow cover one brief period in the life of the mysterious Scotsman named Angus McCallander.

CHAPTER ONE
THE SHAWNEE

THE TALL, IMPOSING TRAPPER was desperate to move his load of furs down the west fork of the Monongahela River to the trading post at the Forks of the Ohio (present day site of Pittsburgh). The winter spent with the Shawnee had been most productive and, at last count, his impressive piles of hides and pelts numbered more than three hundred. While most were deer hides, the soft, shiny pelts of beaver, silken skins of river otter, and heavy hides of elk and bear added considerably to the mass. English fur buyers referred to such an assortment of animal skins as peltry.

The Scotsman, christened Angus McCallander twenty years earlier, had few options. He had originally planned to haul his furs by horseback, following the same meandering trail along the Monongahela that had brought him to the headwaters of this mountain river. But the death of his only horse had crushed that plan, and the Shawnee had no extra horses. This small band had only one horse—an old swayback that could barely drag firewood into their camp, let alone haul over five hundred pounds of furs through 130 miles of wilderness forest.

Angus considered leaving the furs in the Shawnee camp while he returned on foot to one of the trading posts along the Potomac River to obtain two or three packhorses. Unfortunately, he had no gold or other goods to trade, and he could not haul enough furs on his back to exchange for horses. Even if he could hike out of the wilderness to get horses, summer would arrive by the time he returned to the Shawnee camp, and the fur buyers would have closed their trading posts for the year.

Angus had arrived at the Shawnee camp the previous October with a black mare named Night Sky, purchased in the Lancaster settlement of central Pennsylvania. The pack baskets slung over her back had protected the assortment of trade goods that he would trade for furs. Steel needles, sewing awls, and fishhooks occupied space inside three sizes of iron kettles. Merchants in Lancaster had shown him how to save space by nesting his kettles. Knives, files, and axe heads were wrapped in bright cloth and carefully packed inside the smallest kettles. Angus was unable to carry much on his single horse, and soon after arriving in the Shawnee camp his entire supply of trade goods was exchanged for several prime deerskins and bearskins.

This particular clan of Shawnee had previously been part of a large village of a thousand Indians along the North Branch of the Potomac River—a location known as Shawaneese Oldtown. Following several attacks by the Catawba Indians, and the intrusion of white settlers in the region, Chief Tall Turtle and many of his followers moved to the headwaters of the Monongahela River. Although the Shawnee were eager for trade goods, especially iron kettles and axes, the Chief did not want his people to become dependent on European goods.

The Shawnee were primarily hunters, but were also productive farmers. To clear land for crops they first chose a patch of rich bottomland, and then removed a ring of bark from each tree. The trees died in one to two years, after which the Shawnee built fires around the base of each to accelerate the tree's fall and thereby harvest firewood. Some trees fell that same year, while others remained standing for several years. Corn was their most important crop, and their cornfields had presented a strange sight to Angus when he first arrived at the Shawnee camp. Stumps, fallen trees, and standing trees co-mingled with tall, golden-brown cornstalks. Adding to the strange scene were squash vines scattered throughout the field, and bean plants climbing up cornstalks. Never had he seen such a mélange of growth!

Deer were so plentiful and the Indians so skilled with a bow that they readily accumulated piles of deerskins. In contrast, beaver and river otter were difficult to collect. Angus, however, could readily trap these wary furbearers. The Indians did not begrudge him the opportunity, so long as he was willing to provide them trade goods for their deerskins.

Angus reflected on the circumstances that left him stranded. Deep snows would have kept him from departing the Shawnee camp before the end of March, so his plans were to load his furs onto Night Sky and reach the trading post no later than the end of April. Those plans, however, came to an abrupt halt in early January as he and Night Sky returned from checking traps.

It had been a long but productive day; his traps held two beaver and one river otter. As he was checking the last trap the wind became violent, the temperature dropped drastically, and a full-scale blizzard hit with an intensity that filled Angus with fear. Visibility dropped to nearly zero. He was confident the black mare could easily find her way back to the Shawnee Camp, even though the wind was to their backs and she could not pick up the scents drifting from the campfires. Angus dropped the reins loosely on the mare's neck and with a gentle kick of his padded moccasins urged her in the direction of camp. The horse slowly picked her way around the hillside and through the giant trees that dominated the Appalachian landscape. Angus surrendered to the biting wind as he huddled in the saddle with the beaver and otter pelts tied across his lap.

Ahead of him huge boulders were scattered over the forest floor—boulders that eons ago had come crashing down the hillside to rest in a random and treacherous pattern. As the black mare carried Angus toward the huge boulders, he was reminded of the rocky crags throughout the Scottish Highlands of his youth. He recalled many happy days hunting red deer throughout the Highlands, and the massive boulders comforted him. Unbeknownst to Angus, the boulders provided an ideal hunting spot for the numerous mountain lions that frequented the West Fork River drainage. From any one of numerous vantage points, they could ambush an unsuspecting elk or deer. These powerful meat eaters, called panthers by most of the hunters in Pennsylvania, needed at least one deer a week to provide the energy essential for surviving the long, cold Appalachian winters.

One particular mountain lion that frequented the boulders was an adult male. He was nearly fifteen years old and past his prime. His fang-like teeth were not nearly so pointed as when he had been the most efficient carnivore in the forest, and his claws were no longer dagger sharp. Yet he was still a killer, capable of bringing down a white-tailed deer, or even a small elk. Although the cat had been downwind of Angus and Night Sky, the wind gusted so violently that the cat did not detect the human scent. It was overshadowed by the scent of fresh blood on the beaver and otter pelts and the somewhat familiar horse scent.

The big tawny predator routinely sat in a rhododendron thicket high on the hillside above the Shawnee camp. On several occasions, he had carefully studied Night Sky, but the black mare's size had been a deterrent to attack. Like most predators, the mountain lion had learned to select small prey, and a small meal, rather than risk injury attacking a larger animal. As a younger cat, he had successfully killed several full-grown elk, but now in old age he was no longer tempted to attack a horse or elk.

Perched on a boulder that towered above the rhododendron thicket, the cat did not identify the horse's silhouette and certainly did not see the human hunkered down under the snow-covered bearskin robe. As the apparition appeared suddenly out of the blinding snowstorm, the cat first identified it as one of the many buffalo roaming the woods. Three times it had attacked a yearling buffalo that had been separated from the herd. The cat liked the taste of buffalo meat, but it would not risk the threat of stomping hooves and slashing horns. Memory served it well! But as the ghostly shape approached, it no longer resembled a large buffalo.

Hunger overwhelmed caution. Without hesitation, the cat leaped as Angus and Night Sky passed below the giant boulder. One set of front claws sunk into the horse's neck while the other set struck the bearskin covering Angus. The force of the cat's attack knocked Angus off the horse, and the life-saving bulky bearskin fell to the ground. The cat concentrated its efforts on the frightened horse and sank its teeth into the horse's neck, while slashing into its ribcage with powerful hind claws that were designed for disemboweling.

Angus heard and felt the bone snap as he fell awkwardly atop a small boulder. He knew immediately that his left arm was broken, but that was the least of his worries. He searched frantically for his rifle in the snow but quickly realized that he had no chance of using it to shoot the cat. The long barreled, muzzle-loading Pennsylvania rifle required two hands for shooting. Angus thought about propping the barrel in the forks of a small sapling but knew that would accomplish little. He could not distinguish horse from cat. As the two animals went thrashing out of sight into the storm Angus could hear nothing but the wind roaring through the trees.

With temperatures hovering around freezing, Angus knew the horse was lost. He must concentrate on saving his own life. He could sense the general direction of the Shawnee camp, and pictured its many campfires throwing off life-saving heat. It would take him at least three hours to get there, assuming he could maintain his sense of direction and not wander aimlessly—an unlikely assumption given the low visibility. With his left arm dangling helplessly at his side, Angus began the perilous journey to the Shawnee camp. Thankfully, he still had his bearskin coat and his deerskin bag with a few pieces of jerky, and his fire-starting flint and steel. It suddenly dawned on Angus that he had lost his beaver skins in the snow, but he chided himself, "I have bigger fish to fry now. I must survive this blizzard."

After an hour of struggling through knee-deep snow, Angus realized that he did not have the strength to continue. Under normal circumstances he would not have been concerned, since he had spent hundreds of nights in the wilderness without a shelter. This time was different. He had serious doubts about whether he could start a fire with one hand. To be successful, one hand must firmly hold the steel, while the other strikes it sharply with the edge of the flint. Angus had started fires in the dark, in the rain, and even in the wind. A single spark settling into a handful of shredded bark or dried grass would initiate a trickle of smoke, and a few well-directed puffs of air would soon produce a glowing ember. With a few more puffs, a small flame would magically appear. Every person living on the frontier could start a fire with flint and steel—at least every person with two healthy arms and hands.

Night slowly wrapped the injured trapper in a blanket of bone-chilling, murky soup. Through the impenetrable darkness, and though snow drifted nearly waist deep, Angus tried to make out any boulder with an overhang where he could find shelter from the wind. Blindly he stumbled onto a boulder where the snow on the leeward side rose only to his ankles. Feeling his way along this refuge, Angus carefully slid his rifle under the overhang and then commenced packing down the snow to form an area large enough for him to lie down. Although the broken arm greatly limited his efforts, he soon gathered a small pile of dried leaves, twigs, and two small branches. He retrieved a large branch he had seen while approaching the boulder, and used his one good arm to drag it under the boulder. After removing the mitten from his right hand, he quickly found that he could not firmly hold either the flint or the steel with the broken left arm. Without panic, he returned the flint and steel to the deerskin bag and pulled out several pieces of jerky.

The challenge facing him was really quite simple—survive the night and continue his search for the Shawnee camp in the morning. Beyond the snow, ice, and darkness, a warm bark wegiwa awaited. Angus crawled beneath the bearskin, cradled his wounded arm to his chest, and huddled against the boulder. After eating three pieces of the nutritious jerky he fell into a light slumber. As snow settled over him he slept fitfully, awakening once to what he thought was the distant scream of a mountain lion. Then all was silent—silent as a grave. He knew that if the cat had killed the horse it would eat its fill before retiring to the protection of its den. If it had failed to kill Night Sky it might return to the site of the original attack, but there was little that Angus could do, regardless of the actions of the cat. His last thought before falling asleep was, "O Lord, please send angels to help me through the night. But if you can't help me, please don't help that mountain lion."

Temperatures did not drop much below freezing that night, and daylight found Angus still alive. The winter spent with the Shawnee had toughened the young trapper, and the possibility of not surviving the night or the daunting trip back to camp never entered his mind. This was just another challenge thrown at him by the Appalachian wilderness, and he had already survived several. Although certainly not warm, he still had feeling in his toes—the place where frostbite would first appear. He had kept his fingers tucked under his armpits and, as with his toes, had moved them several times during the long night. Still burrowed within the bearskin, Angus had eaten two more pieces of jerky before raising one edge of the heavy, black fur and peeking out.

The sky was still overcast, but visibility was much improved, and it appeared that the brunt of the storm would soon pass. Although it would have been easier to stay huddled within the bearskin under the boulder overhang, Angus knew that would result in only one outcome—death. If he were to find the Shawnee camp he must set out immediately, since his strength would ebb as the day progressed. Shortly thereafter the snow stopped falling, and he began a painful, arduous, slow-going walk. His broken arm had throbbed all night, and every step through the drifted snow increased the sharp pain.

Fortunately for Angus, during the previous night several Shawnee had noted that there was no smoke coming from the vent hole in the top of Angus's wegiwa, situated at the edge of their main camp. He had told several Shawnee that he would return before dark, and they became concerned when a search of the bark dwelling revealed his absence. However, little could have been done at that time of night even if a snowstorm were not raging through the forest. When Angus had still not returned to camp the next morning, they quickly agreed to search in the direction of his trap line.

Around midday, two of the braves discovered the carcass of the horse. The cat had returned that morning for another meal and tried to cover the carcass before leaving, a behavior typical of most large cats. In so doing, it left sign that the ever-observant Shawnee did not miss. Although the snowstorm had made it impossible to backtrack the horse to the spot of the attack, the Shawnees knew the direction to search.

They crossed Angus's trail in early afternoon, and in less than one hour spotted him struggling slowly through the drifts. While two of the braves rubbed his feet, another fed him jerky and a fourth quickly started a small fire. Like an efficient machine, the group gathered larger and larger pieces of firewood so that the first small flames became a medium-sized warming fire. To reduce pain-causing movement, an elongated piece of bark encircled Angus's broken arm, and was held in place by leather strips. After several hours the group began to move the warmed and grateful trapper in the direction of their camp. Four broke trail through the deep snow, two supported Angus, and one carried his rifle. In less than two hours they were back in camp.

The tribal healer was a wizened, weathered, stoop-shouldered old woman with graying hair. Assisted by a quiet young woman named Sweetwater, the healer determined after several minutes of painful pulling and twisting, that the break was between the elbow and the shoulder, in the upper arm bone. As the women wordlessly manipulated the ends of the broken bone back to a normal position, Angus suppressed screams and felt himself pass out. A splint of chestnut wood was firmly secured to the arm with rawhide strips, Angus roused and, with the pain subsiding, he quickly downed a small bowl of rich elk broth. Moments later, he fell into a fitful sleep.

Sweetwater remained at his side to keep vigil, to keep the fire burning, and to supply more of the elk broth each time he awoke. For two weeks following his accident, the Indian maiden daily prepared his food and carried in firewood. As he lay on his thick, warm bearskin he had plenty of time to study the cheerful, young woman who he guessed was probably a couple years younger than he. Her hair, arranged into one long braid, extended nearly to her waist. Her black eyes seemed to be constantly smiling while her long, slender hands adeptly completed the small chores she had assigned herself. In silence, she daily checked his splint, making adjustments when necessary, and moving his fingers to maintain proper circulation. During these visits the Shawnee girl had numerous opportunities to study the trapper. Although he was taller than most of the Shawnee, it was not his size that impressed her, but his hair and bushy red beard. She had seen a few white men at the Potomac trading post, but none with red hair. The first night following the resetting of his broken arm, while he slept fitfully, she had timidly run her hands through his beard. It was surprisingly soft, and she wondered how it would feel against her face.

Though the hot food she brought to him was most welcome, the tender touch of her hands brought greater enjoyment. Angus looked forward to Sweetwater's daily visits, and the girl likewise eagerly anticipated their interactions. Although neither fully understood the words of the other, they were able to communicate all necessary meanings.

CHAPTER TWO
THE CANOE

THE BROKEN ARM ENDED trapping for that winter, so Angus spent the next two months in and around camp, assisting his hosts in whatever ways he could. As his arm began to heal, signs of spring made premature appearances, and Angus grew anxious about transporting his pelts and furs. Without a horse, overland transport was unrealistic. The only logical choice was to float them out on the river. Angus was no stranger to river transport. In his native Scotland he had constructed several boats to travel the Scottish rivers and lochs (lakes). For three years after coming to America, he worked as an indentured apprentice to a shipbuilder near Philadelphia. Having neither tools nor sawn boards, however, he realized he could not build a boat. A log raft would be too risky because of beaver dams, downed trees across the river, and boulders. In addition, he would need to guide the raft into small streams or at least into side eddies as he moved down the west fork of the Monongahela. It would be almost impossible to maneuver a raft loaded with furs to the Forks of the Ohio.

A canoe would be the ideal choice, but should it be a bark canoe or a dugout? In northern Pennsylvania, he had seen a few of the high-prowed, birch-bark canoes and was amazed at the speed and maneuverability they provided. With the help of the Shawnee, he could probably build a bark canoe in a few weeks, but unfortunately, white-barked birch trees were scarce around the headwaters of the west fork of the Monongahela. Angus knew the Shawnee used the bark from the yellow poplar and elm trees to make canoes, but the bark always became waterlogged and the canoe had to be pulled out of the water each night to dry. Such a nightly task would be impossible with a heavy cargo of furs and hides.

The only other option was a dugout canoe—one that required considerable effort to construct. When finished, however, it would be waterproof and provide the maneuverability required for the difficult trip down the Monongahela. Timing was everything—Angus must depart the Shawnee camp and arrive at the trading posts before the fur buyers departed.

Although Angus had dreams of selling enough furs to someday buy land and build his own farm, he had a much more urgent need for the gold that he hoped to receive for his deer hides and beaver pelts. Before fleeing Scotland he had promised his childhood sweetheart, Heather, that he would one day send enough gold back to Scotland to pay for her passage across the Atlantic. After a few years in the colonies, Angus realized that his best means to earn gold was through hunting and trapping; thus his adventure into the Appalachian wilderness had begun the previous summer.

On several occasions, Angus had carefully studied the dugout canoes that the Shawnee kept anchored to the banks of the west fork of the Monongahela—the tributary that he had come to call the West Fork River. Using his considerable experience in building small boats, he could envision some, but not all, of the steps needed to transform a tree into a dugout canoe. He wondered what tools were used to shape the stable watercraft. Were two arms and hands required to do the work, or could he use his one good arm? Would some of the Shawnee help with what seemed to be an impossible task? How many days would he need to transform a tree into a dugout canoe? Could the dugout be completed in time for him to reach the trading posts before the buyers left for their ocean-going ships? He had more questions than answers, more misgivings than confidence.

During the month called February in the colonies, when the "Moon of Flowing Sap" had filled out to a round ball, Angus was ready to begin canoe construction. Although his arm was still in a sling, he was able to grasp small items without experiencing the severe pain that had lingered for weeks following the mountain lion attack. More importantly, he could use his right arm to drag firewood, swing an axe, or scrape flesh from pelts without causing pain to his broken left arm. The first requirement for a dugout canoe was a suitably large tree of soft wood that could easily be hewn into the desired shape. Such a tree would need to have been dead for at least three years to reduce its overall weight in order to float easily.

During his healing period Angus had eaten several meals with Sweetwater and her family in their bark wegiwa. He became close friends with the Indian maiden, as well as with her parents. When it came time to locate a tree that could be converted into a dugout canoe, Sweetwater helped Angus search the banks of the nearby river. During those pleasant outings, Sweetwater taught Angus the Shawnee names of many common trees and animals, as well as numerous other objects. In return he taught her their English names.

Eventually, they located the perfect log a few hundred paces from the riverbank, on a gradual slope where it could be rolled downhill at the appropriate point. The log was the base of a towering, long-dead chestnut tree that had come crashing to the ground during an ice storm the previous winter, falling just outside the area planted to crops. The trunk was straight and limbless, and nearly as wide as his arm span. The tree had broken off a few feet above the ground, at the point where the Shawnee had deeply girdled it, and that end would serve as the rear of the dugout. Angus paced off ten long steps along the length of the limbless trunk and notched the bark at the point that would become the front end of the dugout. While attempting to envision the finished product, he remembered the words of Joseph Myers, the Philadelphia shipbuilder, "A tree is not a mast until it's hewn." Angus added, "And a tree is certainly not a dugout until it's hewn."

When trees crashed to earth, most of their limbs snapped off. These were usually hauled back to the Shawnee camp to feed the many campfires that burned continuously during the long, cold, winter months. Rarely did the Shawnee resort to flint axes or hard-earned iron axes to cut larger tree trunks into firewood. Such efforts were not worth the time and effort. Small trees that could be hauled by their lone horse or by several men were dragged back to camp to feed the larger campfires. Large trees were left to rot in the forest.

With help from Sweetwater, Angus rigged a two-man harness from braided strips of elk hide. Accompanied by Gentle Buffalo, the two strapped on the harness and hauled several large limbs to the point notched for the front end of the dugout. Gentle Buffalo, one of the largest and strongest men in the tribe, was shorter than Angus but appeared to be more than his equal in strength—one of the reasons Angus had asked him to assist with the canoe building. In return for his advice and assistance, Angus promised to leave Gentle Buffalo half of his steel traps. Angus planned to leave the other half of his traps in the village and told Gentle Buffalo that if he did not return, all the traps would be his.

A fire was built at the axe mark and the exciting challenge of building another watercraft began. Angus and Gentle Buffalo would keep the end fire burning day and night, until the log burned in two. The next step baffled Angus. How did the Shawnee remove all the "insides" of the dugout? The walls of their dugouts were only one finger thick. If he had to use his iron axe to chip away all that wood, it would be the next winter before he was finished. Gentle Buffalo began the mysterious process of excavating the inner wood by using a deer-antler rake to dig a long, deep trench under the downhill side of the log. In that trench was built a fire—a fire that would slowly create the hollow insides. Thus Angus learned that such canoes should be called "burnouts," not dugouts.

In nine days the large fire positioned at the notched front end burned completely through the fallen chestnut tree, and the log of the planned dugout was separated from the rest of the tree. The completed dugout would be almost thirty feet, nearly twice as long as the Shawnee canoes used for crossing the river. While the fire at the end of the dugout had needed little attention, and often was fed several large tree limbs at one time, the trench fire required nearly constant attention. It was essential that it be kept small so that the log would be hollowed out without damaging the sides. The trench—and its associated fire—was widened so that in a few days the flames were directly under the log. Although Angus needed little help with the small fires, there was seldom a time when there were not several "helpers" present. The novelty of such a huge dugout caused much debate about whether it would float, or if it would even remain upright without spilling his entire load of furs into the river. The greatest controversy arose over the ability of one person to maneuver such a bulky craft the length of the Monongahela River. Angus spent many hours asking himself these exact same questions.

After twelve days, the small trench fire had hollowed a deep depression on the underside of the log. It was time for the next major step, one for which all the Shawnee men and many of the older boys were needed. The log had to be rolled. Long stout hickory poles were inserted under the chestnut log, while long, braided, elk hide ropes were tied around it. With half the men pulling the ropes and the other half pushing the poles from the opposite side, the ponderous log slowly began to roll. All rocks and hummocks had been cleared away from the downhill side of the log so that it could roll into an upright position. A few rocks were used to brace it in place, and the next phase was ready to begin.

Angus and Gentle Buffalo initiated the demanding task of shaping the outside. With careful chops of iron axes, the front end was slowly formed into a narrow prow that would glide easily through the water. The back end was rounded somewhat, but only enough to improve its appearance and to remove all the charred wood. While the trench fires had been burning under the log, the uppermost part of the log—which was actually the bottom of the canoe—had been flattened to improve stability. Because this required chipping away small slabs of bark and wood, Angus was able to do much of the work. With his healing arm still strapped to his side by soft deerskin strips, he developed a slow but effective technique of safely swinging his axe.

During the next three weeks, as small fires inside the log burned ever deeper, Angus and Gentle Buffalo carefully scraped and gouged the charred wood from the inside. An iron axe and the shoulder blade of a deer equipped with a hickory handle were the only tools they used. Careful to keep the sides at least as thick as their longest finger, the desired shape slowly began to emerge. In broken English,

Gentle Buffalo summarized, "Making a dugout is easy, just take away everything that doesn't look like a canoe and you're left with a boat." His previous experience in the art of building watercraft had instilled in Angus a trait that served him well in many situations—patience. Boat building should not be rushed.

He remembered his grandfather, Harry McCallander, saying many times, "Haste has destroyed more boats than have all the storms in Scotland."

By the time skunk cabbage was poking its bright green leaves up through the late winter snows, and highly-prized ramps were big enough to dig, the dugout was nearly completed. A few finishing touches were all that remained. Angus planned to drill or burn small holes through each end of the dugout, and several more along each side, high enough to be above water level when the dugout was loaded. Those holes would be used to attach elk hide ropes. His craft was less streamlined than the smaller dugouts of the Shawnee, and not nearly so graceful as the birch-bark canoes he had seen around Lancaster, but Angus nevertheless was pleased. No doubt the dugout would float, but could he maneuver it downriver?

Most of the Shawnee village showed up to see the launch. Eight Shawnee, four on each side, pivoted the dugout so that its front end pointed toward the river. As they slid it onto a series of small saplings the dugout slowly began to move downhill. With a final push, the eight Shawnee eased it over the riverbank into the water, and all eight carefully jumped into the dugout. Although it rolled more than Angus would have liked, it did not tip, and with crude paddles the Shawnee soon moved upstream against the current. A loud cheer erupted from those gathered along the river, and a happy smile crossed the face of the Scotsman. They rounded the bend and went out of sight, but in a few minutes returned to the launch site. After pulling it onto a gravel bar and tying it securely to a tree root the jubilant Shawnee jumped ashore and returned to the camp with the rest of the observers.

Every afternoon during the next few weeks, Angus pushed the dugout into the river and slowly gained a feel for handling the long, awkward craft. Although weak from limited exercise, his broken arm had healed sufficiently for him to start using it more. On many days Sweetwater accompanied him in the dugout. It was obvious that two people could guide the canoe better than could one. Two arms would be needed to maneuver the dugout, especially if he tried to paddle across the current or up a small stream. He would spend the next two weeks strengthening his muscles and carving at least three spare paddles.

As his day of departure neared, Angus was faced with a decision, one more troublesome than all the others that confronted him. On several occasions, Sweetwater had indicated that she was willing—and eager—to go with him in the dugout to assist with the paddling and to translate if they should meet any other Indians. Angus had given it much thought and could think of many appealing reasons why her presence would be welcome. Sweetwater said she could safely find her way back to the Shawnee camp by following the same trail Angus had used on his arrival, and Angus had no doubts that she could. However, Angus knew he could never convince Heather he had needed a young Shawnee maiden to assist him during the canoe trip. If he had needed assistance, why hadn't he asked a strong young brave to help?

With the Planting Moon rapidly approaching, the camp began preparing for this critical annual event. All available hands were occupied repairing tools and clearing the cropland of fallen trees. Angus had few visitors during his daily dugout sessions. Although they could survive without corn, no Shawnee wanted to go through a winter eating nothing but deer, or elk, or buffalo. Sunny days and soft southern breezes produced spring-like temperatures, and the forest floor came alive with colorful flowers, confirming that spring would once again heal the earth. The Shawnee's struggle to survive the dreaded depths of winter was finally ending.

As Angus improved his dugout-handling skills, the forest floor seemed to undergo a metamorphosis. He recognized the trilliums with their three white petals, spring beauties with their small pinkish-white flowers, and the May apple with its shiny green leaves and small white bloom. Bird songs once again floated through the forest canopy as the ground beneath absorbed the life-giving sunshine.

With help from Gentle Buffalo, Angus moved the furs from his bark wegiwa down to the riverbank. Then he tied them into bundles so that, if necessary, he could unload them one bundle at a time. The smaller furs of beaver and river otter were piled into the narrow front end, while the much larger deer hides and elk hides were arranged in the middle—all sitting atop a layer of poles that covered the bottom. The final step was to cover the piles of furs with smoked, greased elk hides to provide some protection from the inevitable spring rains. Their work done, the two men made final preparations for Angus's departure. A two-week supply of jerky and smoked meat was wrapped in greased pouches and secured to the inside of the dugout, along with the surplus paddles.

As the moon faded behind the hills to the west, and the early morning sun climbed above the hills to the east, Angus arose and ate a hearty morning meal. He made his way to the river, exchanged farewells, and Gentle Buffalo pushed the dugout, bearing Angus and his load of furs out into the current. The entire village had come down to the river to watch the departure, since most had quickly warmed to the ever-smiling trapper who had brought them trade goods. Prior to launching the dugout, he had promised them he would return the following autumn and bring with him an even larger supply of trade goods.

Many of the Shawnee were shouting best wishes to Angus, but as he drifted with the current he noticed that one Shawnee in particular was not shouting or waving. A solemn, sad Sweetwater stood quietly at the edge of the crowd, with no trace of happiness on her usually beaming face. When Angus had calculated the space needed for his furs and hides in the dugout, he realized that there would be no room for another individual—man or woman. The decision was made. Sweetwater could not accept that he would not want her assistance and companionship on the trip, and their last meeting before he departed was not pleasant. It was an unfortunate event, since his stay in the Shawnee village and time with Sweetwater had been enjoyable and rewarding.

The river width near the Shawnee camp was twice the length of Angus's dugout canoe. Huge trees bordered the river on both

This was different from riding a horse along a trail through the dense woods. A horse would avoid most dangers, stepping over or around obstacles, yet wary of any scents of predators.

The day passed quickly, and the ponderous dugout encountered no obstacles. Angus stopped at mid-day to stretch his legs and eat a meal of smoked deer meat, but he remained in the dugout the rest of the day. When thirsty, he simply dipped a large clamshell into the river and savored the cool, clear water. In early afternoon Angus rounded a bend. On a sandbar along the western shore he spotted a large, white-headed bird feeding on something he could not identify. He had seen many of those birds around the Chesapeake Bay and identified it as a bald eagle. The bird let Angus get almost opposite it before emitting a high-pitched screech and flying away from its meal of fish. From the odor that drifted out to Angus, it must have been dead for several days. Angus had seen bald eagles catch live fish, but he had also seen them feed on dead ones. Apparently these birds were not too particular about what they ate.

As the sun dipped towards the western hills, Angus searched for an overnight stopping place. He wanted plenty of daylight his first evening on the river to safely anchor the canoe and set up camp. He preferred a gravel bar where he would have solid footing to grasp the braided elk hide ropes attached to the ends of the canoe. Because of the weight of the furs in the dugout, he knew he could not pull the craft up on the bank. However, by pulling the canoe into the slow eddy below the gravel bar it would be out of the main current, and he could safely tie it to a log. Everything went as planned, and in a brief time Angus was sitting before a small fire. His meal the first night consisted of smoked deer meat, as it would for most of the journey.

While sitting against a log and staring into his small fire, the warm glow of the rising moon appeared through the trees on the eastern horizon. Angus was tired after nearly ten hours on the river, but satisfied with his progress. Although none of the Shawnee had ever floated from their camp at the headwaters of the West Fork River to the Forks of the Ohio, they estimated he would need three weeks to complete the trip. Spreading one of the tanned deerskins beside the fire, Angus began a nightly ritual that would continue until the canoe journey ended. He heated the tip of his hunting knife in the small fire, and beginning at one end of the deerskin, sketched the shape of the stretch of river he had successfully floated that day. Prominent features such as small tributaries and beaver dams were added to the map. After completing that project, Angus cut a small notch into the handle of his paddle, representing the first day on the river.

As he did every night, Angus slept in his deerskin clothing. He had arrived at the Shawnee camp the previous fall wearing leather boots, plus wool and linen clothes typical of those worn by settlers in the colonies. By early winter they were nearly worn out, especially his leather boots. The repeated wetting and drying had caused them to split in half a dozen places. He admired the deerskin clothing of the Shawnee and had traded the last of the goods he brought from Lancaster for a complete set of leathern clothes.

As the flames from his small campfire flickered their last, he wondered what the sleeping arrangements would have been if Sweetwater were with him. With a bearskin to cushion the gravel, sleep came easily.

Arising with the sun, Angus ate a quick but satisfying breakfast of deer jerky, secured the ropes holding the furs, untied the dugout, and pushed off into the current. His left arm had stiffened during the night, and a dull ache coursed up to his shoulder—a reminder that the broken arm was not yet fully recovered. While eating deer jerky that morning, Angus had heard a series of loud gobbles echo down from the nearby hillside. Based on the locations of the gobbling, there were at least two birds. He identified them as wild turkeys. Angus had only learned of these large black fowl after coming to the colonies, as there were no wild turkeys in Scotland.

Angus was soon floating down the West Fork again. The sun had climbed above the trees on the eastern hillside as Angus rounded a bend. On the western shore—with widespread tail feathers and down-swept wings—were two large turkey gobblers strutting in the open woods. The sun glistened off their feathers and Angus realized they were not actually black, but a mixture of greens and purples and glossy blacks, an iridescent plumage unlike any Angus had ever seen. Their heads were a brilliant mixture of bright red, light blue, and white. Angus was not the only spectator to this show. Five hen turkeys, lacking the long beard that characterized each gobbler, were scratching through the leaves in search of food.

It occurred to Angus that male gobblers could change their appearance more abruptly and drastically than any other animal he had ever seen. Their streamlined body shape, with wings held tightly along the back, and narrow elongated tail held in a somewhat drooping position, could transform within seconds. Suddenly the bird could more than double its size by puffing out chest feathers, spreading wide its fan-shaped tail, and stiffly extending its down-stretched wings. Most incredible of all, the featherless, nondescript black head explodes into the bird's most striking feature. The top of the head miraculously becomes almost pure white, as the face turns a bright blue, and the neck, caruncle, and wattle change to brilliant cardinal red, all showcased against the backdrop of a glossy-black iridescent, tail. The spectacle receded behind him as the canoe slowly pulled Angus away from this wooded stage.

Angus reflected on the appearance of the strutting gobblers, and noted that they were much more impressive than the bald eagles that frequented the coastal bays and rivers. Their deep gobbling that seemed to echo from hillside to hillside was much more entertaining than the high-pitched screech of the bald eagles. In his opinion, no other bird so symbolized the Appalachian wilderness as did the wild turkey—the largest of all birds inhabiting the eastern forests.

The second day passed quickly, and Angus gained confidence in his ability to handle the dugout. By mid-afternoon, he was surprised to see the current slow to a near standstill as water depth increased noticeably. He rounded a bend and the cause became apparent—a large beaver dam extended across the river. Angus slowly guided the canoe through the quiet water that the dam created. Angus had crossed over the remains of two beaver dams earlier in his trip, and he was surprised that the spring floods had not washed out sections of this particular dam.

As he floated closer it was obvious that the dam had indeed

washed out at one spot along the left edge, but beaver had since repaired it. Water seemed to be flowing into the recently repaired spot, so Angus steered the canoe in that direction. Pulling the canoe to the shore he carefully jumped out and snubbed the end of his elk hide rope to the root of a giant sycamore that overhung the river. A quick glance at the dam indicated there was no way he could get the canoe over it. The end of the dugout was too heavy for him to lift up onto the dam, and the water too deep to stand and push his dugout with any force. His only choice was to remove a portion of the dam and create a gap through which the canoe could float.

Angus removed his rifle, the extra paddles, the bearskin, and the elk hide—just in case the dugout capsized. He tightened the elk hide ropes that secured the bundles of furs and then untied the belt around the loose-fitting deerskin shirt that hung half way down his thighs. The large sleeves would be especially cumbersome if he should fall into the river, thus he removed the shirt. Angus cautiously stepped out from the bank onto the top of the beaver dam and began prying away the logs a rifle length from shore.

In a few minutes, moccasins and leggings were thoroughly soaked. As Angus pried away the short logs inserted by the beaver, he marveled at their talents. A dam like this was capable of holding great volumes of water, as the pond behind it grew ever larger. Most dams could withstand all but the heaviest winter and spring runoffs, and only heavy flooding caused real damage. Angus had watched with curiosity as these large rodents felled trees, cut them into short sections, and hauled them to the river. The cut sections were secured to the bottom of the beaver pond, and provided food during the long winter months. Because beaver ate only the bark, many such short sections of trees trunks were needed to sustain them until spring.

More impressive than the cutting of trees was the construction of dams. Sections of tree trunk from which the bark had been eaten were used to form the main body of the dam. Mud, small sticks, and even rocks were used to make a near-waterproof dam. In all his travels he had encountered nothing like it—no other animal could transform its environment like the beaver. Their engineering brought nothing but admiration from Angus, but it was now necessary for him to breach the dam—at least temporarily. As Angus began to lose feeling in his toes, he reckoned the opening in the dam was large enough. Water now flowed through the opening in a torrent that should sweep the dugout through the dam and rapidly down the river.

Angus felt confident that the dugout would slide through the dam so he put on his shirt, tied his rifle and extra paddles securely in the canoe, and cautiously climbed in. He had stopped three boat lengths above the dam, and reminded himself he would have only a few minutes to maneuver the canoe into the slot. Cautiously lowering himself into the canoe, he untied the elk skin rope and felt the current begin to tug. With the pointed bow of the canoe aimed directly at the opening, there was little Angus needed to do but make sure the current pulled the bow into the opening.

Minutes later the bow entered the opening and the rush of water pulled it ever faster. Angus could feel the bottom scraping on logs that remained in the dam, but they slowed the canoe only slightly. With a sudden plop the rear of the canoe cleared the dam and the current swept it far downstream.

The next day he worked his way through the branches of two large sycamores that had fallen into the river and crossed an old abandoned beaver dam without having to exit the canoe. The river was widening, but the current remained steady. In early afternoon, he began to notice a few boulders protruding above the surface and knew he must be extra cautious. In addition to those visible above the water, there were certainly boulders just below the surface that he must somehow avoid. Although he could not see those hidden obstacles, he was often warned of their presence by the water movement. An unusual swirl or a few small ripples indicated some object just below the surface. Angus now wished he had brought someone with him! While kneeling at the rear of the dugout his view of the water directly in front of the bow was blocked, and more importantly, any objects beneath the water were obscured. He cautiously stood up in the dugout, an act that brought extra danger. Sweetwater could have perched on top of the furs at the front of the dugout and watched for boulders in the water, but that option was long gone.

As he felt the rough bottom of the dugout slide over a submerged boulder Angus became alarmed, but he was soon clear. He lost count of the number of boulders that seemed to reach for the dugout, realizing he had no good way to avoid them. Thrusting his paddle as far down into the water as possible, Angus estimated that the river near the shore was about chest deep. He considered moving to shore, exiting the dugout, and guiding it by the elk hide ropes slowly downstream as he walked along the bank. However, the uprooted limbs and protruding roots of those giants still standing would have made such an attempt dangerous. Angus could steer the dugout around obstacles, but only if given plenty of warning. The great unwieldy length of the dugout and the speed of the current made it impossible for him to make sudden turns. If the dugout should ever upset it would be impossible for Angus to roll it upright. The dugout would remain afloat for several hours, or possibly even days, until the hides and furs became waterlogged. However, the current would carry them so far downriver that he most likely would never recover his valuable cargo.

Angus successfully steered the dugout away from a fallen tree along the right bank but was concerned that another tree trunk might have floated downriver and caught on the submerged top. With his attention riveted on the downed tree, he did not spot the subtle ripple in front of the dugout. He felt the dugout shudder, then come to a stop, as the front ran up onto some immovable object in the water. Although Angus could not see the object, he knew that he had struck a submerged boulder. He surmised the dugout had hit it nearly straight on, because there was little tilting.

In the brief interval that Angus weighed the situation, the current began to slowly turn the canoe. With the front end anchored on the boulder, the back end began to swing around with the current. Angus realized there was little he could do, and he was in serious danger of upsetting. Being a strong swimmer, he was not worried about his own safety, but was concerned about his bundles of hides and furs, and of course his rifle. Elk hide straps, fastened through small holes around the top edges of the dugout, would hold those objects essential to his survival in the boat for a time. Rising from

Edwin Daryl Michael

the kneeling position, Angus sat on the rear rim of the dugout in order to better evaluate his predicament. The spring breeze was cold against his neck.

The back end of the pivoting dugout slammed into another submerged boulder and immediately the canoe listed to one side. With such a heavy load there was little clearance between the top of the dugout and the water. As the current pressed against the dugout, this critical distance was quickly reduced to almost nothing and the first small waves eased over the edge. Once water started to pour over the side, the canoe rolled even more, and before he could react, Angus was thrown into the river.

Without Angus's weight, the dugout somehow managed to right itself. Although chestnut wood is somewhat porous and lightweight, the thick solid bottom served to keep the dugout balanced. After Angus fell out, the dugout immediately rose higher in the water and the rear of the canoe eased over the submerged boulder and continued to pivot as it had when it struck the first boulder. The dugout floated free from the boulders and resumed its journey down the river—without Angus.

When Angus came to the surface he was almost a full boat length upriver of the canoe. He sputtered a few times and tried to swim to the dugout, but with no success. The fast-flowing current was pulling the high-floating canoe downstream faster than Angus could swim. Knowing that he had to get to shore, he struggled towards the riverbank and soon felt his feet strike bottom. Angus realized how fortunate he was to be wearing deerskin clothes and moccasins. Had he been wearing heavy leather boots and woolen clothes he would have been lucky to escape the river.

"What a predicament," Angus thought as he scrambled up the bank and bounded downstream. Darting through the giant trees, Angus nervously glanced at the dugout floating with the current. Fortunately the forest was clear of fallen debris, and he soon caught up with the dugout. Continuing his wild run, the soggy woodsman passed the dugout and started to formulate his plan. At ten boat lengths ahead of the dugout, Angus quickly changed direction, pulled off his shirt, and dove into the river. Swimming with all his

26

strength, he drew alongside the dugout and grabbed the elk hide rope that dangled from the rear. Gradually he was able to guide the canoe closer to shore, and, as his strength faded, his feet once again struck bottom. Hanging onto the rear of the canoe, he managed to guide it along the bank to a sand bar. Both ends of the dugout canoe were tied securely before he collapsed onto the sand bar.

Although the water in the bottom of the dugout worried him considerably, his immediate task was to get warm. A cold front had blown in during the night, and that morning he had been greeted by a landscape whitened by frost and a riverbank edged with ice. Hurriedly collecting fuel, he retrieved his shirt and soon had a small fire radiating life-saving heat. Angus removed his clothes, propped them against branches close to the heat, and began searching for larger tree limbs to add to the fire. Although his exertion warmed him slightly, he knew he needed a roaring fire to drive away the cold that had penetrated deeply into his body.

Angus soon dried off, but his only clothes were the ones he had been wearing. However, he did have one large tanned doeskin, bleached almost white and softer than his deerskin shirt. The cloth-like doeskin had been a gift from Sweetwater—before she discovered she would not accompany him on the trip to the Forks of the Ohio. Angus removed the bleached doeskin from its greased elk hide covering, and he once again admired its striking symbols. Using the hot flat tip of a skinning knife, Sweetwater had burned the shape of side-by-side mountain peaks into each of the four corners. Angus had asked her what they represented, and with a shy grin she had answered, "Hills."

With the creamy doeskin draped over his clammy back and shoulders, he turned slowly before the fire. Gradually, his body heat returned. Now he must decide whether to put on his dank clothes or start bailing water from the dugout. His concern for the furs outweighed his own personal comfort, and he began the arduous task that he'd dreaded from the start. The bottom of each bundle of furs and hides was sitting in water, and they would eventually begin to absorb it. Unfortunately, there was no way to bail out the water that was concentrated in the front end of the boat—the end containing the bulk of the furs. The rear of the dugout, where Angus typically knelt, was riding high and dry in the water. The open bottom, from which he might have bailed, held no water. After removing the elk hide straps, Angus lifted each of the heavy bundles out of the dugout and onto the sandy beach.

He had anticipated such a task, so each bundle was made no larger than he could handle. He could not have known, however, that swimming in frigid water would drain his strength. The task was almost too daunting; the wet furs were significantly heavier than dry ones. Angus removed the valuable beaver and river otter pelts from the deepest water at the front, but was unable to continue. The exertion and the cold were sapping his strength to the point of exhaustion. Now crawling, Angus moved to the fire, added more fuel, and wrapped the soft white deerskin around his shoulders. He rotated his still-wet deerskin clothes before the fire and fought off the urge to put them back on, for they would do little to keep him warm.

His flowing curls and beard were nearly dry, and as he pranced nearly naked around the roaring fire he remembered the Shawnee ceremony conducted at the Moon of Flowing Sap. The Shawnee eagerly awaited sap that would flow from cuts made in the sugar maple trees when conditions were right—freezing nights and warm, sunny days. Although they could not make much syrup, the small amount produced was a most welcome gift, coming as it did at the end of winter. The intensely sweet syrup would once again be part of their diet.

They celebrated the occasion with an exuberant fire dance and Angus, dressed only in his breechcloth, had joined the Shawnee in their ritual to express gratitude for the wondrous gift of maple syrup. Close to midnight, by colony time, the ceremony began. Snow covered the ground, and the deep dry cold precipitated the cracking of tree limbs; but the flames of the huge fire that reached higher than most of the bark wegiwas warmed everyone present. Dancing and feasting continued throughout the night until the pile of firewood was nearly spent, and the first hint of daylight appeared through the trees. With Chief Tall Turtle leading the way, the Shawnee had jumped into snowdrifts, then quickly darted into sweat lodges—

women in one and men in another. Angus had been accepted as a member of this small band of Shawnee and was expected to join in all such activities. The thoughts of the dance and the sweat lodge now helped warm his naked body—but only slightly.

Angus reluctantly left the warmth of his riverbank fire and returned to his dugout. He struggled to remove the piles of deer hides. As darkness settled over the land, Angus lifted the last bundle out of the dugout. After a supper of wet jerky, he pulled on his nearly dry clothes and began the one task yet to be done. Each bundle of furs and hides had been quickly placed on the sandbar not far from the water's edge, and now he carried each close to the fire. It was essential that each be completely dry before it was reloaded into the dugout. Although his previously broken arm throbbed constantly, he worked doggedly. With that task completed, Angus crawled into his damp bearskin, positioned himself between the fire and a dry bundle of deer hides, and quickly fell asleep.

The territory defended by the twelve-wolf pack was over forty miles long, while the newly formed pair had a range of only ten miles, covering both sides of the river and much of the adjacent hillsides. The new parents had established their territory outside that of their former pack in an area with adequate prey to support a single pair of wolves.

By hunting together the male and female could bring down a large deer, a small elk, or even a young buffalo. The biggest challenge came when the female wolf remained with the pups during their first few weeks of life and the male had to hunt alone. Late winter is a stressful time for all hoofed animals, and the deep snows that accumulated along the West Fork River resulted in the deaths of several deer and elk.

In the delicate balance of Nature, predators benefit from the misfortune of these ruminants, as much less energy is required to acquire a dead deer than a live one. A winter-weakened deer can still get in a lucky blow with a sharp hoof to break a rib or a leg of a careless wolf, and an elk is even more of a threat. There is no risk, however, in feeding on a carcass. As a result, the black male wolf carefully studied any potential prey before attacking. He would occasionally stalk a wild turkey, a grouse, or even a snowshoe hare, but it was a waste of energy to chase a healthy turkey or rabbit when he could kill a sick or weakened deer. One deer would provide enough food to last the male and his mate for almost one week, while a turkey or rabbit would hardly make a meal for one of them.

After eating all he could hold, the black male would return to the entrance of the den where he regurgitated large chunks of the quickly swallowed meat. Upon hearing her mate approach, the female would quickly join him at the mouth of the tunnel and, with much face licking, show her appreciation for the meal he provided.

The packs of timber wolves that roamed the Appalachian Mountains usually contained fifteen to twenty adults. Most individuals in a pack were closely related, and the resulting family group was extremely successful in meeting the natural challenges common in the mountains. Their size and intelligence, along with pack behaviors that enable them to function as a single entity, made it possible for these 100-pound canines to bring down a 200-pound deer, a 600-pound elk, or even a half-ton buffalo.

Throughout the seventeenth century, all major river drainages in the Appalachians were home to packs of timber wolves. Food sources were plentiful for these predators, and Native American Indians rarely killed them, even though wolves and Indians depended on the same prey. There was plenty of hoofed game to satisfy the needs of both humans and carnivores. In contrast, early settlers took a dim view of the wolf and the mountain lion. Both predators killed the wild animals that the settlers needed to survive, as well as many of their domestic sheep, pigs, and cattle. Real or imagined, the ultimate threat posed by these predators was that of attacking and killing the settlers themselves.

The solitary nature of mountain lions posed a greater threat to humans than did wolves. Wolves, traveling in packs, were much more likely to be seen by the settlers than solitary panthers. Settlers were also much more likely to hear the chorus of howls from a hunting wolf pack, than to hear the occasional squall or scream of a big cat.

Tolerance of predators was another factor distinguishing natives from settlers. The weapons of the Indians were not as devastating as those of the settlers, whose guns were more than adequate to reduce and eventually eliminate wolves from the region. Firearms in the hands of experienced settlers had been responsible for the deaths of thousands of wolves along the eastern seaboard. When guns were not adequate, traps and poison were used. But the single most ominous threat was the reduction and eventual elimination of the wolves' primary food source. Early settlers in the colonies could not, or would not, coexist with the large hoofed mammals. It would only be a matter of time before the last surviving elk and buffalo would be killed. Without elk and buffalo as a food source, packs of wolves would cease to exist as well.

The sun had barely climbed over Cheat Mountain when the mother wolf heard snuffling and growling at the mouth of the tunnel. A month earlier a large, hungry, male black bear had emerged from hibernation in a cave along a steep mountain face. Before entering hibernation, he had fattened on acorns and chestnuts and as a result his weight had increased to more than 600 pounds. But because he did not eat during his prolonged winter sleep, he had metabolized more than 100 pounds of his fat reserves. Less powerful than when he entered hibernation, he was still strong enough to dig down to the wolf den. The odors of wolf pups and the food brought to the den by the male wolf added to the bear's hunger.

A lone bear, even a 600-pound adult male, usually avoids wolves. He is capable of killing a single wolf or even a pair of wolves, but a full pack instinctively brings respect and fear. This bear had encountered no large wolf packs throughout that portion of the West Fork Valley, and he was ravenously hungry. The cunning and defensive nature of wolves probably accounted for the secondary escape tunnel that led out around a hillside where it emerged beside a large hemlock tree. The female alone could easily escape, but maternal instincts prevented her from abandoning her pups—even if it meant losing her own life. Thus, she began to move the pups. Gently she picked up the smallest gray female by the scruff of its neck and carefully dragged it through the escape tunnel.

The bear could not see the wolf emerge because the hemlock tree obscured the tunnel opening, thirty feet from the main entrance to the den. Crouching low to the ground she carried the pup to a large pile of boulders located a hundred yards away. Carefully she dropped the pup into a small crevice and instructed it to stay put and remain quiet. The little female pup had remained calm while her mother carried her to the boulders, but now that she was alone in a strange place fear quickly overwhelmed her. She had never been alone in her entire life. Her mother had not only taken her from the only place she had ever lived, but had immediately left her. Instinct and the mother's sharp orders, however, caused the pup to remain motionless in the small depression where she lay and waited.

The father wolf was loping back to the den, after feeding on a yearling deer, when he heard the bear. Quickly changing from a casual lope to an earth-covering run, the large male wolf was soon within sight of the black invader. Without hesitation he leaped at the exposed rump of the bear and attempted to cripple one of its hind legs. The bear growled in pain and turned to face his lone antagonist. The bear outweighed the wolf by nearly 400 pounds, but the wolf's agility, vigor, and rush of adrenaline nearly equalized the battle. The wolf was experienced enough not to drive for the neck of the bear. The life-snuffing clamp of the wolf's powerful jaws might work successfully on the windpipe of white-tailed deer or even elk, but it would be suicide to try it on a bear.

Instead of charging, the snarling wolf slowly circled while exposing his huge fangs and repeatedly dashing at the bear's legs. He could not hamstring the bear as he might an elk, but he might convince the bear that the risk of injury outweighed the rewards at the end of the tunnel.

Halfway back to the escape tunnel, the returning mother wolf heard the sounds of battle. Torn by the strong urges to move the remaining pups, or join her mate in battle, she chose the latter. Wolves are highly social animals and the short life with her mate had created such a strong bond that the female did not hesitate. The bear would have retreated from a snarling, slashing pack of wolves, but he was hungry, and two wolves were not enough of a threat to cause him to retreat. Instead, he became even more aggressive.

The wolves tried to stay on opposite sides of the bear, but he ignored the smaller female and charged savagely at the larger male. The female wolf seized a hind leg and held an instant too long. Roaring with pain, the bear turned suddenly and the curved claws at the end of his powerful forearm tore into the vulnerable rib cage of the female. With an almost casual swipe, the bear flung the wolf over twenty feet through the air. Knocked nearly unconscious, she struggled to rise. But one of the bear's long claws had punctured her lungs. Blood bubbled out of her nostrils as she made an effort to rejoin the battle, but she would fight no more. She collapsed into a heap on the ground, her eyes slowly closed, and her life gradually slipped away.

The male wolf had no way to know his mate was dying. All he knew was that the bear was a serious threat—one he could not ignore. The heat of battle and the drive to protect his family drove the wolf to greater fury. The flabby skin of the bear, resulting from the fat loss during hibernation, was effective protection against the cutting, slashing canines of the wolf. During one especially aggressive attack, the wolf's jaws clamped onto the loose skin of the bear's front leg. Unable to inflict damage, yet unable to quickly release his grip, the wolf realized too late that he was vulnerable to counter-attack. The bear savagely clamped his powerful jaws around the wolf's back. As his backbone snapped, the life of the male came to a sudden end. The battle was over; the life of the two-wolf pack was abbreviated.

The bear rested a few minutes, licked his wounds, and then proceeded to satisfy his hunger by tearing huge chunks of still-warm flesh from the male wolf. Following his meal, he hauled the carcass of the female wolf into a spruce thicket high on the hillside and buried her remains under a blanket of pungent spruce branches, spruce needles, and soil. Her flesh, along with that of her mate, would enable the bear to regain much of the weight he had lost during hibernation. With several meals easily available and no threat of further attack, the bear lost interest in the den where the four orphaned wolf cubs huddled together.

The wolf pups spent a long frightened night in the den. Although quite hungry, they would not leave their home. The earthen shelter had protected them during their short life and their mother had always provided them with food in the form of milk and meat. The pups would remain in the den until one of their parents returned. But never again would they see their parents. Never again would they rush joyously to meet their mother as she crawled into the den. The den that had provided shelter and security throughout their short lives would now become their burial tomb.

The small pup carried by its mother to the boulders spent an even longer and hungrier night than her siblings. With no littermates to provide warmth and security she was cold, wet, and frightened. Whimpering softly, she spent all the next day and one more night in the rocks. The following morning hunger and thirst drove her out of the rocks. If she did not eat that day starvation would claim her life. But she was too young and much too small to find any food on her own. So weak that she could not walk, the tiny pup stumbled down the hill towards the river. She fell over the edge of the bank and splashed into the shallow water, just as the dugout canoe rounded the bend.

CHAPTER FIVE
THE WOLF PUP

ANGUS MCCALLANDER WAS FULLY focused on guiding his large dugout canoe downstream. Ever alert, he noticed the small bundle of wet fur ahead of him at the river's edge. With powerful paddle strokes he eased the dugout closer to shore but was unable to identify the creature. He first thought it was a small beaver, but as he drew closer he saw the long slender tail and decided it was a river otter, or possibly a mink. As the great chestnut canoe ground to a halt at the edge of the sandbar, Angus stepped out and quickly tied it to an exposed root. Moving slowly and quietly to the limp, soaked creature, he noted the head and pointed ears were dog-like. Too weak to resist, the shivering little wolf pup allowed Angus to scoop her into his large warm hands. Had she been dry and well fed she would have growled and sunk her small, sharp, baby teeth into his hand.

As he carefully lifted the wet bedraggled pup into his canoe, Angus exclaimed, "Ye're one of the sorriest beasties I've ever seen!" He wiped the pup dry, gently wrapped it inside the soft, white deerskin and then slipped it inside his deerskin shirt, but not before noting that the pup was a female. Warmth slowly transferred from his body to hers and she snuggled close to the comforting heartbeat of Angus's torso. Fatigue overwhelmed hunger as she succumbed to a deep sleep.

The newly found tiny cargo securely stowed inside his shirt, Angus eased the canoe back out into the current and continued his trip downriver. Vivid memories of the Pennsylvania hound that accompanied him when he left Lancaster flashed through his mind. Although not nearly the equal of the hounds he had owned in Scotland, it had been a good companion. It had warned him of dangers on several occasions and had even tracked a retreating bull elk that Angus shot on one hunting trip. Angus was riding his black mare, Night Sky, over the Appalachians, with the hound trotting in front, when the incident occurred. The hound, having picked up the scent of some animal that crossed the trail, was nosing around a rotting, moss-covered log as it had done so many times during their trip from Lancaster. Next the dreaded, unmistakable sound of vibrating rattles penetrated the silence of the forest.

The hound, with no inherent fear of rattlesnakes, suddenly jumped backward, yipping with both surprise and pain. After striking the dog, the large snake slithered away to the protection of a fallen tree. Angus could see that the reptile was nearly as long as he was tall, and its middle appeared to be as thick as his leg above the knee. It was clearly the biggest snake he had ever seen.

There were few snakes in the Scottish Highlands, and Angus had been both surprised and alarmed to learn that poisonous snakes were common throughout the mountains. He had seen a few small rattlesnakes and copperheads near Lancaster, but nothing so fearsome as the huge, nearly coal-black reptile coiled beneath the fallen tree. The snake fascinated Angus, but his hound was in trouble. He jumped from the black mare, threw her reins around a tree, and ran to the hound.

The venom-transmitting fangs had penetrated one of the worst places possible, as evidenced by the swelling on the hound's neck. As the hound's heart pumped the poison through its body, Angus hoped that death would come quickly. He did not want his hound to linger in agony for days, swollen and convulsing. As the hound lay sprawled on the forest floor, Angus knelt beside him and searched for the spot where the fangs had punctured its skin. Ten minutes passed. As Angus tried to comfort the dog, it began to shake, and violent jerking convulsed throughout its body. Angus cradled the dog's head as the last breath passed from its nostrils. Angus had watched many animals die, and it was always an emotional experience if they suffered. He would miss this companion.

As he buried his faithful companion, Angus reverently voiced the words he had often heard his mother express, "The Lord giveth, and the Lord taketh away."

As the canoe drifted downstream, Angus's thoughts turned to Scotland and the many hounds he had hunted with. Memories of many pleasant outings in the Highlands brought a warm feeling. Angus had acquired three different dogs in America, but none of them was anything special. They would tree a raccoon or chase a wounded deer, but they were not worth the feed it took to keep them.

The locals said it was impossible to keep a wolf as a pet, as wildness never left the animal. But perhaps this little pup was young enough to imprint. Angus stopped for lunch on a gravel bar and built a small fire of driftwood that had washed up along the bank. He warmed some of the venison he carried with him and, after eating his fill, offered a small piece of thoroughly chewed meat to the now-dry pup, still wrapped in deerskin. The sweet taste of the warm cooked deer meat was quite different from the raw meat she was accustomed to, but her hunger overcame any aversion to this strange flavor. Too weak to bolt down the pieces, as she normally did when fed by her mother, she slowly chewed on the meat. Juices ran down her throat and caused her to chew even harder. After several minutes she had masticated the deer meat enough to swallow the small pieces.

Angus fed her five more bites and decided not to give her too much at one time. Wrapping her securely within the white deerskin, he carried her to the canoe and placed her on a bundle of furs. After pushing off into the slow-flowing river and jumping into the dugout, he tenderly slipped her inside his deerskin shirt.

With the pup's hunger temporarily sated, the warmth of the shirt and Angus's body induced a deep, two-hour sleep. Although she no longer shared her den with her brothers and sisters, two of her three needs were satisfied—food and shelter. The warmth provided by Angus and his deerskin shirt would substitute for the comfort formerly provided by her littermates. Several soft whimpers escaped from inside Angus's shirt that afternoon, but they seemed to be whimpers of comfort rather than whimpers of distress.

As the afternoon sun began its western descent, Angus searched for a campsite where he could spend the night. A short time later he spotted a gravel beach sheltered by a high bank where driftwood was plentiful. Angus steered the canoe onto the beach, placed the wolf pup and its deerskin cover under his bearskin, and then stepped out of the canoe onto a protruding stone. He pulled the back of the canoe up onto the beach and stretched a strong elk skin cord from the end of his canoe to a large log that had been stranded on the gravel bar. He was eager to make camp and feed the pup.

Angus would have preferred to build a temporary lean-to under the trees, but that would put him too far from his canoe. It would be easy for another trapper or an Indian to cut the rope and let the canoe drift downstream with the current. The furs were too valuable to risk a loss when it could be avoided. Angus tied a slender cord to the side of the canoe, partially buried the string under some sand and gravel, and tethered the other end near his campfire. Before going to sleep he would tie the end of the cord to his leg and thus be warned if the canoe moved any distance. This was a trick he had been using and would continue to use each night of his journey to the Forks of the Ohio.

After gathering a small pile of driftwood, Angus scooped out a fire pit near the stranded log, shredded a handful of grass, and then added loose bark and fine twigs. Three quick strikes of flint on steel, and a spark flew into the fire starter. It was second nature to nurture a spark into a small flame that produced a crackling fire. In a short time he had a bed of coals that he scraped to one side of the fire pit. After filling his small kettle with water from the river, he set it in the middle of the coals. Supper was the same, night after night. A large slice of smoked venison was held in the fire with a sharpened stick and four handfuls of cornmeal were thrown into his small kettle. He would cut off pieces of the meat and add them to the corn mush to make a stew, or he would let the cornmeal bake in the bottom of the kettle to make johnnycake. This night he decided to make a stew. Shortly thereafter he was sipping the nutritious mixture with the wooden spoon he had carved from a chestnut limb.

During the entire time that Angus prepared camp and ate his supper, the wolf pup had remained huddled under the bearskin in the bottom of the canoe. As darkness settled over the wilderness valley, Angus walked to the canoe and carefully lifted the bearskin off the wolf. Because it was still wrapped in the deerskin, the pup was not overly alarmed at being moved. She was still weak from spending nearly two days in a pile of rocks, and hunger caused cramping pains in her small shrunken stomach. Awakened from her nap, she nevertheless remained quiet, just as her wolf mother had taught her.

Angus was certain the pup was hungry and weakened. But if she could eat enough to survive the long night she just might escape death. Sitting with his back against the log so that the pup could not see the fire, Angus pulled the deerskin back from her head and placed a small piece of meat that he had been chewing into her mouth. Hunger outweighed any natural fear the pup had of her strange surroundings, and she began chewing the meat. She did not like the bright light and closed her eyes while chewing. Angus fed her several small pieces and by the fifth piece she was bolting it down with no chewing, as was her normal feeding behavior.

After partially unwrapping the deerskin so that the pup's feet rested on the gravel, Angus began to gently stroke her back. As he had hoped, the pup squatted then peed a small yellow stream. Angus continued the stroking and the pup pooped a small squishy pile. Encouraged by her appetite and the functioning of her kidneys and bowels, Angus thought the pup just might survive whatever ordeal had orphaned it and brought it to the river's edge that morning.

Enough activity for one day! The exhausted canine was once more wrapped in the deerskin, and placed on a bearskin beside his pile of firewood. The pup was soon asleep, and Angus sat by the fire as darkness enveloped his campsite. After watching the flames of his small fire for a short time he spread his bearskin on the ground between the stranded log and the fire and placed his rifle where it was within easy reach. Angus added one more notch to his canoe paddle and burned additional features of the river onto his deerskin map.

As he waited for sleep to come, Angus reflected on the pups he had raised, and recalled that the most faithful were those taken from their mothers at an early age. Although Angus did not know the age of the wolf pup, its size indicated that it was just barely old enough to leave its mother. He knew that a pup would bond with its new master if taken from the mother at the critical time. If weaned too early, however, the pup would not receive all the milk necessary for the strong teeth, bones, and muscles of a full-grown dog. Weaned and transferred too late, the pup would never become permanently imprinted to the human who raised it. "Consider, however, that this is a wolf," he argued to himself, "one of the most ferocious carnivores in America." Young wolves tied near lodges in Indian camps would attack anything and anyone that approached. Either the Indians had not caught the pups early enough, or they did not know how to tame them. Would this pup be any different?

The sight of the helpless wolf had triggered protective feelings that surprised Angus. He preferred to be alone on his trapping trips into the wilderness; but "alone" meant without human companions, not necessarily without canine companions. Angus needed a dog and had planned to start looking for one as soon as he returned to Lancaster. A colonist with a litter of pups would gladly let him select one with a suitable disposition. The Indians had offered him several dogs, but he had politely refused them, as none would have been a suitable hunting dog. Chances were that none would have become the devoted companion he was looking for.

Angus reminded himself that a wolf was not really a dog, although the two were probably cousins. The spirit of wildness ran through the wolf's veins. Wolves hunted to kill, for without the kills there would be no food and without food there would be no wolves. To domestic hounds, however, the chase was reward enough; their owners would feed them when they returned home. Angus figured that a wolf companion would be something special, and decided then and there to try to tame the orphaned pup. Somehow he had to get the pup to forget her mother and look to Angus for food, warmth, and security, but more importantly, leadership.

Among his many past canine friends, one hound had bonded more strongly to Angus than any other. Without his mother's knowledge, a young Angus had sneaked the pup into his bed for the first five nights after it was weaned from its mother. That pup had quickly switched its affection to Angus, and the two became inseparable pals. Angus would now try the same thing with the wolf pup. After covering the fire with ashes he lifted the pup, still swaddled in the deerskin, to his bearskin. He tied the canoe cord to his leg, pulled a second bearskin over him, and almost tenderly nestled the pup against his body. Although Angus sensed small kicks and wiggles of the pup and heard every small whimper, they both slept soundly that night.

Angus awoke as the first faint hint of daylight pushed darkness from the sky. Crawling slowly into the frosty air, he left the pup to enjoy the heat trapped between the two bearskins. He started the fire for his morning meal, cut off a slab of venison, and prepared to bake some more johnnycake in his iron kettle. Although eager to push the canoe into the river and continue his float downstream, he was also eager to see how the pup would respond to his presence. After the food was ready, Angus removed the still sleeping pup from the bearskin and carried her to the fire.

The pup was much more active than she had been the previous day and squirmed inside the deerskin. When Angus pulled the hide back from the pup's head she emitted a low growl. Her health was improving, even if her disposition was not. She ducked her head back under the deerskin when Angus offered her a bite of venison, but the odor caused her quickly to change her mind. She grabbed the meat and quickly swallowed it in one gulp. Angus fed her several more bites of meat, bigger and more numerous than she had consumed the previous evening. Her appetite had returned to normal, but she was still too weak to jump or walk or run.

After she relieved herself, Angus again cocooned her in the white deerskin, carried her to the canoe, and bundled her in the bearskin. Launching his craft into the water, he lightly stepped in, picked up his paddle, and deftly guided the canoe out into the current. Another day had begun. There would be nearly fourteen hours of daylight and Angus did not want to waste any of them. He was eager to reach the trading post where he could sell his furs, purchase some depleted supplies, and receive the latest news. Although he greatly enjoyed the solitude of the wilderness, he coveted news of the latest French-

British conflicts. Hopefully, the wolf pup would sleep most of the day and cause no trouble that might delay his progress.

The river coursed smoothly between lofty hills wrapped in dense forests that bordered it on the east and west. It was easy to avoid the occasional boulders, so the canoe and its two occupants continued their uneventful northward journey. The river had widened considerably, and no longer did tree branches form a canopy overhead. Angus was comfortable with his ability to read the river—the ripples, the swirls, the rapids, and the calm, flat stretches. He was confident in his ability to avoid lurking disaster in the form of hidden snags and boulders. Angus estimated that it would be another two days before he reached the junction of the West Fork and the eastern fork of the Monongahela. Unless storms dumped several inches of rain upriver he should experience smooth water all the way to the trading post at the Forks of the Ohio.

Angus had carefully chosen this river because, unlike the eastern fork of the Monongahela, it contained no dangerous rapids. Stories abounded about trappers who attempted to bring loads of furs down the dangerous waters of the eastern fork, losing not only their canoes and furs, but also their lives. If he ever trapped in the headwaters of the eastern fork he would need horses to pack out his furs. He would possibly try it next year, but for now he must deliver this load of furs safely to the traders, or there would be no gold to pay Heather's passage from Scotland. Angus constantly fretted that he had abandoned his beloved in Scotland. Along with his frustration at having so little gold, he felt guilty that he was enjoying the freedom and excitement of the American frontier while his beloved was facing the hardships dealt by the English.

To cover even more river miles, Angus chose to eat the mid-day meal in the dugout canoe. The weather was good, and he could just as easily eat his venison while drifting downstream as sitting on the riverbank. Before packing the canoe that morning, he had cut off several large slices of cooked venison and placed them where they were within easy reach. He also kept a bag of buffalo jerky and pemmican handy and chewed on that when he felt hungry.

The Shawnee taught him to make pemmican, an important

part of their diet. Dried, smoked deer meat (or elk or buffalo) was pounded into a coarse powder, then mixed with melted bear fat, dried berries, and the kernels of whatever nut meats were available to create a highly nutritious, easily preserved food.

The pemmican mixture was typically rolled into walnut-sized balls, which could be easily carried on hunting trips. Although the bear fat would get a little rancid and soft during the warm summer months, it kept indefinitely during winter months.

He floated for hours without stopping, dipping his cup into the river to sate his thirst. Although Angus could stand upright in the canoe, doing so was risky. Thus, when the need to relieve himself got too strong he pulled the canoe to the shore, and took the pup out to do likewise. Such stops provided an opportunity to stretch his legs, since the long hours spent kneeling in the bottom of the canoe cramped his leg muscles.

While constantly alert for possible dangers in the river and on the adjacent hillsides, his thoughts often returned to the wolf pup. Coming from a breed that had combined toughness and cunning to exist for tens of thousands of years, he did not doubt that it would survive. If it stayed with him it would need a name. A special animal needed a special name. His hounds had been given such names as "Bonnie" and "Ruffee" and "Lucy." A wolf deserved a name that recalled the wilderness—one that reflected the qualities of the mountains or the skies, the rivers or the storms, or the dangers that were ever present. The name should be two syllables, so that it was easily recognizable to the pup. A one-syllable name was too easily missed or misunderstood. Most dogs only identified and responded to the first one or two syllables of a name, even if the name actually had three or four syllables. The second syllable should be one that could be drawn out when calling to the dog. Angus liked a name that ended in an "e," so the "e-sound" could be as long as he wanted. Bonnie was a good name for a gentle dog, but not appropriate for a timber wolf. This name selection was going to take days or weeks to resolve, but the pup must have a name for training to be successful.

The pup slept through the morning, and, although Angus could not see her beneath the bearskin, her movements during early afternoon told him that she had awakened. He was sure she was hungry, but he did not want to risk feeding her while the canoe was in the water. The pup would have to wait for her evening meal until he beached the dugout. Angus reasoned that if hungry, she was more likely to let him handle her and feed her. Although she had been nursing her mother several times each day, the nursing frequency would have decreased as she and the other wolf pups were slowly weaned from milk to a meat diet. They were usually fed solid food once per day, but if the male wolf was unsuccessful in his hunt there was no meat for the pups.

By mid-afternoon Angus started searching the shoreline for a suitable campsite. Had he been alone he would have needed only one hour of daylight to set up his camp. To spend some daylight working with the wolf, however, he needed at least two hours. Gravel bars were numerous along the river, and in late afternoon he spotted a nice broad bar along the inside bend of the river. It was bordered by a high bank, which had two large logs and an adequate supply of driftwood. Huge towering sycamore trees formed a canopy over the gravel bar. He pulled onto shore, tied up his canoe, and prepared his fire pit alongside one large hemlock log. He was eager to unload the pup and see how she would react to his presence. She was surely hungry, but would certainly have more energy than she had the previous night. He did not know what to expect, but he was sure it would be interesting. Angus wanted to have warm meat to feed her, since she was used to feeding on the warm meat regurgitated by her mother. He would have to gradually switch her diet to raw meat, but that could wait.

Slicing off slabs of a dried venison shoulder, he placed them on broiling sticks that were propped close to the fire. As the meat sizzled, the juices dripped into the fire and gave off the aroma that Angus always looked forward to. He thought that he could eat venison everyday for the rest of his life and never get tired of it. Of course, buffalo and elk, plus an occasional turkey, would add a welcome variety to his meals, but an all-meat diet was adequate if plenty of fat was available. As the meat warmed, Angus bit off a large chunk and slowly chewed it into softened pieces that the pup could handle.

Lifting the deerskin-wrapped pup from the dugout canoe, he carried her to the fire, and kneeled down on his bearskin. Again shielding her from the flames, he removed the deerskin from her head, and offered her a piece of the warmed and softened deer meat. A puny low growl rose from her throat, but she did not hesitate to grab the meat. In one quick gulp it was gone. After feeding her enough to distend her stomach, Angus decided it was time to give her some exercise. After all, she had been wrapped in the deerskin for nearly two days.

Gently unwrapping the pup from the deerskin, he placed her on the bearskin and stroked her fluffy coat to mimic the mother's licking. For the first time he got a good look at the pup and saw she bore little resemblance to the half-drowned creature he had first seen along the river's edge. Her small rounded ears and long fluffy tail identified her as a wolf. Angus estimated that she weighed almost three pounds.

Her sky-blue eyes stood out against her soft gray fur, gray like the clouds that scudded across the winter sky. Not white like the big puffy clouds that forecast good weather, and not black like the storm clouds that forecast an imminent snowstorm, but silvery gray like the clouds that warned of the unknown. He thought she was one of the most beautiful creatures he had ever seen. All pups are charming, but the combined looks of a cute puppy and a wild predator made this one special. He really wanted her to be a faithful companion— to share the joys and the dangers of life in the wilderness.

The pup recoiled as she gained her first full, daylight view of Angus; her natural instincts warned her that this was an enemy to be avoided. The only living creatures she had seen were wolves. This was certainly not a wolf, although the long red hair made the creature kneeling before her look somewhat animal-like. While its appearance was strange and threatening, the strange creature's scents were somewhat familiar. She could detect scents that reminded her of the den—deer and bear and beaver, and a mixture of dozens of other vaguely familiar wild animal scents. But one overtone was strangely different. She had picked up hints of that odor while in the canoe and while being fed bits of meat. The pup had never seen or smelled a human. Although the weathered deerskin that clothed Angus had been tanned and later exposed to hundreds of smoky fires, it smelled somewhat like the pieces of deer hide that lay around the mouth of the wolf den. Had it been summer, the pungency of human sweat would have dominated all other scents, but dozens of rainstorms during the winter months had removed much human scent from the deerskins.

Smoke from the fire irritated the wolf pup's nostrils more than the human odors. While the clothes, bearskins, and deerskins gave off smoky odors, she was not too disturbed. Angus had built a small fire with the driest driftwood he could find, but it still gave off a little smoke. When the wind changed, the smoke drifted over the pup and she shuddered. It burned her eyes and stung her sensitive nostrils. She suddenly jumped from the bearskin and ran away from the smoke. She ran to the steep bank, but turned as she reached its base. She then ran pell-mell towards the river, falling into the water before she could stop.

Although shallow, the current caught her and pulled her downstream. Awkward paddling with her short front legs did little to get her out of the water. Angus had not chased after the pup when she first bolted off the bearskin for fear of frightening her even more. But as the current started sweeping her downstream he jumped to his feet and ran into the water. Fortunately she had not drifted far from the shore and Angus had to go in only up to his knees. Grabbing the pup by the scruff of her neck, he carried her back to the bearskin. The pup shook herself a few times and then crouched as if ready to run again. Angus slowly dropped the deerskin over the now shivering pup and scooped her up so that she could not see him and would be sheltered from the campfire smoke. He would have to figure how to gradually orient the pup to a campfire, and to a human.

CHAPTER SIX
EARLY TRAINING

—————————

THE PUP WOULD DEFINITELY need a leash. She would have to be tied up at campsites, and would certainly have to be tethered while in the canoe. No pup ever liked a rope around its neck; all fought it at first. The sooner the rope was used, however, the quicker it was accepted. His experiences in Scotland had taught him that a rope should be tied around a pup's neck as soon as it was weaned from its mother. The loose end of the rope should drag after the pup and would actually become a plaything. While chewing on and chasing the rope, the pup would become accustomed to the slight tugging against its neck. Angus had expanded the rope training with former pups by gradually pulling on the rope, especially when offering them food. To get them accustomed to the tether, Angus would fasten the rope to a post only when he fed them. Most pups soon came to accept the rope as a normal part of their lives. Thus, the first steps to tame the wolf pup were determined.

After retrieving a five-foot deerskin cord from the canoe, Angus approached the swaddled pup. He tied a small loop in the end of the cord, reached under the deerskin, and placed the loop around its neck. The pup trembled but did not resist him. To prevent injury he had placed a stop knot in the rope so that it could not tighten around the pup's neck. Angus lifted the deerskin and the pup shivered slightly as the cold air hit her damp fur. After sitting on her haunches for a few minutes she walked from the bearskin to the steep bank. She sniffed at a piece of driftwood and then squatted to relieve herself for the fourth time that day.

Meandering over to the river's edge, she sniffed at the water. She stuck her nose in the water but jumped backward as water entered her nostrils. The pup had never drunk water and had never really seen water, other than the few minutes she lay in it when Angus first discovered her. Now she returned to the water and timidly sniffed at the small waves that washed around her paws. She jumped back, sniffed, then tried to bite the water and in so doing got a few drops in her mouth. Although cold, it was refreshing. The dry deer meat had made her thirsty. She began awkwardly biting, and licking, and lapping at the water. Only a little water entered her mouth, but it was enough to convince her that this was fun. She continued playing at the water's edge for several minutes, grabbing bites of water. Then tiring of the game, she wandered back to the high bank. While this whimsical lesson was taking place the feather-light cord was trailing behind her, but she was barely aware of its presence.

Angus left the bearskin, crawled on his knees towards the pup and stopped ten feet away. With head tilted sideways, intent blue eyes watched him curiously, but she did not attempt to run. Ears pointed alertly upward, but her tail was held down. Angus had a mouthful of deer venison, and made a show of spitting in out on the gravel in full view of the pup. This behavior triggered fond memories of her mother entering the tunnel with a meal of venison, and the pup advanced a few steps closer to Angus, her nose twitching nervously. He retreated a bit, crouching on the gravel much as the mother wolf would have done. Enticed by the odor, the pup crawled slowly towards the small pile of partially chewed venison, with ears now held flat.

As she began eating the meat Angus crawled within reach of the deerskin cord fastened around her neck. He crouched on the gravel and slowly inched closer to the feeding pup. Shortening the cord between him and the pup, Angus was within an arm's length before the pup finished eating. Slowly reaching out, Angus grasped the cord just behind the pup's neck. As she finished eating, she turned to move away, but Angus scooped her up into his large hands. She growled and snapped. Angus gently grabbed her muzzle, held her jaws closed, and uttered a low, guttural drawn out, "No. No." The pup cringed slightly, but remained quiet when Angus released her muzzle.

Fearing that his voice would frighten the pup, Angus had been hesitant to speak previously, reasoning that the sound of a human voice was unlike anything she had ever heard. He was also aware that successful training depended on the pup obeying his voice commands. Angus suspected that a deep, guttural "No," somewhat resembled the growl that the wolf mother would have used to extinguish some behaviors. Although he had spoken frequently to the hound pups he previously raised, he would delay talking to the pup until it became accustomed to his presence.

Walking slowly to the fire, Angus placed the pup on the bearskin and covered it with the white deerskin. He tied her leash to a limb protruding from the log, against which he now reclined. As he stared into the hypnotic flames from his small campfire, he concluded that the first lesson in taming this fascinating little wild creature had gone rather well. The eight-hoots of a barred owl announced the arrival of night and Angus crawled into his bearskin bed. The pup was already asleep and dreaming of her former den, especially the warmth and comfort provided by her brothers and sisters. The warmth provided by Angus's body replaced that provided by the pup's mother and, in response, she snuggled up against him. Conscious of every sound and every movement, Angus felt it keenly when the small sleeping pup snuggled against him. He realized that the pup was responding to his body warmth and not to him as a person; but the fact the pup did not avoid him gave hope that he might become a surrogate for the mother.

Angus and his bedfellow slept soundly during the night. At first light, Angus picked up the bearskin-wrapped pup, and moved the wriggling bundle to the far end of the big log. He tied her where the smoke would not be a problem and started the campfire. After a hearty breakfast, Angus fed the pup some mush-soaked venison. All dogs liked cooked mush, and they seemed to put on more weight with a corn meal and meat diet than with meat alone. As he expected, the pup gulped down the pieces of flavorful venison as quickly as Angus dropped them before her.

As the pup watched, Angus readied the canoe for another long day on the river, but this time he built a small recess for the pup.

Her eyes locked on his every move. Turning a basket on its side he layered a deerskin in the bottom and partially covered the retreat with a bearskin. This would be the pup's bed and her sanctuary in case of bad weather. Every young canine needs a private place of its own, and a small, enclosed place is preferable to a large one. A pup is less likely to relieve itself in its own retreat than if given the entire run of a large canoe. No pup, wild or domestic, would inhabit a feces-filled space, unless it had no choice.

Angus thought of Sweetwater and wondered what the Shawnee maiden would say if she saw the effort he was making to accommodate the pup in the canoe. Surely she would question how he could make room for a wolf but find no room for her.

Angus now crouched and slowly approached the pup on all fours. He fingered the deerskin cord as he drew closer and eventually was able to pick her up. She growled at him and once again nipped at his hand. In response, he grasped her muzzle and growled back, "No, No!" to her. The pup was deposited into the deerskin-lined basket and Angus pushed off. The current soon caught the heavily-loaded canoe and swept it downstream. Only occasional paddling was needed to keep the canoe facing downriver, and a wary Angus kept a watchful eye on his surroundings. The pup was still regaining her strength, and the morning's activities had taken their toll. She was soon asleep in her basket. It was clear to Angus that some dogs were much more intelligent than others, and thus easier to train. But Angus suspected that wolves were more intelligent than domesticated dogs. Hopefully, both man and wolf would learn much as the training continued.

The day passed much as had the previous one, although Angus found himself stopping more frequently than before to let the pup play and relieve herself. By stopping he was delaying his arrival at the trading post, but a few minutes spent with the pup would not add more than one or two extra days to the trip. Angus was amused that the pup became quite playful and spent several minutes biting at the water and chewing sticks she found at the water's edge. He realized that this was not only good exercise but was a necessary foreplay for drinking and a way to keep her occupied in the canoe. He found it rewarding that she constantly peered back at him to gauge his reactions.

That night and the next morning were uneventful, although the pup entertained him by spending considerable time digging in the sandy bank. At the lower end of the gravel bar where they camped Angus found the dried out remains of a small elk that had drowned while trying to cross the flooded river. Using his axe he removed the kneecap and two of the short toe bones. He gave the pup a kneecap with vestiges of dried elk skin and she began chewing her newfound treasure with gusto.

Angus had started talking to the pup in an attempt to get her comfortable with his voice. At first she seemed to be frightened of this strange sound, but he was careful to speak deeply and softly. He wondered whether he should attempt to make wolf sounds or man sounds, or a mixture of the two. He wished he knew what sounds the mother wolf made when she brought food, or called the pups, or reprimanded them for undesirable behavior. He knew nothing of wolf language, other than the howls that were frightening but fascinating. Should he try to teach the pup to howl, or would the pup know how to howl without training? Angus still had not decided on a name for the pup. When talking to her, he simply called her "puppy," with a drawn-out "eee." He made an effort to call "puppeee" each time she wandered away from him on the gravel bar. Sometimes she turned and looked at him, but most of the time she ignored him.

It was time to load the pup into the canoe, so Angus deposited her in the middle and handed her one of the elk bones. She immediately settled down with her prize and began chewing earnestly. Although her baby teeth were small, they were sharp enough to gouge the ends of the water-softened bone. Chewing occupied her nearly an hour, before a full stomach and a warm sun brought on a deep puppy sleep. Angus pulled the bearskin over her basket and let his thoughts wander to the past winter.

The visit with the Shawnee had been enjoyable, as well as educational. He had learned things about the wilderness that he would never have learned otherwise. He had made many acquaintances, and there were even a few Shawnee he could call close friends. Not surprisingly, his thoughts returned to Sweetwater. Her smiling dark eyes remained quite vivid in his memories, and he would have been thrilled if she suddenly appeared at one of his campfires during the trip downriver. But that was not likely to happen, even if she had pursued him. His canoe traveled much faster than she could walk and even faster than she could ride a horse through the rugged mountains. He might never again see her shining face or hear her delightful laugh.

Somewhat pensively, he envisioned a different river trip with Sweetwater seated in the front of his dugout. As the afternoon sun reached full strength, she would have casually slipped off the top of her doeskin dress. Paddling would accentuate the firm muscles in her bare back and her smooth golden skin would glisten as each strong stroke drove the paddle into the passing river. Although only the sleek back would have been visible to Angus, it took little imagination for his thoughts to wander beyond the shoulders. As he mentally enjoyed the scene, he acknowledged the associated distraction of that attractive body. How could he remain constantly alert for danger when his attention was focused elsewhere? Smiling wistfully, he weighed the advantages and the disadvantages of her company.

He wished she could see the wolf pup. She seemed to like animals—especially dogs—more than she liked many of the Indians in the camp. This was not surprising to Angus, for he shared similar feelings about many of the settlers along the Monongahela. He preferred traveling with one of his hounds to the company of settlers, trappers, or hunters. He was reminded of the Scottish proverb, "Better alone than in ill company." He did not really enjoy talking to other humans, wanting to keep his thoughts to himself. He was at ease talking to his hounds when they were alone, and both he and his dogs seemed to enjoy the monologue. Talking to Sweetwater had been surprisingly easy. Even with a language barrier, they had enjoyed conversations about the trees, and the animals, and all the natural things that made the wilderness so special. He was even comfortable sharing some of his ideas with her, although he never revealed his deeper, more personal thoughts.

Angus grew concerned when he realized that his thoughts had first turned to Sweetwater, and only later to Heather. During the long, sometimes tedious trip across the Atlantic, Heather was constantly on his mind. Angus wondered how she would be able to survive such a daunting trip. It was tough enough for a strong person like himself, whereas a dainty girl like Heather would face problems that he could not even imagine.

Angus had been forced to endure hardships most of his life. From his life in the stone huts of the Scottish Highlands to the many hunting trips through rocky crags searching for the elusive red deer, he had been seasoned for the rigorous sea voyage and life in the Appalachian wilderness.

In contrast, Heather had spent most of her time in and around the farmhouse near Loch Ness. Life had certainly not been easy at the farm, but she had never survived extended trips into the Highlands and had certainly never endured cold wet nights sleeping only in the shelter of a few boulders.

Day after day, while working with the boat maker, Joseph Myers, near Philadelphia, Angus thought of Heather. But as he made the exciting and dangerous trip across the mountains to the Monongahela, he was forced to block out all but the immediate challenges. During that journey his childhood sweetheart had been the lead character in most of his dreams, but now as he transported his load of furs down the West Fork River she was absent many nights. Angus still longed to see her, to have her join him in making a life in the Appalachian wilderness.

Possibly they would build a cabin along one of the rich bottomlands so abundant throughout the mountains. While wild animals would provide most of their food, they would clear a few acres for a cornfield, raise a few sheep and cows, and probably have several hogs running free through the hills. There certainly would be constant danger, but Angus could make friends with all but the most warlike of the Indians. He would build a small trading post. Hopefully, the Indians would value him as an important source of the goods they wanted, and thought they needed, rather than an enemy.

Before Heather could join him in the Appalachians, he had to get enough money to pay her passage across the Atlantic or buy her release from indentured servitude. While the current load of furs and hides in his canoe would not bring enough to pay for the trip, it would be a mighty good start.

Angus wondered whether Heather would accept a wolf as a companion. Her family had sheep dogs on their farm, but a sheep dog was not a hunting dog. The sheep dog had one job, and apparently one joy in life—to herd sheep in the way and manner signaled by its master. Sheep dogs were good at what they were bred for, but they were not hunters. The task of hunting was best handled by a hound.

If Angus could tame the wolf, the biggest challenge would be to train the pup to hunt. A hound in the Appalachian wilderness had to be quite skilled at helping its master in the successful pursuit of deer, elk, buffalo, and turkey. It also had to be skilled at handling bears, panthers, and wolves. The hound had to be big and powerful, but most of all it had to be intelligent. It had to recognize whether the task at hand was to trail a deer, drive off a panther, or warn of an Indian.

A wolf pup would normally have been taught all the finer points of hunting by its parents and other members of the pack. But his pup would never have the opportunity to follow along as the pack chased an elk for miles, or stalked a lone buffalo, or pulled down a deer. Its teaching would be up to him.

While a canoe floating down a wild river and loaded high with furs was not a great place to train a pup, it might not be a total loss. The first few weeks would involve only a few simple commands, with no serious hound training. Discipline would certainly be important, as would acceptance. The pup had to accept Angus as her pack leader—providing food and shelter, protection and leadership.

Just as it was important to Angus to have a canine companion, it was even more important that the pup have a leader—in this case a human leader. Wolves are social animals and, given the choice, they never live alone. They need the cooperation of other wolves to make kills of animals larger than themselves, but they also need the social structure of a pack. Dominant leaders are necessary for a wolf pack to exist, but there must also be subservient followers. Angus concluded that the next seven days spent on the river would be crucial to developing the social structure of this two-member pack.

Angus tied the loose end of the sleeping pup's leash to the bundle of furs immediately in front of his feet. In this way the pup could either rest in her own basket retreat, or sit and look out over the sides of the canoe, or even climb up onto the pile of furs. When she awoke, the pup became aware of the uprooted trees floating past them and the few large animals that moved onshore. Angus observed that the pup could not spot large animals that were motionless. She had never seen deer, elk, or buffalo, and thus did not recognize them as living things if they remained stationary.

As the canoe rounded the bend Angus spotted a lone bull buffalo standing at the river's edge. The canoe would pass within a few feet of the animal and Angus instinctively reached for his rifle, which was tied across the load of deer hides. Although he longed for a nice buffalo tongue for dinner that night, shooting the beast made no sense. He would end up wasting most of the meat. He had no room in the canoe for the hide, and he had enough deer venison and pemmican to feed him and the pup until the end of the trip. Also, the rifle fire would attract the attention of any Indians, or unscrupulous white trappers, who might be in the area. Yes, a buffalo tongue roasted over his campfire would taste mighty good, but it was not worth the risk of losing his load of furs.

Buffalo are not known for their keen eyesight, and because the canoe was floating slowly and Angus sat motionless, the giant bull did not spot the canoe until it had drifted to within twenty feet. Although the wolf was carefully studying the shoreline, to her the buffalo was nothing more than a large black lump, not unlike the many uprooted tree trunks they had passed. To Angus, the buffalo was one of the most awesome land animals he had ever seen; it was larger than any of the hairy beef cattle that his family had raised in Scotland and even larger than the shaggy horses his clansman had used to travel through the Scottish Highlands. Although this beast somewhat resembled one of the oxen used to haul wagons in the seaboard colonies, the huge head—with flat forehead, prominent beard, and shiny black horns—convinced Angus that the two were only distantly related.

To further justify this opinion, Angus studied the towering hump situated behind the neck, the thick mane over the head, neck, and shoulders, the huge dark eyes that were deep as Loch Ness, and the smooth wooly hair that covered the rear quarters of this strange animal that the French trappers had first called boeuf, buffe, and buffle. Only later did the French term "buffelo" become the widely used "buffalo."

Angus wondered what would happen when the buffalo saw the canoe, but he was more concerned about how the wolf would react. The buffalo detected a slight movement in the canoe at the same time he caught the strange mixed smells of man and wolf. He snorted, turned with a loud splash, and crashed through the willow bushes growing at the river's edge. The pup was so startled she tumbled headlong off the pile of furs and landed in the bottom of the canoe. But curiosity, not fear, took over. Instead of cowering inside her basket, she quickly stood up with her front paws on the side of the canoe and began yipping bravely at the rapidly retreating buffalo.

Angus was not surprised at her reaction, but was not pleased to hear her yip. A good hound must never bark except on command. Barking advertises your presence, and that is rarely advantageous in the wilderness. He immediately grasped her muzzle in his hand and in a low voice uttered, "Qui...et, qui...et." The pup was understandably excited, and although she had never seen a buffalo, her instinct told her that this running creature was something to chase.

Had she been with the wolf parents there would have been a chase. While her short legs would have limited the duration of her pursuit, she would have learned that wolves are supposed to chase prey animals, regardless of their size. She would have watched her parents chase the buffalo and would have learned by imitation. Angus knew she must be taught not to chase every animal she encountered. She must chase only on command. Otherwise, she must trail quietly and avoid detection. She must learn to wait for Angus's signal; he was the leader of her pack.

With the buffalo out of sight, the pup soon shifted her focus to objects floating in the river, flying overhead, and moving along the shore. She had climbed back onto the pile of furs when a small tree limb, riding high in the water, suddenly floated beside them. The pup thought it would make a nice thing to chew on and reacted by jumping unabashedly from the furs into the water. She disappeared from sight but quickly surfaced, and instinctively began paddling. She managed to keep her head above the water, but her eyes displayed her apprehension. The water was cold and she wanted back in the canoe. Angus reacted quickly; clutching the deerskin cord tied around her neck, he pulled her closer to the canoe. Reaching over the side he clutched the scruff of her skinny neck and hauled her into the canoe. She looked as bedraggled as she had when he discovered her alone at the water's edge. This time, however, she only needed to shake a few times, lick some water from her belly, and roll over three times on the deerskin before she looked almost normal. As she looked up at Angus, she panted heavily and he could almost see her heart beating wildly under those scrawny ribs.

Fear was quickly replaced by excitement as she confidently stood up to search for the tree limb that had caused all the trouble. Her self-assurance was becoming as clear as her personality and her experiences were teaching her a great deal.

Angus and the wolf shared several pieces of deer venison in the canoe and several more later when they stopped for their mid-day meal. They made four short stops during the day. A full two hours before sunset, Angus paddled the canoe onto an ideal sandbar where they would stop for the night. Storm clouds were gathering in the western sky and the temperature was dropping. There would be rain before morning. He must find and cut enough saplings for a lean-to that would provide some protection from the weather. He could throw deer hides over the frame, and they would repel pouring rain. It was equally important to gather a large pile of dry wood.

The wolf pup had found a nice teething stick and Angus tied her to a log while he prepared camp. Angus was able to chop several dead birch into long logs that he rolled down the riverbank to their campsite. Remembering the long hours she had spent chewing on the elk bones in the canoe that day, Angus set out to find some more small bones for the next day's trip. A few minutes of searching revealed a thighbone and several small foot bones of a deer. He put the thighbone in the canoe and dropped the foot bones into his deerskin shoulder pouch. He would give them to the pup tomorrow when they were once again on the river.

CHAPTER SEVEN
THE BLUE STONE

LIGHTNING FLASHED ACROSS the western sky several times during the night, and the booming thunder awakened both Angus and the pup. The resulting rainfall was light, and the storm had passed over them by the time faint light to the east announced that the night was nearly ended. Angus removed the pup from the bearskin and tied her to the end of the canoe. She could play in the water and lap up a few drops as he prepared breakfast. While water was boiling in his small kettle, Angus decided to add a few more deer bones to his shoulder pouch. The pup seemed to relish chewing them, and they kept her occupied in the canoe.

As he reached into the pouch, Angus felt the strange blue stone he had discovered in a cave during his stay with the Shawnee. His thoughts meandered back to the early season snowstorm that suddenly appeared as he was scouting for beaver dams west of the Shawnee camp and to the strange circumstances surrounding the appearance of the mysterious mineral. He recalled how he had set out his traps in a series of beaver ponds upstream of the camp, and then searched for several more pond complexes to relocate his traps during the fast-approaching winter.

Recalling a small cave he had discovered earlier in the day, Angus retraced his steps and was soon out of the biting wind and the blowing wet snow. The cave, situated high on the hillside, had been large enough for him to stand upright, and after a cursory examination Angus had decided to spend the night. He often did not return to his bark wegiwa in the Shawnee camp and had spent many nights camping beneath an overhanging boulder, or out in the open if the sky promised no precipitation. Resting his muzzle-loader against the side of the cave, Angus gathered enough branches to maintain a small fire inside the cave throughout the night.

The floor was dry and wide enough for him to spread his bearskin. Angus lit a pine knot and began to explore the cave when he found mysterious markings on one wall and what appeared to be an old fire pit. The markings closely resembled the etchings Angus had seen in various caves throughout the Scottish Highlands. They were known as Ogam, an ancient Irish alphabet composed of lines, not letters. Apparently he was not the first human to spend time inside that particular cave. Angus calculated that the cave was large enough for as many as six persons to make it their home for an entire winter.

After supper he sat by the small fire inside the cave, studying the shadows that flickered constantly on the walls. There were plenty of small branches at hand to maintain the fire; he carefully placed his flint and steel at the edge of the pile of branches.

As Angus rested in the cave, his thoughts returned to life in the Scottish Highlands, where he had spent many nights huddled beside a small fire within the friendly confines of a small cave. The memories of those adventurous days in Scotland reminded him that he sorely missed his homeland. In his relaxed state, Heather floated into his thoughts and he soon fell into a deep sleep that lasted the entire night. A hint of daylight appeared at the entrance of the cave and urged Angus out of his bearskin. Noting that no glowing coals were evident, he added a small pile of dried bark and grass to his now-blackened fire pit and reached for his flint and steel. Much to his surprise, both were missing, but in their place his fingers discovered a smooth stone.

Angus spent several minutes searching around the small pile of branches and finally concluded that his flint and steel were not where he had left them the previous night. What in the world could have happened to them? Although he really did not need a fire for warmth, he wanted one for light. Kneeling near his fire pit, Angus had carefully fingered the ashes. Rewarded by slight warmth and then definite heat, he spotted the glow of one small ember. After carefully adding bits of dried grass, a small wisp of smoke appeared, followed within minutes by a small flame. As it had done countless times, fire—the most important of all human discoveries—reliably appeared.

While eating a breakfast of smoked deer jerky, Angus had added wood to the fire until it was throwing light onto all walls of the cave. Picking up one of the pine knots he had purposefully saved, Angus began another search of the cave. On a ledge halfway up one wall he carefully examined a pile of small sticks that he had missed the previous night. As he had held his burning torch closer to the pile, he spotted a small reflection and, to his surprise, recognized his steel and his flint. How could his fire-making tools have moved during the night?

Angus curiously poked at the pile of sticks and was surprised to see a small gray animal scamper out and make its way along the ledge. After moving only a few feet, the critter stopped and sat up on its haunches. In the light of his torch, Angus saw it was a rat, but not the kind of scruffy rat he had seen on the large sailing ships that crossed the Atlantic. This rat had soft gray fur, big ears, long whiskers, and large black eyes that stared at the intruder. Its belly was a clean whitish color, and its tail was covered with soft hair. This certainly was not a ship rat. Angus remembered the Shawnee tales of rats that lived in caves—"cave rats" they called them. These fascinating rodents would take any small items they could find, especially shiny ones. However, they did not really steal them, because they would always leave something in exchange. It might be an acorn, a chestnut, or a small stone.

Angus had felt a twinge of remorse about recovering his flint and steel, because he wanted to keep the strange smooth blue stone and maintain the integrity of the "trade." Having nothing else to leave the cave rat, he placed two pieces of deer jerky near its nest of sticks. Hopefully, the cave rat, or "wood rat" as Sweetwater had called it, would feel that it had received a fair trade for the blue stone.

Angus relinquished his memories as he watched the wolf pup, remembering how the blue stone had become warm when he rubbed its surface. Once again he slowly caressed the smooth blue stone in his large weathered hands, and as before it emanated warmth.

Could this be his imagination or did the temperature of the stone actually increase?

Angus figured that if you rubbed any stone, friction would create a little warmth. He picked up a smooth river rock almost the same size as the blue stone, and rubbed it in his right hand and the blue stone in his left. After several minutes, there was no doubt in his mind that the blue stone was considerably warmer than was the river rock.

As Angus was rubbing the blue stone he noticed that the pup had waded out into the water. Keeping his voice calm, he whistled and called, "Back … back." Much to his surprise, the wolf immediately turned and stared intently at him. Then quickly, but purposefully, she stepped out of the water onto the shore. Angus was incredulous. It appeared that she understood exactly what he wanted her to do and actually obeyed.

He had indeed been successful in training some of his hounds to respond to certain commands, but it had required months of repeated trials, with rewards and punishment, before they showed even the slightest indication that they understood. Was the wolf so much more intelligent than his hounds? Angus put the blue stone back into his deerskin pouch and began to chew on a piece of deer meat. Crawling toward the pup on all fours, he spit the meat onto the ground before the pup, which lay flat, focused on the man approaching her. As she waited, he softly spoke, "Good lassie. Good lassie." The pup seemed to pay little attention to his voice, but instead snatched and then gobbled down the offering. When finished, the pup cautiously approached Angus and, for the first time, licked at his mouth.

Angus could hardly contain himself. The pup had overcome its fear of this strange creature and recognized it as a source of food. Angus crawled back to the fire, chewed up some more venison, and again spit it out before the pup. Once again she licked his face, ears back and tail wagging. The pup had apparently accepted Angus as a provider and a leader.

As much as he wanted to hold and pet the pup, Angus realized they were wasting daylight. They must finish breakfast, break camp, and get onto the river. Hurriedly, he carved "AMc" with his hunting knife into the bark of a giant sycamore, to match the location he had burned into his deerskin map the previous night.

The sky had cleared to a brilliant blue as westerly winds pushed the storm clouds over the horizon to the east. There had not been enough rain to raise water levels and the dugout canoe floated steadily downriver. Although little paddling was necessary, Angus had to steer clear of the few floating trees that had fallen into the river during the high waters of the previous winter. It occurred to him that he no longer felt pain in his broken left arm, and it seemed almost as strong as his right. With strong strokes of the paddle, Angus had no trouble avoiding all obstacles and was still able to scan the shoreline and nearby forests for any movement.

They passed several deer and a small group of buffalo that morning, and the pup reacted excitedly when their approach caused a small flock of wood ducks to take flight noisily from a quiet eddy. Angus quietly spoke to the pup, "Ea . . . sy. Ea . . . sy." This time the pup did not yip, or jump into the river, and this pleased Angus greatly.

As he paddled, huge towering trees crowded in on the river, making Angus a bit nervous. He tried to stay in the center of the river and not get too close to either bank. He did not expect to meet any other humans in a canoe, but there was a chance that someone on foot could spot his canoe with its huge bounty of furs and hides. In most places the river was wide enough that he felt no threat from the bow and arrow of an Indian. However, he was never out of range of a Pennsylvania rifle, and in the hands of a white hunter or trapper he would be an easy target. The smoke of a campfire high on the hillside had caught his attention that morning, but no humans had been visible.

Gigantic sycamores on the left bank reached out to those on the right bank, their trunks and exposed roots scarred deeply by the thousands of ice chunks that had been swept downriver during spring floods. In other places, dense stands of hemlock created a thick screen, and Angus could see only a few feet into their foreboding darkness. While Angus was ever watchful, the pup ignored the forest landscape, growing excited only when some large object floated past or some large animal went crashing through the trees. The pup alternately slept, chewed on a deer bone, or gulped down the few bites of deer meat that Angus offered her. But most of the day she would lie on her bearskin and watch Angus for hours at a time. Occasionally she would close her eyes and take a quick nap; but upon wakening, her sparkling blue eyes would fasten on this strange creature that was always nearby.

Thoughts of her past were only vague memories, flashing quickly through her dreams. In those dreams, she recalled her life in the den, of playing with her brothers and sisters and snuggling against the warm body of her mother.

As with most wild animals she remembered few, if any, specifics of the past and thought nothing of the future. She lived in the moment. But the experiences, instincts, and knowledge of her parents, their parents, and the bloodlines of all their ancestors had been passed on to the pup. Although she had much to learn, she had the essential knowledge instilled in her brain that would make learning come easy.

The pup continued to be curious about the big creature that shared the canoe. He seemed friendly enough, feeding her and keeping her warm. But instinctively she remained wary of his close presence. Several times she had crawled close enough to smell his leggings and moccasins, and even licked his hand when he extended it with a piece of venison. She enjoyed being near him, lying against his knees as he kneeled in the bottom of the canoe, or sitting with her back touching his leather clothes. He had not attempted to hold her when they were in the canoe or even when they were sitting near the campfire. Only subconsciously did she sense that he would often caress her soft fur when they slept by the fire under the warm bearskin.

Angus was not surprised that the pup had become friendly with him. Most of the pups he had raised relished human contact, responding by much licking of hands and face. The wolf had slowly accepted his voice, and he now felt comfortable talking to her. She would tilt her head and stare at him as he spoke. Angus was gratified that the wolf pup showed signs of bonding.

As they rounded a bend in the river, Angus saw that it widened significantly. The West Fork more than doubled in size as it joined an even larger river from the east—a river that would one day be known as the Tygart. Angus remembered passing the mouth of this particular river the previous fall when he had led his packhorse up the west side of the West Fork River. The speed of the dugout canoe increased as they floated past the junction. Angus estimated that they now had at least ten more days of floating to reach the trading post. If those ten days went as smoothly as the previous seven, he would be surprised and extremely grateful.

Gravel bars became more numerous as the river meandered through the broad, forested valley that stretched ahead as far as Angus could see. Although the river waters flowed faster than Angus liked, the wider river meant a safer trip. He would be farther from the banks, with more room to maneuver his canoe should danger appear.

With so many gravel bars to choose from, Angus had some difficulty selecting one for their nightly camp. He scanned the shore for a large one with a high bank, since he wanted to let the pup run and play without fear of her going into the forest. He spotted a suitable bar, and carefully paddled his canoe into the shallow waters at the bar's upper end.

After stepping into the cold, clear water he carefully tied the end of the canoe to a large, flood-swept log. He untied the deerskin cord that held the pup and called, "Come. Come." As usual, she was so eager to get onto shore that she leapt from the top of the bundle of furs, which acted as both perch and resting area. Landing in the shallow water, she quickly splashed ashore and relieved herself. Angus walked with her around the gravel bar, looking for any sign that a large animal or a human had recently been there. Fortunately, he found no human tracks, but he did find the tracks of a large bear that had apparently crossed the river. He led the pup to the bear tracks and tried to get her to smell them, but she was indifferent.

With delight, she discovered something wonderful—the dead carcass of a large catfish that had washed ashore. After considerable sniffing she followed her instincts and rolled in it! Dogs and their wolf ancestors cannot resist the temptation to roll in something dead—the ranker the better. Angus did not want to share a canoe with a foul-smelling pup, but former experiences had taught him he could never change this behavior. He would have more luck teaching a dog not to bark, or gulp its food, or walk in mud puddles, than extinguishing the urge to roll in putrid dead things. It puzzled Angus that a dog or wolf would want to smell like something dead. Was it instinctive to mask the natural canine odor in order to be more successful in stalking a deer or a rabbit?

The pup required plenty of opportunity to play and dig, so Angus fastened a long deerskin cord to the one already tied around her neck, and then tied the extension to the end of the canoe as he began to set up camp. As she played, Angus quickly carved his initials on a tree that could be seen from the river. Sheathing his knife, he reached into his deerskin bag for the flint and steel to start a fire and his fingers again brushed against the round blue stone. Until the previous day, he had not thought much about the blue stone since he found it in the cave. Nothing specific happened on the river to trigger his thoughts about the blue stone; they just suddenly surfaced. Angus admitted to being superstitious, and it almost seemed as if the stone was trying to send him a message. But just as quickly as thoughts of the blue stone had materialized, they evaporated when Angus's attention was drawn to something more pressing.

After the pup had rolled on the dead catfish a few times Angus gently pulled her away. Walking across the gravel bar he guided the pup to his left side and commanded, "Heel. Heel." He continued walking around the bar, calling "heel" several times. The pup ignored him and tried to run ahead when she spotted a large log lying on the bar. Angus firmly held the deerskin cord so that the pup remained alongside or slightly behind him. When they were four feet from the log Angus called, "Whoa ... Whoa." The words "heel" and "whoa" were two of the most important commands for a dog to learn. These commands would be especially important when hunting, or when stalking an animal close enough to use his Pennsylvania rifle.

Angus wanted the pup to walk at his left side. Being right-handed, he carried his long-barreled flintlock muzzle-loader in his right hand so that he could cock the hammer and quickly swing it up to his right shoulder. The ability to fire quickly often meant the difference between chewing dried jerky or enjoying fresh deer liver for supper. A dog walking at his right side would prevent the smooth swing of the rifle to his right shoulder. As he made several more circuits around the gravel bar, Angus repeated the "heel" command. It would take many repetitions before a dog, or wolf, would walk naturally at his left side.

After tying the pup to the end of the canoe and assuring himself that the site was safe, Angus made camp. A careful examination of the surrounding hillsides revealed no smoke that would have indicated a campfire. Every time he searched the nearby hills for campfire smoke he thought of Sweetwater and the many campfires they had shared the past winter. Usually he had a vision of her engaging smile and her long black hair, before her face faded away. A few times he had envisioned her standing on the riverbank when he departed the Shawnee camp—her smile replaced by a frown of disappointment.

Sweetwater's image eventually morphed into Heather's, but the features of his Scottish sweetheart were usually blurred, often appearing quite hazy. On some days he would try hard to recall Heather's lovely physical attributes—lengths of chestnut hair falling along her slender neck; the doe-like brown eyes shaded by thick lashes; the long shapely legs of a dancer. Yet even those images became fleeting as he returned to the present.

When the venison and corn mush stew was ready to eat, Angus brought the wolf pup to the fire. The pup was now familiar with flames and even seemed to bask in their warmth. She especially enjoyed lying on the bearskin close to the fire and eyeing Angus as he sat nearby. If Angus happened to step close to her she would raise her head and slowly wag her tail with pleasure. She had never known warmth from any source other than her mother and her littermates, but now she had discovered the satisfaction of soaking up the sun's rays in the canoe, or the fire's heat when on a bearskin.

The pup watched closely as Angus put several pieces of meat into his mouth and began chewing; she began to salivate. She stood up and hungrily edged closer to Angus. As he crouched down, she licked at his mouth and beard. In response he spit out some pieces of meat on the ground and then offered her several more from his hand. After quickly swallowing all the meat she began licking his hand, and Angus gave her some more slices of the smoked venison. She gulped those down but still seemed to be hungry.

Because the pup was now eating so much, Angus worried that his supply of smoked venison would run out before they reached the trading post. Deer were plentiful along the river, and the canoe often passed close enough to shoot one, but firing his Pennsylvania rifle could alert nearby humans to his presence. But what could be caught with the least amount of time and effort?

The Shawnee had built funnel-shaped traps in streams to capture fish, and at night they speared fish from the riverbank or from a canoe. The light from a burning pine knot made it easy to approach a fish swimming near the surface and to thrust a two-pronged spear into the finned prey. Large catfish were often speared, wrapped in cattail leaves, and roasted in coals. The Shawnee also set snares and deadfalls along animal trails to catch small critters such as rabbits, squirrels, or even small deer. Angus reckoned that the wolf pup would rather eat a rabbit than a catfish. At Sweetwater's urging, he had brought three slender cords made of woven yellow poplar bark to make snares.

Leaving the wolf pup tied to the log, he searched along the riverbank for animal runways. In a short time he found one narrow runway through tall grass and a second that emerged from under a fallen hemlock tree. He would set two snares in the grass runway and one in the runway below the hemlock tree. After making a small loop in the end of a cord, he expanded it into a circle about four inches wide. The snare had to be wide enough for an animal's head to pass through, but narrow enough that the shoulders and front legs could not. The loop of the snare was set across the trail and was held open by small tree branches pushed into the ground. The end of one snare was tied to the base of a bush while the ends of the other two were tied to small logs.

An animal traveling along the runway would be caught by the neck when the pressure of its shoulders and front legs pushed against the snare. Struggling would cause the snare to tighten around the animal's neck and in a few minutes it would lose consciousness. Death would come quickly, unlike the prolonged suffering if caught by a hawk or owl or bobcat.

After setting the three snares, Angus returned to his campfire. The wolf pup was so happy to see him return that she ran and jumped up on him. This was the first time she had ever jumped up onto his leg. While Angus was pleased to see that she had missed him, he was annoyed with her jumping. This was one of the most exasperating traits that a dog could have, and showed a lack of training on the owner's part as well as a lack of discipline on the dog's part.

As the pup was standing on her hind legs with her front feet against his deerskin leggings, Angus lightly stepped onto her hind toes. Due to her small size, her feet were not very far apart and Angus's deerskin moccasin covered both her hind feet. Although his moccasin was soft, the pup's toes were caught between the weight of his foot and the solid gravel. Though not seriously hurt, the pup yelped in surprise and pain. At the same time Angus stepped on her toes, he commanded, "Down. Down." The pup quickly dropped onto all fours and began licking her pinched toes.

Angus did not want to lessen the pup's feelings for him, but he could not permit the pup to develop bad habits. He knew that if he struck the pup with his hand or a switch the pup would associate him with the pain. Because she could not see his feet when she jumped on him, the pup would not associate the pain in her toes with anything he did. Now Angus dropped onto his knees and began rubbing the pup's head and neck. She began wriggling and wagging her tail and was soon licking his hands and his face. She forgot all about the pain in her toes and followed Angus back to the campfire.

As they sat before the fire, the pup sprawled on the bearskin and laid her head on Angus's moccasin. Her eyes soon closed, her body relaxed, and she drifted off. Angus watched as she let out a few low whimpers while breathing deeply. With her lips partly separated, she seemed to be smiling. Angus smiled also. Other than the one obvious thing, what more could a young man want? He had the flickering flames of a small cozy campfire, a wolf pup resting its finely-shaped head on his moccasins, a river gurgling nearby, and he was surrounded by a deep, fascinating wilderness. Night sounds added to the moment as green frogs called from the riverbank, barred owls hooted from the opposite hillside, and the smacking of a beaver tail in the river joined the calls of a night bird as it flew upstream. He felt fortunate to have solitude, freedom, and unlimited opportunities.

Angus and the pup both slept soundly through the night, although Angus dreamt of the disastrous Battle of Culloden. The English slaughtered more than two thousand of Bonnie Prince Charles' highlanders, and both Angus and Prince Charles had narrowly escaped with their lives. The Prince and many of his faithful fled from the Scottish Highlands to the Isle of Skye where they eluded their British enemies. From there Angus fled to Ireland where he found passage on a ship leaving Belfast for America, in the company of 180 other Scotsmen. The miseries of the wretched two-month Atlantic voyage posed a stark contrast to the comfortable and rewarding four years he spent as a boat builder's apprentice along the Delaware River. It required those four years of indenture to pay for his ship's passage across the stormy Atlantic seas.

The pup was also dreaming. But her dreams centered on events in her newfound life—a warm campfire, a cozy bearskin, juicy deer meat, a smelly dead catfish, and a kind companion.

At the first hint of daylight, Angus awoke and slipped his lanky frame from under the bearskin, careful not to awaken the pup. Eager to check his snares, he hurried up over the riverbank and eased through the underbrush to the snare at the downed hemlock. To his disappointment the snare was untouched. The second snare, set in the grassy runway, had been pulled loose as if some large animal had ventured through, but like the first snare, it was empty.

Angus had set many snares around Loch Ness and found that on any one night only a few snares were likely to be successful. He knew precisely where to find the large warrens that provided homes for hundreds of fat hares and those were his targets when he roamed the Highlands. A fat hare roasting on a spit over a small campfire, with the juices slowly dripping into the fire provided enough rich meat to sate even the hungriest Highlander.

Angus approached the last snare, and his heart raced as he

noticed the trampled grass. The snare was no longer attached to the branches over the runway. Edging closer, he saw a large cottontail rabbit hanging limp. Collecting the rabbit and his other two snares, he hurried back to the campsite. The rabbit was still limber, so Angus was confident it had been snared shortly before dawn. The Shawnee recounted how wolf parents would bring dead animals to pups, as a precursor to killing their own food.

The wolf was still asleep under the bearskin, and Angus called quietly to her as he approached. The bearskin moved slightly, and a tiny black twitching nose slowly eased out, followed by a small pointed muzzle, then two inquisitive blue eyes, and finally a pair of rounded ears standing straight up. With only her head out in the open, she looked around, nose wriggling. Angus called, "Puppee come. Puppee come." The pup crawled out from under the heavy bearskin, yawned, stretched, and then sat on her haunches. When he called the third time she located him and bounded in his direction.

As he dropped the dead rabbit on the gravel in front of the pup, she stopped, backed up, and then began sniffing at the strange furry thing. Cautiously she inched forward close enough to sniff at one of the long hind legs, then she moved around to the head. A drop of blood, still liquid, hung from the rabbit's nose. The wolf pup sniffed at the blood, then quickly licked it off. Instinctively, she bit at the head and neck, although her baby teeth were inadequate to tear into the rabbit. The rabbit weighed nearly as much as the pup, but by now her adrenalin was surging, and she managed to pick it up. After proudly dragging it around the gravel bar several times, she dropped her prize and lay down beside it, panting. Was she smiling as she looked at him, Angus wondered. After a brief rest, the pup began to chew on the rabbit's head.

Angus wanted the pup to associate this furry creature with eating, not play. He knelt beside her and with his knife sliced open the rabbit's belly, while she watched intently. Reaching into the body cavity he pulled out the still warm innards and carefully separated the lungs, liver, heart, and kidneys from the long string of intestines. All rabbits have tapeworms and he must prevent the pup from becoming infected with those nasty internal parasites, so he threw the intestines into the river and shoved the other organs back into the body cavity.

As soon as he placed the rabbit back in front of the pup, she snatched the liver. As she chewed on the juicy lobes of the liver, the bright red blood oozed out around her mouth and onto the gravel. This was her first experience with fresh blood and her taste buds immediately sensed this was something to savor. Although she had never killed a living animal and had never lapped the warm salty blood from torn flesh, her instincts conveyed that this was the life of a wolf. Warm blood meant a successful hunt, which in turn meant a belly full of high protein energy.

With gusto, the pup ate the entire liver, and then she tackled the heart and both kidneys. After briefly chewing on the spongy lungs, she lapped up the blood that had collected in the rabbit's body cavity. Her first raw meat was quite different from the partially digested meat that her mother had brought her. Although this raw meat was not so warm as that regurgitated by her mother, the pup found it much more satisfying. Fresh blood was the difference. Angus removed the mangled rabbit from the pup's possession and quickly skinned it. After cutting off the rabbit's head and feet, he skewered the remains on a long sycamore sapling.

Quickly rekindling his campfire, he propped the rabbit carcass directly over the flames and then sat back to watch the pup. He had given her the rabbit's head, and she was intent on licking the blood and chewing the fleshy cheeks. Her baby teeth were sharp enough to gnaw off a few pieces of meat, and she attacked the head with relish.

Angus felt sure he could capture plenty of small animals to feed the pup, but how could he teach her to hunt and kill on her own? Some of the hound pups he had owned were natural hunters, first chasing and digging out mice, then later stalking and capturing larger prey. Angus hoped that the wolf's natural instinct would augment the complex skills necessary to be a successful hunter. However, for the next few months he would be the chief hunter of their pack, trapping rabbits and groundhogs and chipmunks and even mice. He must fill the roles of mother and father wolf.

Fat dripped off the rabbit into the fire, prompting both diners to relish the mouth-watering scent of roasting rabbit. In less than thirty minutes the rabbit was golden brown and no more juices dripped onto the fire. Angus pulled on one of the front legs and as expected, it easily separated from the rest of the rabbit carcass. In four bites he had stripped all the meat off the front leg and was ready for more. While he would never tire of venison, there was no doubt that the roasted rabbit was the best meal of the entire canoe trip. He wondered why he had not taken time to set more snares. Angus shared some of the roasted rabbit with the pup, and she eagerly ate it, although with less appetite.

Angus saved one of the substantial hind legs for a mid-day snack. After wrapping it in the tender young leaves of a river birch, he placed it in his deerskin pouch. As his hand entered the pouch, there was the blue stone. It was as if his hand sought the stone. For some reason, he could not resist taking the stone in his hand and slowly caressing it. Instantly the stone grew warm. As Angus continued to rub the stone, the warmth spread from his hand into his arm and then into his body. It was a strange warmth, not like the discomfort of a hot stone that had been near a fire, but more like a pleasant internal tingling from a hot cup of sassafras tea. Now months later, he was more stymied by this strange sensation than he had been the first time he felt the warmth.

Still clutching the blue stone, he untied the pup and started across the gravel bar. At each previous night's stop, he had given her a lesson in obeying commands. Like children, pups have a short attention span and several short lessons are more effective than one long lesson. As they moved away from the canoe, the pup, predictably, started to run ahead. Just before she reached the end of the deerskin cord that Angus held, he called, "Whoa." To his surprise she came to an abrupt stop and instantly turned to look at him quizzically. Angus was flabbergasted. His thoughts were drawn to the stone in his hand. The warmth seemed to be pulsating, continuously changing from hot to cool to hot again.

The pup had not moved, but her azure piercing eyes continued to stare at Angus. With his focus on the blue stone, he began walking forward, almost subconsciously directing, "Heel, heel." The pup promptly moved to his left and followed closely at his side as Angus crossed the gravel bar. He walked a little farther and then quietly said, "Whoa." The pup stopped and sat down on her haunches still staring intently at Angus. Angus was completely befuddled. In one hand he had a vibrant blue stone with life-like energy, and in the other was a leash to a wolf pup that obeyed every command as if she anticipated what he was thinking.

Still confounded, Angus placed the blue stone back in his deerskin pouch and loaded the pup into the canoe. "We're trading daylight for dark," he told her. It was time to get onto the river, or forego reaching the mouth of Buffalo Creek before mid-day. This was the stream where he had seen the herd of buffalo on his journey up the West Fork the previous autumn. He remembered the expansive thickets of wild plums growing on the hillside above one of the small side streams. He longed for some of those juicy yellow plums, could feel the sweet juice running down his beard. He wondered if the wolf pup would chew a juicy plum. At this time of year, there would be no plums on the trees or on the ground. While the plums were a treat to Angus, they were an important staple for the many animals whose home range encompassed that small valley. Deer and bear, squirrels and chipmunks, turkey and grouse would have consumed every one of the plums last fall. On a return trip, he might fully explore that place, which on twentieth century maps would be labeled Plum Run.

CHAPTER EIGHT
THE MONONGAHELA

ANGUS WAS NOW FLOATING on the river called Monongahela by the settlers and trappers, the same one called "Mohongeyela" or "Menaungehilla" by the Indians. Only two days' travel remained before they would reach the mouth of LaCheathe, the large river that entered from the east. Angus had been told to look for traders named Samuel Eckerlin and James LeTorte at the junction of LaCheathe and the Monongahela. When he had passed this way the previous fall, however, they were nowhere to be found, and he surmised they lodged on the point only for a short time during spring, and then departed with their furs and hides to the Potomac.

Another trading post, this one called Frazier's, was three days' float past the junction of the two rivers. Angus could not decide whether to trade his furs at a post on the Monongahela, or continue downriver to the French trading post at the Forks of the Ohio. Indians told him that he could float the Monongahela from LaCheathe River to the Forks of the Ohio in five days. John Frazier would be most eager to trade for Angus's furs, to prevent the French from getting them.

On Angus's trading list of needs were flour, corn, and salt, plus powder and lead for his Pennsylvania rifle. He must also acquire some jewelry, iron axes, bright-colored cloth, and other goods for future trading with the Indians. More than anything, however, he sought gold and a horse or two. Finding a horse at LaCheathe would be unlikely, so he would wait until arriving at Forks of the Ohio to trade. Settlers and explorers coming by horseback from the Potomac or Lancaster would be more than willing to trade a horse for his dependable, sturdy dugout canoe. The canoe would get them downriver farther, faster, and more safely than a horse. Even more advantageous, the dugout needed no feed, held more baggage than three horses, and required only the river current for power.

As Angus and the wolf pup floated slowly downriver, tree-covered hills flanked both sides. The ever-changing river sometimes lay at the base of steep cliffs or rolled sluggishly through landscapes stretching broadly for several hundred yards. Around mid-day, the mouth of Buffalo Creek emerged from the left and the land surrounding its vast shores resembled meadows. Angus visualized this spot as his farm. At the completion of his indentured apprenticeship he had secured a fifty-acre grant from William Penn, but now wondered if he really wanted to settle close to civilization. He had no doubt that the area from Philadelphia to Lancaster would eventually become border-to-border farms and small towns. Angus acknowledged that the valuable area around Lancaster contained farmland superior to anything he had seen in Scotland, but it held no wilderness. At this time in his life, he preferred wilderness. The Scottish proverb came to mind, "Eagles fly alone, but pigeons flock together."

By noon Angus and the pup needed a respite and stopped for a brief stretch. As the pup scampered around a small sand bar, Angus observed that the hills on the eastern side seemed taller, encroaching on the river. Soon after resuming the river journey, emerging rills, several with interesting torrents, eased into the Monongahela through numerous clefts in the hillsides, adding their volume and voices to those of the river and the surrounding forests.

The main body of river water flowed slowly, but in some places Angus had to steer skillfully around the boulders that waited to grab his wooden dugout. The days were obviously longer than when he had started his downriver journey, yet he still had only fourteen hours of daylight. With high hills to the west, sunlight waned sooner than Angus's energy and zeal. However, he had no choice—he certainly was not going to float at night. A sightless night journey held unjustified risks of crashing into a partially submerged tree, or a hidden boulder. He was too near the end of his journey to take risks.

Emerging from a big S-curve in the river, the canoe entered a straight, mile-long pool. At the mouth of a small stream on the west side of the river lay a gently sloping gravel bar, bordered by a large grassy meadow. It was an excellent site for setting snares. After weeks of skillfully maneuvering the dugout, he deftly guided it into shallow water and then up onto the gravel, scraping easily to a stop. The tethered wolf jumped out before the canoe had stopped, running and splashing in the water before returning to the gravel where she shook a few times, and then ran unabashedly back into the water. Perhaps she sensed the extent of her leash, because she never exceeded it or choked herself.

Angus gathered his snares from the canoe. Should he take the pup with him to experience all the new scents that filled a grassy meadow? If she traipsed alongside him, would she leave a scent that rabbits would avoid? "Surely a little pup would not leave as much scent as a big man such as I." A rabbit would more likely avoid a strange man scent than wolf scent, which was a natural part of the field.

Calling, "Come. Come," Angus scrambled up over the four-foot high riverbank. The short legs of the pup could not get a good foothold, and she tumbled back down to the bottom. She quickly jumped up, shook herself a couple times, and made another attempt to climb to the top. This time she used her short claws, and with Angus gently pulling on the rope, she got her front feet over the top edge of the bank. Angus grabbed her by the scruff of the neck and lifted her up. She licked his hand then began cautiously exploring the unfamiliar, but interesting, grasses covering the meadow.

Her first exciting discovery was the small winding trail of a meadow mouse. Sniffing excitedly, she began trailing until the scent descended into a small round hole at the base of a clump of grasses. Pushing her nose into the hole she sniffed several times and then began digging excitedly. Angus let her dig a few minutes, but when she failed to find the mouse he beckoned her to follow. Reluctant to leave the attractive scent, she finally responded to Angus's gentle pulling on the cord.

Her next great discovery was a pile of rounded brown droppings, the size and shape of small, flattened marbles, which Angus identified as rabbit droppings. After sniffing at the pellets, the pup picked one up in her mouth and started to eat it. Angus immediately grasped her muzzle firmly in his giant fist and ordered, "No, no! No, no!" The pup reluctantly dropped the enticing novelty and followed Angus as he searched for a fresh rabbit trail. Angus had dropped the cord, giving the pup her lead. She was scampering back and forth beside him, somewhat reluctant to leave his side and venture out into the grass.

Reaching into his deerskin pouch to get a snare, Angus felt the blue stone and the familiar but strange warmth once again penetrated his fingertips. Removing the stone from the bag he began to gently rub its satiny smooth surface.

The pup had moved off a short distance, once again sniffing and tasting something on the ground. Angus hurried over, and saw that she had picked up another brown pellet. This one was shaped like a teardrop, and resembled a small, elongated blackberry. Although smaller, the droppings were similar in shape to those of red deer, common throughout the Scottish Highlands. Angus guessed its source was one of the many white-tailed deer that frequented the area.

It was common for all young dogs—and probably all young wolves—to eat deer and rabbit droppings. After several months of being scolded and scutched with a thin tree branch, most pups dropped this habit, but others continued as long as they lived. Angus was unaware of parasites in deer or rabbit droppings, and concluded he had more serious challenges than trying to halt what was natural instinct.

Still holding the warm blue stone, Angus commanded, "No, no. No, no." The pup immediately looked up at Angus, dropped the deer pellet, and sat down on her haunches. It seemed uncanny that the pup had processed his spoken words. Angus calmly told her that he did not want her to eat any more droppings; regardless of whether they were from rabbit, deer, elk, buffalo, or bear. He told her, "It's a disgusting habit, and although there's little danger of them making you ill, no self-respecting wolf should be eating trash. A wolf should eat raw bloody meat, not the remains of partially-digested food dropped by some other animal."

The pup's blue eyes gazed at him intently and, as he spoke, she walked over and sat down at his feet. She then opened her mouth and offered a few short yips. Was she attempting to respond? It seemed preposterous to Angus that not only had she understood him, she had even tried to answer him. He imagined her telling him that the pellets were really interesting, and tasting them was how she learned about them. She could not feel them with fingers as he could, and the only way she had to learn about things like deer droppings and rabbit droppings was to sniff them and taste them.

It occurred to Angus that as impossible as it might be, he had just intuited the logic of the wolf pup. He quickly laughed off that thought as wishful thinking. No one could actually talk to animals, he told himself. It might be possible to get some of them to understand simple one-word commands, but it was fantasy to suppose they could comprehend a person's reasoning. And even more fantastic was the possibility of a person discerning the sounds made by an animal, let alone its thoughts.

Twilight was rapidly overcoming daylight, and Angus must promptly set the three snares if they were to have fresh rabbit for breakfast. Replacing the warm blue stone in his deerskin pouch, Angus ordered the pup to heel. She obediently moved to his left and trotted beside him as he headed for a nearby rabbit trail. The grassy meadow was crisscrossed with freshly disturbed rabbit trails, and Angus had no problem finding three likely spots for his snares.

With the chore completed, Angus and the pup turned back to the riverbank. Two exposed roots provided a good foothold and he carefully eased down to the gravel. Somewhat apprehensive about the three-foot drop, the pup ran back and forth along the top edge. Finding a spot where a tree root provided a good foothold, she stepped down with her front feet; but the root was too small and her feet slipped off. Down she rolled, stopping only when she plopped onto the river gravel. After shaking herself several times to get rid of the sandy soil in her short gray coat, she began to run around the gravel bar in small circles. Then she headed to the river for a drink and a playful romp in the shallow water.

A few short obedience lessons followed a quick supper, and it was time for the simple pleasures of another campfire. The wolf seemed to enjoy the fires even more than Angus. With the sun far behind the western hills, darkness came quickly, but clear skies were the prelude to a half moon later in the night. As the campfire flames transitioned into glowing red coals, Angus and the pup dozed off. While the sun was certainly critical for navigation, the moon with its distinct phases and varied, yet predictable, times of rising certainly made life interesting—especially when one camped out every night.

As Angus and the pup slept, the faint glow against the high hills to the east indicated the point of the moon's ascent. A small edge of bright light appeared through the trees atop the ridge, followed rapidly by the glowing arc of the top of the moon. In a matter of minutes, the partial moon had cleared the treetops.

Ever alert to any unusual sounds, Angus suddenly jerked awake as a loud splashing broke the quiet of the night. The moon was suspended above the trees. Its brilliant soft-white rays illuminated the river so that Angus could identify the silhouettes of his dugout canoe beached on the gravel bar, several boulders in the river, a dead tree, and a large dark moving mass less than a rock's throw upriver. A light breeze was blowing down the river, preventing the creature from detecting the scents of human, wolf, or hides and furs. Although the intruder was bathed in moonlight, Angus was not certain of its identity. It was large enough to be an adult black bear, an elk, or even a big draft horse.

The wolf pup heard the splashing, perked up her ears, and stood alertly on the bearskin. Angus closed his left hand around the pup's muzzle as he reached for his rifle with his right hand. He whispered, "Qui-et, qui-et, qui-et." Another large animal lurched raucously over the riverbank into the river, thirty yards away. One by one more of the bulky animals gravitated to the water as Angus counted at least twenty. They slowly raised and then lowered their massive heads to reveal by their slurping sounds that they were drinking. With a smile of relief, he muttered, "Buffalo!"

After a few minutes the lead animal waded farther into the river and moved towards the opposite shore. The remainder of the herd followed. Their initial splashing, as they entered the river, broke the quiet of the spring night, but as they reached deep water and began swimming Angus strained to detect even the slightest sounds from the herd. The only sound that echoed back to the gravel bar was the quiet lowing produced by a few of the burly black animals. The stillness of the night was once again broken as the huge animals clambered up the riverbank of the opposite shore, and a few small trees cracked as the herd toppled them. In less than ten minutes the parade was over, and all was quiet once again. Angus released his hold on the pup's muzzle and quietly spoke, "Good girl. Good girl." With enough moonlight to brighten the river, Angus and the pup strolled around the gravel bar before returning to their bearskin and settling in for a welcome night's sleep. Angus and the pup snuggled together under the bearskin as the moon climbed towards its zenith.

Since the sky was nearly too bright for him to sleep, Angus intently studied this celestial sphere that illuminated the gravel bar. He remembered the last full moon when he and Sweetwater had sat along the riverbank for a few hours with an especially warm spring breeze blowing in from the south.

He remembered many of the full moons that he had been fortunate to experience. More than one hundred full moons had been spent in the Scottish Highlands, two more while on the ship crossing the Atlantic, and several dozen in this wonderfully amazing country called America. Where would he be when the next full moon crossed the nighttime sky? Perhaps he would work his way back across the Alleghenies and inquire about news from Heather. Although he greatly enjoyed the Appalachian wilderness, he had savored the plump oysters, delicious blue crabs and shrimp, and all the other seafood that made the coastal region so attractive. As Angus drifted into sleep, he delighted again in his current good fortune. In this soporific state, he was without a care or desire.

The faint light behind the trees on the western hilltops revealed the moon's earlier descent toward the horizon. At the same time faint light on the eastern horizon signaled that the sun would soon be marking the end of another restful night. The pup nuzzled anxiously against Angus, signaling that she was ready to crawl out from under the bearskin and play on the gravel bar. Angus spoke to her as he did every morning, "Are ye awake, little lassie? Ready for a wee romp on the beach before breakfast?"

What would they have for breakfast—more pemmican or fresh roasted rabbit? Stirring the ashes, a couple coals glowed at him like bloodshot eyes. With the addition of small pieces of bark and a few dry sticks, he soon had a small fire going. If he caught a rabbit he would add some larger sticks and have a nice roasting fire ready by the time he had cleaned and skinned the animal.

Angus estimated there was enough venison and pemmican to last five more days. He was still hesitant to shoot his rifle until it was absolutely necessary, but he would have to replenish their meat supply soon. After passing the mouth of LaCheathe it would be a couple hours to the Dunkard settlement, an ideal place for him to do a bit of hunting.

What would he do with the pup while he hunted? He had never left the pup alone, except for a few minutes while he explored the riverbank. Should he take the pup with him? It would be a great chance for the pup to use all her senses on a newly killed animal. There was one potentially serious problem. The pup had never heard the loud explosion of gunfire. Some pups were so frightened by the loud noise that they would take off running for hours before returning. Those pups predictably became gun-shy and were nearly useless as hunting dogs.

Angus had begun exposing the pup to louder and louder noises when he started banging on the side of the canoe with the flat side of his axe each time he fed her. Although the banging on the canoe was nothing like the loud explosion of his rifle, it was loud enough for the initial lessons. Had they been on the river with no concerns about dishonest Indians or trappers, Angus would have used small amounts of powder in his rifle and fired it without a lead ball in the barrel at the same time he gave the pup some fresh meat. The next step in the progression would have been to fire increasing amounts of gunpowder, after which a dead rabbit would be thrown in front of the pup.

It was essential that she associate the sound of the rifle with a dead animal and fresh blood. While floating down the river, Angus had frequently slapped the flat blade of his paddle against the water surface, resulting in a loud smack. At first he did this only when feeding the pup, later he had repeated the paddle smacking while petting the pup with one hand and softly telling her, "Ea..sy. Ea... sy. Ea…sy." The training at first alarmed the wolf pup, but she soon ignored the banging on the canoe and the paddle smacks.

The pup had been playing only a few minutes on the gravel bar when Angus called, and they scrambled up over the riverbank. Using the handy tree roots, the pup easily made it to the top. They moved directly to the snares, where Angus found a recently killed rabbit. Calling the pup, he let her chew on it awhile then picked it up and carried it along with the snares back to the campfire. He fed several pieces of driftwood into the fire and then pulled his hunting knife from his belt sheath.

Angus had dropped the rabbit so that the pup could continue with her tasting and chewing—another essential lesson in becoming a meat-eating wolf. After picking up the rabbit, Angus sliced open its belly, pulled out the pale yellow intestines and the dark red liver. He threw the intestines into the river, and handed the liver to the pup. As she began chewing, Angus banged his paddle loudly against the side of the canoe. With only a quick glance at Angus, the pup continued eating the fresh liver.

Angus pulled out the kidneys and the heart and then the lungs. After stripping off the fur and cutting off the head, he jabbed a sharpened stick through the rabbit carcass and propped it over the fire. His own breakfast would take a little longer to fix than had the pup's. The pup had almost finished the liver, so Angus handed her the heart and then each of the two kidneys. With three quick gulps they were gone and the pup began licking the hairs around her mouth that were stained by rabbit's blood. Angus smiled and pronounced, "That blood makes ye look like a real wolf, rather than some auld sissy village dog."

Upon completion of a leisurely breakfast, their trip continued. Angus anticipated that they would reach the mouth of LaCheathe that day or the next. With the Dunkard settlement a few hours downstream of LaCheathe, they would spend one more night on the river, and a second at the Dunkard Settlement.

The river flowed steadily past steep-sided hills that partially blocked the morning sun. The pup had adjusted to life in the canoe and spent most of the day perched atop the load of pelts in the middle of the dugout. Because of the risk of her falling, or more likely jumping, into the river, Angus kept the cord attached to her neck. She maintained a constant vigil, peering from one side to the other, ever alert for movement. Only when sleeping or watching Angus, did her blue eyes not scan the river for some strange floating object or the riverbank for some animal. She occasionally let out a yip or puppy bark, but a gentle, yet firm reprimand from Angus quieted her almost instantly.

Although the dense forest hid most wildlife from sight, calls and songs revealed a forest teeming with a multitude of birds and other animals. Many of the calls were similar to those Angus had heard around Lancaster and throughout the Appalachians. He seldom observed a bird actually singing, so he had no way of knowing the color or size or shape of the birds he heard. It would take him many years and countless sightings to associate a bird with its unique song. Angus recognized the birds as summer residents, and although he had no idea where they spent the winter, he figured they must have migrated farther south where more food was available.

Occasionally Angus saw a few birds flying over the river, but only crows were noisy. Soaring above him daily were both bald eagles and golden eagles. He was awestruck by the sheer size of the bald eagle, magnificent with its white head and wide white tail. By contrast, the golden eagle's head shone metallic golden when turned just right into the sun. He recognized several kinds of raptors, especially a large, brown hawk with an orange-red tail that had been common around Delaware Bay. It was called a redtail. Turkeys were abundant on both sides of the river. Huge flocks of passenger pigeons crossed the river, often stretching in a solid plane from one hillside to the other. Although there were few ducks or geese, several long-legged herons waded in the shallows, searching for minnows or frogs or snakes. Angus was disappointed that the Monongahela did not have more shorebirds and ducks. He found them fascinating to watch and identify, having learned their names from Joseph Myers during the days they were trapping in the marshes around Delaware Bay.

It was around mid-day that the Indian appeared on the eastern bank at the edge of the woods. Angus spotted him standing along the bank with his hand raised high above his head, apparently signaling to Angus. Although no bow or gun was visible, Angus was certain that no Indian would be in the woods without a weapon of some sort. The Indian called out, but the words were not familiar to Angus. While living in Lancaster, Angus had been warned about the dangers of travel in remote areas. Some settlers had cautioned that undertaking trade with remote Indians far from the Pennsylvania settlements would be in vain. Valuable goods would be a great temptation to Indians, and other traders. By himself, Angus was vulnerable to attacks by either.

The Indian remained at the edge of the river as Angus prudently angled his canoe slightly toward the opposite shore. Angus suddenly remembered a hunting trick he and his brother had successfully used on small lakes at home. When they spotted a flock of ducks or geese one of them would run along the shore yelling and waving his arms in the air. The ducks or geese would usually swim to the opposite shore, where the other brother, who was well hidden in the marsh grasses on that shore, would jump up and manage to bring down a couple of birds as they flushed from the water. As Angus drew even with him, the Indian's words, "Trade. Trade," echoed across the water.

Pulling his rifle from alongside the furs, Angus called out in response, "No trade goods. No trade goods." The Indian continued to wave his arms and shouted something else, but Angus could not understand what he was saying. As the dugout canoe moved around the bend Angus was on high alert not to be duped like the hunted birds in Scotland. He continued to scan both banks of the river for any suspicious signs, but nothing appeared. During this encounter, the wolf growled, but did not bark.

The mid-day stop was delayed until they were well past the Indian. Even then it was a short break before they were back on the river. For their delayed lunch, he gave the wolf pup a few pieces of smoked venison, while he ate two of his pemmican balls. The afternoon was uneventful, except for the curious howls of a wolf high on the hilltop to the east. Always suspicious, Angus wondered if it really was a wolf, or perhaps an Indian sending a signal. In the absence of answering howls, Angus relaxed and continued towards the mouth of LaCheathe.

There had been other howls on their journey; most had been lone howls, causing some concern, but many sounded like howls from a pack. The howls always evoked immediate responses from the pup. Ears erect, her head tilted quizzically at an angle, she stood up on the side of the canoe peering toward the calls that matched vague memories of howling outside her den. Her father wolf had announced his return from a successful hunt with several howls from the hillside.

But now the wolf howls also evoked an even older response in the pup, one passed from one generation to all the successive ones. As long as there had been wolves, there had been howls—howls signaling the finding of a crippled elk that could become an easy meal; howls signaling a successful hunt after the pack had brought down a winter-weakened buffalo; howls signaling possible danger from a black bear or a mountain lion within the pack's territory; or howls made just for the pleasure they provided.

Angus considered floating all night rather than risking a surprise attack while he slept on a gravel bar, but without moonlight such a nighttime float would be too risky. While the Indian had not really appeared threatening, Angus avoided any campsite that had a small stream nearby. The noise of the stream entering the river would muffle sounds of an intruder attempting to invade their camp.

Just as the sun slid behind the western hills, he spotted a large gravel bar bordered by a very high bank. Angus pulled the dugout onto the upriver end of the gravel bar and conducted a careful search for any human sign. Finding nothing, he pulled the bearskins from the canoe and spread them beside a small log. The weather was mild enough not to have a campfire that might advertise their presence.

For supper, two hind legs from the rabbit snared the previous night were supplemented with cold venison and pemmican balls.

With clouds still hiding the moon, it would be difficult to spot any movement on the gravel bar during the night. Angus would rely on his sense of hearing to detect any unusual sounds. As part of their night ritual, Angus tied a long cord from the canoe to his ankle before he and the pup curled up together in their bearskin bed.

Angus woke from his light slumber several times during the night, to noises from the river and the nearby woods. At this time of night, one's imagination could exaggerate events. In the words of the Shawnee, it was "The time when shadows stalked shadows." Thick heavy clouds gave way to wispy, fast-moving ones and, sometime after midnight, the moon slipped clear of the clouds and lit objects around the gravel bar and riverbank. Trees and other shapes were obvious; Angus felt confident no one could encroach on their camp without detection. A check of the powder in his rifle proved it was dry enough to fire if needed.

The pup slept soundly through the night, although her low whimpers wakened Angus twice. On one occasion he felt a sudden jerk and her feet began moving as if she were digging. Angus wondered if dogs and wolves dreamed. He reckoned that one did not need to be able to talk to have dreams. One needed only a mind that registered experiences, and the pup obviously experienced joy and fright, pleasure and fear. When she slept, she must relive portions of the previous day's events.

As the faint light of dawn replaced inky night, forest songbirds began heralding the day. Angus roused from his slumber, stretched his robust frame, silently rose from his bearskin, and detached his leather tether. The canoe lay moored at the edge of the gravel bar and his rifle still lay by his bearskin. Although it seemed his worries had been for naught, Angus reminded himself that caution was the watchword of all outdoorsmen. Peril was a constant companion, whether in the form of Indian or white man, mountain lion or rattlesnake. After a quick breakfast of cold venison, Angus loaded the canoe and another day on the Monongahela was underway.

The clear sky promised fair weather, although a slight headwind meant their time would be slowed. With the sun now shining brightly onto the western hills, the new spring foliage of the hardwood forest colored the hillsides a picturesque blend of greens—pale green of oaks, dark green of chestnuts, and the blackish green of hemlock and spruce stands. As the sun warmed the valley, the pup was soon asleep with her head across Angus's foot, and Angus felt his own eyelids drooping lethargically. The hills to the east climbed sharply from the river's edge and seemed to rise even higher than those they had passed upriver. To the west the hills were gentle and more inviting to foot travel.

After a few hours, the canoe entered an extensive straight stretch. At the far end, the river widened appreciably and made a hard turn to the west. As they approached the bend Angus could see another river flowing in from the east. Although not so wide as the Monongahela, the joining river seemed to be flowing much faster. This had to be LaCheathe, the river that would later be known as the "Cheat." The current became swifter as the waters of the two rivers merged, and Angus surmised they were only a short distance from the Dunkard settlement. He was looking forward to some conversation with Johannes, Gisela, and their children. He was also eager to learn if any fur-buyers had passed through the area.

How would the wolf behave when faced with a small crowd of people? She would certainly recognize them as creatures similar to Angus. But compared to the only human she had known, they would smell, talk, and dress differently. Farm animals and buildings would be alien to her. Dogs could present problems. Although the wolf was too young to fight a dog, Angus did not yet want her to meet one. Did a wolf pup smell any different than a hound dog pup? Would a hound dog be likely to attack the pup? Angus had many concerns, but none of them outweighed his eagerness to spend time with the Dunkard families.

As Angus approached the point of land where LaCheathe flowed into the Monongahela, he steered the dugout onto shore. He saw no sign of smoke and reasoned that the traders, Eckerlin and LeTorte, had packed up their furs and headed for the Potomac. He felt disappointed, but he had known that his late departure could jeopardize his chances of reaching the traders before they left. However, he must still investigate their camp. After securing the dugout, he cautiously worked his way up the riverbank. There lay the cleared area littered with many large stumps, along with the bark huts built by the traders. To his regret there was no sign of life, no horses, no hounds, no smoke, and no humans. Closer examination showed that someone had been there that spring, but had abandoned the camp.

Although Angus hoped to obtain some gunpowder, lead, and possibly even gold, he had not been overly optimistic. But he was confident there would be traders at Frazier's, a year-round trading post not far from the Forks of the Ohio. Angus and the wolf pup returned to the dugout and resumed their journey. After passing a high, steep bluff on the east side of the river, he began searching eagerly for a stream entering from the opposite shore.

Shortly before noon, Angus confirmed the small stream flowing in from the west was Dunkard's Creek. Maneuvering the dugout to the mouth of the creek Angus turned the bow into the slow-moving current. This was the first time he had attempted to move the canoe against a current, and he realized that the size of the canoe and the added weight of the furs made the task nearly impossible. After advancing ten boat lengths up the creek, Angus jumped ashore and secured the canoe to a large maple. Lifting his rifle from the canoe and calling the wolf pup, they worked their way up the bank and onto the open field that bordered the river.

CHAPTER NINE
THE DUNKARDS

NONE OF THE DUNKARD settlers were in sight, but there were familiar sounds of farm life—someone chopping wood and a cow bawling. The log buildings, sitting atop a small grassy knoll and surrounded by pasture fields and cropland, were visible from the river. They were too distant, however, to determine if any new structures had been added since his visit the previous autumn. Carrying his rifle in his right hand, and gently grasping the pup's lead cord in his left, Angus ordered the wolf to heel as they began their slow ascent up the gently sloping field towards the Dunkard buildings. Part of the field had been recently plowed, and, although no green sprouts had yet emerged from the rich bottomland soils, the width of the rows indicated that corn had been planted. Stumps scattered throughout the field broke the symmetry typical of the flat, fertile farmland around Lancaster.

Nothing much appeared to have changed since his last visit. The small settlement consisted of two log cabins, one large barn, a smokehouse, a lean-to shelter, a small springhouse, and a two-seater outhouse. As Angus came closer to the buildings he could see that a second log barn was under construction, and a few small trees had been planted around the two log cabins. The Dunkards wished for shade trees to provide relief from the afternoon sun during summer months.

It occurred to Angus that settlers, unlike hunters and trappers, regarded the forest as a liability, rather than a source of wealth. Whereas settlers believed that if they did not conquer the forest it would conquer them, Angus believed that if he took care of the forest it would, in return, take care of him. Along the Atlantic coast, the colonists had cut and burned and razed the forests to clear land for cultivation. In a surprisingly short time, settlements were established and the farming frontier pushed ever closer to the great Appalachians.

As he drew near enough to make out the windows and doors, Angus could see a small plume of bluish smoke drifting from the stone chimney of the larger cabin, and the door to the main barn stood wide open. Obviously people were around somewhere. Angus stopped and began shouting to announce his arrival, "Ho in the house. Ho in the house." Country custom—whether in Scotland or the Appalachian wilderness—demanded that a stranger approaching a house announce his presence before coming within rifle distance. Hearing no response, Angus ventured a little closer and repeated his greeting. Someone stepped out of the barn, while another person appeared in the doorway of the larger cabin. A third person stepped from behind the pile of logs that were being hewn for the new barn. Angus was too far away to be recognized or understood if he shouted his name, so he walked closer.

After a short distance, one of the figures called, "Who comes? Who comes?"

Angus stopped and called loudly, "Angus, Angus McCallander." With that response, two more persons exited the barn, and two more emerged from the small one-room cabin.

Someone yelled joyously, "Welcome, welcome."

Angus and the pup advanced slowly through the cornfield past blackened stumps, until he was close enough to recognize his greeters. All wore black clothing typical of the Dunkard sect, and the men had full beards. There were Johannes and Gisela, with their daughter Katrina standing slightly behind. Her two younger brothers, Fritz and Jonathan, had started to run down the hill towards Angus, but their father sternly ordered them to come back. Also recognizable were Dieter and Bertha, the childless couple who lived in the smaller cabin. Apparently all had survived the winter and no new settlers had joined the group. The Dunkards readily recognized the tall, husky Scot dressed in leathern hunting clothes.

His ruddy face, weathered by several years of wind and rain and sun was quite prominent.

As Angus neared the main cabin where Johannes and his family lived, he stopped and ordered the pup to sit. She had pressed close to his leg and was obviously distressed by the loud yelling and unfamiliar people with strange voices. While running his hand gently along her back, he kneeled and began talking to her softly, "Easy, little Lassie, easy. There's nothing to fear, I'll protect ye." He continued for several minutes, during which she calmed somewhat and sat back on her haunches. As the group watched his actions intently, Angus explained to them that he had a new pup and did not want her alarmed with all the sudden activities. Most likely the pup would be more at ease with a small person, so Angus asked that only Jonathan, the youngest of the two brothers, come quietly and slowly forward.

Always eager to do something that his older brother could not, ten-year old Jonathan at once approached Angus. When he was about eight feet away Angus told the boy to stop and let the pup get a good look at him. The pup was curious, but obviously a little nervous. She had moved slightly behind Angus and was peeking out around his leg at the boy. Angus continued to rub his hand along her back and told her, "Everything's alright, ye have nothing to fear." He knew she did not understand anything he said, but the steady tone of his voice and the calming effect of his hand would reassure her that there was no danger. Angus told the boy to come closer and stop a few feet from them. The short gray hair on the pup's back rose slightly, and she gave out a low growl. With a soft, "No. No," Angus moved close to the boy, shook his hand, and suggested that he kneel down on the ground. The pup cautiously moved forward and began sniffing at the boy's bare feet. Angus told Jonathan not to move and not to touch the pup, but to give her time to learn his scent and lose her fear.

Meanwhile, the other settlers were watching the boy-pup encounter with fascination and wondering why Angus was so cautious. They knew the boy would not hurt the pup, and certainly the small pup would not hurt the boy. Momentarily, the pup's curiosity and the strange odors of the boy's feet caused her to circle him and relax her initial fear. Angus told Jonathan to put out his hand so the pup could smell it. When she did, he could lightly rub her ears, so that the pup began to wag her tail. It was obvious that, given time, the two would be friends.

Angus arose, called the pup, and approached the group. Asking them not to touch the pup, Angus told the Dunkards the little he knew about her history. While he explained how he found her nearly dead in the West Fork River seven days earlier, the pup began sniffing everyone's shoes and feet. Twelve-year old Fritz, somewhat jealous that his younger brother had been first to touch the pup, was soon on his knees rubbing the pup's soft gray fur. Noting that the daughter was still somewhat bashfully waiting behind the others, Angus said aloud that the pup had never seen a woman, and he thought it might be a good idea for her to meet Katrina.

Angus called, "Come. Come," but the pup, reluctant to leave these two new interesting creatures, did not obey. Gently pulling the deerskin cord still fastened to the pup's neck, Angus again called, "Come. Come." Finally Angus managed to get the pup close enough to Katrina so that its interest turned to the new person. The long black dress that touched the ground was especially intriguing. The pup sniffed at the dress, and at one bare foot that peeked out from beneath, then pushed her muzzle up under the dress. The girl had not moved, but when the wet nose touched her bare leg she jerked back. The pup jumped backward, sat on its haunches, and stared curiously up at the girl.

Angus told the girl that if she wanted to make friends with the wolf pup, the best way was to kneel down and let it sniff her hands. The ongoing competition with her brothers erased any reluctance, and she was soon down on one knee. The pup learned that not all human hands smell the same. While the boy's hands smelled only slightly different from Angus's, the mixture of strange odors on the girl's hands captivated the pup. As the pup licked her hands, the girl giggled and began softly rubbing the pup's ears and neck. The pup rolled on her back, as if inviting Katrina to rub her belly, and the girl responded. The pup wriggled in pleasure and a warm feeling filled Angus as he watched the comely girl playfully roll the pup in the grass.

Angus was gratified that the initial encounters had gone so well. As the youngsters continued their frolicking, Angus reported that he had a canoe full of furs and skins and needed some help in pulling the canoe far enough up the creek to hide it from view of anyone floating past the settlement. Angus asked for a long rope to tow the canoe, and a strong one was soon retrieved from the barn.

Katrina was disappointed when her mother told her she would need to help with supper, for she wanted to go with the men. She told her mother she would really like to see the canoe and all the furs and hides, but what she really wanted to do was talk to Angus and play with the fascinating little wolf pup. The men and boys headed for the mouth of the creek, relishing the challenge. In no time they pulled the dugout upstream around a small bend where it would not be visible from the river. After tying both ends securely to large tree roots that protruded from the bank, they placed several leafy box elder branches across it to break its outline and obscure it even further.

While the men were securing the canoe, Gisela began planning supper. Angus was such a pleasant young man, and everyone enjoyed his company so much, that Gisela wanted this supper to be special. And of course her reputation as a fine cook was at stake. Gisela knew exactly what she had to work with, and it wasn't much. They had no fresh meat and no vegetables left from their harvest last fall. In addition, it was much too early to have any fresh vegetables from this year's garden. While the potatoes and peas had been planted three weeks earlier, they had planted the corn only two days ago. It would be several months before any fresh vegetables were ready to harvest.

They had enough corn meal to fix some corn pone, but what would they do for meat? They had eaten the last of their bear bacon the previous week and had only some deer jerky, but Gisela figured Angus had had his fill of jerky during his long canoe journey. The boys had been catching fish in the creek the last few weeks, and she felt sure that they could catch enough for supper.

They needed some vegetables, but even the sauerkraut was long gone. Because they had been able to haul only one stone crock over the mountains from Lancaster, they were not able to make enough kraut to last through the long winter months. Although they rationed carefully, there was only a little left in the bottom of the crock by the end of November. They had consumed that on New Year's Day when, according to German custom, you should eat sauerkraut if you expect the coming year to be rewarding. They were not really superstitious, but the Dunkards did not want to tempt fate—they needed all the help they could get to survive life along the Monongahela.

The only vegetables they had eaten since the last of the shriveled potatoes were boiled with deer jerky in February were wild greens they managed to collect along the creek bottom. Three large baskets of seed potatoes had been buried in dried grasses several feet deep to escape the destructive freezes, but those could not be eaten, even if no other vegetables were available. Everyone knew that without the seed potatoes there would be nothing to plant; as a result, there would be no bright green potato vines and no golden brown tubers to dig the coming September.

The Dunkards had learned about edible wild greens while living near Lancaster and were pleasantly surprised to find most of the same plants growing near the Monongahela. They never ceased to be amazed by the abundance of foods that grew wild, free for the taking. Although none of them were good hunters, the abundance of big game animals made it possible to have a constant supply of meat hanging in the smokehouse, whether it was deer, elk, buffalo, or bear.

Bear were the easiest to kill, especially during October, when they were preoccupied with eating chestnuts. As they gorged on the bountiful nuts the bears were not especially wary. Thus one could get close enough to shoot them easily with a musket. Not only did bear meat provide roasts, steaks, and bacon, but the hulking bodies yielded large quantities of tallow that could be substituted for hog lard to make shortening, candles, soap, leather dressing, and lubricants.

No food was so welcome to the Dunkards as wild berries. Large juicy raspberries, followed a few months later by even larger and juicier blackberries, supplied treats for nearly every meal. Because raspberries and blackberries could not be dried and stored, and because they had no glass jars in which to preserve the berries, the

Dunkards had eaten berries for breakfast, berries at mid-day, and berries again for dinner. Not only were their hands stained reddish-purple, but their mouths, tongues, and teeth remained a gaudy color for several weeks during the hot summer months.

As the cool nights and colorful leaves of autumn forecast that summer had ended and winter was indeed on its way, every one of the Dunkards had joined forces for weeks to gather basket after basket of the rich, sweet chestnuts that fell from the trees—"Manna from heaven," the father had described it on many occasions.

The woods and fields had provided more natural foods than they could possibly eat during late summer and early fall. But the super abundance of fall was replaced by the utter paucity of late winter. Unfortunately for Angus and the Dunkards, there just was not much available in the way of plant foods during February and March. However greens such as pigweed, wild mustard, and onion-like ramps, though not abundant, were available if one knew where to look and how to identify them.

Pokeweed, because of its unusual height, was one of the easiest wild plant foods to identify in summer and fall. Unfortunately, the thick bulbous root was poisonous and the large shiny leaves would cause seriously upset stomachs. Only in spring, when the young tender leaves first pushed up out of the fertile soils of the Monongahela Valley, could the Dunkards add those nutritious greens to their diet. During the previous September, hundreds, or even thousands, of tall pokeweeds were prominent near the barn, along the creek, and at sites they had cleared for crops. The mature plants grew taller than the boys, taller than Katrina, and some even reached above the black hats worn daily by Johannes and Dieter. Besides the pokeweed's distinctive height and shiny leaves, the long clusters of dark purple berries also indicated its presence.

Unfortunately for Katrina, her brothers had discovered that the juicy berries could be easily pulled off the tall plants and thrown at targets to leave a prominent purple stain. At first the targets had been rocks, tree trunks, and the side of the barn. Later the cow and horse were targets, and, as might have been predicted, Katrina was next. The purple stains caused by the soft, ripe pokeberries squashing against her black dress were not really obvious, but when several smashed into her hair she was not amused. She had chased her two younger brothers around the barn several times, but her unwieldy long dress guaranteed she had no chance of catching them. The pokeberry attacks ended when purple stains appeared on one of Gisela's special aprons. Stern warnings from Gisela and father Johannes convinced the pesky brothers that the consequences would be severe, so they discontinued that good-natured fun.

The Dunkards not only craved fresh vegetables, but knew that their health depended on them. Thus, when it was evident that the dreadful winter was at last finished, they began looking for the long-dead, dried stalks of last year's pokeweed that had been smashed flat by winter's winds and snows. The first small leaf tips of new green pokeweed plants were met with an excitement that matched the welcome given to the first ripe raspberries. Within a few days after those first prized leaves were discovered in April, they became a steady part of the daily meals. The family soon tired of them, but other edible greens began appearing in the rich fertile soils of the Dunkard's farm. When Angus arrived at the Dunkards, pokeweed was still small enough that it could be fried into a tasty dish. In addition, there was also some watercress growing near the woods at the upper edge of the cornfield.

While her portly mother was ruminating on the menu for the evening meal Katrina asked, "Mamma, can I fix a pie?" Sixteen-year old Katrina had been helping in the kitchen since she was only five years old and could cook nearly as well as her mother. She often helped with meal preparation and there was no doubt she could make an excellent pie. But why was she eager to take on that chore? It did not take much thought for Gisela to figure out the reason— any girl who shared the lonely life of the wilderness with only her family would jump at the chance to impress a good-looking lad who stopped by for a brief visit. She remembered one of her own mother's favorite sayings, "Kissing don't last, but cooking do."

Gisela answered, "Of course, Katrina, but what kind of pie will you make?"

Katrina had already made her choice before volunteering to

make the desert. "Strawberry-rhubarb," she immediately answered. "The rhubarb clumps growing out behind the barn have several stalks ready to be pulled, and I know where there is a nice patch of wild strawberries not far up the creek."

Gisela smiled knowingly, nodded her head, and said, "You better get started." As Katrina grabbed a basket and quickly ran out the door, Gisela asked Bertha to pick a mess of greens for supper. Katrina headed first to the strawberry patch and was thrilled to find that wild critters had not eaten all the juicy red berries. Unable to fill her basket with strawberries, she nevertheless found enough to combine with the rhubarb and create one succulent pastry. She was so excited that she ran part of the way back to the barn, where she pulled nearly two dozen small rhubarb stalks. With the small hunting knife they kept inside the barn Katrina whacked off the leaves, then cut the stalks into bite-sized pieces. Carefully toting the basket that was nearly overflowing with red and pink fruit, Katrina returned to the house to show her mother the beautiful bounty she had gathered.

Gisela started her meal preparation by adding a few pieces of oak firewood to the small fire in the fireplace. In a few minutes the strawberry-rhubarb mixture was simmering in a blackened iron pot suspended over the fire. Unfortunately, they had no sugar. They had a small amount of maple syrup that would have to substitute, but Katrina would have preferred to use honey for sweetening the strawberry-rhubarb mixture. The Dunkards had been disappointed to find there were no honeybees along the Monongahela. Although honeybees were not native to America, some were brought to the colonies from Europe and eventually spread westward. Wild swarms of honeybees were present near Lancaster, but apparently they had not yet migrated over the Appalachian Mountains.

Anyone could cook the filling to go into the pie, but skill and experience were necessary to produce a flaky piecrust. Unfortunately for Katrina, the main ingredient for a flaky piecrust was flour, and all the flour they had brought from Lancaster had been used long ago. Katrina gathered her fixings in the middle of the table, but instead of soft, white flour she had a yellowish meal of ground acorns and chestnuts. Acorn meal, especially when made from sweet white oak acorns that had been leached to remove the bitter tannins, was almost as good as wheat flour in pies.

The Dunkards had been rationing their acorn/chestnut meal all winter, since it would not be possible to replenish their supply until acorns and chestnuts dropped the next October. Chestnut meal was somewhat coarser than acorn meal, since the nearly rock-hard dried chestnuts were impossible to pulverize. Katrina had spent countless hours pounding and grinding dried chestnuts with a tough, lightweight, ash pole for the pestle and a mortar made of a short section of hollowed hickory log. She had yet to discover a method of turning dried chestnuts into chestnut flour.

With gentle stirring, Katrina began to cut bear lard into the acorn/chestnut meal, added some salt, and sprinkled cold water over the rich dough to bind it all together. After rolling the pale yellowish dough on the table until it was flat, Katrina cut out a round piece that she placed in the bottom of the one large pie pan they owned. That pan was placed inside the small stone oven they had built in one corner of the fireplace. She then covered the front of the oven with the square stone that had been shaped to fit snugly. Katrina put one shovel of red coals on top of the stone oven and piled another shovel of coals against the side; temperature could be adjusted only by adjusting the amount of hot coals. She fondly remembered the beautiful wood cook stove they had used in Lancaster and how easy it was to brown a piecrust just right in the separate oven chamber.

Because heat had to slowly build up inside the primitive stone oven that her father had designed, it was essential that the stone not be removed from the front. Thus, it was not possible to check the progress of the browning. Her mother had learned to judge when the crust was browned just right by the aromas that emanated from around the stone front of the oven. On a few occasions, however, the piecrust they pulled out of the stone oven was a disgusting black rather than golden brown. If burned inedibly black they would grudgingly throw it away. Even in the Monongahela wilderness, where food was always scarce, no one wanted to eat a burnt piecrust. What if the rhubarb-strawberry pie was more black than brown? Katrina would be so embarrassed that she would not want to face

Angus, and she was certain he would remember the burnt rhubarb-strawberry pie as long as he lived.

Katrina gathered the remaining dough and once again rolled it flat. This she shaped to form the top crust of the pie. After the bottom crust was lightly browned, Katrina would fill it with the sweet strawberry-rhubarb mixture, add the top crust, and return the pie to the oven for the final browning. She wanted it to be warm and fragrant when she pulled it from the oven and set it in front of Angus. She considered topping it with a few shapes or even a letter "A," but finally decided to be even more creative. Taking the one butcher knife they owned, she cut the round piece of dough into long strips, about as wide as her thumb. She would later lay them out in a fancy crisscross pattern that would let some of the red rhubarb-strawberry filling show through between the golden brown strips of piecrust. This pie must be the very best she had ever made.

Hearing men's voices outside, Gisela moved to the door and asked her sons, "Do you boys think you could catch enough fish for supper?"

Eager to show off their fishing skills, they shouted, "Sure," and headed behind the barn to unearth a few dozen worms. They grabbed their long hickory poles from the barn and headed to the creek where a deep hole always seemed to hold a few hungry fish— especially during spring months. Although their horsehair lines were only long enough to reach a short distance out into the creek, they usually caught fish that were close to shore waiting for some tempting bug or worm to drop into the water.

Jonathan had the first bite and soon had a pan-size bass flopping on the bank. Before he finished throwing it into the bark basket, Fritz managed to hook an even nicer one. The fish were hungry, but probably not so hungry as Angus and the others who would sit down to supper. The boys figured at least two fish for each person, or sixteen fish. Several sunfish were pulled out, but they were too small to eat so they threw the flopping little "sunnies" back into the creek. In a short while, the boys had filled their basket with bass and headed back up to the house. Their dad would clean the bass and fillet them into boneless, or nearly boneless, pieces that would sizzle in the fat and fill the frying pan.

When the two brothers reached the house, they proudly showed everyone the fish they had caught. Gisela was especially proud because now her supper would include meat to go with the cornbread and greens—and hopefully pie as a finale.

As the tantalizing smell of baked piecrust floated out of the house, Gisela told Katrina that her crust was ready to pull out of the oven. She should not leave it a minute longer or she knew what would happen. Katrina removed the stone and was relieved to see that the bottom crust was indeed a light golden brown. After adding the still warm strawberry-rhubarb filling, Katrina somewhat nervously added the crisscross top strips. When the edges were crimped, she returned the pie to the stone oven and piled glowing hot coals onto the oven's top and sides. Now was the critical time, but the mélange of smells from the entire dinner would make it difficult to judge just when the pie was ready. Katrina knew it would be nearly an hour before the pie was ready to eat, and she wanted to play with the wolf pup—and see Angus. Telling her mother she would be outside, she wiped her hands, took off her apron, fixed her hair, and hurried out the front door.

CHAPTER TEN
SCHATTO

ALL THE MEN HELPED clean the fish alongside the small creek that ran behind the barn, while the boys played with the wolf pup. Katrina seemed a bit bashful about joining the men and boys and stood at the corner of the front porch while watching the activities near the barn. Timidly stepping off the porch, she moved like a shadow towards the barn. About halfway there the pup spotted her and raced to the girl. The pup relished all the attention the boys provided, but it was somehow fascinated by the girl's long dress and the appealing odors on her hands and bare feet. Katrina did not move as the pup sniffed her toes, then her dress hem that brushed the ground, and once again her bare leg. Kneeling down, she began rubbing the pup's ears, which prompted the pup to collapse on its side in the grass, close its eyes, and bask in the pure pleasure of puppy massage.

After a few minutes, Angus left the men cleaning the fish and walked towards Katrina and the pup. As he neared, he said, "It's time for the pup's lessons." With all the distractions, Angus realized that this was a poor time for lessons, but he wanted to reinforce everything the pup had learned on the various sand bars. As Katrina rubbed the pup's small ears she reflected on watching Angus hold the wolf pup, and her gaze shifted to his hands. She realized that his weathered hands were large and powerful, yet capable of being gentle with the small pup. The thought entered her mind that she had always valued men with big hands.

Taking the slim rawhide rope from his deerskin bag, Angus looped it around the pup's neck and in so doing his hand gently brushed the hand of Katrina, who had continued to pet the pup.

Neither Angus nor Katrina moved for a few seconds, both being acutely aware of the contact. With a little embarrassment, Katrina pulled back and stammered, "I would certainly like to see how you train a wolf."

Angus asked Katrina to go back to the porch, where she would not be a distraction, and he would see if the pup would respond to any of his commands. The pup tried to follow the girl, but Angus gently held it back. When Katrina had reached the house and sat down on the front porch, Angus firmly commanded the pup, "Sit," and in so doing gently pushed down on her rump. This command was usually successful, since it was natural for a pup to sit on its haunches.

As expected, the pup sat quietly, although she stared intently at Katrina. Angus ordered the pup, "Stay," and walked a few feet away. Although the pup wanted to run over to the girl, it obeyed and remained sitting on its haunches. Angus returned and, among many compliments, told the pup, "You're one of the smartest pups I ever owned and I'm really proud of you." To reward her and reinforce the lesson, he pulled a small piece of smoked deer jerky from his bag and offered it to her. With one gulp the meat was gone and, true to form, the pale blue eyes begged for more. Angus stood up, held the rope firmly in his left hand and, while walking slowly forward, commanded, "Heel." With only slight hesitation, the pup began walking at his left side.

The Dunkards stood and stared, obviously impressed, as man and wolf moved around the barn and back to the house, finally stopping beside the front porch near Katrina. She was smiling broadly as she observed, "The pup is just like your shadow." Angus had ordered the pup to sit, and it obediently dropped onto its haunches. With a sudden inspiration, Katrina proclaimed, "Schatten shall be the pup's name! That means shadow in German."

Angus thought a few minutes while he repeated the word, "Schatten, Schatten, Schatten." He knew the pup needed a name and the sooner the better. For whatever reason, he had not been able to come up with one that seemed to fit the pup's personality and likewise would be appropriate for giving commands or calling her from a distance. "Schatten" was distinctly different from any of the commands he was using to teach her obedience, and the pup should be able to easily recognize the word. After rolling several combinations through his head, Angus declared, "Her name will be Schatt-o; not Schatt-en, and whenever I call her name I will be reminded of the German girl who named her."

Katrina was pleased, if somewhat embarrassed, as she smiled and petted the wolf pup. She murmured quietly, "Schatto, Schatto, Schatto." The pup cocked its head to one side, listened to the word being repeated by the girl, and opened its mouth in what appeared to be a slight grin. Although the pup had no idea what the word meant, she seemed to like the sound of the word.

As Angus, Katrina, and Schatto sat at the edge of the front porch, a burning odor suddenly drifted out of the house. It was not the odor of something slightly burned, but of something burned to a crisp. Katrina hesitated for a few seconds, while the implications of the horrible burning odor registered in her brain. Jumping quickly to her feet, she shouted, "Mama, Mama, Mama. It's burning! It's burning!" and quickly ran into the house. "I was watching Angus and the wolf pup when I should have been watching my pie." What would Angus think? She so badly wanted to impress him with her cooking skills, but what would he conclude when he saw the burned pie—one that she had made with her own hands. He would certainly be impressed, just not in the right way.

As tears started streaming down her cheeks, she noticed that her mother was not in the cabin. She had gone out to the small creek behind the barn to help clean the mess of greens that Bertha was able to collect. Black smoke was rolling out of the small stone oven. As she desperately searched for a towel to remove the hot stone front and pull out the pie, she cried out, almost in pain, "Oh no, why was I so careless?" As she pulled away the stone in front of the oven she thought she heard boyish giggling coming from outside the back door. Certainly they could smell the pie burning, she reasoned. Why had they not yelled for her, or her mother? Certainly they would not let the pie burn just to embarrass her?

Frantically pulling away the hot stone, she failed to notice that the black smoke was coming not from inside the oven, but from the glowing coals on top of the oven. From around one corner of the cabin, the brothers had listened secretly as Angus and their sister talked about a name for the wolf pup. Ever anxious to play another trick on their older sister, the two young boys had put a day-old piece of cornbread under the coals on top of the stove and then added more hot coals. It didn't take long for the cornbread to blacken and then begin smoking.

Reaching into the small oven with her towel, Katrina was surprised to see not a blackened piecrust, but one almost golden brown. Only then did she realize that the smoke was coming from the coals on top of the oven. Her brothers giggled wildly as they ran towards the barn. Although their sister was a girl, she was bigger and older than either of them and could deliver a painful whack or kick whenever they upset her, which was about every day.

As she lovingly put the pie back into the oven to keep it warm for supper, Katrina wiped the tears from her eyes while quietly laughing and crying. At any other hurtful prank she would have chased after the boys to try to get even. But this time she realized that running childishly after them, while shouting threats, would only lead to embarrassment for her. Angus, meanwhile, wondered what in the world was going on. He felt badly for Gisela, whom he assumed was preparing the meal. Because he was sure that she would be upset by the burned food, he remained on the front porch.

After throwing the burnt piece of cornbread out the back door, Katrina returned to the front porch. With a slight grin, she explained to Angus, "It was nothing serious, just a piece of cornbread that mysteriously fell into the hot coals." The pie would be a surprise. Reluctant to leave her dessert unguarded, she told Angus that she must help her mother fix supper and quietly returned to the kitchen.

Angus replied that he must give the pup some more lessons and called, "Schatto, come… come." Leading the pup in the direction of the meandering creek where his dugout was hidden, he commanded, "Schatto, heel… heel." He was concerned about his furs and needed to be sure they were safe, and this was a good opportunity to work with the pup to reinforce her training. As they approached the canoe, Angus thought about the new name and repeated it aloud several times. Each time he spoke the name he looked at the pup and gently pulled on her deerskin cord, to get her attention and, if possible, get her to look at him. He realized it would be many days before the pup would recognize his name.

Gisela waited until she saw Angus coming back up the hill from the creek before she started to fry the fish and greens. She poured the yellow batter of cornmeal, salt, and bear tallow into the skillet, and placed it directly over the hot coals as soon as she returned to the house, and the fried mixture, which they called corn pone or cornbread, was now crisp on the bottom and cooked through to the top.

As she lowered the last of the fish fillets into the skillet, Gisela called to the men and boys that they should wash up and come to the table. The alluring kitchen smells had them hurrying behind the barn where a large chestnut log had been hollowed out like a canoe, and positioned beside the small stream so that a trickle of water kept it filled. Although constructed primarily to water horses and cows, it also served as a washbasin. Hands were washed directly in the trough, while water was splashed liberally on faces. Running boys beat the men to the cabin just as Gisela took the last skillet-full of fish from the fire.

Angus tied Schatto to the front porch, since he was unsure how she might react inside four walls. Besides, some people did not like dogs under the table when a meal was served. At first, the pup had pulled against the cord, but she could see inside the log cabin and settled down shortly to watch the strange spectacle. She could hear the voices and could watch Angus as he ate. Gisela asked if the pup might like a little milk, and Angus agreed that milk would indeed be a welcome treat for her.

Although their two cows barely gave enough milk to feed both families, Gisela said that they could certainly spare some for such a charming little pup. She dug out a small, scarred wooden bowl, poured in some milk, and then added a piece of cornbread and some small scraps of fried fish. Quickly lapping the milk mixture and licking the pan clean, the pup whined for more. Angus responded by grasping her muzzle and repeating, "Schatto, quiet…quiet." Before returning to the cabin he had given her an old leg bone of a deer found behind the barn; this would keep her occupied until they finished supper.

When he first entered the one-room cabin, Angus was immediately impressed with its neat, orderly appearance. The log walls were lined with wooden pegs that held all the clothing the Dunkard family owned, which was not much. The overhead rafters were lined with even more pegs from which hung cooking utensils, tools, woven baskets, and two long-barreled muskets. While the outdoor clothes lining the walls blended visually with the logs, the various paraphernalia hanging from the rafters stood out prominently. Angus had no difficulty recognizing the carved wooden cooking spoons, forks, dippers, and mixing bowls. What held his attention though, were the baskets—baskets of all sizes and colors. Some were made from the smooth bark of tulip poplar trees, some from rough grapevines, some from split oak strips, and a few from stems of sedges found in wetlands along the river bank.

Living with the Shawnee had revealed that by using various colors and styles it was easier to identify the basket contents, even when the basket was hung at head height. Several baskets in the Dunkard cabin were piled high with dried roots, probably to cure various ailments that might threaten the health of the frontier family.

This cabin was built three logs taller than most frontier cabins, so that a small loft area in each end supplemented the usable floor space. No boards covered the bare floor, but the packed earth had been swept clean. One loft was over the large bed where the parents slept, while the opposite loft was above Katrina's bed. The boys slept in one loft area, and the other held storage. Two small window openings, one at each end of the cabin, were positioned under the lofts. The cabin's doors and windows were carefully made of tightly fitted, vertical wooden planks suspended by wooden hinges, and braced with horizontal planks. Angus reckoned they would be kept closed and covered with insulative animal skins during the cold months, but propped wide open during summer months to provide relief from the heat of cooking fires. "Surely the settlers, like Indians, do most of their cooking outside the cabin during the hottest months of summer," he thought to himself.

The two boys anxiously called, "Sit by me," interrupting his careful study of the cabin's interior. Gisela directed Angus to sit between the two boys on one side of the table while she, Katrina, and Bertha sat on the other side, with their backs to the fireplace. Johannes and Dieter sat at opposite ends of the long, wooden chestnut table.

The place settings around the table were a mixed assortment, with no two matching. The oblong plates and two-tined forks had been carved from chestnut and were similar to those Angus had used during his journeys through the mountains, but his attention was drawn to the clay mugs. Some were burnt orange; some were dusky gray, while others displayed alternating bands of orange and gray. But most striking, each mug bore the outline of a tree-leaf deeply incised into its side. Angus recognized a chestnut leaf on one and a white oak leaf on a second. Other mugs were adorned with a mitten-shaped sassafras leaf, a tulip-shaped poplar leaf, a sugar maple leaf, a holly leaf, a basswood leaf, and the five needles of a white pine. Angus had seen an assortment of Indian pottery, but none held such intricate designs.

In the colonies, mugs were commonly glazed. These orange and gray mugs with the leaf outlines were not glazed, but they seemed more appropriate for the wilderness setting. He picked up the mug with a chestnut leaf and asked, "How did you manage to haul such fragile clay mugs over the rough trails between Lancaster and the Monongahela Valley?"

Gisela smiled and proudly answered, "We didn't bring them over the mountains. Katrina made them here with her own two hands."

Angus gingerly rotated the mug in his large weathered hands as he studied the fine leaf detail. He glanced at Katrina, who blushed slightly and lowered her eyes to her lap, and then he asked, "How did you ever learn to make such fancy mugs?" Katrina continued to stare downward, too embarrassed to speak.

After a long pause, she quietly pronounced, "I learned from an old Irish neighbor in Lancaster."

Gisela interjected, "The food is getting cold; let's get on with the meal."

Fortunately, they had an extra plate for Angus, and in a few minutes each wooden plate was piled high with a piece of cornbread, a small pile of greens, and two pieces of fried fish. Each mug had been filled with refreshingly cool buttermilk from a crock they kept in the springhouse, positioned over a small spring that flowed year-round from the hillside above the barn.

As usual, Johannes offered the blessing, "Deep peace of the running waves. Deep peace of the flowing air. Deep peace of the quiet earth. Deep peace of the shining stars. Deep peace of the Son of Peace to you." Immediately following the final "Amen," everyone began eating like famished orphans. With little conversation, the cornbread and greens soon disappeared; Gisela brought the last of the fried fish to the table.

Angus remarked, "These fried fish are truly delicious. You boys surely did your share to make this a special meal." The boys grinned broadly as Angus explained that this was the first real meal he had eaten since beginning his canoe trip. He added, "The buttermilk is really exceptional. I haven't had milk, buttermilk, or butter since I left you last fall." As the eating slowed, he told them about the foods that he and the wolf pup had eaten during the canoe trip: smoked venison, buffalo jerky, and roasted rabbit. The families were obviously charmed by his tales, and pressed him with many questions.

With bare plates begging the question, Gisela asked, "Does anyone want dessert?" They were all keenly aware that something sat in the stone oven like a lady-in-waiting. Only Katrina had actually seen the finished product. Tearfully, she had divulged to her mother the mean-spirited trick her brothers had played. With motherly understanding, Gisela consoled her and said, "All's well that ends well."

When she asked Katrina what type of punishment would be appropriate, the girl immediately answered, "They should get a scutching and not get any pie to eat." Her mother's instinct deemed this consequence too harsh, and therefore proposed to make them skip dessert some night after Angus left. They had, after all, made a significant contribution to the dinner.

As everyone relaxed in anticipation of the promised dessert, Angus asked about their meat supply. Johannes responded, "We're clear out of fresh meat and have only a little dried venison left. We have been busy from daylight to dark preparing the fields, and only last week finished planting the corn."

Angus was keenly aware that the Dunkard men were not very good hunters, and their survival depended on getting the crops planted at the proper time. He pronounced, "I'll get up early tomorrow morning and shoot a deer."

Almost unnoticed, Katrina had left the table and moved to the stone oven. As she removed the pie and returned to the table, all eyes focused on the showpiece in her hands. The penetrating smell of the rhubarb-strawberry mixture now dominated the room. Almost dramatically, Katrina enthroned the pie in the middle of the table and stepped back to give everyone a chance to admire the golden crisscross crust before she cut it. There were well-deserved, "Ooohs," and "Ahh's," for the desert had indeed turned out beautifully, and her father commented, "That just might be the purtiest pie I've ever seen."

She knew her brothers would have something smart-alecky to say, and sure enough, Fritz, the older brother, loudly stated, "I hope the bottom crust isn't burned." Secure in her success, Katrina was not ruffled. Gisela, however, glared at both boys, warning them to be careful or they might go to bed without dessert.

Angus asked where they had gotten the tin pie plate, remarking that he had seen very few when he lived in the colonies. Gisela explained that they had brought the plate from Germany and added that they had purchased a pewter platter in Lancaster. Angus noted that it would be a great advantage to have a tin plate and cup on his journeys, and he would try to trade for them. He'd been told that eating utensils of tin were invented in Germany nearly one hundred years earlier, but not until the early 1700s were they made in England. Although tin utensils were not yet being made in the colonies, Angus predicted it would not be long before they would become common. Silver and pewter utensils were too expensive and too heavy to carry on trips.

Gisela casually informed everyone, while looking at Angus, that Katrina had picked the strawberries, cut the rhubarb, rolled both crusts, and baked the pie entirely by herself. With blushing cheeks, Katrina cut the pie in half, then in fourths, then again into eighths. Gisela realized that Katrina was trying to impress Angus and announced that their special guest should have the first piece. She nudged the lovely dessert and a large fork in front of him. Carefully removing one piece, Angus managed to slide it onto his plate with only a small amount of the luscious, reddish-purple filling spilling out. The pie then quickly made its way around the room.

Katrina sat across from Angus so she could watch him eat and see the look on his face as he took his first bite. Angus realized that this was a critical moment for Katrina and her mother, since the quality of the pie would reflect on both of them. He had to compliment the dessert without being excessive—false praise might be worse than none at all. What if the pie was too sour, or the top crust was not flaky, or the bottom crust was too soggy?

After taking his first bite, he slowly chewed and then swallowed—without a word. He hoped that someone else at the table would be the first to comment, and he could then support or refute what they said. Aware that the others were indeed waiting for him to comment, Angus knew he could not wait too long before paying his compliments. Katrina had been the last to start eating, delaying each bite, assessing the quality, waiting expectantly for any comments. Angus took a drink of buttermilk, cleared his throat, wiped a small amount of pie filling from the corner of his mouth, uttered an "Ummm," and then boldly stated, "I declare, that was the best pie I've ever eaten in my entire life. Katrina, you really know how to bake a pie."

Katrina beamed, as the words seemed to echo through her head. She thought that was one of the most wonderful compliments anyone had ever paid her, and she would always remember his exact words.

Johannes also voiced appreciation for his daughter's skills, then pushed back the bench and announced that while the women cleaned up the kitchen he and Dieter would milk the two cows. After the chores were finished they would all move to the front porch where Angus could continue regaling them with stories about fur trapping.

Gisela, still annoyed by the boys' pranks, ordered them to each fetch a bucket of water from the water trough and then rinse off the plates and cups. With typical boyish grumbling, they slowly picked up the wooden buckets and headed for the slow-flowing creek. Anxious to hear the stories that lay ahead, Gisela, Bertha, and Katrina had tidied up the kitchen in record time and the boys quickly finished rinsing the plates and cups. Angus expressed a need to check his furs, so he untied the pup and walked down to the creek. The trip to the canoe was interrupted several times by commands to "sit," "stay," "come," and "heel." The repetitions were preceded by the name, "Schatto." Finding the canoe tied securely, Angus headed back up hill to the log cabin.

Soon the small group gathered on the porch. The boys and their sister sat along the edge with their feet dangling, while the adults sat on log benches with their backs against the rough wall of the log house. As Angus began relating his adventures, the boys argued over who should hold the wolf pup. Katrina thought she should be the one to hold Schatto, as she now called the pup even in her thoughts, but she did not want to appear childish and thus said nothing.

Angus began the narrative with his departure from their settlement the previous fall. He recounted how he had followed the west side of the Monongahela upstream for twelve days, guiding his horse across two large streams. Many smaller streams, which his horse easily forded without swimming, also entered the main river. For the first time, he mentioned the Shawnee and his countenance changed. Unsure of how the Dunkards would accept his living with people they considered possibly dangerous, he grew hesitant to describe the events of the past winter.

Providing only the barest of details, he related how he had discovered a bronzed Indian maiden as the pack of wolves were circling her. When he shot one of the wolves, they ran one direction and the girl another. His shot had alerted a hunting party returning to the Indian village, and they immediately took him captive. By killing one of the wolves to save the girl from what appeared to be a deadly attack, he had violated one of the sacred taboos of the Wolf Tribe.

All the Dunkards had become completely silent, spellbound. In the hushed quiet, he explained how Sweetwater, the maiden, explained to her father, Chief Tall Turtle, that Angus had actually saved her life. Thereupon, he was released from the rawhide ropes and was accepted as a member of the tribe. An audible sigh escaped from the group, followed by a few nervous laughs from the boys, who were the most impressionable.

At the mention of Sweetwater, a frown came across Katrina's face and her lips tightened. Angus happened to see the drastic change in expression and was perplexed. Katrina seemed almost upset with his tale, but he could not imagine why. Had he been too explicit with his description of Sweetwater's charms?

With few enhancements, Angus continued to detail how he hunted and trapped, stretched and dried the furs and deer hides, built a dugout canoe, and then floated down the Monongahela to their farm. Jonathan asked about his hunting knife, and Angus explained that the handle was made from the jawbone of a black bear he had killed when staying with the Shawnee. Angus slid the knife from its sheath and demonstrated how the teeth provided a firm grip, preventing the knife from slipping in his hand.

Johannes was deeply impressed with how matter-of-factly Angus recounted his accomplishments, any one of which would have been a major feat for most settlers.

The boys kept interrupting Angus's story, wanting to know more about the Shawnee. Several times their mother ordered them to shush, while Angus finished unfolding his adventure. Katrina asked no questions and made no comments. She was deep in thought. This trapper was unlike anyone she had ever met. She knew little of his life in Scotland, or the years he spent as an apprentice near Philadelphia and Lancaster. She suddenly realized that she did not even know if he was married. Was it possible that he had a wife somewhere? Would a responsible man abandon his wife to spend the winter with Indians? She knew she could not be so bold as to ask him pointedly, but somehow she must find out—before he left, if possible.

CHAPTER ELEVEN
THE DEER HUNT

As TWILIGHT SETTLED over the Monongahela Valley, Angus announced that he would have to finish the story another time. If he were to be successful in his hunt the next morning, he must be in the woods before the first light of day outlined the giant tree trunks. From the opposite shore, eight hoots of a barred owl echoed across the river like a harbinger of bedtime, and Angus realized that the pup had slept through the entire evening. The running, playing, and excitement had worn her out. Angus asked permission to sleep in the barn with the wolf pup, and Johannes replied, "Of course. There's a small pile of hay to cushion the hard ground, and it will be far better than the hard gravel bars you have been sleeping on."

Angus presented a small problem, "The pup has never been with me on a hunt, and I fear the shooting might frighten her, or more likely, she'll spook the deer." He asked, "Could someone sleep in the barn with us, and stay with the pup while I slip away before daylight?" Both boys volunteered insistently, and Angus could see that there was no way to choose one over the other. If Katrina had been younger she might have been allowed to join the boys, but at sixteen years, joining them was out of the question. With resignation, Katrina moved into the house and declared that she was tired and ready for bed.

Angus had brought his bearskins up from the canoe earlier that day and while the boys each grabbed their blankets, Johannes led Angus and Schatto to the small barn. Before retiring for the night Angus placed his long rifle, powder horn, and skinning knife near the barn door. He would sleep in his moccasins and clothes. It would be

117

a simple matter to rise quietly from the hay, move to the door, gather the hunting gear, and head for the woods. The boys, jabbering more than Angus wanted, obsessed about Indians and wolves, and more Indians. This boyish jabber might have gone on for hours, but Angus ordered the boys to quiet down so that he could get some rest. Both youngsters were well aware of their meatless smokehouse, and they drifted to sleep with thoughts of fresh deer liver frying in the big black skillet. Angus and Schatto soon joined them in a deep sleep, made pleasant by the sweet scent of hay that filled the barn.

Like a true woodsmen, Angus could set his internal clock to awaken at any time he chose. He would typically open his eyes, examine the stars or moon, and determine how many hours remained before daylight. Twice during the night in the barn he awoke, and each time he was temporarily confused by the starless sky. Smiling to himself, he realized that he was looking at the barn roof and would get no clues about when to retreat into the woods. When he awoke the third time, a hint of daylight through the open barn door sent him to the woods. Better to be in the woods too early, than too late. With only this one morning to bag a deer and replenish the empty smokehouse, Angus deeply wanted to repay the Dunkards for their hospitality.

When Johannes outlined where deer had been sighted in recent days and described where they often came to drink, Angus had consciously visualized and memorized these descriptions, so that even in darkness he was completely oriented. It took only a few minutes to pass through the newly planted cornfield and reach the edge of the woods. There was little food for deer in the woods at this time of the year, since the last of the chestnuts had been eaten by January. Very few young trees or shrubs survived in the mature woods to provide browse, so the deer would be attracted to the fresh green growth where woods met clearings. He selected a spot where the sun would be at his back and the wind in his face, and quietly sat down against a large poplar tree. With an hour to wait for enough light to shoot, Angus easily slipped into a light sleep.

A twig snapping to his right alerted Angus, and without opening his eyes he pictured the direction and strained to identify the source. It was much too dark to see, let alone shoot, so Angus remained in his comfortable seat with his eyes closed. As a young hunter, his father had taught him that he could hear better with his eyes closed. As another twig broke, Angus visualized the distance and direction the animal was moving. After further evaluation, he concluded it was a single full-grown deer. But only in daylight could he positively identify the animal. White-tailed does were heavy with fawns and he would not shoot a doe. Bucks had dropped their hardened antlers in January, and the new velvet-covered antlers would be so short at this time of year that he must be close enough to distinguish bucks from does. His preferred target that morning would be a young buck, but any buck would do.

As quickly as the snapping sounds began, they ceased, indicating the animal had bedded down or quietly moved beyond hearing. Angus settled back into a relaxed half-sleep, confident that with daylight would come a deer. The calls of forest birds alerted him that daylight would soon meander through the adjacent field.

Try as he might to identify the songbirds issuing their spring calls, few were familiar. A wild turkey gobbled from its roost in a tree on the hillside above him and was answered by a second, and then a third further around the hill. A male ruffed grouse, the English partridge, began its drumming on a large fallen chestnut log. The grouse began to "beat" its wings faster and faster, producing the quaint drumming so characteristic of Appalachian forests in springtime. As he listened, Angus salivated thinking about the fried breast meat of a turkey or even a grouse. Either would be most welcome, but he needed quantity more than quality. And in his mind, fried deer liver, heart, or tenderloin would rival even the most tender grouse breast—an opinion not shared by those people who considered that golden-fried grouse breast had no equal.

Before the sun's rays edged over the hill to his back, an outline materialized at the edge of the field. It was an impressive four-legged hulk, and Angus's eyes fairly popped to see a yearling elk rather than a white-tailed deer. He was chagrined, however, not to distinguish its gender. With better light he could spot antler nubs, if any were present. He could now hear other animals, probably deer, walking in the woods behind him, and yet he could barely recognize three deer feeding about two hundred yards directly ahead of him.

A thin wispy fog was settling over the open field, at times completely engulfing the deer that were feeding before Angus. Morning sunlight added a welcome shimmering golden sheen to the fields as Angus brought his long rifle to his shoulder in a slow fluid motion. In a matter of minutes he would be able to determine the elk's gender, and thus settled the front sights of his rifle on the elk's shoulder. Resting his elbows on his knees, he waited patiently, as he had done hundreds of other times when his rifle was all that stood between him and starvation.

Angus's keen eyes tagged the elk as a young bull and he calmly shifted the sights to the small spot at the rear edge of the shoulder blade. Ever so lightly he squeezed the trigger. The spark from the flint ignited the powder, the bullet spiraled swiftly out of the barrel, and as the smoke from the barrel cleared slightly, the blast silenced the forest chorus. Angus watched the young elk collapse on the ground. As with most hunts, the actual killing was anticlimactic. Angus lowered the barrel slowly to his knees, and remained motionless against the trunk of the ancient poplar. The Dunkards would have plenty of fresh meat for the next two weeks and Angus felt an overwhelming sense of satisfaction.

He saw no further movement from the short grass where the elk had fallen, and was confident that the animal had died instantly. Patience was a virtue in many situations, but especially so in hunting. To move immediately following a shot would alert animals and humans alike, whether they were deer or elk, cougar or wolf, Indian or another hunter. In ghostly fashion, Angus poured a load of gunpowder from his powder horn down the barrel of his rifle and then soundlessly rammed in a fifty caliber lead bullet, wrapped in a small piece of greased cloth, until it reached the powder.

After fifteen minutes, Angus noted that the animal sounds of the forest had slowly returned to the frequency and volume prior to his shot. He rose to his feet and cautiously moved from tree to tree along the edge of the woods until he was opposite the fallen elk. He could easily make out the white belly hair of the elk, but was in no hurry to leave the protective cover of the trees. Holding his rifle at the ready, Angus moved towards the yearling bull, or stag, as it was called in Scotland.

As he approached the downed quarry Angus quietly broke off the end of a mountain laurel branch, and placed the green-leafed twig in the mouth of the animal. Like his kinsmen before him, he believed it was essential to acknowledge the spirit of an animal killed for food. Wordlessly he released the animal's spirit to join the spirits of all the other animals that had once roamed the hills along the Monongahela Valley.

After strategically placing his rifle within reach, he removed his skinning knife from its thick leather sheath, and with a long, swift slash he quickly opened the body cavity from breastbone to tail. The razor-sharp, foot-long blade sliced through the tender belly skin like a knife through butter. Angus rolled the elk onto its side, spilling the bulbous stomach and the long intertwined intestines out of the body cavity. Two more careful cuts separated the heavy organs from the carcass and the warm steaming mass plopped onto the grass. Angus skillfully separated the reddish-purple liver and the oval kidneys from the other belly organs, then pushed them back into the body cavity with the heart and lungs so that all the edible portions would be hauled back to the Dunkards.

Johannes had arisen at the first sign of daylight, and was relaxing on the front porch watching the sunrise over the tree-cloaked mountain ridges to the east when he heard the shot. In the absence of a second shot, he grew confident that Angus's hunt had been a success. Johannes stepped off the porch, grabbed the heavy rope from its wooden peg, and headed towards the smaller cabin.

Dieter had also heard the shot and met Johannes on the run as they hurried to join Angus. Johannes could picture in his mind the exact location where Angus was waiting and they located him quickly. After a quick and happy congratulatory greeting, the three of them slid the elk carcass through the dew-covered grass downhill to the barn. With considerable effort, the 200-pound carcass was hoisted up to a beam so that any blood remaining within the body cavity would drain to the ground.

The wolf pup heard the men outside the barn, even though none had spoken. Its squirming and whimpering had wakened both boys, prompting the youngsters to abandon their cozy beds of hay and scurry out the main door. The pup made a beeline for the small drops of bright-red blood and like a scavenger lapped them up as quickly as they fell to the ground. Angus gave the "sit" command, cut a few small pieces of meat from the still-warm carcass, and offered them to the pup. Johannes and the boys were quite impressed that Schatto had obeyed Angus's order to sit, even though initially she had tried to jump up and reach the legs of the hanging elk carcass. She was sitting patiently near Angus, waiting for the next tidbit, when Katrina came around the barn. The wolf pup immediately spotted the girl and moved a few steps towards her bare feet before sitting down to wait for the next morsel that Angus offered.

Angus smiled at Katrina, and said, "I brought an elk for you and your family, but there may not be any meat left after this starving wolf pup eats her fill." Angus handed Katrina the liver and heart of the elk and jovially remarked, "If ye'll take these to the house, your mother can get them ready for the skillet. We'll finish skinning this elk and hurry in for breakfast." Working like a smooth machine, Angus, Johannes, and Dieter slipped the hide from the animal and propped open the body cavity to cool in the shade of the barn. As they washed their hands at the water trough, voluminous chimney smoke promised fried elk meat would soon be placed on wooden platters for all to enjoy.

Johannes announced, "A short grace is good for hungry folk," and offered a brief, but heartfelt thanks for the successful hunt. During a leisurely breakfast, consisting of nothing but fried elk liver and heart, Angus recounted the details of his morning hunt. When they'd eaten their fill, the butchering process began. The shoulders and hams were easily separated from the hanging carcass, then Angus carefully removed the two back straps, which Johannes called tenderloins. These elongated cuts of meat, positioned on either side of the backbone, were the most prized of all because they were even more tender and flavorful than the liver. Each back strap was three inches wide and over two feet long. Similar, but smaller versions of the back straps were located inside the body cavity, along the backbone. Angus carried the shoulders, hams, and back straps inside the barn where wide planks cut from a tulip poplar tree had been set up to form a rough, functional table.

Gisela began cutting the back straps crosswise into one-inch thick pieces, while Johannes, Dieter, Bertha, and Katrina cut the meat from the shoulders and hams into long narrow strips, each an inch wide and six to twelve inches long. Johannes sent Fritz and Jonathan to gather wood for the slow fire that would soon be sending small clouds of smoke billowing out of the narrow openings in the roof of the smokehouse. He reminded them, "Be sure to get plenty of green hickory, it produces the best smoked meat."

In late fall or winter, they would have simply hung the elk carcass in the barn and cut off pieces just before mealtime, but at this time of year the hanging meat would spoil before much of it could be eaten. The only means of preservation available to the Dunkards was smoking and salting. The combination of low heat and dense smoke that filled the smokehouse would keep away the flies and dry up all moisture from the long pieces of elk meat. There was no danger of spoilage if the meat was well dried.

By late morning the carcass of the elk had been reduced to the backbone and ribcage, from which most of the meat had been stripped. The wolf pup had spent the morning lying in the sun outside the barn chewing on the lower elk legs that Angus had given her. The larger bones had been put into a slow-simmering pot set over the fire in the cabin fireplace and the resulting broth would provide dinner for the following evening. All the elk meat, other than the back straps, was hanging from slender poles set near the ceiling of the smokehouse, where it would remain for the next two days. Although the smoked meat would last for months if kept dry, it would all be consumed in two weeks.

With the hard, messy work finished, everyone washed their hands and headed for the cabin. In a short time the sweet smell of frying back strap and liver filled the cabin. With little talk, like breakfast, the meal consisted solely of elk meat and was soon finished. Everyone moved to the porch where Angus announced that he must head downriver to find a trader who would be interested in his furs and hides. Everyone expressed their regrets he had to leave after such a short visit.

The look of happiness faded like blood in water from Katrina's face. She abruptly stopped rubbing the pup's belly and begged, with her eyes and facial expression, for Angus to stay just a little longer. She had known he would leave, but had not realized it would be so soon. The boys once again bombarded Angus with questions about the Indians he might encounter, while Johannes pressed him about his plans for the coming summer. Angus responded that he would likely proceed to the Forks of the Ohio to trade his hides on his way to Lancaster for an extended stay with the gunsmith who had taught him how to make long rifles. He intentionally did not mention that after trading his furs his main goal was to find answers to his questions about Heather. Had she sent a letter to his last-known Lancaster address? Had she left Scotland? Was she already working in the colonies as an indentured servant to repay her passage across the Atlantic?

As Angus told of his plans for the summer he reached into his deerskin bag hanging from a peg on the front porch to count the number of small bones he carried to occupy the pup. Perhaps he should take some of the small leg bones of the elk in the canoe. His fingers brushed the smooth blue stone resting among the bones, and he immediately lifted it from the bag. After explaining how he had found it in a small cave, he passed the stone around for everyone to touch. Angus did not tell them about the strange warmth that had flowed from the stone, since he wanted to see if any of them would experience the same sensation.

As he passed the stone to Fritz, who was sitting beside him, he suggested, "Rub this stone and see if you think it is the smoothest stone you ever felt." While Fritz agreed that it was certainly smooth, it was not remarkably warm. Angus told him to pass it to the others so that they also might see how smooth it was. Each person in turn rubbed it for several minutes as they examined its strange blue color. No one noted any warmth coming from the stone until Katrina at last took it into her hand. A strange look came across her face, and she shook her head as the stone surged warmth to her hand. A look of apprehension crossed her face as she handed it back to Angus who then began to massage the blue stone.

As he did, he studied Katrina and thought that she was especially fair of face, with sparkling blue eyes, a pert little nose, and an enchanting smile. He realized that no longer was she the teen-age child he had met during his visit with the Dunkards last fall; she had blossomed into an attractive young woman. The thought also passed through his mind that he would like to spend more time with her. Katrina began to blush, as if reading his mind, and beat a hasty retreat back inside the cabin. A befuddled Angus wondered what had come over her.

Angus's musings were interrupted when Johannes asked, "When might we see you again?" That question was one Katrina had wanted to ask, but was too shy to do so. Although she was inside the cabin, she was hanging on every word uttered on the porch.

Angus replied, "I plan to return sometime early next fall on my way back to the headwaters of the Monongahela. I intend to spend another winter trapping for furs and hunting for deer and elk." His answer became a farewell as Angus slowly rose from the porch and announced that he planned to float at least five miles that afternoon. Picking up his rifle, he called, "Come, Schatto, come."

Katrina winced when she heard the word, Schatto, the name she was responsible for. Would Angus think of her when he used the name, Schatto? Certainly he would not forget that Katrina was the first to declare that the pup behaved like a shadow. Katrina was a bit preoccupied recalling the way Angus stared at her, but would not forego his departure.

Angus, Schatto, and all the Dunkards slowly paraded down the hill from the cabin, almost ceremoniously passing through the recently planted rows of corn towards the mouth of the small creek. As they reached the dugout canoe loaded with furs, the boys rushed over the bank to remove the branches that camouflaged the boat. When the cover material was removed, Angus lifted the pup onto her familiar perch atop the load of furs. He handed her an elk foot, stepped into his craft, and asked the boys to untie the ropes mooring the canoe. The task gave the boys a feeling of importance to allay the disappointment of Angus's departure.

With a broad smile, Angus bid them a lively farewell. All waved and shouted their good-byes as the current slowly swept the canoe out of the small stream into the main river. Katrina called good-bye and waved her hand ever so slowly, but her faint smile faded as a tear slowly trickled down her cheek. She spun around to hide the now sad expression on her face, and began trudging back to the cabin.

The boys ran along the top of the bank accompanying the canoe for a short distance before Gisela called for them to come back. As the strong river current caught the canoe, Angus glanced back and was as surprised as he was disappointed to see Katrina slowly moving up the hill while the others remained on the creek bank. The mental image of the small, stoop-shouldered figure trekking slowly up the hill was not the one he wanted to carry with him for the next few months. Puzzled by her conduct, Angus remembered a saying he had heard several times in Lancaster, "Glasses and lasses are brittle ware." He preferred to remember her smiling face as she rubbed the belly of the wolf pup or the look of triumph when she heard him proclaim, "Katrina, you really know how to bake a pie."

CHAPTER TWELVE
THE DEPARTURE

_____

GUIDING THE BULKY DUGOUT into the main current of the Monongahela took great skill. Angus was relieved to note a lack of obstructions as far as he could see, for the river was getting deeper and faster every mile he traveled. Two moderately large streams would eventually enter the river from the west, adding even more water volume to carry the canoe steadily northward. Barring any unforeseen delays, he should reach the Forks of the Ohio in four days.

Katrina was halfway to the cabin before the others abandoned their lively sendoff. A flood of nostalgia swept over her, but with it came many questions about Angus. Vivid impressions lingered. His bushy head of red hair and matching reddish beard had been intentionally trimmed in preparation for arrival at their cabin. Although his large hands, muscular arms, broad shoulders, and tall lanky frame stood out sharply in her thoughts, his quirky smile and easy-going manner evoked the strongest feelings. Katrina had met several boys her own age in Lancaster and some who must have been about the same age as Angus, but none had the looks, personality, or charisma to match this rugged Scotsman.

By the time she reached the cabin her joy had evaporated and was replaced by sadness. How could an exciting visit with someone like Angus become painfully depressing when he departed? Katrina assumed that Angus had so many vivid memories of exciting past adventures that images of his short stay with her family would disappear long before he reached the Forks of the Ohio. How could thoughts of a girl he had never really talked to, or had never been alone with for more than a few minutes, enter his mind when he was busy trying to trade furs and survive the Appalachian wilderness? She wiped a tear from her cheek, entered the cabin, and mumbled to herself, "Were it not for hope, the heart would break."

"A person needs three things to be happy," Katrina thought: plenty of work to keep busy, something significant to look forward to, and someone to share your life with. With only two of those three elements, she feared that the rest of her life would be spent living with her family in the wilderness. There were an endless number of chores to occupy her time, and now she had something to look forward to—the day when she would once again see Angus. Many times she wished they had never left Lancaster, where there were girls and boys her age. She fondly remembered the days spent at school and the weekly church services that provided so many opportunities to meet other young people.

As she had reminded herself on many occasions, it did no good to mope around the cabin. Things only got worse. Her mother often told her, "Don't stay long at a pity party." Katrina knew from experience that she must find something to do without delay so that she did not dwell on the departure of Angus.

Soon after the family had arrived at the site of their new home along the Monongahela, Katrina realized that one of their pressing needs was baskets. Everything grown or collected was gathered in baskets—beans and corn, acorns and chestnuts, strawberries and blueberries, ginseng and yellow root. An equally important use of baskets was the storage of dried foods. Although she had made several dozen functional baskets that first summer, it was evident that they needed hundreds, not dozens. Before the first winter along the Monongahela was even half over, Katrina realized that basket making served another purpose. Being imprisoned with her two annoying brothers during the long dark days of winter was often depressing. The slow, tedious crafting of a basket offered relief and gave her life a badly needed purpose. With time, her basket-making skills improved, and by the end of that first winter she could complete a small basket in one day. Now, however, she could easily turn out two or three small baskets if she devoted the entire day to the task. The larger ones, such as those used to gather ears of corn, still required more than one day to complete.

Her father wanted her to construct two large deep pack baskets to hang on either side of his horse. He would use them to haul ginseng and yellow root to the Potomac. If his trading were successful, he would return with baskets full of items they badly needed. Katrina had already prepared her list, which included sewing needles, cloth for a new dress, and a book—any book.

She had been able to bring only two dresses with her when they left Lancaster, and each had been patched so frequently that she would be embarrassed to wear them around anyone except her own family. She wore her best dress for their dinner with Angus, and was consoled that it was clean. A very observant Katrina noted how Angus's deerskin leggings and shirt appeared tough, yet comfortable. She decided that a deerskin dress would be a future project.

With all the other chores and tasks assigned to her, Katrina wondered how she would find time to tan a deer hide and make a dress. Such a dress project might be postponed until the following winter. If Angus returned during early autumn as he had forecast, however, she would want to have the deerskin dress completed so that he could see she was capable of handling the responsibilities of a frontier woman. Pie making was only one of her skills.

As if there weren't enough demands on her time, Katrina also needed more clay for the numerous pieces of pottery that made life in the wilderness more comfortable. The family felt a crucial need for five-gallon crocks to hold sauerkraut. Although the tasks of creating baskets and pottery were solely her responsibility, Katrina was also expected to help with most of the other daily chores. Some she enjoyed; others she almost despised. Among the joyless duties were hoeing the endless rows of corn scattered among the blackened stumps; grinding basket after basket of acorns, chestnuts, and corn; and hauling the thousands of limbs and logs for the cooking and heating fires that must be kept burning day and night throughout the long winter.

Digging ramps, picking berries, hunting ginseng, and even hauling baskets of clay from the riverbank were somewhat enjoyable. All those tasks took her into the woods where new adventures seemed to await each visit. Of course there was always the possibility of danger—in the form of rattlesnakes or copperheads, wolves or panthers, or even the black bears that occasionally tried to break into the barn. The settlers also feared Indians, even though they had experienced no problems during their two years along the Monongahela.

Gathering acorns and chestnuts was an arduous task, but it was Katrina's favorite. Those bountiful crops of early autumn fell at the time of year when she most enjoyed being in the woods. Summer's heat and humidity had finally ended, and the first frosts of the year were followed by the dazzling colors of the deciduous hardwood trees. It seemed to Katrina that wildlife prized the early fall bounty even more than her family. The multitude of animals concentrated under the groves of chestnut trees included deer, buffalo, black bears, wild turkeys, passenger pigeons, and gray squirrels. Every animal in the forest was attracted to the sweet nuts that tumbled from their spiny hulls; each prompted to increase its weight and energy reserves to survive the forthcoming winter.

Some of the chores required concentration, while others were so routine that Katrina's mind could wander. Those were the times when she wished she could talk to a girl her own age. She could and did talk freely with her mother, but some fantasies could only be shared with a same-generation soul mate.

While Katrina wandered in a near daze back to the cabin, each family member was enrapt with separate thoughts of life in the wilderness. Her father carefully studied the ground for any sign of sprouting corn. Like most farmers, Johannes enjoyed working the earth. When the soil began to warm each spring he felt the urge to initiate the annual cycle that farmers had repeated for tens of thousands of years. Spring is the favorite season for those who work the land. The planting season prompts optimism and renews confidence.

Preparing a site for planting had been the most difficult task they faced to establish their home in the wilderness. Johannes and Dieter had girdled many of the larger trees, most of which later died while standing. Others had been cut down with the two-man crosscut saw hauled over the mountains from Lancaster. Those harvested logs had been used to construct their two cabins, and later the barn. Some of the girdled trees now stood like quiet sentinels guarding the cornfield. They were, in reality, poor sentinels, as they gave no warnings when the crows and wild turkeys arrived to eat the newly sprouted corn. In fact, they provided tall perches from which marauding crows could be on the lookout for humans.

The Dunkards had brought from Lancaster a lightweight iron plow, which Johannes had attached to a wooden handle. As the horse pulled the plow past the many stumps and standing dead trees, Johannes had struggled constantly to hold the iron cutting edge just below the soil surface. Plowing had become easier the second year, and would become easier with each passing year. Johannes knew they needed more cleared land, at least double what they now had, and therefore they would repeat the back-breaking process of converting virgin forestland to cropland.

Johannes planned an overland trip to the Potomac the following week, hoping to return with some additional livestock. They needed chickens, another cow and, if possible, some pigs. Their needs were so numerous that the few baskets of ginseng and yellow root would not be enough to exchange for all the desired goods. Some essential commodities included flour, sugar, salt, gunpowder, lead, and cloth for clothes.

And now they needed to replace their old auger, one of the most valuable tools the Dunkards had carried over the mountains from Lancaster. A gouge auger drilled a round hole into a board or a log, creating clothing racks when wooden pegs were driven with a wooden mallet into those holes. The augers were also used to make holes for the hickory legs on furniture. The long rough-hewn log table, for example, was the nucleus of most activities inside the cabin. The crosscut saw and axes were irreplaceable for constructing log cabins and barns, but augers made life more orderly and civilized.

When Katrina completed the two large pack baskets, Johannes would begin his journey over the mountains. Everyone in the family had listed for him several times the items they needed most. Johannes pondered what else he might take to trade at the Potomac, when it occurred to him that there were additional items with trade value—Katrina's mugs. If the process of glazing could be developed, he was certain the mugs would be highly prized. He must add to his list of priorities, improvements to their kiln to fire pottery.

Upon his return from the Potomac, Johannes would be faced with more projects than he would have time to complete. Some ventures were critical. If he could attach a shed at one end of their cabin, for example, it would serve as a bedroom for the boys during summer and a place to keep firewood dry during winter. Their sleeping loft became unbearably hot during summer, compounded by meals cooked in the fireplace.

Cutting and hauling firewood was a constant never-ending chore. Any girdled trees that fell were promptly cut into sections and skidded by horse back to the cabin. Johannes estimated that a pile of wood the size of their cabin was sufficient to survive a normal winter, while an unusually cold winter would require considerably more. His rule of thumb was that the volume of their winter wood supply must be equal to the structure being heated. There was never a shortage of wood, surrounded as they were by forest. The wood was useless, however, until cut into lengths that would fit into their fireplace.

Although sturdy and strong, Johannes seemed to run out of energy before nightfall every day. His day started with guiding the plow, hoeing corn, and then girdling more trees. The few remaining hours of daylight after dinner were devoted to splitting firewood. On those nights he longed for more sons, and sons old enough to share the workload. He made mental notes to his list to add another axe, another crosscut saw, and certainly one or two more files to keep tools sharpened. Finally, to the Dunkards back in Lancaster, he must write of the vast opportunities and resources, urging them to move to the Monongahela. Life would be much better, and much safer, if two or three more families settled in the area.

Johannes reflected on the life-changing decision he and Gisela had made to leave Germany and escape the harassment and intolerance faced by their religion. The first of the German Dunkards had left Germany in 1719, eventually settling northwest of Philadelphia in a community now known as Germantown. They lived a simple life, advocating non-violence, and practicing no strict church ritual. To live a true Christian lifestyle, Johannes felt they must isolate themselves from the evils of society, and therefore moved his family to the frontier in the Allegheny Mountains. Their decision was sweetened by the promise from William Penn—Governor of the Pennsylvania Colony—of economic freedom, religious freedom, and of greatest importance, cheap land.

Gisela was preoccupied with more domestic thought. Each of them desperately needed new clothes; the boys were growing so rapidly that nothing seemed to fit them. During summer months they could go barefoot and wear pants that came to their knees. For winter though, they must have new shoes, pants, shirts, and coats. She pleaded with Johannes to bring back some durable cloth, along with thread and needles, so that she could make new clothes.

They had been successful in tanning a few deer hides, and Angus had given Gisela several suggestions on making the leather softer. He had carefully explained that hides must be stretched, dried, scraped, stretched again, and then scraped again. To create the thin deerskins that could be converted into comfortable summer clothing, it was necessary to scrape off the hair, rub deer brains onto the hides, and then soak them in a stream for two to three days. After the hides were pulled back and forth around a tree sapling hundreds of times, they would become pliant enough to wear as dresses, shirts, leggings, and moccasins. So now she would set out to make some deerskin garments, although there weren't enough hours in the day to complete any single task that lay before her.

As she continued walking back to the cabin, Gisela's thoughts turned to her vegetable garden. They had brought a few seeds over the mountains from Lancaster, but they must acquire a broader array if she were to offer her family varied meals. On her list for Johannes were cabbage and carrot seed, beans and corn seed, and different types of squash seed to plant between the rows of corn. She also requested a sausage grinder. In Germany she had made hundreds of rich, juicy sausages known as bratwurst. Bear meat was fat enough to substitute for pork, and with a meat grinder, their smoke house next fall would be hanging heavy with strips of smoked venison and long loops of bear sausage.

Of all the things Gisela desired, a book was foremost. She liked to read, but their only book was an old Bible they had brought from Germany. With a book written in English, Gisela could teach the boys to read, and Katrina could improve her reading.

Gisela also craved a calendar, even though she realized there were hundreds of things more essential than a calendar. They brought no calendar with them when they had left Lancaster, nor had Johannes carried one back from the Potomac on his trip the previous year. Within a few months of arriving at the Monongahela they had lost track of time. They had anticipated many of the challenges of living in the wilderness, but the inability to track time was unexpected.

Other than celebrating birthdays and Christmas, the Dunkards did not need to know actual dates. It was evident when spring, winter, summer, and fall arrived, just as it was apparent when they must perform seasonal chores like cutting firewood and planting crops. They had their Sabbath-stick to number days of the week, so they were always certain to observe the Sabbath, but they had no device to keep track of weeks or months. They had tried cutting notches in a stick to record the date, but as they became overwhelmed with sheer survival in the wilderness, they often forgot to cut the notches. They did make a special effort to celebrate the children's birthdays and had worked out a moderately accurate system. The flowers, trees, and wildlife provided plenty of clues about the time of year, even the actual month.

Katrina's birthday, June 22, was approaching. They celebrated her birthday on the first full moon after the mountain laurel and serviceberry bloomed. Jonathan, her ten-year old brother, was born on November 10. His birthday was celebrated on the first full moon after the chestnuts and acorns dropped and the high-flying flocks of geese migrated southward. Poor Fritz had been born on February 14. No natural events announced the arrival of February. The appearances of trees and animals remained relatively unchanged from the end of October through the end of February. Heavy snows arrived in November and the creeks usually froze over in December.

But those events were not consistent enough from year to year to accurately determine the arrival of February.

The Dunkards had celebrated Christmas at the first full moon following Jonathan's birthday in November, and then celebrated Fritz's birthday on the second full moon following the Christmas full moon. The settlers had spent nearly two years along the Monongahela and everyone, other than Katrina, had celebrated two birthdays in their wilderness cabin. Her birthday would be celebrated at the next full moon. But unless Johannes obtained flour and baking powder on his trading trip to the Potomac, Katrina would not have a pie or cake to celebrate her seventeenth birthday.

Gisela studied Katrina as she reached the cabin, and once again pondered her daughter's future. How would she ever meet any young men while they lived in the Monongahela wilderness? More families would eventually settle in the area, of course, but Katrina was almost seventeen years old, and well aware that her mother had married when she was seventeen. When her daughter asked to make the pie for Angus, Gisela remembered poignantly when she had baked an apple pie for Johannes, many years ago in Germany. Although she doubted Angus would ever court Katrina, she was certain that her daughter would invite his attentions. She smiled as she remembered her own mother's advice; "Marry your son when ye will, but your daughter when ye can."

Today was not hot, but it was warm enough that Gisela was reminded of the hours spent cooking meals inside the cabin last summer. It was so stifling that on some days they ate cold smoked meat on the porch to avoid cooking. That schedule sufficed for many days, but when beans and squash were ready to pick, cooking would follow. A logical solution to the insufferable heat would be a lean-to summer kitchen attached to the opposite end of the cabin from where Johannes planned to build a summer bedroom for the boys. Gisela designed the summer kitchen with a small stone fireplace just large enough to hold a skillet or a small pot.

While the others had returned to the cabin and the chores that awaited them, Fritz and Jonathan lingered at the riverbank, watching Angus until the last ripples of his dugout had faded from sight.

The two young boys skipped a few rocks across the river and then reluctantly retraced their steps back up the hill just as their mother called. They had each other's companionship, and to them life on the frontier was exciting. Their main responsibility during summer months was to protect the sprouting corn from marauding crows and blackbirds that descended on the new growth during daylight hours. Later in summer, when corn reached the ear stage, the two boys would need to be alert at night for any deer or buffalo that might find their crops. They had more than enough chores to keep them occupied, except during winter months when life inside the cabin became boring.

Fishhooks were always in demand. No other piece of equipment yielded a greater harvest relative to its size or cost. Along with heavy fishing line, the boys asked their father for a gun small enough for a boy to shoot. Johannes informed them that the price of such a gun would be more baskets of ginseng than they already had gathered. After seeing Angus's dugout, and hearing his description of how it was made, the boys also wanted a canoe. With boyish enthusiasm, they agreed to begin looking for just the right log to build one.

Meanwhile, on the river Angus was anxious to once again be alone, without human companionship. Although he was reluctant to leave the Dunkards—he was committed to trading at the Forks of the Ohio. Actually, he looked forward to this trip, just as he had eagerly anticipated the leg of the trip down the Monongahela from the Shawnee camp. For Angus, life without challenges would be tedious. In just twenty-two short years of life, he had survived every challenge that emerged and was confident he could handle whatever occurred for the remainder of his present adventure. Overconfidence must be avoided, for arrogance was more dangerous than fear. While fear honed the senses like a strop sharpened a razor, overconfidence caused nicks in the keen edge of an otherwise sharp mind.

As the warm afternoon sun began its descent towards the western horizon, Angus removed his deerskin shirt and laid it atop the load of furs in front of the sleeping wolf pup. Once again, Angus entered a cerebral zone of constantly scanning the river ahead and the banks on either side, while subconsciously processing the sounds emanating from the surrounding forest. Although he relished the fervor of a hunt, mile for mile he savored the quiet satisfaction of transitioning river and mountain scenery.

Like a meteor across the galaxy of his mind came the question of what it would be like to share his canoe, or his life, with another person. He asks himself, "How much of another person's presence can I tolerate?" Would the presence of another person be more beneficial than disruptive, more conversant than acceptable? For now he had the only company he really wanted—Schatto. As he studied the pup sleeping on the pile of hides, he remembered that she now had a name, and he must begin using that name as he issued commands and tried to communicate. He repeated the name several times to himself, "Schatto, Schatto, Schatto." In so doing, he was reminded of the person who had suggested the name and repeated to himself, "Katrina, Katrina, Katrina."

CHAPTER THIRTEEN
HAGGIS

THE MOUNTAINS BORDERING the Monongahela reminded Angus of the Cairngorm Mountains of Scotland, but the river itself was quite different. A trip down the Orchy, the Findhorn, or the Spey in Scotland was the ultimate excursion through rapid currents, life-threatening boulders, and small waterfalls. Travel on the Monongahela reminded him more of his serene travels across the many Scottish lakes, his favorite being Loch Ness, with all the mystery surrounding it. He wondered if he would ever again see Loch Ness, or Loch Loman, or any of the other beautiful lakes that had been such an important part of his former life in Scotland. He missed the lakes, and questioned why were there none in the Appalachians.

While he missed his family and Heather, he could not be homesick in such a wonderful country as America—a land with a superabundance of varied wildlife, desolate but magnificent scenery stretching to the horizon, forests of gigantic towering trees, and limitless stretches of river to explore? How had he been so fortunate to end up in this magnificent place? Life in the Highlands had been difficult. His family had the bare necessities to survive, and little else. Their clan raised or rustled enough sheep and cattle to supplement the meat from red deer and hares they harvested from the countryside. While a few of his elderly relatives had indeed starved, and a few had frozen to death in poorly heated stone huts, he had been strong enough—or fortunate enough—to escape such fates.

He grew concerned that the English redcoats were still trying to exterminate the clans of the Scottish Highlands. King George II had banned the playing of bagpipes and wearing of the kilt.

Persons convicted of such crimes were imprisoned for six months, while those convicted for a second offense were transported to one of His Majesty's colonies beyond the oceans for seven years. Angus would have willingly returned and fought with Bonnie Prince Charles against the English to gain the separation from England that had been such a long-lived dream. However, most clan members had conceded that amassing an army large enough to challenge England was nothing more than fantasy. Thus, Angus had fled his homeland.

Angus contemplated owning a farm, specifically along the small stream with dense thickets of yellow plums. But with a farm came endless confinement. Continuous oversight and management were necessary to protect the sheep and cattle and any other livestock he might accumulate. In addition, livestock needed barns, hay, corn, and water. He could not fathom the amount of work needed to maintain the crops and animals just to make a living on a farm. "Perhaps I can build a small cabin and just live off the land, without all responsibilities of farming. I would then be free to travel, unhindered by duties and routine chores." Happiness for Angus was synonymous with freedom, and freedom was paramount.

As the heavily loaded dugout floated ever northward, the river widened and the surrounding hills became less lofty. He had not departed the Dunkard's small settlement until early afternoon, so Angus planned to float until dusk. Schatto had exercised exhaustively that morning and would sleep most of the afternoon. The soft gurgling of the river, the gentle rocking of the dugout, and the warm rays of sunshine combined with the short night's sleep caused even Angus to nod off several times. To his dismay, while his eyes were closed, the dugout had started to turn sideways. Although not yet perpendicular to the slow current, the dugout was nevertheless in a potentially dangerous situation. He remembered what had happened the last time the dugout turned sideways, and reprimanded himself for his lack of focus. Fortunately, there were no submerged boulders or trees in the vicinity, and he deftly maneuvered the craft back into the current.

Angus beached the dugout on the requisite gravel bar as the sun passed behind the western hills. He set up camp, conducted a few obedience lessons with Schatto, and built a small fire near the riverbank. Angus and the pup ate their supper of elk meat in silence as two bullfrogs began their nightly chorus. Several bats followed erratic flight paths over the river in search of insects, while two great blue herons flapped slowly upriver. A soft elk skin was the only blanket they would need that warm spring night. The pup snuggled against Angus, and the two dreamed of the girl called Katrina and the Dunkards who made their short visit so delightful.

Angus stirred at first light and noted that during the night, dark clouds had invaded the blue sky of the previous afternoon. The warm breeze blowing from the south warned of coming rain. Angus would have to observe the clouds and the wind more closely before he could make an accurate prediction about the rain's intensity and duration. He had indeed been fortunate on the trip, averting long periods of heavy rain, and now was resigned to the likelihood of precipitation. After a hurried breakfast of smoked deer, Angus tightly secured the smoked and greased elk skins that covered his bundles of furs and hides, and prepared to depart. Schatto had found a nice stick to chew and was reluctant to enter the dugout. She ignored Angus's call to come, and rather than let her continue to ignore a command, he moved to her, grasped the rawhide rope that never left her neck, and lifted her by the scruff into the canoe.

The sky darkened and the wind increased as they floated downriver. The clouds were not the roiling, ugly clouds that portended a severe thunderstorm, but instead were the heavy, low-hanging clouds that forecast a steady, prolonged rain. Wind gusting upriver buffeted the flimsy branches of birch trees lining the riverbank and exposed the pale undersides of their leaves.

As the first few drops fell, the tiny splashes and the subsequent ripples spreading outward from each impact point fascinated Angus. He dreaded rains so heavy that they ruined this spectacle. Schatto stared intently at the river as the drops fell, but as her soft gray fur became soaked, she turned to licking the annoying water. Angus noted her discomfort and gently lifted the pup into her basket, covering it with one of the greased elk skins. Schatto poked her nose out a small opening but was satisfied to remain secluded from the incessant drops that ran off the greased hide like water off a duck's back. Angus pulled another elk skin over his own deerskin shirt and focused on guiding the dugout in the river current. His attempt to bail the rainwater from the bottom of the dugout became secondary to managing the direction of the canoe. The large clamshell he used for bailing was ineffective against the relentless rain that persisted for hours.

With dusk overtaking them, Angus deftly maneuvered the dugout into the shallow water on the downriver side of a bar. Stepping into the water, he roused the pup, and began emptying the dugout. Several inches of rainwater had accumulated, and the bottom layer of furs was thoroughly soaked. He used several large branches from the nearby woods to construct platforms on the gravel bar for the furs and hides. Removing his deerskin shirt, he wrapped it securely inside a greased elk skin and, uncovered to the waist, began transferring bundles to the gravel bar. It was an arduous task, and Angus accomplished it while great jagged streaks of lightning punctuated the eastern horizon, indicating that the storm had departed the river valley. The rain dwindled to a light drizzle, the bundles were all on shore, and the greased elk skins would protect them from all but heavy downpours.

Angus did not attempt to build a fire, but did gather a large pile of dead branches to light if the rain stopped. Huddled under an elk skin, Angus and Schatto enjoyed a meal of smoked deer meat, supplemented by three pemmican balls kept dry in one of the bundles of deer hides. Angus was worried that the bear fat might upset her delicate stomach. He would not welcome a pup with an upset stomach in his dugout the next day. Schatto must be exposed to new foods gradually since she would eventually be eating a variety of strange items. Biting off tidbits, he offered Schatto something new for her diet. Without hesitation, she gulped down the pemmican just as she did any other meat.

As Angus slowly chewed his pemmican, he was reminded of a similar food commonly eaten in Scotland called "haggis." It was considered by some to be the national food of Scotland. The stomach of a sheep was emptied of its contents, turned inside out, thoroughly washed, soaked overnight, and then boiled for several hours. The prepared pouch then became the container for a mixture of toasted oats, onions, beef suet, and various spices, added to a blend of minced sheep heart, liver, and lungs. The resulting "porridge" was stuffed into the sheep's stomach, the ends tied securely, boiled for three hours, and then served hot. Angus remembered fondly the delicious haggis that his mother often prepared for the family, but he also remembered the many times he had carried a cold haggis on one of his extended hunting trips through the Highlands. A wave of nostalgia swept over Angus and at that moment he would willingly trade all his pemmican balls for just one of his mother's hot haggis.

The rain stopped as darkness engulfed the river bottom. Angus and Schatto huddled together under a somewhat dry elk skin; sleep came easily for the pair.

CHAPTER FOURTEEN
THE REVELATION

MORNING DAWNED BRIGHT and clear as Angus arranged a small pile of dried bark and leaves. With aid of flint and steel he soon coaxed a small flicker of flame to life. The dry sticks he had covered with an elk skin were added, and a comforting blaze soon resulted. To dry the sodden pelts, Angus pushed several wet branches close to the fire and turned the bottoms of the bundles of furs and hides towards the fire. His deerskin shirt was spread on tree branches stuck like tall skewers into the ground near the flames. His next crucial step was to replace damp powder from his muzzle-loader.

After the contents of his soaked deerskin bag were emptied onto a deer hide, the bag was hung near the fire. Against a sky of panoramic promise, the sun cast its first golden rays onto the gravel bar, and immediately one beam struck the blue stone. It did not glow like one of the coals in the fire, but was instantly transformed. The blue sheen became luminous, as sparkles of light burst from within the stone itself. The constant rubbing of the soft deerskin against the stone had worn away some of the original surface tarnish, and now its blue luster was unearthly. It projected a shade and brightness different from anything Angus had ever seen. He could not resist picking it up.

Angus decided they had time for obedience training while his belongings were drying. Still holding the blue stone, Angus called to the wolf pup who was exploring the gravel bar, "Schatto, come. Schatto, come." The pup, with the same quizzical look on her face that Angus had seen previously, turned and promptly trotted back to her master. At Angus's command to heel, the pup moved to his left side and followed him around the gravel bar. Angus gave the order, "Whoa," followed by "Stay," and he slowly moved away from the pup. Sitting patiently on her haunches, Schatto stared intently at Angus. To reinforce the "Stay" command, Angus slowly crawled up the steep bank, while repeating the order, "Schatto, stay. Schatto, stay." At the top of the bank he halted, extended the palm of his hand towards the pup, and firmly repeated the order, "Stay. Stay." Angus then moved behind the trunk of a large sycamore and remained motionless.

While standing there, he realized he still held the blue stone in his hand, and it seemed even warmer than when he had first held it that morning. Angus would not leave the pup so long that she moved from her position, or the lesson would be a failure. If he failed to reinforce the response he desired, he might encourage an unacceptable behavior. Quickly moving to the edge of the bank, Angus was fascinated to see the pup still sitting on her haunches. With the palm of his hand facing the pup, he repeated the "Stay" command and then carefully dropped down off the high bank to the gravel bar. Angus stopped and called, "Schatto, come." Eagerly she bounded to Angus and sat at his side. Dropping to one knee, he tenderly rubbed her ears and scratched her belly, telling her, "Good girl. Good girl." As an even more compelling reward, he stooped so that she could lick his face—an act that would reinforce the bond between the two. A warm feeling came over Angus, as he contemplated the obedience of the pup. The bonding and submission moved him more than most of his other accomplishments. He marveled at the ability of a pup not quite three months old to master basic commands that most hounds accomplished only after a year.

Returning to the fire, Angus replaced the still-warm blue stone into his deerskin bag, along with his flint, steel, some dry tinder, and several pieces of pemmican and smoked deer meat. While Schatto played at the water's edge, Angus bailed water from the dugout. Next he reloaded the dried bundles of furs and hides into the dugout, and carefully secured his long rifle and his extra paddles.

As man and beastie consumed their light breakfast, Angus projected arrival at Redstone Creek to be late that afternoon.

Johannes had informed Angus that a trading post was being built at the mouth of the creek, about two days north of the Dunkard's cabin. There would certainly not be a full supply of trade goods available, and moreover there would be no gold. Even if a trader lived at the site, he had likely departed with his load of furs for the Atlantic colonies. Angus was eager to find the post, and if it were indeed an active trading post, there would be obvious signs such as a rough boat landing, or well-worn paths leading up the riverbank.

The fire had consumed all its fuel, leaving only a few glowing coals, and as Angus rose to his feet, Schatto scampered to the canoe and tried to jump in. The wolf seemed to sense they were preparing to start another day's journey. Although she was maturing daily, her legs were still much too short to jump very high. Angus picked her up, deposited her in the dugout, freed the boat from its mooring, and stepped into the rear. In a few moments, both were comfortably settled into position, and the current took control. Schatto perched atop a load of deer hides, sniffed the air, and scrutinized every detail of the shore, while Angus kneeled on a bearskin with paddle in hand.

On this day, the river was so wide that Angus had expansive views of the surrounding country. For the first time on his downriver float, vistas opened, and he could survey the horizon from ridge to ridge. The dense forest and its hidden splendors, however, remained dark and mysterious. Even though the gigantic trees were widely separated, newly unfurled leaves blocked sunshine from reaching the forest floor, so that in very few places did golden rays penetrate. The river had not only broadened, but had become quite shallow in many places. Small wooded islands appeared, and Angus had to choose whether to pass right or left. In a few places, the water was so shallow that the bottom of the dugout scraped through loose gravel, making a grating sound.

As morning waned, Angus's inquiring mind once again contemplated the river—a living entity as truly as the neighboring forest. He mulled over the significance of a river's banks as well as the water itself. Without banks a river would have no form. Angus had perceived many times that a river was a unique entity; it could be experienced through all five senses. Through touch, his fingers sensed the wetness, velocity, and temperature. He could taste the river, sometimes sweet and sometimes acrid. Gazing at the river, his eyes beheld the direction of its flow and objects floating on its surface. His nostrils disclosed whether it was fresh, musty, or stagnant. His ears could detect the water gurgling over rocks or lapping against the shore.

As the dugout drifted slowly through one of the deep pools occurring so frequently in the lower Monongahela, Angus spied something floating at the surface dead ahead, and he noiselessly maneuvered the dugout alongside the object. He recognized the head protruding from the water, attached to a round shell barely breaking the water surface. As he drew even with the animal, Angus was startled to see that the massive head was larger than his upper arm. The moss-covered shell and long spiny tail revealed a huge snapping turtle. Through the Shawnee, Angus had become familiar with snapping turtles, some crawling awkwardly across land to lay their eggs and others swimming smoothly through the water in search of fish. He had even sampled snapping turtle stew, and found it delicious.

Angus instinctively reached for its tail. Turtle stew! What a welcome change from smoked deer meat and pemmican. With both hands, Angus partially hoisted it out of the water and, to his utter amazement he saw it was nearly as wide as the dugout and as heavy as sixty pounds. Now that he had it in his grasp, what was he going to do with it? Minus the wolf pup, he might have attempted to heave it into the dugout. However, as the uncontrollable turtle fought violently, Angus concluded that with or without Schatto, he could not haul such a monstrous reptile into the dugout. Even if he could, why risk a serious injury to himself or his frantically curious pup?

Schatto was both frightened and fascinated by the strange creature in Angus's grasp. When the turtle splashed water into her face, the pup yipped wildly. Angus shouted, "No! No!" but the excitement was too much, and the yipping escalated. Angus estimated that the turtle was larger than any beaver or river otter he had trapped, larger and more dangerous than any fish he had seen. Judging by the size of its powerful jaws, the turtle could easily bite off several of his fingers or toes, and could certainly do major damage to an arm or leg. As his grip on the wildly struggling turtle began to weaken, Angus shook his head, grinned, and released the impressive, ancient reptile.

As the turtle slowly submerged, the canoe floated onward, Schatto became subdued, and Angus's thoughts flashed back to the legendary prehistoric reptile that he had seen in Scotland. While boating on Loch Ness, Angus had been frequently startled by a lake serpent with a small head atop a long slender neck, three to four times larger than his dugout. Many of his relatives and friends had also seen the lake serpent, but no one had ever been harmed. The Monongahela would never support such a creature, and the snapping turtle was surely one of the largest animals to live there.

The current slowly drew the dugout further downriver, and the pup again settled atop a bundle of pelts. Schatto and Angus relaxed, but both remained alert for any other strange entities that might materialize in the river. By late afternoon, there was no evidence of Redstone Creek and the associated trading post. It would be useless to search on foot, so Angus continued to search the sky for smoke and the riverbanks for human sign. As the sun began its westward retreat, Angus sighted a well-worn path leading from a gravel bar to the top of the riverbank. He hurriedly coaxed the dugout to the eastern shore, easing it onto the gravel bar. An examination of the river's edge revealed no sign of canoes being dragged ashore or human footprints. Although beaver had downed several trees, the path was too wide to have been made by the large rodents. Deer, elk, or buffalo had not made the path, he concluded, because their rounded hoof prints would have lingered, in spite of recent rain.

The wolf pup tagged along after Angus to the top of the bank. There a large area had been cleared of trees, and construction of a log cabin had commenced but lacked a roof. Angus approached a bark-sided lean-to, where several fires had once burned. Angus abandoned the inspection and returned to the dugout. A gnawing concern overtook him that all traders had left the region. Although the gravel bar would have made a good overnight camp, Angus decided to press on for the three remaining hours of daylight.

As the western sky turned various shades of red, orange, and purple, Angus beached the dugout on a small gravel bar and repeated his nightly routine. After a short training session for the pup, the two travelers settled down before a campfire. Although he had nothing to cook, Angus wanted a fire just large enough for heat and comfort, but too small to produce detectable acrid odor and smoke. As long as Angus could remember, fire had been an integral part of his life. Firewood had been scarce in Scotland, but they always managed to find enough for a small blaze. In this wilderness, however, firewood was available in inexhaustible amounts. According to his grandfather, forests once covered much of Scotland, but humans with their sheep and cattle had transformed the forestland to scrubland, and now low-growing heath dominated much of the countryside. In this vast wilderness along the Monongahela, Angus could not imagine enough people and livestock to strip the mountains of the beech, chestnut, yellow poplar, oak, maple, and hemlock timber.

Angus and the pup sat quietly, both seemingly mesmerized by the fire. Was the fascination for fire passed down by his Scottish ancestors, or was it a natural attraction inherent in all humans? Why did the wolf pup seem to be equally drawn to a phenomenon that was not a natural part of her world? The warmth was certainly lulling to both human and dog, but the movements of the fire seemed seductive as well. Flickering flames are unlike anything else in the world, crackling, sputtering, and smoking. Are humans and animals attracted to objects and events that activate several of their senses?

Angus and Schatto departed the gravel bar as the morning fog slowly lifted, and the upswept, undulating hills dominated the landscape, as well as Angus's respect. Dense stands of hardwood trees, interspersed with hemlocks, started at the water's edge, clung tightly to the slopes, and eventually faded into the blue haze that accentuated distant ridges.

After a day marked only by a small herd of passing buffalo at water's edge, a large gravel bar appeared on the western side of the Monongahela, and Angus decided it would make a good campsite. On this rewarding day they had covered several river miles. By the time they reached the Forks of the Ohio, Angus and his dugout canoe would have covered almost two hundred miles. He had no way of knowing the actual distance or, for that matter, any of the distances between landmarks, since no person had ever floated from the headwaters of the West Fork to the Forks of the Ohio, and no maps existed for the area.

Angus was hopeful that their camp the next night would be at the Forks of the Ohio. Angus secured the dugout, gathered firewood, and set out to explore the gravel bar and nearby forest. They had stopped only once during the day, and Schatto deserved intense exercise before they reached the trading post. It might be necessary to keep her tied while he attempted to sell his furs. When Angus first tethered her to logs each night, he had kept her secured only for short periods, and always when he was nearby. Later, he began moving away from her while giving the command, "Stay...stay." She had pulled against the deerskin rope then, but now she accepted it, remaining motionless and attentive.

Angus wanted fresh meat for Schatto; she'd had none since they left the Dunkards. Smoked venison had kept the pup from starving, but she would not grow at a normal rate without plentiful raw meat. Deerskin leash in hand, Angus commanded the pup, "Schatto, come...come." After circling the gravel bar twice, the pair darted up the bank and began a search for rabbit runways. Several trees had been blown down by a windstorm sometime in the past, and a dense blackberry thicket now occupied the area around the fallen tree trunks. Rabbits rarely lived in a dense forest, where no grasses, briars, or tender shoots grew to provide the food they needed. In contrast, a blackberry thicket offered food and protection from predators such as red-tailed hawks, great-horned owls, and gray foxes. Along the Monongahela, they were constantly on the lookout for an unsuspecting rabbit, gray squirrel, or ruffed grouse in the open.

Angus chanced upon several recently used trails, and began setting his snares. In the meantime, the actions of the wolf pup indicated that she was inundated with interesting scents along the trails. The first litter of young rabbits, born in April, had left the nest and one could carelessly wander into a snare that night, so after setting his snares they returned to the gravel bar. It would have been good training to let her follow the scents that her wolf nose found so fascinating and he must begin to provide these opportunities on a regular basis, but on this night Angus did not want Schatto to frighten any rabbits out of the blackberry thicket.

As they dropped onto the gravel bar, Angus resumed obedience lessons. Angus gave the first command, "Schatto, heel." After a few circuits of the gravel bar, he issued the command, "Whoa…whoa." Ordering her to stay, he moved in the direction of the dugout. Much to his disappointment, the pup only partially obeyed his commands. She had first wandered slightly to the front and then behind him, instead of walking slightly behind his left leg. She had paused at the "whoa" command, but then she moved several steps before coming to a halt. She remained on her haunches at the "stay" command, but fidgeted nervously before slowly crawling on her belly to Angus. On previous nights, he had felt reassured by her training exercises. However, on this night he was sorely disappointed when she acted like a willful pup.

Angus realized he had not provided the usual rewards so essential in reinforcing the lessons. Could that be the reason she was not responding? As Angus reached into his deerskin bag for a piece of deer meat, his fingers brushed the blue stone and he was disconcerted at its warmth. Acting on impulse, Angus ordered, "Schatto, sit." Immediately, the pup stopped fidgeting and crawling, and sat upright on her haunches fully alert. Angus thought to himself, "This is more like it, this is how a well-trained pup should respond." Moving quickly to the pup to reinforce her response, he offered her a piece of deer meat, which she gulped down. Still clasping the blue stone, Angus resumed the lessons. The pup's heightened responses exceeded his expectations!

Angus deposited the stone back in the bag before he and Schatto returned to the small fire. While Angus gathered more firewood from the gravel bar, the pup meandered down to the water's edge and pursued a retreating crayfish into deep water, Angus called, "Schatto, come…come." She completely ignored him. Angus was perplexed. How could she obey his every command one minute, and the next minute be unresponsive? Angus did not repeat the command, but instead returned to the fire with his load of fuel, carefully watching to make sure she did not venture too far.

As Angus pondered the situation, he suddenly experienced what Grandfather Harry McCallander had called an "Ah, ha" moment. The pup had responded faultlessly when Angus held the blue stone, but without it, she responded like any ordinary three-month-old pup. How could a stone enable the pup to understand his commands? Now confused, Angus realized this idea could be easily tested. Once again he called, "Schatto, come." Once again she ignored him. He retrieved the blue stone, rubbed it softly, and repeated, "Schatto, come." The pup at once turned her head and ran splashing through the water to him. Moving directly to his side, she sat attentively on her haunches. Several more trials, with and without the stone in hand, convinced Angus that the blue stone was bewitched. He was more bewildered than ever.

During their dinner, questions whirled like a tornado through the Scotsman's mind. Did the stone solely reinforce the commands previously learned, or did it disseminate pathways to new commands? When the two had finished supper, an anxious trainer extracted the blue stone from the bag, held it tightly as the warmth spread through his fingers, and then spoke, "Schatto, to the canoe, to the canoe." The wolf pup sat upright then moved, tentatively, to the canoe. Angus stared in disbelief. Quietly, Angus said, "Schatto, come." Without hesitation this time, the pup left the canoe and ran directly to his side. Angus rubbed her ears while she wriggled in delight, then he rolled her onto her back and rubbed her belly. Both Schatto and Angus were requited; the pup because of the reassuring caresses, and the Scotsman because of the amazing spectacle he had just observed.

To satisfy his skepticism, Angus conducted several more trials while holding the blue stone. He directed the pup to go to the river's edge, and she went to the water. He bade her to go to the riverbank and lie down; she trotted to the target and stretched out. To Angus it was undeniable that the blue stone possessed some penetrating force that enabled the wolf to understand his words and possibly his thoughts. Questions flooded his brain till he thought his head would explode. How far away could Schatto grasp commands? Could she follow two or more simultaneous commands? Did he have to rub the stone, or simply hold it? Did the stone have to radiate warmth before his commands were transmitted to the pup?

In spite of the gnawing questions, Angus decided not to test the pup anymore that evening. As he rotated the stone in his hand, one disturbing query arose. Could the pup respond to his thoughts as well as his words? That question would be easy to test. While holding the tepid stone, Angus concentrated on the command, "Schatto, fetch a stick. Schatto, fetch a stick." Abruptly, the pup darted across the gravel bar, found a water-soaked stick near the river's edge and carried it back to Angus. Ears straight up and tail held horizontal, she quietly held the stick until he accepted it from her mouth. Angus smothered her with affection and unbridled praise.

Angus pondered these events, and reflected on the various times he had held the blue stone in his hand while instructing the pup. He suddenly remembered the incident on the Dunkards' porch the day he left. He had been holding the blue stone and thinking about Katrina when she began to blush and suddenly left the porch. Could the stone have facilitated her insight to his thoughts? He distinctly remembered thinking that she was a most attractive girl and he would like to spend more time with her. Assuming she had indeed perceived his thoughts, Angus wondered whether any of the other Dunkards had understood them. Because none had responded in word or expression, Angus concluded that his thoughts were transmitted only to Katrina.

The last night of their two-week float trip down the Monongahela was anything but serene and peaceful. Staring up at the stars, Angus tried all night to make sense of his monumental discovery. Magic, mystery, and persons with special powers were an accepted part of life in the Scottish Highlands, but Angus had come to believe there were logical explanations for every action and every reaction. Now doubts clouded logic. The wolf pup's sleep that night was interrupted with considerable squirming and whimpering. Was she also responding to the evening's strange events?

When Angus awoke to a pink glow in the East, he decided he would retrieve his snares before daylight signaled the start of another day. Angus began gently scratching Schatto's belly. The pup stuck her nose out from under the elk skin, stretched her growing limbs, and moved to lick Angus on the face. In complete jest, Angus said, "Schatto, go up the riverbank, check the snares, and bring back any rabbits that have been caught." The pup yawned, squirmed out from under the elk skin, and continued her affectionate licking. The blue stone was tucked inside the deerskin bag, and Angus would have been dumbfounded if Schatto had obeyed any part of his command.

After their morning drink from the river, Angus and Schatto headed for the snares set the previous evening. Schatto made a beeline for the briar thicket, a perfect site for her to learn about scents of different animals. With animated tail, the pup sniffed her way through the blackberry thicket. Angus watched intently as she wove back and forth, following one trail and then another. Suddenly a full-grown cottontail burst from a dense clump of briars and darted down a trail. Schatto spotted the rabbit and instantly took chase. The excited yipping of the pup and the occasional glimpse of the prominent white, powder-puff tail of the rabbit told Angus the route of the chase. The rabbit exited the briar thicket and, with leaps nearly six feet long, was soon out of sight in the dense woods. Schatto promptly lost the scent of the rabbit and returned to the delightful array of scents in the thicket.

Her search through the thicket eventually led to a snare that yielded a half-grown cottontail. She paused and then crouched low to the ground. With a low puppy growl, she jumped on the rabbit, and by the time Angus arrived she was biting its head. Angus kneeled to the ground, untied the snare, and spoke, "Good girl. Good girl."

To positively reinforce her reaction, Angus removed the long-bladed hunting knife with its bear jaw handle from its sheath and sliced open the belly of the rabbit. He pulled out the heart and liver and fed them to the pup. With a minimum of chewing, they were soon devoured. Angus collected the rabbit carcass, retrieved the other snares, and returned to the riverbank. The pup followed alongside, trying to lick the blood that was dripping from the rabbit.

Angus had determined earlier that morning that if they caught a rabbit, he would expose Schatto to the sound of gunfire. At the edge of the bank, Angus dropped the rabbit over the edge and urged Schatto to run down after it. Just as she reached the now-dead rabbit, Angus turned away, aimed his rifle in the direction of the forest, and fired. As expected, the sound reaching the pup was greatly diminished, and she exhibited little alarm while licking the blood from the belly-cut.

At their campsite Angus reloaded his rifle, but put in a much smaller amount of gunpowder than usual and did not insert a lead bullet into the barrel. He removed the lungs and kidneys from the rabbit, handed them to Schatto, and then quickly stepped to the end of the gravel bar. Aiming away from the pup, he fired the rifle, quickly returned to her side, and petted her affectionately. While she ate, he hurled the intestines far out into the river for snapping turtle food and pulled the fur from the rabbit.

Without delay, Angus suspended the rabbit by a green birch branch over a small fire. After Schatto finished eating the lungs, Angus gave her the head. The diversion would keep her occupied while the pink meat finished cooking. As the fat dripped into the fire and appetizing aromas drifted across the gravel bar, Angus relaxed on the bearskin that had been their bed for so many nights. Contentment flooded over him.

The trading post at the Forks of the Ohio and all that lay beyond beckoned to Angus, but he was in no hurry to depart the gravel bar. Angus ate both hind legs and one front leg of the rabbit and fed the meat from the other front leg to Schatto. He wrapped the back, with its small tenderloins, into some grass from the riverbank and slid it inside a bundle of beaver pelts at the front of the dugout. He let the pup run around the gravel bar for a few minutes before loading her into the boat.

Although the sky was overcast, a warm breeze from the south offered the promise of a pleasant day on the final leg of the trip. The pup was soon asleep in her basket, and Angus kept the dugout in the middle of the tranquil river. His thoughts soon turned to the perplexing blue stone. In the labyrinth of his mind whirled the many ways to test the limits of its magical powers. He was anxious to determine if other animals, especially horses, would respond as Schatto had. Would wild animals—deer, hawks, or snapping turtles—respond to its sorcery? That possibility was mind-boggling.

His paramount concern was whether his thoughts could be transmitted to humans. Angus felt angst as he realized there were alarming implications if the blue stone did indeed transmit his thoughts to other persons. Rarely would it be acceptable for other people to read his mind. Angus had always guarded his thoughts and now risked having them exposed. This development could be dangerous with regards to an enemy. But it could be useful if he and another did not share the same language. Language barriers had caused problems communicating with Sweetwater and the other Shawnee. While a few of the Indians had understood some English words when he arrived, several months had passed before he was able to communicate easily with them.

Another enigma suddenly surfaced. Were the sorcerous powers assigned to the holder of the stone? Katrina was the only one of the Dunkards who had held the stone and experienced its radiating warmth, but Angus did not remember grasping any of her thoughts. Did her thoughts dwell on the stone and not on him? Considerable time and experimentation would be necessary to answer these questions. In the meantime, guarding the blue stone would require more vigilance than guarding Bonnie Prince Charles.

Although the blue stone muddled his reasoning he continually scanned the river and the nearby forest for signs of trouble.

The river flowed steadily with no obstructions, and late that morning Angus spotted the junction of a large river flowing from the east. That had to be the Yogh-yo-gaine, for no other large rivers entered the Monongahela after it passed LaCheathe. Similar to the Monongahela and LaCheathe, the Yogh-yo-gaine flowed northward. Angus had been forced to cross the Yogh-yo-gaine the previous autumn when he made his trip across the mountains from Lancaster. At that time, the river had been at its shallowest, but now it would be flowing much faster and deeper. Angus would not wish to cross the river when it was running full. As the dugout approached the mouth, the Yogh-yo-gaine came rushing into the Monongahela with volume far greater than LaCheate. The conjoined river appeared almost double in size. This junction was the journey's final landmark before reaching the Forks of the Ohio, where the Monongahela and the Alligane (later spelled Allegheny) merged to form the mighty Ohio.

Johannes told Angus that an Indian village—the only one he knew of along the Monongahela—was located slightly upstream of the mouth of the Yogh-yo-gaine. A few individuals from the village had visited the Dunkard's settlement, and had been surprisingly friendly. They had offered to trade some deer hides, but Johannes had nothing to trade, and the Indians had departed without incident.

Christopher Gist calculated that upwards of twenty Mohawk families resided near the mouth of the Yogh-yo-gaine. Gist, a surveyor and explorer who resided further upstream on the Yogh-yo-gaine, had reported to Angus that these Mohawks were governed with great authority by Queen Allaquipas (later spelled Aliquippa). This old Indian woman, who had led the band for many years, was one of the very few matriarchal leaders of Indian tribes in the region.

Angus spotted smoke drifting over the treetops a short distance up the Yogh-yo-gaine, but saw no other signs of life. Although he might have visited with the Mohawks to learn more about the Allegheny River, the Mohawks had no use for his furs, and they certainly would have no gold.

As the dugout was swept around a sharp bend, there lay parallel to the shoreline an enormous recumbent sycamore. The relentless erosion of the river current and the forces of a powerful spring windstorm had uprooted the ancient tree. This motionless and partially submerged tree was no different from hundreds of others Angus had passed during this trip. Resting on this particular tree trunk, however, was a sight that made him catch his breath. Suddenly he was within four boat-lengths of the sycamore, and at that close distance Angus had no difficulty identifying the object as an Indian, resting full-length in the mid-day sun with feet positioned downstream, head pointed upstream, and coal-black tresses floating lazily on either side of the log. Angus was slack-jawed at the sex of the Indian, who he reasoned was probably one of the Mohawks from Queen Allaquipas' camp.

The well-developed perky breasts jutting skyward mirrored the nearby hills, and it appeared that the vulnerable Indian maiden lying on her back in the nude posed no danger. One leg rested flat against the tree trunk, while the other knee bent upward. Silky black hair, hanging loosely around the maiden's head, contrasted sharply with the smooth white sycamore bark. One long slender arm hung over the side of the giant tree trunk, and the other rested comfortably on the girl's midriff. Her auburn skin glistened in the sun, as if still wet from the river's cool water.

Ever wary, Angus weighed the possibility of the alluring vision being a decoy for Indian attack. Danger could come in many forms—bows and arrows, guns, or a fleet of canoes. Glancing at both banks, the trapper detected nothing suspicious and then turned to survey the river behind him. He inadvertently tapped the side of the dugout with his wooden paddle, and the maiden instantly sat up. Startled by the unexpected dugout and its occupant, she visibly appraised the situation much as had the Scotsman.

Angus's shirt and hat had been removed earlier that day, and now his imposing muscular body caught the eye of the girl, much as her body held his fascination. Showing surprising control, in one soft motion the maiden gracefully stood fully upright on the anchored log. The sight of her perfect proportions triggered a sensuous reaction and a momentary cessation of Angus's breathing. With her body silhouetted, her rounded buttocks, uplifted breasts, gentle contours, and long graceful legs reminded Angus that a voluptuous woman is one of Nature's most aesthetically pleasing creations.

Unpretentiously bold, the girl stooped and picked up her deerskin dress, draped it over her arm, and with a coquettish smile, nodded to Angus. He silently asked, "What in the world went through your mind as you viewed a burly trapper and a wolf pup floating past in one of the largest canoes you've ever seen?" Angus was tempted to approach her, but only smiled broadly, and with a slight wave of his hand, called, "Nice day." Regrettably, the current forcibly swept the dugout past the fallen sycamore with its feminine adornment and Angus was caught up in resuming his voyage.

Among the thrills and spills of his float from the headwaters of the West Fork River, this experience would be burned in his memory for years to come. As the dugout rounded the bend, Angus could not resist a backward glance. His reward was another breath-taking view of the shapely maiden still standing upright on the giant sycamore log looking after him with her dress hanging limply in her hand. With a pensive smile, he said aloud, "A few years ago, when I was younger, I might have traded a boatload of furs for a lassie like ye."

Many times during his trip, the Monongahela River had briefly changed directions, alternatively flowing east and west, but persistently northward. The river was making a long sweeping curve towards the northwest when a stream entered the Monongahela from the east. This must be Turtle Creek, where, according to Johannes, a man named John Frazier expected to build a trading post. After beaching the dugout at the river's edge, Angus and Schatto made another exploratory trip. Several trails led from the river to a fair-sized clearing, which had been carved out of the dense forest. Two bark-covered lean-tos stood at the edge of the woods, but there was no recent sign of the trader who had vacated this post. Angus and Schatto once more boarded the dugout, and a strong push sent the canoe floating downstream towards the river called Ohio. In desperation, Angus acknowledged there remained one, and only one, opportunity to trade the results of his labor.

CHAPTER FIFTEEN
FORKS OF THE OHIO

ANGUS COULD SEE that ahead a large river was emerging from the north, almost certainly the Allegheny, marking the confluence known as the Forks of the Ohio. The French trading post should be on the north, where the point of land between the Monongahela and the Allegheny offered the best building site. Maneuvering the dugout over to the right, Angus searched for signs of human activity. First, he spotted pale-blue smoke drifting above the trees. Floating closer, he could see a bark canoe moored on the riverbank. He grew excited and apprehensive as he deftly guided the dugout onto the bank. Ordering Schatto to stay, Angus jumped into the water and secured the canoe to an exposed tree root used many times before.

On the point of land between the two rivers, a clearing held several hundred large black stumps. A short distance up the point sat a log cabin and two bark-covered buildings. The two smaller structures were three-sided lean-tos, crudely built, and obviously not intended to be permanent. Although the larger structure was more solidly built, it likewise appeared to be built for short-term use. Lifting the pup from the dugout, Angus firmly held her deerskin rope in his left hand while holding the Pennsylvania rifle in his right. Smoke was coming from the log cabin, where Angus hoped he would find a trader. With Schatto trailing obediently at his left side, Angus scanned the area for dogs that might attack the pup. Angus saw no dogs and heard no barking. If dogs were present, they would have spotted him with the pup as he beached the dugout and the clamor would have alerted every living thing in the area. Angus became hopeful when he saw six hobbled horses grazing in a grassy area near the woods. He would like to trade his dugout for a couple of horses. If he could not trade for gold with the French traders, he would settle for a packhorse to haul some of his furs back to Lancaster or the Potomac.

As he approached the cabin, Angus noticed a person sitting on the porch of the log cabin. A red-bearded Scotsman faced a clean-faced Indian, both wearing buckskin clothing. He appeared to be slightly older than Angus, though shorter and weighing considerably less. This Indian's broad muscular shoulders told of many hours spent paddling canoes up the Allegheny River. Pointing to the Indian, Angus asked, "Shawnee?"

The Indian shook his head, and answered, "Iroquois!"

Angus felt disappointed because he knew how to communicate with Shawnee, but he didn't know if he could communicate with an Indian from another tribe. Angus asked, "Fur trader?" The Iroquois pointed inside the cabin, while intently studying Angus, his handsome rifle, and the charming wolf pup. The Indian's intense scrutiny was, in fact, disquieting, and Angus felt his instincts activate as he stepped onto the porch and entered through an open door.

Inside were several piles of furs and deer hides, along with numerous wooden barrels and crude wooden boxes. Hanging from the rafters were dozens of woven baskets of various sizes. A large, plank-constructed wooden table filled the middle of the room, and between the table and the stone fireplace sat two men. Angus asked, in English, "Fur traders?" The one with the black beard answered in French, "Oui."

The Indian followed Angus inside and moved like a shadow to one end of the cabin. Angus noticed the Indian's attempt to hide his limp and observed that one leg was shorter than the other. The words of his Grandfather flashed through his mind. When faced with something that was obvious he would repeat, "Doesn't a man with one short leg always have one long leg?" Angus's apprehension began to mount and the hand holding Schatto's leash moved to his tomahawk. He knew nothing about any of these men, and would be forced to trust his instincts.

By pointing to the piles of beaver pelts and deerskins and then to the supplies spread out on the table, Angus communicated to the Frenchmen that he wanted to trade. They responded in French, and Angus could not understand a word they said. Using gestures and some of the Shawnee words he had learned, Angus turned and explained to the Iroquois that he wanted to trade furs for supplies and sell deerskins for gold. The Indian seemed to understand and with total lack of inflection explained in broken French to the traders.

The black-bearded Frenchman moved to the porch, and motioned Angus to follow him. It was evident that he wanted to see the furs and skins in the dugout. As they moved off the porch, the Frenchman pointed to himself and stated, "Maurice," then pointed to Angus and asked, "Your name?"

They moved wordlessly down the hill to the river, and Angus noticed that Maurice kept glancing sideways at the pup trailing obediently at his left side. Angus decided not to reveal that Schatto was a wolf. The fact it was a wolf, coupled with its unusual obedience, might make the pup a target for covetous thieves. Hopefully those at the trading post had never seen a three-month old wolf and would not identify Schatto as such.

The Frenchman began conversing and likely asked several questions, but Angus could only guess what he was saying, and therefore responded, "Yogh-yo-gaine," while pointing back up the Monongahela. Angus declined to show his map to the traders and had no intention of revealing his trapping sites. Maurice nodded his head as if he understood, and they continued in silence towards the dugout. At the river's edge the Frenchman carefully examined each peltry bundle, while making marks with his knife on a piece of flat bark he had carried from the cabin.

As the Frenchman continued to examine each bundle, Angus pulled a small piece of deer hide from the dugout. He showed the Frenchman the piece of hide on which he also had meticulously recorded the numbers of each kind of pelt and skin: forty-five beaver, twenty-six river otter, two hundred deerskins, and twenty elk skins. Pointing to piles of each kind of pelt and hide he tried to explain his marks to Maurice.

Angus would allow no ambiguity about the numbers and types

of skins. The Frenchman continued his scrutiny, while studying the marks Angus had made on the piece of hide. When the Frenchman had satisfied his curiosity about the numbers and condition of all the skins, he made several more marks on his piece of bark and returned to the cabin. Angus carried with him one deerskin, one elk skin, one beaver pelt, and one river otter pelt.

Maurice led the way into the cabin past the Iroquois who was once again sitting stone-faced on the porch. Inside the cabin, Angus approached the other Frenchman and said, while pointing his finger at his own chest, "My name is Angus. What's your name?"

He responded, "My name Jean Claude." Angus repeated it twice, and the short Frenchman smiled and nodded his head up and down. Angus examined the contents of the boxes, barrels, and baskets, in search of items he needed. To illustrate what he wanted, he placed gunpowder, lead bullets, fire-starting steel, knife, fishing hooks, small axe, bag of cornmeal, salt, wool shirt, and wool hat on the table. Angus remembered from his visits to trading posts at Lancaster that beaver pelts and deerskins had nearly equal trade value. He had memorized the exchange values for specific trade goods. A musket was worth thirty-five skins; an axe—five skins; a wool shirt—five skins; a hatchet—three skins, and a knife—one skin. The French Traders, however, still had to transport their furs up the Allegheny River to Montreal, then overland to eventually reach the river that would later be known as the St. Laurence. The precious cargo would finally be loaded on ocean-going ships to satisfy the European appetite for leather and fur.

Angus had no guarantee what his furs were worth this deep in the wilderness, but the trader would surely underestimate Angus's trading prowess and therefore try to exploit him. Angus could only wait to learn what the Frenchman offered for his furs, and then demand more. With his father, Colin, Angus had learned much about trading on their many trips to sell sheep and cattle. While serving as an indentured apprentice to the boat builder, Joseph Myers, Angus trapped and sold furs of mink, muskrat, and river otter. Those experiences had honed his trading skills.

While living along the coast near Philadelphia, Angus was

informed that the French controlled the lands north of the colonies, and many English feared they would try to gain control of the lands west of the Appalachians around the Ohio River. Little did Angus know that in a few short years the English, the French, the colonists, and several Indian tribes would all be embroiled in battles to determine who would control the great river and its rich surroundings.

The Ohio Company was organized in 1748 by a group of prominent Englishmen and Virginians under a royal grant from the English government. They were deeded 500,000 acres west of the Appalachians and south of the Ohio River, between the Monongahela and Kanawha rivers. The huge acreage was granted free of rents for ten years, contingent upon their building a fort, maintaining a garrison, seating one hundred families on the land, and protecting the settlement.

As enticement to settle the region, a family of six was offered five hundred acres: each of the first four members of a family was entitled to one hundred acres and each additional member, fifty acres. The Ohio Company had not yet established a trading post at the Forks of the Ohio, however, so the French seized the opportunity to hurriedly erect a few rough buildings and establish contacts with the Indians living in the area.

And now, with difficulty, Angus attempted to convey to the Frenchmen what goods he required. In response, they countered with the number of furs or skins they wanted in exchange. After much frustration, Angus turned to the Iroquois who had been standing quietly at the end of the cabin. Using Shawnee words, Angus told the Indian what he wanted and was pleased to hear him translate to the Frenchman. Angus could not understand what the Iroquois was telling the Frenchman, but gradually an understanding was reached.

Although Angus was not completely satisfied with the details, he agreed to exchange all his beaver and river otter pelts for the much-needed gunpowder, lead bullets, fire-making steel, knife, axe, fishing hooks, cornmeal, salt, shirt, and hat, plus two pack baskets to haul the items he received. Finally Angus tried to explain that he wanted to exchange his deerskins for gold. He made a rough sketch of a coin, and eventually Maurice pulled a French coin from a leather bag to show that he understood. Angus was uncertain what a deerskin or an elk skin was worth, and thus proposed one gold coin for each deer or elk skin. Maurice shook his head rapidly, and Angus interpreted his words to mean, "Too much!" Bartering continued for much of the afternoon, but no compromise was reached. Angus experienced a heightened awareness of his plight of being unable to communicate directly. He could not quite judge the character of a man if he could not gauge his words or look him in the eye as he spoke. The disadvantage he suffered from naiveté was offset, however, by his innate sense of caution bordering on distrust.

Angus decided that he would now propose trading his dugout for horses, and on a piece of bark he sketched his dugout and then the crude outline of two horses. In addition, on one horse he sketched a saddle. Maurice again said what Angus interpreted to mean, "Too much!" but gestured to Angus to follow him outside.

During the bartering inside the cabin, Schatto had chewed on one of the old bones that Angus carried for just such an occasion. Untying her rope, he commanded her to heel, and they followed the Frenchman out of the cabin. It became evident that he intended to show Angus the horses, and perhaps to discuss a trade. Angus figured that settlers coming west across the mountains from Lancaster or the Potomac had traded the horses to the Frenchman for supplies or a raft before continuing down the Ohio. The French traders should be willing to trade horses for his dugout because more settlers would arrive at the Forks of the Ohio that summer, and most needed some form of water transportation to float the Ohio River.

Of the six horses corralled, two were large powerful workhorses, the type used to pull plows and other farm equipment. They would make good packhorses. Three others were smaller, riding horses, similar to Night Sky, his black mare that was killed by the mountain lion. The last was a medium-sized gray mare, with black mane and tail. Angus had momentarily forgotten about Schatto and realized that she was crouching behind his legs. She had seen deer and elk, and even a herd of buffalo along the riverbank, but she had never been this close to such a large animal. Kneeling down, Angus talked to her while softly rubbing his hand along her back.

Angus knew that some horses tolerated and even interacted with dogs, while others became quite nervous in their presence. Angus called Schatto and led her towards the horses, which were hobbled to prevent them moving far from the trading post. The hobbles consisted of short pieces of elk skin, about four feet in length, tied around the ankles of two legs on the same side of the horse. A horse restrained by hobbles could take small steps, but could not run. With its movements greatly restricted, a hobbled horse seldom wandered far from where it was released to graze.

As Angus and Schatto approached, the three small riding horses moved away, while the two large workhorses only stood and gazed. In contrast, the gray mare moved in their direction, lowered her head, and began sniffing at the pup. Schatto issued a few low growls, then moved out from behind Angus. Stretching her head towards the mare, caution was overcome as the wolf and the horse made nose contact. Both quickly jerked backward, but almost then quickly recovered and stretched forward to repeat the nose contact. The horse snorted loudly at the pup, showing curiosity rather than fear. The pup licked at the horse's nose, and Angus sensed that the two could readily become friends.

Angus placed his hand on the gray mare's back, then on her neck. When she seemed to welcome his touch, he softly moved his hand up and down her face and let her smell his hand. Grasping the halter she wore, Angus curled back her lips to examine her teeth, which were in good condition and revealed she was four to five years old. Apparently she had been well cared for most of her life.

One additional question had to be answered, was the gray or any other horse frightened by gunshots? Maurice carried a small French pistol in his belt, and Angus successfully conveyed that he wanted the Frenchman to fire the pistol into the air to observe the horse's response. Leading Schatto around the side of the nearest cabin, Angus knelt by her side and then signaled the Frenchman to fire his pistol. As the gunshot exploded across the clearing at the Forks of the Ohio, Angus handed Schatto a piece of deer meat as he spoke calmly to her, and then he quickly noted the reaction of the horses. Although Schatto started at the sound of the shot, she calmly began eating the meat. Angus was gratified to see that none of the horses reacted to the explosion. Most frontier horses were accustomed to guns being fired nearby.

Angus indicated that he wanted the gray mare and one of the small riding horses in trade for the dugout. Maurice motioned to Angus and they walked to one of the small lean-tos, which appeared to be used for storage. Inside were several saddles and bridles. Angus examined them carefully and selected one saddle and two bridles. Although both showed considerable wear, they appeared to have been well made and received good care. Unknown to Angus, the Frenchman had been duly impressed with the size of the dugout, and figured that if Angus had brought it downriver by himself, then it should be easy to trade it to the next settlers who arrived.

After returning to the trading post, they continued negotiating but did not make any real progress. As the afternoon sun began approaching the western hills, Maurice and Jean Claude invited Angus to eat with them. They threw some corn meal, slices of smoked meat, and some unidentified greens into a kettle hanging inside the fireplace.

With little conversation, the two Frenchman, the Iroquois, and the Scotsman hastily finished the stew and moved out to the porch. As the sun dropped behind the hills, Maurice indicated that Angus could bed down in one of the small lean-tos, but Angus declined the offer. He had ongoing concerns for his safety, and did not want to be confined to a small cabin with only one exit. He opted, instead, to sleep on the riverbank where he could watch over his furs. Calling to Schatto, the two moved down the point to the riverbank where Angus built a small fire.

Angus was not satisfied with the discourse that had taken place, but he was not discouraged. He had reached the Forks of the Ohio, and the Frenchmen were willing to trade. From Maurice's reactions to his furs and skins, Angus concluded that the Frenchmen valued their high quality and definitely wanted them. There was no doubt they would reach an agreement, although it probably would not involve as much gold as Angus wanted. The language barrier made trading so difficult that Angus actually considered using the blue stone. However, he quickly discarded the idea after considering the potential pitfalls associated with transmitting his thoughts to Maurice. The possibilities were too risky until he conducted trials to determine the stone's powers.

Angus let the fire die out before surreptitiously moving his bearskin a short distance from the dugout. Although the Frenchman and the Iroquois knew the vicinity of his camp, he would conceal the exact spot. Fortunately, the moon would not rise until after midnight and even then would be only a small crescent. It would be too dark for anyone to spot the bulky form of human and pup huddled together under an elk skin. Besides, he had placed a decoy close to the campfire site. After carefully tying a long deerskin rope to one end of the dugout and the other end to his ankle, Angus bedded down a short distance from the river's edge.

The river flowed quietly along the point, and Angus was certain he could hear any intruder approaching from the river. He knew he was in a potentially dangerous situation, and could be easily overpowered by the Frenchmen and the Iroquois. During daylight he felt less vulnerable, although he was outnumbered. There had been no indications they might assault him, but it was often difficult to discern people's malevolence. Given France's aspirations to control the fur trade west of the mountains, Angus concluded the government certainly did not favor trappers trading with the English. It made no sense to jeopardize future trades by stealing furs or killing trappers.

The night proved uneventful, and after a breakfast of pemmican and deer meat, Angus and Schatto returned to the large cabin. After tying the pup to the porch and giving her a bone, Angus entered the cabin as the two Frenchmen and the Iroquois were finishing their breakfast. They offered Angus coffee in a tin cup and he accepted, although he had never learned to enjoy the strange drink.

With little attempt at conversation, the four sat around the table and sipped their coffee. Angus carefully studied the Iroquois and each of the Frenchmen. Angus attempted eye contact, taking careful note of their facial expressions and hand gestures. The Iroquois seldom changed expressions or used his hands to make gestures. He remained sullen and uttered little.

While the two Frenchmen had openly admired the Pennsylvania rifle, the Iroquois cast many covert glances in its direction. The Indian also spent long periods of time studying Schatto. Although this might simply be curiosity, Angus had a premonition that the Iroquois was deeply attracted to the pup. The black-bearded Frenchman named Maurice laughed constantly and kept a steady smile on his face. Angus concluded that he was truly a jolly person and was not putting on a show to impress Angus.

In contrast, the other Frenchman, Jean Claude, seldom laughed but maintained a shy grin. Angus felt at ease with the two Frenchmen, but he felt troubled around the Iroquois. Angus had learned to observe people critically; in the same way he observed animals. He had become skilled at correctly intuiting their motives and accurately predicting their actions.

As the coffee cups emptied, the trading resumed. Using symbols scratched on a piece of bark, Maurice indicated that he would offer Angus one gold coin for every two deerskins and one gold coin for every elk skin. With quick calculation, Angus determined that he would receive one hundred coins for his deerskins, and twenty coins for his elk skins. Angus had learned that passage across the Atlantic would cost at least two hundred gold coins, possibly more depending upon Heather's point of departure. Angus indicated to Maurice that he wanted one gold coin for every deerskin, but would accept one gold coin for each of the skins, regardless of whether they were elk or deer; two hundred and twenty coins total.

Maurice startled Angus when he offered two hundred coins if Angus would throw in his muzzle-loading rifle or the pup. The muzzle-loader, with its fancy curly-maple stock and sleek barrel over four feet in length, presented a stark contrast to the rustic, bulky, short-barrel muskets that the Frenchmen owned. Angus had scoffed as he emphatically refused to let them shoot it or even touch it. During the entire stay at the trading post, the rifle was either in his hand or at his side. He would never part with the rifle, since his very survival in the wilderness depended on it. Angus was certain that the Iroquois had identified Schatto as a wolf and had convinced the Frenchmen that when fully grown, the wolf could be sold for a huge profit.

Angus categorically refused the offer for either the rifle or Schatto, and the amicable bartering continued through the morning. He explained by gestures, that he had made the rifle, and he would make another one that coming summer. He pledged to bring his old rifle on his return trip and would sell or trade it to them. With assistance from the Iroquois, they finally came to terms. Angus would receive one hundred forty gold coins, plus the gray mare, one of the small riding horses, one saddle, two bridles, and two saddle blankets.

Angus ate lunch with the Frenchmen, and then announced that he would be leaving as soon as he was loaded. Gathering all his newly acquired trade goods, including a leather bag filled with gold coins, Angus went to catch his horses, assisted by the Frenchmen.

Much to his relief, the gray mare was easy to approach and comfortable with saddle and bridle. Apparently she was used to being ridden and welcomed his attention. All three of the small riding horses were about the same size and appeared to be in good condition. Angus caught the largest, but it would not stand still when he tried to throw on the saddle blanket and pack baskets. The smallest of the three riding horses, a dark brown mare stood quietly watching the activity. Angus caught her and was surprised that she stood patiently while he threw on the saddle blanket and pack baskets. Apparently, she had previously carried baskets.

Leading the horses back to the cabin, Angus tied the gray to the porch and loaded all his supplies into the pack baskets on the brown. The Iroquois watched closely as Angus carefully packed the bag of gold coins in the bottom of one of his pack baskets. With everything loaded, Angus had one more problem—and not a minor one. What about Schatto?

Angus had contemplated this dilemma many times during the previous sleepless night and decided on three options. The pup could ride in one of the pack baskets on the brown mare, in a pack basket thrown behind Angus on the gray, or she could walk beside the horses. Angus knew she would enjoy walking more than riding, but unaccustomed to long treks, she would tire easily. The pack baskets were large enough for the pup to ride comfortably, on a cushion of deerskin. As she grew stronger, he was confident that she could follow alongside the horses all day.

To start the journey, he decided to put her in a small basket thrown behind his saddle on the gray. Bidding the Frenchmen and the Iroquois farewell, Angus gently kicked his moccasin heels into the gray mare's sides and headed towards the forest behind the cabins. One journey had ended and another had begun. Angus told the Frenchmen he planned to cross the Allegheny Mountains to reach Lancaster. In truth, he had not actually finalized his plans.

With the horses came several new options. He could follow the trail south to Wills Creek (current site of Cumberland, Md.) then hitch a boat ride down the Potomac River to Chesapeake Bay. From there he could move up the coast to Philadelphia to seek word of Heather. In addition, he wanted to consult boat maker Joseph Myers about making bigger and better dugout canoes—canoes that could haul two persons and large loads.

Another route would take him back over the Alleghenies to Lancaster, where he had asked Henery Gumpf, the gun maker, to watch for Heather and to save any letters from her that might arrive. If he chose to return to the colonies, he would spend the summer working with Henery, to learn more about making Pennsylvania rifles. He was convinced he could make one even better than his original. He was proud of the fine rifle he had made last summer, but he had a mental concept of an improved rifle that would serve him even better. He would have no problem selling the original.

A third option was to follow the Monongahela back to the Dunkards. He had considered spending the summer with the Dunkards, then return to the Shawnee camp for the coming winter, trapping and hunting. A summer with the Dunkards was inviting because he could determine whether he really wanted to be a farmer. There would also be endless opportunities to get acquainted with Katrina.

Reports had circulated about a settlement along the western shore of the Ohio River on a point of land where a river called the

Muskinghum joined the Ohio. Angus sought to learn more about those lands west of the Ohio known as the "western frontier," and felt now would be an opportune time. The Ohio River, named La Belle Riviere ("the beautiful river") by the French, was irresistibly attractive to Angus.

As Angus rode the gray mare into the woods between the Allegheny and the Monongahela rivers, he decided to travel eastward for a short distance, following a rough trail that the Frenchmen said would cross the Allegheny Mountains. Darkness would quickly envelope the deep forest because of the dense canopy of trees through which he now rode, so he would travel for only a few hours before stopping for the night. Although he could not see the pup behind him, he could reach around and rub her head. She seemed to be content, riding quietly behind him without whining. The gray mare was a pleasant surprise, riding even better than Night Sky. The small brown mare followed submissively, as if she had previously traveled as a packhorse.

Every riding horse should have a name, though the actual words comprising the name are more important to the rider than to the animal. Angus wanted a name related to the animal's coat color, but nothing came to mind. Perhaps the name would come to him as they headed ever deeper into the forest. The gray and the brown mares had been fortunate choices and Angus now felt confident they would carry him and his goods safely across the Alleghenies—if he indeed followed that route.

As dusk settled over the land, Angus stopped the horses, climbed down, and lifted Schatto from her basket. The giant trees were widely spaced, and Angus had his choice of suitable campsites. He selected a plot near some downed trees where grasses and low shrubs provided food for the horses. As Angus built his fire pit and gathered firewood, he began to fret about the gold coins. Was there any danger of the Iroquois or the Frenchmen following him to steal the coins? He must be on guard tirelessly tonight as he made camp, since a fire would reveal his location and make him especially vulnerable.

As Angus and the pup sat around their first campfire in the wilderness forest, he studied his defensive strategies and weighed the potential of an attack. His two horses would catch the scent of any other horses or humans that might approach, and any whinnies coming from his horses would be an adequate warning. He would smother the small campfire, so that his location could not be detected from a distance. With supper finished, Angus and Schatto settled into their bearskins. Angus was comforted as the wolf snuggled close to his body. As he nodded off, Angus sighed, "Life on the frontier is the life I was meant to live."

CHAPTER SIXTEEN
THE FOREST PRIMEVAL

SCHATTO WAS SOON ASLEEP and emitting a strange mixture of whimpers. Although Angus was aware of the whimpers, his subconscious was focused on the numerous night sounds and prevented deep repose. Absent were the familiar sounds of river animals that brought such diversion during his float trip down the Monongahela. Also missing were the lapping and gurgling sounds created by the river itself. While many early settlers dreaded the darkness of the deep forest, Angus welcomed the solitude and comforting stillness of the towering trees. As he vacillated between periods of light sleep and of being fully awake, he analyzed every sound that moved through the treetops, around the giant tree trunks, and across the forest floor—such sweet sounds, the night music of the forest. The eight-hoots of the barred owl were easy to identify, as were the high-pitched chirps of the flying squirrels gliding from tree to tree and the shrill calls of tree insects.

Most difficult to distinguish were the sounds originating along the forest floor—the sharp snap of a small twig, the slight rustle of leaves, and the soft brushing of hair and hide against a low-growing shrub. Experience enabled Angus to determine the size of the animal responsible for each sound and to discriminate between the stealthy movements of a meat-eating predator and those of a plant-eating deer. Always more difficult to distinguish were the sounds made by humans. Native wildlife often gave the first clue that some foreign entity was moving through their forest—the call notes of songbirds would suddenly stop, birds took flight, squirrels initiated their alarm chatter, and deer nervously stomped their feet, snorted, or bolted.

The night passed uneventfully, and as dawn filtered into the forest, Angus and Schatto roused and stretched their stiffened muscles. Once fully awake, Angus concentrated on the cacophony of early morning sounds and was comforted to hear only the mixed chorus of familiar songbirds, mingled with the scampering of chipmunks and gray squirrels. No intruders prompted the forest animals to emit warnings. During the night, the southerly winds ushered in comfortable temperatures, eliminating the need for a morning fire.

As Angus and Schatto shared a breakfast of savory smoked elk, he pictured Gisela roasting one of the elk haunches in the fireplace. She would have the boys regularly turn the meat so that it cooked evenly on all sides. As the cooking fire made their cabin unbearably warm, she would once again remind Johannes that he must begin work on the summer kitchen to eliminate the need for a fire inside the cabin during the hottest days of the year. Angus chuckled to himself at the struggles of domesticity.

At the command, "Come, Schatto, come," the two campers moved to the horses hobbled nearby. A thin ground fog blanketed portions of the forest, and Angus was surprised how well the gray mare blended into the vaporous background. It suddenly occurred to him that "Fog" or "Foggy" was a possible name for the gray mare. The gray anxiously proceeded toward Angus, pausing to rub noses with the wolf pup. Angus softly rubbed the mare's neck, and then gently let his hands work down her shoulder and onto her face. She remained motionless as the welcomed caresses affirmed her new master's temperament. Reflecting on the name of his previous mare, Night Sky, Angus pronounced, "I shall call ye, 'Night Fog,' lassie."

Schatto sniffed curiously around the mare's legs and then began to explore the nearby trees. At the base of each large tree were numerous captivating scents, each pungent enough to excite the predatory instincts of the wolf.

Angus worked the bridle onto Night Fog then approached the brown packhorse standing quietly. She shivered nervously as Angus worked his hands over her neck and shoulders then moved to her sides, back, and rump. It was apparent that the brown horse had not received as much personal attention as the gray mare, and Angus wanted both horses to welcome his touch. He was confident that after a few days this neglected animal would be competing with the gray for his attention. After saddling the gray mare he secured the pack baskets on the brown.

Angus decided to let Schatto run alongside the horses for a while on the trail and thus began their first full day. Mounted on a horse, Angus typically carried his Pennsylvania rifle across the saddle in front of him. His left hand held the reins while his right hand rested on the rifle. In that position, he could instantly drop the reins and in one fluid motion fire at any target to his left. Facing almost directly into the rising sun, Angus shielded his eyes as he attempted to discern the faint trail that led off to the east, identified occasionally by a tree blazed with a tomahawk.

The trail was originally used by small herds of buffalo as they commuted between the Potomac and Ohio rivers, but later it became a route used by Indians to move through the forest. Years of travel by buffalo, Shawnee, Iroquois, and Cherokee left signs that any experienced woodsman could detect. Unfortunately, the trail was not always distinct enough for the horses to follow on their own, causing Angus to divide his attention between scanning the forest for danger and reading the trail.

To some extent, the soft plodding of horses' hooves in the forest duff muffled the sounds of forest wildlife. Schatto quickly learned to avoid the horses' hooves and trotted quietly beside Night Fog unless some interesting scent caught her attention. Then she followed it a few feet before realizing she was being left behind. Breaking into a run, she caught up with the horses and continued her slow trot. Angus noted that Schatto was tiring and it would soon be necessary to place her in the pack basket behind him.

Suddenly, off to their left a deer snorted and a blue jay scolded at something in the same general area. Instantly halting the gray mare, Angus pivoted in his saddle to locate Schatto. As his torso rotated, he felt something slice through the fleshy edge of his left shoulder, and an arrow thudded into one of the giant poplar trees on his right.

In an incredibly coordinated series of movements, Angus jerked his left moccasin out of its stirrup, clenched his rifle as he bent forward, and slid like water down Night Fog's right side to the ground, where Schatto sat at attention. He had barely escaped critical injury and would not make himself an easy target for a second arrow. Angus gently placed his hand on Schatto's rump and firmly ordered, "Stay. Stay," as he slipped behind the poplar tree where the quivering arrow had sunk deeply into the bark.

Assuming his attacker was the Iroquois from the trading post, Angus figured the Indian wanted him dead so he could purloin the rifle, wolf, horses, and gold coins—everything Angus owned. Although he had no way to judge the skills of the Iroquois, Angus coolly regarded his own skills equal to those of any Indian. Almost smugly, he knew his long rifle gave him the edge in any shooting contest, although it would be useless in hand-to-hand combat. If survival depended on such a defense, he would fearlessly rely on the razor-edged hunting knife and iron tomahawk stashed in his belt.

The duplicitous Iroquois had left the trading post on foot shortly before darkness settled in. Moving silently through the forest, he remained far enough from the trail to avoid detection. He had smelled the wood smoke from Angus's evening campfire but was too cunning to risk being seen or heard while stalking close enough to use his bow. He opted instead to set an ambush near the trail, where he could send an arrow into Angus as he passed on horseback. He chose a sheltered spot behind a large sugar maple with a double trunk when Angus approached. Unfortunately for the Iroquois, Angus reacted to the warning cries of forest wildlife just as the arrow was released.

As Angus dropped to the ground, the Indian calmly notched another arrow into his bow and slipped behind the tree trunk. As long as each of the two combatants stayed behind tree trunks there would be no injuries. Each knew the other would shoot to kill if given the opportunity. The Iroquois must murder Angus if he wanted to abscond with all his belongings; Angus in turn must slay the Iroquois or be pursued all the way over the Alleghenies.

Trunks of the giant hardwoods, several centuries old, stood widely separated, with very little underbrush growing in the shade of the canopy's dense foliage. Sunlight dappled the forest floor, providing just enough light to make each of the combatants easily visible. The Iroquois' preference was to slip away and set up another ambush, but it was too late and he was boxed in. His unequal gait, caused by a stunted leg, would hinder him so that Angus would spot him moving from tree to tree, and make him an easy target for the long-barreled rifle. Had the Iroquois not been over-confident in his ability to eliminate Angus, he would have selected an ambush site from which he could have easily retreated.

If the situation hadn't been so dire, it might have been comical. Each adversary traded glances with the other, trying to prevent an advance to a different tree. Angus evaluated the situation, and at once recognized that the Iroquois might well try to retreat rather than attack. Angus wanted him to attack, wanted to resolve the issue rather than postpone the inevitable. If the stalemate lasted until darkness fell, the Iroquois would easily escape to attack another day. Waiting would accomplish nothing for Angus.

How confident was the Iroquois? Did he think he could shoot an arrow before Angus could fire his rifle? Angus estimated that they were about thirty yards apart. Because of the slight delay required for his flintlock to send a spark into the powder and the subsequent explosion to send the lead spiraling out the barrel, an arrow would reach him before his bullet reached the Iroquois. Of greater significance, the Indian could shoot a second arrow before Angus could reload and get off a second rifle shot.

Cautiously easing his rifle around the tree trunk, Angus peered out at the Iroquois, who was likewise glancing around his respective tree trunk. Angus quickly aimed as if to fire, and the Indian ducked back out of sight. Instantly, Angus dived towards a large tree located about ten feet away, then rolled into a seated position at its base. He heard the arrow thud into the ground beside him as he reached safety and quickly rose to his feet. Resting his rifle barrel against the side of the tree, he took careful aim at where he calculated the Indian's head would reappear. Sure enough, the black topknot adorned with eagle feather slowly eased around the tree trunk, but not far enough to give Angus a clear shot. Angus decided to repeat the same bold maneuver.

Twice more Angus leaped out and rolled behind a nearby tree and twice an arrow barely missed. While the Iroquois was still cautious, Angus noted that he had inched slightly farther out from the tree trunk with each arrow. Angus had been working his way closer to the Iroquois and was now less than twenty yards away. Could he risk one more move?

As the Iroquois peeked around the maple, Angus again leaped and rolled. But this time he reversed direction and headed for the tree he had just left. The slight hesitation for the Indian to readjust his aim provided ample opportunity for Angus to reach the safety of the tree trunk, and the arrow thudded harmlessly into the giant chestnut. Quickly easing his rifle around the tree, Angus took careful aim, and this time as the black topknot and tawny face reemerged, Angus firmly squeezed the trigger. Through the small cloud of smoke, he watched the bark explode from the side of the tree at the exact location where he had aimed. Confident the lead bullet had continued its path through the bark and towards the face of his foe, the emboldened Scot sprinted directly at the Iroquois. He had selected a tree that would provide some cover if the native should jump out and shoot his bow.

With no sign of his enemy, Angus quickly lengthened his giant leaps. Nearing his adversary, Angus dropped his impotent firearm and in one smooth action clutched the belted tomahawk with his right hand while extracting the long-bladed hunting knife with his left.

Suddenly, Angus experienced a flashback. He was on the Scottish moors with Bonnie Prince Charles and wielded not tomahawk and hunting knife, but heavy broadsword and dirk. The adrenaline surged and from somewhere deep within came the unearthly snarl of a Highland yell. The predatory Iroquois had grossly underestimated his prey, for the Scot's skills had been tempered by the trauma of a battle so savage that survivors could not run far enough to escape their gory memories.

As the snarling Scot rounded the sugar maple, his tomahawk began its deadly downward arc and his knife flashed forward. As fate would have it, the Indian was confounded by the bullet that grazed his head and the bits of bark blown into his eyes. Unable to counter the threat of Angus a few feet away, the Iroquois dropped his bow and clumsily reached for his own tomahawk. But he was much too slow! The sharp blade of the iron tomahawk sliced through his brown neck, partially severed the head, and if that injury had not proved fatal, it was followed a second later by a knife blade plunging into his side, the bear jaw handle affixed solidly to the ribcage. As the Iroquois crumpled to the earth, Angus removed his knife from the limp form and stepped cautiously backward—ready for another attack. But none came; the fight was over.

As the rush of adrenaline subsided, Angus was again carried back to Drumossie Moor, where as many as two thousand of his countrymen lay bloodied and dying after only one hour of the Jacobite rebellion. Those who survived were forced to retreat, but there was no safe haven anywhere in Scotland for true Highlanders. The battle of Culloden ended, but the killing did not. The day after the battle, the Duke of Cumberland sent patrols back to the killing fields to butcher seventy injured Jacobites. The next day they found seventy-two more to torture, thirty-two of whom were deliberately burnt alive. The victorious general was given the title "Butcher" Cumberland. Faced with overwhelming numbers of cannons, survival at Culloden had dictated retreat.

Angus leaned against a sugar maple, inhaled deeply, and relaxed his entire body. After wiping the blood from his knife and tomahawk, he returned them to his belt and moved to retrieve his rifle. He retrieved the Indian's tomahawk along with his bow and the five arrows remaining in the quiver.

As his heartbeat slowed, Angus suddenly realized that he had left Schatto beside the horses. Was she still there, or had his rifle shot so frightened her that she ran off into the woods? This would have been the first loud rifle shot she had ever heard, and Angus feared she had panicked.

As Angus approached the horses, he could not see Schatto. It appeared that she had indeed run off. However, as he came closer he was amazed to see her sitting calmly on her haunches between the front legs of Night Fog. The thrill of having the pup behave in such an unexpected manner brought joy to his heart. Dropping to his knees, he appealed, "Come, Schatto, come." She quickly bounded to his feet, and the two of them rolled in the leaves, as two wild animals overwhelmed by a sudden, unexpected reunion.

The good-natured wrestling ended with Angus commanding Schatto to heel. He returned to the dead Iroquois and proceeded to gather leaves, branches, and a few large rocks. As he tossed on the last handful of leaves, Angus pronounced, "You are sleeping your last sleep!" Although the thin covering would provide little protection against scavengers, Angus believed that every human deserved some semblance of a burial.

As Schatto licked the blood seeping out of the Indian's fatal neck wound, Angus wondered if he could teach her to avoid the hazards of villainy waiting in every settlement and on every trail. They would meet many Indians, hunters, and trappers on their journeys, and most would pose no threat. However, he must teach Schatto to be wary of them.

Angus, with Schatto at heel, searched for the arrows that the Iroquois had fired, and managed to find four. All were undamaged, except for one that had snapped at the point when it struck a chestnut tree. Angus gathered even that one, which he would repair during his travels.

Returning to the horses, Angus loaded his rifle, secured the bow and quiver of arrows into one of the pack baskets, and lifted Schatto into her own basket. After mounting Night Fog and tying the lead rope of the brown packhorse to his own saddle, he resumed the journey. The unfortunate encounter had cost them some two hours of daylight. The Frenchmen from the Forks of the Ohio could not afford to follow, and no one he met on the trail could know he had gold coins in the pack basket. Now the danger of attack was greatly diminished.

The trip settled into a comfortable routine as the strange quartet moved southeast. Angus spent most of the day riding but occasionally dismounted and walked beside Night Fog so that he might be closer to Schatto. It occurred to him that he had spent too many days cramped in the dugout. The foray with the Iroquois had driven home the need to regain the strength in his leg muscles to sprint short distances or sustain long walks. Naps and short rests in the pack basket behind Angus's saddle quickly rejuvenated Schatto, and it seemed that no sooner had he put her in the basket than she was ready to get back down again.

Wolves depend more on their ability to detect and recognize scents than their ability to identify objects visually. Angus wondered what scents the pup was discovering, while envying the pup's inherent competence. Most likely chipmunks, gray squirrels, and wild turkeys left most of the odors but, based on the fecal droppings, he knew Schatto was also picking up scents left by deer, elk, and black bear.

Travel through the forest presented one problem they had not faced when traveling down the river—the availability of drinking water. In the dugout, Angus could dip his clamshell into the river and drink whenever thirsty. Schatto had learned to lean over the side of the canoe and lap up water to satisfy thirst or mischief. Water was present in the forest, but not predictably. The trail typically paralleled the Monongahela, and thus no lack of small tributaries flowed westward into the river. All streams they crossed that day were small enough to wade across easily, and each was cool and clean.

The Frenchmen at the trading post had told Angus to be alert for a fork in the trail, where one arm led east to Lancaster while the other headed south to the Potomac. As the sun dipped towards the western horizon, prominent tomahawk slashes on the trees clearly marked the spot where the two trails diverged. A small stream passed nearby, and Angus decided to go no farther that day. Moving back into the forest, he saw an opening that would provide limited grazing for the horses. He removed the bridles, saddle, and pack baskets, providing much-needed relief for the animals.

After hobbling the two mares, he gathered fallen branches for their nightly campfire and plopped down with his back against one of the many giant tulip poplars that never ceased to amaze him. As a youth in Scotland, he could never have imagined trees that grew so huge. His backrest was at least eight feet in diameter, and contained enough firewood to heat a cabin for an entire year—if a person had the means and time to cut and split such a behemoth.

Earlier that afternoon, while on foot, Angus decided to try

a new command on Schatto. That command was "Back." There were occasions when a hound must stop running and immediately return to its master's side. The "back" command was a combination of "whoa" and "come," but, by the tone used when issuing the command, the hound understood that it was an urgent command—one that should not be ignored.

Although constantly distracted by sights and sounds of the forest that afternoon, Schatto had consistently obeyed the "back" command. In close pursuit of a chipmunk running through the forest, however, she would get so excited that she would not abandon the chase and return to Angus. This was a common problem, requiring constant repetition to reinforce obedience.

Although they needed no campfire for that night's meal, Angus coaxed a small fire to life, and as the pup stretched out near the small amount of heat the flames provided, she immediately dozed. Angus realized that she had expended more energy that day than in her entire life. He must get her some fresh meat tomorrow to keep her young muscles growing.

The trail to the left was a more direct route to Lancaster, but a few extra days would matter little. Johannes had told him that the trail to the right was well marked and would require four to five days to reach the Potomac River. Both trails crossed the highest ridges of the Alleghenies, but neither would create any hardships for the horses. He wanted to visit the region along the Potomac River and determine for himself the number of settlers that were pushing westward.

According to Johannes, the Ohio Company had built a small trading post along the Potomac River at the site called Wills Creek. Next spring, Angus might want to take his furs to the Wills Creek Trading Post, rather than to one of the trading posts on the Monongahela. The decision, while not a troubling one, had been on his mind most of the afternoon as he weighed all the possibilities. With all options considered, the die was cast. They would go south to the Potomac and then on to Lancaster.

CHAPTER SEVENTEEN

OVER THE ALLEGHENIES

ONE OF THE EARLY-MORNING pleasures of floating downstream was watching the sun make an appearance, but now a dense mass of foliage obscured the actual sunrise. As a youngster it was Angus's habit to waken in time to view the sun's rays first illuminating the undersides of any low-lying clouds. Next came the arc of the sun's sphere bulging over the mountains. Finally, the entire globe escaped from the depths of darkness, and a new day commenced.

Angus, the boy, had enjoyed sunrises more than sunsets. A sunrise gave promise of an exciting new day—a hunting trip, a fishing excursion, or a boat trip on Loch Ness.

Rarely did Angus, the frontiersman, witness a sunrise without reliving the most memorable sunrise of his life. According to a pre-arranged plan, before first light he and Heather had arisen early, quietly slipped out of their respective stone huts, and climbed the nearby hill to where a rock outcropping provided an unbroken view of the eastern horizon. Snuggled together against a large boulder, with eyes closed, the two innocent and happy teenagers shared their first romantic kiss. As Angus had opened his eyes, the sun burst gloriously into view. It was irrelevant whether the sunrise was as spectacular as Angus remembered, because now every time he closed his eyes while watching a sunrise he could still taste the sweet affection of that kiss.

Angus, Schatto, and the two horses moved steadily along the well-established path through the mountains towards Christopher Gist's cabin. There they would pick up the well-marked Nemacolin's Trail, leading them directly to Wills Creek on the Potomac.

Angus began the day's journey walking alongside the horses with Schatto at heel. He required her to heel for only two or three minutes. Kneeling beside her, he rubbed her ears and neck affectionately while telling her what a smart pup she was. Rising to his feet, he waved his arm down the trail and commanded, "Hunt ... hunt." She hesitated, and then bounded to a fallen tree next to the trail. Angus had spotted a gray squirrel running alongside the tree and he knew Schatto would pick up its strong scent. Sure enough, she ran excitedly back and forth along the tree as the fresh scent permeated her nostrils. As the squirrel scaled a nearby tree, Schatto abandoned the quest.

By late morning, the trail swung to the south and Angus noticed they were descending out of the foothills. Soon thereafter he recognized the waters of the Monongahela through the trees and thought the gravel bar on the opposite side of the river was precisely where they had stopped two days earlier.

At this point, the steep hillside provided little space for a trail. Angus thought the brown mare, being an experienced pack animal, must have followed many narrow trails during her lifetime. The gray mare's prowess, however, was untested, and she would be leading their caravan with both Angus and Schatto on her back. He did not want to take a nasty spill down the steep hillside into the river.

Having ridden horses through the steep Scottish Highlands, Angus knew it was best to give a horse its head and not try to guide it by use of the reins. This would be a serious test of Night Fog's skills. Dropping the reins onto her neck, Angus gently urged her forward. Firmly grasping his rifle, he carefully lifted the pup from her basket and placed her on the saddle in front of him. Holding her in place, he ordered, "Stay, Schatto, stay." The gray slowed her pace and moved ever so carefully along the trail. At one point, her right front hoof slipped, but her left front was on a solid spot, and she easily regained her balance. Gradually Angus relaxed, as it became evident that the trail was widening and the gray mare had expertly traversed the worst section.

After a mile or so, the trail turned away from the Monongahela, and slowly ascended a long, gradual ridge. For the remainder of the morning they followed the summit on foot, before the trail dropped down to cross yet another creek. Placing a weary Schatto in her basket, Angus mounted the gray mare and they proceeded at a slow walk towards the Potomac, crossing several creeks that left Angus with wet feet and legs, but dry pack baskets.

Near mid-day a wild turkey suddenly flushed from alongside the base of an old sugar maple as the horses came abreast. Eggs were visible, so Angus reined in the horses. The nest, which was nothing more than a bowl-shaped depression between two protruding roots, consisted of a deep layer of leaves and several turkey feathers. Five tan-colored, speckled eggs were present. Several hens with poults had been scratching for insects alongside the riverbank as they floated down the Monongahela, a sign that the nesting season was nearly over.

This hen turkey, whose first clutch of eggs had probably been eaten by a raccoon, was now nesting again. If the second nesting failed, the hen would make no more attempts this year. Carefully removing three eggs from the nest and partially covering the remaining two with leaves, Angus mounted his horse and continued down the trail. Turkey hens typically lay at least ten eggs, so the hen would certainly return to the nest and lay several more eggs before she began incubating.

Angus relished the thought of fresh eggs. Since turkeys lay one egg per day, those he collected would be no more than five days old, and one of them might be only a few hours old. Angus had not wanted Schatto to find the eggs and thus had ordered her to stay in her basket when he dismounted.

He vividly recalled his grandfather ordering him to destroy one of his favorite hounds when it developed the bad habit of robbing hen nests. Grandfather McCallander proclaimed that there was nothing worse than an "egg-sucking dog," the label given hounds that broke apart eggs and lapped out the insides. There would be free-ranging chickens at the Potomac and Lancaster, and Angus could not have a wolf that was a thief. Wolves, like all meat-eaters, would eat every egg encountered in any bird's nest—whether grouse or turkey, duck or goose, or barnyard chicken.

Angus stopped at the next stream they reached, and while he gathered firewood, the pup played in shallow water as the horses grazed and drank. After starting a small fire, Angus pulled a small iron kettle from the pack basket and placed it directly in the flames. As it heated, he poured in some water, added a large handful of cornmeal, and waited while it cooked.

When the cornmeal had formed a soft mush, Angus broke one of the eggs onto a curved piece of bark he had cut from a poplar tree. The egg looked and smelled fresh, so Angus dropped it into the kettle with his cornmeal. He broke the second and third eggs onto the bark and they appeared equally fresh, so they were also added to the mush. Embryonic development of turkey eggs does not begin until the last egg of a clutch is laid. As a result, every egg of the clutch hatches the same day, the last within a few hours of the first. From the standpoint of cooking, the first egg is just as fresh as the last one laid.

As the three eggs began to cook in the bottom of the kettle, Angus stirred in pieces of smoked elk meat, giving pungency as enticing as the best stew. In minutes the meal was ready. Calling to Schatto, who had been chasing crayfish in the small stream, Angus scraped out a portion of the egg/elk/cornmeal mixture onto a piece of bark. He ordered her to sit, and she obediently waited as he blew on the food to cool it.

Angus had been training her to wait until he gave the command before she started to eat. Aware that he must not make her wait too long, he set the food before her while issuing the command, "Wait, wait." Not five seconds later he gave the command, "Aye, aye," and before he had time to scrape his portion onto a piece of bark the pup was eagerly gulping down the delicious mixture. She finished almost before Angus had time to sit down, but since she was preoccupied with licking and scraping the last bits of egg/meat mixture from the bark, she did not immediately beg for more. Using a wooden spoon he had carved from a piece of chestnut wood, Angus soon cleaned his platter, and set it on the ground for Schatto to lick.

After cleaning the kettle, Angus returned it to a pack basket, along with the two pieces of bark, and prepared to start the afternoon's journey. Calling, "Come, come," he led Night Fog down the trail with Schatto trotting at his side. The deep forest might offer a variety of foods for man and wolf, but it offered little food for the horses. Scant grass, seedlings, or shrubs grew in the shaded areas where light was such a scarce commodity. Angus was constantly on the lookout for natural openings where low-growing, green vegetation provided grazing opportunities. Around mid-afternoon they came upon one such area where a tree had fallen, and resultant shrubs and grasses provided limited food for the two mares. Angus and Schatto explored the woods while the horses ate their fill.

In late afternoon Angus saw another blow-down tree some distance ahead. This one was considerably larger than the first. In the space where giant trees once stood, sunlight streaked through the canopy and fell upon the leaf-covered forest floor. As they approached, Angus detected what appeared to be a thick black tree limb in a bright patch of sunshine that brightened the trail. At thirty yards, Angus began to question if the shiny black object was really a tree limb. At twenty yards, he was positive it was not. Over six feet long, it was thicker than his muscular upper arm, but tapered at each end. The black object soaking up the sunshine in the trail was a dreaded timber rattlesnake!

Schatto was running in front of the horses, and Angus quickly grasped the deerskin bag with the blue stone as he reined the gray to a stop and shouted loudly, "Back, Schatto, back." Angus was typically calm in the face of danger, but this situation was different. If the pup continued running down the trail she would encounter the huge reptile. Curiosity would cause her to sniff at its body, at which time it would surely coil into the deadly strike position and commence rattling. That would further excite the pup, and she would bark at the snake or even jump at it. From the coiled position, the snake could successfully strike an object half a body-length away. If the snake injected its full load of venom into the small pup, she would be dead before Angus could reach her side. All this flashed through Angus's mind as he rubbed the deerskin bag and repeated, "Back, Schatto, back!"

At the first urgent command from Angus, Schatto had stopped

running, turned, and stared in his direction. At the second sharp command she began to retreat towards him. With a sigh of relief, Angus dismounted and dropped to one knee. When she reached his side, he grabbed her in his arms and hugged her against his chest. Such a move was unexpected, and the pup wiggled happily in surprise. Angus removed the elk skin leash that he kept near the top of a pack basket and tied it around the pup's neck. Holding the leash firmly in one hand, he removed the bow and quiver of arrows from a pack basket and softly commanded, "Heel, heel."

Angus wondered how wolf parents taught their young to avoid such dangers. Many lessons can be learned from sustaining painful injuries, but a wolf must survive the injury if it is to avoid the threat the next time. If adult wolves seldom survived the bite of a full-grown timber rattlesnake, wolf pups certainly would not.

The lesson that Angus was about to administer was possibly the most important lesson he would ever provide to Schatto. When they were within twenty feet, the reptile recognized the threat and instantly coiled in the center of the trail. With its triangular head held menacingly above the coils, it began flicking its tongue in and out in an attempt to identify the intruders. From the deerskin pouch he constantly wore around his neck, Angus removed the blue stone and stroked it softly. As the stone glowed and warmed, Angus repeated the word, "Snake, snake, snake," and told Schatto never to go near such a dangerous animal.

Because rattlesnakes are often heard before they are seen, Angus wanted Schatto to learn to recognize their telltale rattle. The distinctive rattling was designed to protect the snake from being stepped on by a large animal such as an elk or buffalo, not to protect humans from being bitten. As he continued to warn the pup of the dangers, Angus tossed a few stones at the snake. It immediately began vibrating its tail and, just as Angus anticipated, the rattling began. He was not close enough to count the number of rattles on its tail, but Angus estimated there were at least eight—enough to create an ominous alarm.

The pup was wary of such a large animal, but started a frenzied barking when the snake threw its body into a series of coils. Although the reptile was much larger than the pup, it would have difficulty swallowing her. The rattlesnake's diet consisted primarily of gray squirrels, although it could easily swallow full-grown rabbits. Securing the leash to a tree, Angus slipped the blue stone back into the bag, ordered the pup to sit, and approached within ten feet of the coiled serpent. Scotland had few snakes, and Angus had run across only a couple while roaming the Scottish hills. There was a venomous adder in Scotland, but it seldom reached two feet in length and was not dangerous unless aggravated.

Notching an arrow into the bow, Angus slowly pulled back the bowstring, took careful aim, and smoothly released the arrow. Angus had used a bow most of his life and was confident he could hit the coiled rattlesnake in the head.

His mind flashed back to practice matches with the Shawnee, and to his youth when his father had taught him to shoot a long bow. A typical English long bow was nearly twice as long as Shawnee bows, but the shooting technique was similar. The English bow was a long-range weapon, capable of accurately flinging an arrow over one hundred yards, while the Indian bow was designed for short distance targets.

Angus could have thrown stones and sticks at the snake until it crawled off into the thick underbrush. However, because the blow-down provided abundant vegetation for the horses, he wanted to make camp in the area. There was also a more utilitarian reason to shoot the snake. It would provide fresh meat for that night and perhaps enough for one or two more meals.

The arrow leaped downward from the bowstring and stuck the snake slightly behind the eye. Continuing through the head it penetrated deeply into the ground. The snake began thrashing its tail wildly, but was pinned so tightly to the ground that even its powerful body could not pull the arrow loose. Angus dropped the bow, retrieved the blue stone from the pouch, and continued to warn the pup about the dangerous reptile.

The huge snake thrashed around for fifteen minutes as life drained from its body. Then all was still. Although it appeared to be dead, Angus had been warned that even limp, lifeless rattlesnakes must be handled carefully. In Lancaster, he heard the story of a farmer who had killed a big rattlesnake in his cornfield. Later that day the farmer's son picked up the snake to carry home and show the family, only to have the fangs sink into his hand. The boy began to feel dizzy, and by the time he reached the cabin his hand was swollen. He died that night.

Angus untied the pup and with her at heel, slowly circled the blow-down. Although he did not expect to find another snake, he felt obliged to conduct a thorough search. Uncovering nothing, he hobbled the horses and set up camp near a spring flowing from the hillside.

After gathering wood for a fire, Angus tied the pup's leash to a tree and returned to the snake. He had contended with many animals in his life, but had never tried to handle such a dangerous animal as the rattlesnake lying dead in the trail. Upon reaching the snake, Angus prodded it with a long stick, then grasped it by the tail and stretched it full length. Even in death, the snake's strength was impressive. It was all Angus could do to pull it straight as its muscles contracted in reaction to his pull. After slicing off the rattles with his hunting knife, Angus placed a large rock on the snake's tail to hold it in a fully stretched position. With the arrow still pinning the head, Angus could safely use his hunting knife to sever the head from the body.

Somewhat nervously, Angus grasped the feather fletching of the arrow and neatly sliced through the snake's neck a few inches behind the head. He extracted the arrow from the ground, with the snake's head still attached. Angus carried the arrow to one of the blow-down trees and jabbed it, along with the snake's head, into the trunk where it would be out of Schatto's reach.

After retrieving the body of the snake, Angus slipped the point of his hunting knife just under the skin and carefully sliced the body open from the neck to the tail. Grasping the skin in his left hand and the fleshy carcass in his right, he peeled the scaly hide from the snake like a man peels wet long johns from his legs. He laid the carcass across a tree limb so it would not get dirty and sliced open the body cavity to remove the innards. Angus considered feeding the innards to Schatto, but reconsidered.

The skin, which was over one foot wide and six feet in length, was spread out along the ground, and Angus exclaimed, "Astounding!" He wished he could somehow preserve the beautiful, velvet-black snakeskin to display on the wall of a cabin or inside a Shawnee wegiwa, but the weather was so warm that he knew it would soon spoil. Angus carried the snake's carcass back to his campsite, cut it into pieces the length of his hand, and placed them on a bed of thick green moss.

Angus had never eaten rattlesnake, or any kind of snake, but the pinkish meat resembled frog legs he had eaten in Philadelphia. It should be tasty, like any meat grilled over an open fire in the wilderness. Sharpened sugar maple sticks, each three to four feet long, were inserted into the pieces of rattlesnake. With the bases of the sticks securely inserted into the ground and the meat suspended over the flames, the cooking process began.

The snake was exceptionally fatty, so that the sizzles and scents created by grease dripping into the fire triggered Angus's appetite. Schatto sat a few feet from the fire, staring intently at the cooking meat. She had watched closely as Angus prepared the meat for cooking and anticipated being given a liver or heart or some other raw meat, just as when he skinned rabbits.

As the snake pieces browned, Angus turned them to cook evenly. In fifteen minutes he removed a section of meat with no ribs that would be safe for the pup to eat. He knew that a dog could choke on chicken bones and figured the same danger might occur with snake rib bones. As the pup salivated, Angus chewed off a small piece of the well-browned meat. Although a bit tough, Angus thought the flavor was surprisingly good. "Possibly not as good as rabbit or squirrel and certainly not as good as salmon," he said out loud, "but it's far better than some of the fish from Loch Ness!"

Handing the cooled piece to Schatto, Angus removed another piece from the fire, and man and wolf began eating their first rattlesnake. The pup finished three pieces while Angus was eating two. There would be plenty remaining for breakfast and lunch the next day.

A few hours of daylight remained before darkness, so Angus set out a few targets and practiced shooting the bow. Angus wanted to use the bow to augment their meat supply. Although he had no plans to shoot something as large as an elk, deer, or buffalo, he knew he could hit a gray squirrel or a wild turkey. Whether running across the trail, hanging from the side of a tree, or sitting on the forest floor, there were always gray squirrels visible. Most were not within range of the bow, but frequently one would sit quietly as the small caravan passed nearby. Angus decided to strap his rifle to the horse the next day and have ready only the bow. He was likely to miss more than he hit, but it was important to hone his archery skills. A bow had many advantages over a gun, and the addition of a freshly grilled squirrel to their supper would be welcome.

After fifty-some practice shots, Angus was hitting a small, squirrel-sized target more than he missed. Tomorrow, he would target live squirrels while astride his gray mare. Angus practiced with the bow as Schatto practiced scent trailing. Scents crisscrossed the forest floor, so the pup had no difficulty finding and following the trails of squirrels, chipmunks, deer, turkey, and a multitude of other forest dwellers. Although she never saw any of the animals, following a specific trail provided not only enjoyment but also invaluable training.

Returning to the small campfire, Angus threw a handful of small twigs onto the fire and prepared their bed. Bearskins and elk hides were spread near the fire, and the two hunters reclined before the flames as another day ended. The nightly routine of sitting quietly before the fire, reflecting on the day's events, and studying the flickering flames was a finale that Angus eagerly anticipated. Schatto appeared to enjoy it as well. As the last of the small flames flickered out, human and canine crawled under the elk skin and fell asleep, comforted by the reassuring contact with each other.

CHAPTER EIGHTEEN
FOREST WILDLIFE

AFTER A BREAKFAST of cold rattlesnake, Angus saddled up the horses, swung onto the gray mare, and continued the southeasterly trip towards the Potomac. The trail was distinct through that particular stretch of woods, so Angus dropped the reins. Angus surmised Night Fog had traveled this, or a comparable forest trail on many occasions; she would need little guidance from him.

Lightly holding the bow, with an arrow firmly notched into the sinew bowstring, Angus scanned the trail ahead for the bushy tail of a gray squirrel. Because he held the bow in his left hand, the most successful shots would be to his left. It would be awkward for him to twist and shoot at a target on the right side of the trail; he would not even attempt a shot in that direction.

Gray squirrels are very active the first few hours of daylight, searching for food after a night's fasting. This increased Angus's chances of getting a good shot. A dozen gray squirrels crossed the trail and searched through the fallen leaves, but all were too far away. Several more hung onto the sides of the massive chestnut trees that dominated the forest, but Angus would not risk a shot at any squirrel not on the ground. An arrow that missed its mark would go flying through the forest. He could not take time to hunt an arrow midst leaves blanketing the forest floor.

There was no reason to take shots having little chance of success, so the small caravan bypassed several dozen squirrels. An hour later, a gray squirrel sat digging at the base of a large sugar maple along the left side of the trail. Slowly raising the bow, Angus pulled back the arrow, and with right hand resting gently against right cheek, he instinctively aimed and released the arrow in one fluid motion. Night Fog was advancing slowly, and Angus had not adjusted correctly for her movement, so the arrow narrowly missed its target. As the squirrel bounded behind the tree, Angus concluded he should have stopped the mare before he shot. He dismounted to retrieve his arrow. The undamaged arrow could be reused on the next target.

Angus missed three more shots that morning and decided he needed to practice from horseback, both while the horse was standing still and while it was moving. Around mid-morning Schatto awakened and began fidgeting in her basket. Angus assumed she needed to relieve herself so he dismounted, swung her lightly to the ground by the scruff of her neck, and the two walked alongside the horses as they continued down the trail. In most stretches the trail was relatively open with only an occasional fallen limb that the horses needed to step over. However, as the sun announced high noon Angus could see that the trail ahead was completely blocked.

One of the ancient chestnuts had fallen. With a diameter exceeding ten feet, Angus was unable to see over the recumbent giant. Had he been alone he would have climbed over, but the barrier was insurmountable for wolf and horses. The fallen chestnut created such a barrier that Angus could see nothing on the opposite side. It occurred to him that the tree provided an excellent campsite— as well as an ideal ambush site. A small army of soldiers could be waiting on the other side, obscured from sight.

Hoofed animals had created a path around the tree, paralleling the trunk for nearly one hundred feet before reaching its end. It appeared that the tree had died of old age and a windstorm had toppled it many years ago. The fallen trunk was covered with moss and small ferns were taking root in the decomposing bark. Two sugar maple seedlings, roughly two feet in height, had also taken root in the seedbed created by rotting bark and leaves. Angus wondered how long it would take for the two seedlings to reach the size of the one that had fallen. There were no deciduous hardwood trees in Scotland, so he estimated that at least a hundred years would be needed. Years later he would learn that five hundred years was a better estimate.

Continuing their circuit around the fallen chestnut, they soon returned to the trail at a point opposite where they had stood an hour earlier. Angus decided this was a fine place for their mid-day meal, so he unpacked some of his smoked deer meat, turned the horses loose to graze, and selected a moss-covered spot where he could sit with his back to the log. As Angus fed small pieces of deer meat to Schatto, he noted that her appetite had increased appreciably in the past week. Although they had enough smoked deer to get them to the Potomac, he could foresee a time in the not-too-distant future when significantly more meat would be needed to complete a trip.

Following a nap and a short hike to drink from a spring of cool water gurgling out from under a boulder, Angus rounded up the horses and resumed the trek. Two more gray squirrels went untouched by his arrows before he stopped for the night. The trail crossed a mid-sized stream, climbing banks with adequate forage for the horses, and Angus was gratified with the distance they had covered that day. He hobbled the horses, arranged the pack baskets, positioned the rifle and powder horn for easy access, collected fuel for the fire, and spread their bearskins. Satisfied with the camp, but not the hunting, archery practice commenced.

As darkness fell, Angus heard a familiar sound coming from the hillside not too far away. A wild turkey was gobbling from the tree where it had gone to roost. With the exception of hens sitting on eggs, turkeys typically spend the nights high in the tops of trees. Even when temperatures are below zero and cold winds are wildly swaying treetops, turkeys hunker down far above the forest floor with their toes firmly locked around a tree limb. Angus rose from beside the fire, picked up his rifle, grasped Schatto's braided elk skin leash, and quietly moved in the direction of the gobbling. He was confident that a turkey had made the gobbling, although he had listened to Shawnee imitate a turkey gobble quite convincingly. A second gobble allowed Angus to correct the direction he was traveling, and a third enabled him to pinpoint the source of the call. Satisfied with the location, Angus returned to his campsite and outlined exactly what he would do the next morning.

Arising before the faintest light, Angus fastened the rope around the drowsy pup's neck, picked up his rifle, swung a rolled elk skin over his shoulder, and the two began a slow stalk towards the tree where the turkey was roosting. Approximately twenty yards from the tree, Angus stopped and spread the elk hide on the ground. Angus tied the end of Schatto's leash to a fallen limb, wrapped the edge of the elk hide around the pup, and as she huddled against Angus, sleep returned to the pup. It would be necessary for him to leave her and stalk directly beneath the roosting turkey to get a clear shot.

As Angus stood up he softly fingered the blue stone. Gently holding his hand on the back of the sleeping wolf, he commanded, "Stay, Schatto, stay." Noiselessly, Angus crept through damp leaves to the roost tree. Angus could see at least three turkeys outlined in the treetops. But he did not have a clear shot at any one of them. Shifting so the birds would be better silhouetted against the sky, Angus selected his target and sat down to wait. The turkeys would not fly down from the tree until dawn.

Ever so slowly the sky lightened. The soft thud of a squirrel jumping to the forest floor announced the awakening of diurnal wildlife. Angus hoped that Schatto would remain asleep, but he did not want to tempt fate by keeping her waiting too long. Again he clutched the blue stone, and mentally commanded the sleeping pup to stay. Angus could see the turkeys moving their heads, and knew he could not wait much longer. He could barely see the sights of his rifle, but after firing that particular muzzle-loading rifle several hundred times, he knew intimately every inch and every moving part.

Confident the turkeys could not see him, Angus imperceptibly raised his rifle, rested the barrel against the side of a tree, and settled the front sight onto the chest of the largest gobbler. The distance was only a hundred feet, considerably shorter than the distances he had commonly hit deer, but the target was much smaller. While feathers made the target appear larger, Angus knew that he must send the bullet into a space the size of his hand.

As his finger gently squeezed the trigger, the flint sprang forward and immediately a small burst of flame shot from the barrel. Before the turkeys had time to react, the lead bullet struck the bird and it fell earthward. Schatto, tethered to a log, jumped from the elk skin and looked for Angus. As the bird fell, Angus again fingered the soft deerskin pouch holding the stone and softly commanded, "Sit, Schatto, sit." Although his command was not audible, Schatto understood and obeyed.

Quickly retrieving the fallen turkey, Angus returned to Schatto and dropped the turkey on the ground while repeating, "Turkey, turkey, turkey." Schatto responded by locating the drops of blood seeping from the bullet hole and recognized this large object as food. Although it had feathers rather than hair, the blood taste was familiar.

Angus began pulling feathers from the back and sides of the turkey and Schatto grabbed a mouthful before realizing that they could not be eaten. An amused hunter smiled at the antics of his confused pup and continued to add to the pile of feathers. After plucking all the iridescent black breast feathers with their brown tips, Angus removed the pointed black and white banded wing feathers and the broad tail feathers. Collecting the ten-inch long beard and six of the most striking tail feathers, Angus headed back to the camp. With the turkey in one hand, his rifle in the other, the elk skin flung over his shoulder, and Schatto following closely at his side, Angus made plans for cooking the turkey.

Angus had little choice in how and when to prepare the turkey. He would have preferred to slowly cook the turkey after that day's travel. But to avoid spoilage, he prepared to cook it right away. Angus sliced open the turkey to remove the innards and gave the heart and liver to Schatto. He removed the intestines, hung them over a low limb out of reach of the pup, and set aside the gizzard. He would later open and clean it for Schatto to eat. After separating the wings and legs from the carcass, Angus removed the large breast in two separate pieces. Carefully slicing the pale breast pieces into long slender strips, Angus inserted sharpened branches through the turkey meat and suspended it over the flames. Schatto finished the heart and liver, and patiently awaited the next juicy morsel that Angus would offer. She was soon rewarded with the near-meatless carcass, which had the head still attached—the largest single food item she had ever been given.

Sitting comfortably beside the campfire and eating golden strips of turkey breast, Angus turned the legs and wings to prevent their burning. Angus studied Schatto as she had shoved her pointed snout into the body cavity and removed the bloody kidneys and the soft lungs. After quickly consuming those prize pieces, she alternately chewed on the head, back, and large breastbone.

Angus worried about the pup choking on a small piece of bone, but at her age she was not yet capable of biting off bones and swallowing them. Bones from birds are much more dangerous to pups than bones from mammals. Birds' leg bones and wing bones are hollow and could fracture into dagger-like small pieces to stick in the pup's throat when swallowed. Although wolves seldom capture birds, they occasionally find crippled, sick, or dead turkeys, which are then fully consumed.

Angus would eat the wings and legs for his mid-day meal, and the remaining breast strips would suffice for his evening meal. Turning the legs and wings one more time, Angus rounded up the horses and prepared to depart. Now that the meat was well cooked, Angus wrapped it in green leaves and placed it in one of the brown mare's baskets. After spreading the coals, he kicked some dirt over them and splashed a few bowls of water to finish the task.

Calling Schatto, he took the turkey carcass from her and loaded the pup into her basket atop the gray mare. The carcass went into the brown mare's other basket, and Angus mounted up. Shortly before mid-day the group was progressing down the well-traveled path. The steady rocking motion of the gray mare soon put a sated Schatto to sleep, and Angus dozed briefly. Although he still wanted to test his skill at shooting a squirrel with the bow, they did not need any extra meat.

Because of the shortage of grasses, Angus was always alert for a spot where the horses could graze, no matter how small it might be. Fortunately, the forest canopy was occasionally opened when trees fell from old age, ice storms, or violent windstorms. The resultant grasses, briars, and seedlings attracted deer, elk, and the itinerant horse. At a small blow-down some distance from the trail, Angus urged Night Fog to leave the trail, bound for the opening. At the edge of the blow-down, Angus dismounted, rifle in hand, and scoured the area for sunning rattlesnakes. Resting place secured, he lifted the wolf pup from her perch to stretch and explore. Angus chose a soft moss-covered site where he could rest his back against one of the giant poplars, and hungry travelers prepared for mid-day nourishment.

Flies attracted to the turkey carcass as they rode along the trail now settled onto the raw meat, but Angus was not concerned. Wolves, dogs, and many other wild carnivores regularly eat slightly spoiled meat that most humans would consider a health hazard. His hounds in Scotland occasionally ate such food, but their digestive systems adjusted to the bacteria. A few of his hounds had vomited after consuming rotten meat, but none had ever died as a result. It was important to expose the pup gradually to slightly spoiled meat so that her digestive system would adapt. Certainly adult wolves were scavengers, and frequently fed their pups meat from long dead or rotting carcasses.

Following their meal, Angus and Schatto napped as the horses continued grazing. Angus was suddenly awakened by a cacophony of unusual sounds emanating farther down the trail. At first he was dumbfounded. Then slowly the sounds jogged memories of cattle on the Scottish countryside. Fastening the elk skin leash around Schatto's neck, Angus took cover and focused his attention on the trail. From the forest shadows emerged several dark brown hulks, walking single-file along the trail. Their sinewy hindquarters were covered with short wooly hair, while their heads, forelegs, humps, and shoulders were protected by coarse, shaggy hair. Under his breath, Angus exclaimed, "Buffalo!" The bulky creatures lumbered slowly but steadily along the trail, unaware of the Scotsman and his animals. Angus had seen a few small herds on his way from Lancaster to the Monongahela, but this was the closest encounter.

It was obvious that these massive animals were designed to face danger, rather than flee. The Shawnee described how wolves and mountain lions would occasionally cull an old or injured buffalo, but they would never attack a healthy adult. The consolidated herd vigorously defended against any predator foolish enough to attack.

With broad, massive heads that seemed out-of-proportion to the rest of the body, the huge bulls were markedly contrasted to the smaller cows with their noticeably smaller horns. A few medium-sized animals were obviously yearlings from the previous summer.

Out of the herd's eighteen animals, Angus counted four reddish-tan calves. The herd, led by a matriarch cow, was migrating from the bottomlands along the Potomac River to their summer grounds along the Ohio River. Grazers such as buffalo found little to eat in a mature forest, so it was necessary to move constantly, as they quickly consumed all available forage in any one location. Grasses were their preferred food, and such herbaceous growth was found in abundance only along river floodplains.

Schatto spotted the herd only a few minutes later and now sat shuddering and whimpering anxiously. Angus commanded, "Quiet, Schatto, quiet." Angus removed the blue stone and whispered, "Buffalo, buffalo, buffalo." The frontiersman slowly reached for his rifle and centered the front sights on the shoulder of one of the yearlings. The buffalo were within fifty yards, an easy shot for his Pennsylvania rifle. The two-hundred-pound animal would provide more than enough meat for Angus and Schatto to reach Wills Creek. Unfortunately, Angus had no way to smoke such a large amount of meat and did not believe in utilizing just the tongue, the liver, the heart, and a few of the choicest cuts.

Had they been near a settlement, such as the Dunkard's farm, Angus would have shot one of the animals. If he shot the yearling now, however, much of the meat would go to waste. Slowly lowering his rifle, he clutched the blue stone, and repeated, "Buffalo... buffalo...buffalo."

After the herd was gone, Angus led Schatto to the trail and urged her to investigate the mixture of odors. A small, steaming pile of dung immediately caught her attention and after sniffing it eagerly, she took a small bite. Angus knew that would happen but did not try to prevent it. It was one more avenue for learning to relate the animal to its scent. However, after the one small bite, Angus sternly commanded, "No! No! No!" As Schatto sniffed a wet spot where one of the cows had urinated, Angus again repeated, "Buffalo...

buffalo…buffalo." Firmly convinced that the blue stone was the conduit for communicating with the wolf, Angus slowly rubbed the stone while continuing to repeat the word, "Buffalo."

Schatto's future as a hunter depended on her innate ability to distinguish among the scents left by various animals. There would be times when Angus would want her to trail a bear. At other times an elk or a wild turkey would be their quarry.

A smile crossed his face as Angus recalled a story about a hunter's feisty terrier. The hunter used the dog to kill small animals for their valuable fur. Depending on the time of year, the weather, and the price of certain furs, the hunter would decide what kind of fur-bearer he wanted to hunt that day. To convey the day's target to the terrier, the hunter would show the dog a tapered drying board used to stretch the pelt of that specific animal. Weasels, rabbits, opossums, and raccoons each had individual boards, long-used, and strongly scented from past hunting.

One day the hunter's wife asked him to take her ironing board out onto the porch so she could work in the warm, fall sunshine. The terrier had been asleep on the front porch when it awoke and spotted the hunter with the ironing board. A wide-eyed, frightened dog took off running to the barn, where it did not emerge for three days. An animal large enough to fit over an ironing board apparently was more than the small terrier wanted to tackle!

After reloading the horses, Angus resumed his journey in the direction from whence the buffalo had come. As the small caravan reached the banks of yet another small creek flowing westward to the Yogh-yo-gaine, tracks indicated the buffalo had crossed there, trampling vegetation and grazing. To find forage for his horses, Angus turned Night Fog upstream and paralleled the small creek until they reached an open swale with untrampled vegetation. Here they would spend the night.

As Angus unsaddled the gray mare he realized that he must repeat her name enough times that she would become accustomed to hearing it. Pulling gently on the reins as he led the mare to a grassy spot downstream from where they would camp, Angus called, "Night Fog, here, Night Fog." After hobbling and rubbing both horses, Angus handed Schatto the pungent turkey carcass—a plaything more than a source of nourishment.

Angus collected enough firewood for their evening fire and turned his attention to bow practice. Six small squirrel-sized patches of green moss were placed near the base of a large tulip poplar, and from fifty feet away Angus sent six arrows into all six without a miss. Of the next six shots, he missed one, but now felt confident of hitting the next squirrel he shot at. Although several pieces of smoked deer meat remained in his food cache, the turkey would last only till breakfast.

Angus set three snares that evening, fully aware he was not likely to catch a rabbit. The forest offered little for those animals needing green vegetation for food and thick briary escape cover. Although a border of green vegetation lined the small stream where they camped, the narrow strip was too small to support rabbits. Angus wished he could catch squirrels in a snare, but unlike rabbits, squirrels did not follow easily recognized trails through grass.

A wolf howled to the northwest, followed by a second and then a third, and Angus speculated that they might have picked up the scent of the herd of buffalo. If the wolf pack spooked the small herd, individual buffalo would probably go running wildly through the forest, and if the calves were unable to remain with their mothers, he envisioned the wolves eating buffalo that night.

Schatto also detected the wolf howls, and as another of the eerie calls floated over the small watershed Angus spoke, "Wolf. Wolf. Wolf," as he held the blue stone. It seemed strange to be trying to teach a wolf the word, "wolf." Would he ever have the occasion to use the word in a command? What would happen when Schatto became an adult and heard the call of her own species? Future encounters with wolves would likely be rare, unless they spent extended times in the remote portions of the wilderness. Because Schatto would not reach sexual maturity for another three years there was little to worry about at this time.

Angus asked, "Do you hear those howls, wee Lassie? Did your mamma ever show you how to howl?" On several occasions, Schatto had heard her parents howl outside the den, but she'd never observed the act of howling. Angus figured that all dogs and wolves knew instinctively how to howl, but surely they learned some facets of the unique canine vocalization by mimicking. Cupping his hands around his mouth, Angus leaned back, pointed his nose skyward, and produced a long drawn-out howl. Schatto cocked her head sideways, and stared quizzically at the source of this odd but somewhat evocative sound. Angus repeated the howl a second and then a third time, as the wolf stared attentively. As Angus began his fourth howl, Schatto raised her nose, opened her mouth, closed her eyes, and created her own version of a howl. It bore little resemblance to the howl of an adult wolf, but the high-pitched, extended sound was definitely not a bark or a yip. Man and wolf repeated their strange chorus several times before Angus called a halt to the game. He would repeat the lesson on future occasions when they were serenaded by real wolves.

Before going to sleep that night, Angus's thoughts returned to the blue stone. Sorcery was not a strange concept to Scots. Witchcraft had a long history dating back to the Celts, but Angus had no intimate knowledge of how it worked. If the stone was a talisman what should he know? What was its relationship to the Ogam-like runes on the cave wall where it came into his possession? Was there a distance beyond which he could not transmit his thoughts? How complex could he make his commands? Was it always necessary to rub the blue stone to transmit his commands? Of even greater interest, would other animals respond to his commands? Now that the gray mare had a name, he could test her reactions. Resolving to begin new trials the next morning, Angus offered thanks for the day and slowly drifted into a restful sleep.

Angus lay quietly the next morning contemplating the tests he would conduct with the gray mare. As Schatto began to stir, Angus arose, relieved himself, and called Schatto to check their snares. As expected, all three snares were untouched. Schatto would have no rabbit organs to eat that day. Returning to their camp, they ate breakfast of turkey and venison while serenaded by breeding songbirds. Hundreds of warblers, vireos, grosbeaks, tanagers, and woodpeckers created a mélange unlike any Angus had ever heard in

Scotland. Bird populations in the Scottish Highlands were restricted to ground dwellers and species around lakes and rivers.

Calling Schatto to heel, Angus strode toward the horses. With the wolf at his left side, Angus removed the blue stone from the soft deerskin pouch around his neck. It was a distinct possibility that Schatto as well as the horse could perceive his commands, so Angus decided to reserve unique commands for the horse. "Come," "Stay," and "Heel," would be used strictly with the wolf. When within ten yards of the horses, Angus stopped and began to softly rub the blue stone. Making a concerted effort to concentrate his thoughts on the horse he whistled, then called her name. The gray mare responded by raising her head, which she often did upon hearing his voice.

He had called to the horses every morning while on the trail, but they had never come to him. Although each appeared to look forward to his coat brushing and neck rubs, neither had overtly sought his attention. This was not unusual because some horses were slow to respond to new owners.

Angus stood patiently as the gray mare continued to stare in his direction. Concentrating his thoughts even more on the gray while softly rubbing the blue stone, Angus again whistled and called, "Night Fog, here, here." A faint smile appeared on his face as the mare slowly moved in his direction. Although her steps were restricted by the hobbles, she quickened her pace when Angus repeated the command. Moments later she reached his side and began nuzzling his shoulder.

To his dismay, Angus had no treats to reward the mare. Slices of apples would have been perfect, but no apple trees grew in the Appalachian wilderness. Serviceberry and an occasional persimmon tree grew along the wider streams, and raspberries and blackberries grew in the larger openings scattered throughout the forest, but none of those fruits were ripe at this time of the year. Not even acorns or chestnuts were available. The only reward that Angus could provide was the gentle touch of his hands. Horses are social animals, similar to wolves. They need the security of other horses and must have a leader to follow. Angus would function as the alpha male wolf to Schatto, while serving as the herd stallion to Night Fog and the brown mare.

As he repeated her name, Angus ran his hands firmly, but softly, over the mare's neck, back, legs, and face. He removed her hobbles and turned back to camp. He fingered the blue stone in its pouch, while whistling and calling, "Here, here." Much to his satisfaction, Night Fog followed close behind, and Schatto heeled alongside. The brown mare had observed all the attention given to Night Fog. Now she followed them, hobbling, back to camp.

Angus saddled Night Fog and tied her reins to a tree, then waited patiently as the brown made her way into camp. The pack baskets were soon loaded, hobbles removed, and the group once again embarked on the Catawba Trail, bound for the Potomac. Angus walked slightly ahead of the gray mare while Schatto scoured the trail and trunk of every tree.

Late that morning the trail descended from the highlands, and Angus saw in the distance what must be the Yogh-yo-gaine. The trail led to a convenient ford across the river, where the water was shallow enough for Angus to keep his feet dry by lifting them out of the stirrups and holding them up near Night Fog's neck. Schatto perched at the front of her basket, carefully studying the passing objects in the swiftly moving waters. Without hesitation, the two sure-footed horses made their way across the river and climbed the bank onto the bordering flood plain. Neither dwellings nor other sign of human habitation existed, and Angus saw no indication that a town later called Connellsville would eventually spring up at this location.

CHAPTER NINETEEN
CHRISTOPHER GIST

DURING A BRIEF MID-DAY break along the banks of the Yogh-yo-gaine, the horses grazed, Schatto played, and Angus rested. When the four sojourners continued their southward journey, the trail passed several gigantic sycamores, gradually ascending to the nearby highlands where the mountains appeared rolling, rather than ridged and pointed. The next stop would be the Christopher Gist Plantation, another five miles down the trail. Like most Indian paths through western Pennsylvania, this particular trail followed the higher elevations and thus provided the driest and the easiest route to travel.

Christopher Gist had hosted Angus for a night the previous year, and prepared a rough map for him showing the tributaries of the lower Monongahela and most of the Youghiogheny, as Gist spelled it. Gist had cleared a small tract of forest where he erected a small log cabin and planned eventually to clear at least one hundred acres for his "plantation." Although Angus had never seen a plantation, and had no idea what one looked like, Gist explained it as an expansive farm, supporting a variety of crops and livestock. Christopher had brought his family and several others to the Youghiogheny area the previous year. Angus was eager to learn how they had survived the winter and how much had been accomplished since his last visit.

On the western horizon, a descending sun decreed that darkness would soon cloak the land. Angus spotted a clearing through the trees, and the southerly breeze that carried a whiff of smoke revealed that the Gist Plantation was ahead. As the horses emerged from the dense forest, it became apparent that Gist had chosen some of the best-lying land in the area; gently rolling was the best way to describe it. The small cabin, sited at the southern end of a cleared field, was now enlarged by the addition of a new room. Halfway through a cornfield Angus dismounted and stopped the horses. Loudly announcing his presence, he called, "Hello in the cabin. Hello in the cabin." When there was no answer and no one appeared at the cabin door, Angus advanced further.

When he yelled a second time a husky, middle-aged man with black beard appeared at the cabin door and responded, "Who goes?"

The frontiersman answered, "Angus, Angus McCallander."

The man stepped down off the porch and invited, "Angus, you old Scotsman, come on up." Gently lifting the wolf pup out of her basket, Angus ordered her to heel, gave a tug to the gray mare's reins, and approached the cabin.

After exchanging a firm handshake, Gist told Angus to unpack his horses and hobble them in the grassy area where his own two horses were grazing. Surreptitiously, Gist furtively studied Angus, his clothes, his horses, their packs, and the wolf. When they met the previous autumn Angus was a novice frontiersman, making his first trip into the Appalachian wilderness. Now he was an experienced explorer, as evidenced by the easy way he handled his horses and rifle, the deerskin clothing he wore, and the wolf who walked obediently at his left side. Gist looked forward to hearing all about his adventures.

As Angus climbed the cabin steps, Gist's first question popped out, "Is that a wolf pup?" It was nearly an exclamation.

Clearly, he would have to tell the story of Schatto to every person he met. As they sat on the cabin porch, Angus once again repeated the story of finding the half-drowned wolf pup.

With the basic details out of the way, he introduced his companion, "Christopher, this is Schatto." Angus asked him to hold his hand down for her to sniff and thus meet the stranger. His hands carried an earthy mix of odors from trees, horses, soil, and deer meat. Sensing this was someone Angus trusted, Schatto wagged her tail and sniffed curiously at their host's pants leg. The slight smile that spread through Gist's black beard signaled to Angus that the wolf pup was welcome in his cabin.

As he headed for the cabin door, Gist proclaimed, "Come in and tell me about your winter in the wilderness while I fix supper. My family's away, helping a neighbor over the hill with a barn raising, and I'm alone tonight. I had to stay to help a cow that was having trouble dropping her calf."

Angus detailed how he had moved westward to the Monongahela after leaving Gist's cabin the previous October, visited with the Dunkards, traveled upriver to the headwaters of the West Fork of the Monongahela, and spent the winter at the Shawnee village. Tales of the mountain lion attack, the death of his horse, his broken left arm, and building a dugout canoe were fascinating to Gist.

As the stewing aromas of venison, corn meal, and wild greens drifted from the fireplace, Angus grew hungry as he explained how he had traded his furs to two Frenchmen at the Forks of the Ohio, had subsequently been ambushed by an Indian, and now was headed south to the Potomac. From there he would return to Lancaster and spend the summer building a new muzzle-loader under the guidance of gunsmith Henery Gumpf.

Gist was full of questions about the adventures and expressed great interest in the French trading post. He wanted to know specifics about its size, the number of people who worked there, how many furs they had, if they had horses and canoes, and whether Angus thought they intended to develop a permanent trading post. Angus answered Gist's questions the best he could, concluding that the trading post was obviously temporary. Angus added, "The Frenchmen have erected a cabin, but it wasn't well built and there's no evidence they're planning to build permanent cabins and warehouses."

Aware that his numerous queries reflected undue curiosity, Gist explained, "I'm employed by the Ohio Company. They've been deeded 500,000 acres in the region by the British Crown and the Governor of Virginia, and plan to build several trading posts in the next two years. They already have one small warehouse and trading post at Wills Creek on the Potomac and will be building one at Redstone on the Monongahela later this year."

Over the splendid supper, Angus asked about the trail to the Potomac, and Gist explained, "It's well marked and will be easier to travel than the section you followed from the Forks of the Ohio to the Youghiogheny. Nemacolin, a Delaware Indian, and Thomas Cresap, who lives on the Potomac, were hired by the Ohio Company to blaze and clear the trail from the Potomac to the Monongahela." Gist explained that the Ohio Company wanted the trail cleared so that families from the colonies could move westward and settle on company lands. "Nemacolin's family lives in a cabin on a creek west of here. He stops in to visit on his trips to and from the trading post at Wills Creek, and brings us news."

Angus inquired about Gist's plans for his farm, and Christopher explained that he would be building a barn and more cabins, clearing more land, planting more crops, and starting an orchard. Gist chuckled, "I need a few more acres of sky."

It occurred to Angus that a settler could not survive in the forest. His land's most valued characteristic was open sky, gained only after he cleared enough trees to expose sunlight, which in turn produced crops in the fields, hay in the meadows, and flowers to feed the soul. An open sky also provided vistas: to evaluate crops, to count grazing livestock, and to enjoy the comfort of distant hills that lent a feeling of security.

"You surely picked a great spot for your farm. I wish I could decide where to locate my own fifty acres." Angus then admitted his reluctance to settle down on a farm. "There's so much more of the Appalachian wilderness that I want to see and so much more that I want to do before settling down on a farm."

Christopher responded, "Some people are meant to be farmers and some are not. Until you try it, you'll never know. But it takes time to decide either way." In his mind's eyes, he could not see this young frontiersman as a farmer.

As the flames in the fireplace flickered faintly, a yawning host announced that he was ready for bed. His dreams that night would revisit the many exciting adventures of which he was slightly envious. Gist told Angus he could sleep in the cabin or outside, whatever he pleased. Angus replied, "It's a clear night with no rain likely, so I'll make my bed in the soft grass beside your porch." With his saddle and pack baskets piled together on the porch, Angus spread his bearskin in the grass and soon he and the pup were asleep.

At breakfast the next morning, Gist advised Angus he should be able to reach the Potomac River in two days. The trail would leave the rolling highlands and climb the steep, rugged mountains of Chestnut Ridge, the name given to the extended mountaintop covered with huge chestnut trees.

After crossing Chestnut Ridge, the trail would pass through a broad meadow, which would offer the best grazing for horses until they reached the Potomac. Beyond the meadow, named Great Meadows by the Indians, the trail would pass around two more mountains before finally dropping down to the Potomac. Once Angus reached the narrow pass parallel to Wills Creek, however, he would be in Maryland, and the Potomac River only a short distance beyond.

The two men shook hands genially as Angus thanked him for all his hospitality and advice, and then Angus nudged Night Fog down the trail towards the rolling highlands. As Christopher studied the wolf that trailed obediently alongside the gray mare, he looked forward to seeing them again some day.

Toward mid-morning the trail began a marked, but gradual ascent to a ridgeline barely visible through the woods. Trees at lower elevations had leafed out, blocking the sunlight and greatly restricting distance viewing. As they moved up the mountainside, leafless chestnut trees replaced tulip poplars and the surrounding forest floor was cloaked with elongated chestnut leaves. Empty spiny chestnut burrs had encircled delicious, nutritious nuts the previous autumn, and now Schatto picked her way through the irritating burrs. Angus lifted her out of her misery into the basket atop Night Fog. The trail did not cross directly over the highest ridgeline, but instead passed through one of the many low gaps to eliminate considerable climbing.

By late afternoon they dropped off the ridge and Angus gawked at Great Meadows, the largest treeless opening Angus had encountered on his journey. Still within the deep shadows of the hardwood forest, a wary Angus stopped Night Fog and dismounted. Stealthily working his way from tree to tree, he carefully perused the extensive fields, especially the edges. An experienced woodsman like Angus knew to conduct his surveillance from the dense edge. By moving out into an opening, directly onto a ridge top, or onto the river's edge without first stopping to fully study the area, a man's presence was easily detected, by wildlife or other humans.

Peering around a large white oak, Angus scrutinized the borders of the opening, and then scanned the middle. He was gratified to see ten white-tailed deer, one small herd of elk, and at least twenty turkeys scattered throughout the opening. Christopher Gist described the meadow as a natural grassy opening, burned by the Indians when grasses dried out during late summer or early fall. In so doing they preserved the grassy nature of the site, prevented woody shrubs and trees from becoming established, and thereby guaranteed that it would attract deer, elk, and buffalo.

Although parts of the meadow were soggy, Angus now felt secure enough to select an elevated spot for a dry campsite along the forest edge, near a small stream flowing off the hillside. Even before he had secured their hobbles, the horses were munching on the grasses. They would certainly fill their bellies this night. While Angus gathered firewood, Schatto searched through the grasses for fresh scent. The meadow was crisscrossed by a multitude of animal trails. The broader ones were made by hoofed animals, while narrow trails told of groundhogs, rabbits, foxes, and other smaller-sized mammals. Schatto focused on the smallest trails, not visible until the grasses were parted. These runways were the travel lanes of lemming-like rodents called meadow voles. The pup's instinct had never been so aroused and, with her tail wagging wildly, she began digging into a small mound. As her front legs removed loose soil and ejected it between her hind legs, she gradually created a hole several inches deep and as wide as her head. Suddenly she yipped, jumped at a small brownish critter, and caught her very first prey. It was a meadow vole, common throughout grasslands but absent in forests.

Angus had been watching her intently, and as soon as he realized she had made a catch, he called, "Schatto, come, come." The pup hesitated and dropped onto her belly while still clenching the wriggling rodent. She had captured it and was reluctant to give it up.

Angus realized that this was an excellent opportunity to reinforce the "fetch" command. He rubbed the blue stone and beckoned while repeating his command, "Fetch, fetch." Schatto rose to her feet and moved to Angus's side. Angus grasped the vole and sternly ordered, "Drop, drop." Although the pup had not yet learned the "drop" command, she comprehended its meaning. She released her grip and Angus took the rodent in his hand. A close examination revealed that it had small beady eyes, no visible ears, and a short tail less than half the length of the body. Schatto sat quietly, but watched closely as Angus held the charcoal gray vole by its tail. "Good girl, good girl," he exclaimed and returned Schatto's first capture to her. Quickly grabbing it, she moved off a short distance and proceeded to mouth and bite the limp and lifeless rodent. Her sharp teeth soon tore off pieces of fur and the taste of fresh flesh enticed her to chew. Schatto savored the first animal she had tracked and captured on her own. Angus was quite satisfied as he observed her swallowing small bites.

After setting up camp, Angus called Schatto from her amusements. With snares in hand, he led her to a clump of alder that bordered a small stream. Bark had been chewed from the bases of several of the smaller alder stems, no doubt by rabbits. Well-worn trails through the grasses growing under the alder revealed that cottontails frequented the area, and Angus anticipated that by sun-up his snares would hold a rabbit.

Snares set, Angus set off for the pine trees growing at woods' edge where he gathered four of the largest pinecones to brush the horses' coats. Stepping out into the meadow, Angus gave a shrill whistle that started low then quickly increased in frequency. Schatto stared curiously, fascinated by a sound she had never before heard. One of the ponies in Scotland was so attuned to his whistle that it would come from long distances, and Angus wanted these new horses to respond to his whistle. Now he lifted the bag containing the blue stone, as he whistled again and silently commanded, "Here, Night Fog, here."

Night Fog reluctantly stopped biting off mouthfuls of grass, raised her head, and headed toward Angus. Steps restricted by hobbles, her progress was slow, but as she approached, Angus moved quickly to her side and began rubbing her head and neck. Firmly grasping the pinecone, he ran it through the long black hair that formed her mane and her tail. Night Fog stood motionless, obviously enjoying the attention and the pleasant sensations created by the gentle pulling. Finishing with the mane and tail, Angus brushed her shoulders, sides, and rump. Although most of her winter coat had been shed, several patches of shaggy hair yielded to the makeshift brushes. Stepping back, he admired the silvery coat accentuated by the black mane and tail. She was a striking picture, and certainly more impressive than a horse all one color. Slapping Night Fog on the rump, Angus said, "Go back to eating now. I'll call you in the morning."

Returning to his campsite, Angus heated a mixture of cornmeal and smoked elk in his iron kettle. Schatto's meadow vole was not enough for a growing pup, so the two shared the cooked elk-cornmeal. As darkness dominated the forest and dusk settled over the great meadow, Angus sat with his back to a white oak and scanned the huge opening. Several more deer and elk had entered the grassy field, along with a bear and her two cubs. The turkeys had ended their quest for insects, and were at roost high in one of the larger trees, while the deer, elk, and bear continued to graze on the abundant meadow grasses. They would continue to feed into the night and most would bed down in the meadow only to begin grazing again before dawn arrived.

Angus threw a few more small branches onto his fire and his thoughts drifted. He wondered whether Heather was still living in the Scottish Highlands. Drifting away from Scotland, images of Sweetwater and Katrina found him subconsciously comparing his relationship with each of the three young women. He and Heather had spent countless days roaming the Highlands. He could see her long wavy hair, red as his own, and the freckles that spread across cheeks accentuated with happy dimples. The many days spent in the hills surrounding the Shawnee camp with Sweetwater in some ways made him feel closer to her than to Heather. The girl's intense dark eyes could communicate more than many words, and when she tossed those silky raven braids, she knew her own charisma. Although he had seen Katrina on only two occasions, the quiet brunette German girl with the deep green eyes fascinated him. She wove baskets, made clay cups, baked pies, and named Schatto, but it was something more than this that drew his thoughts to her.

As the fire faded to embers, Angus reminded himself that he now had enough gold to pay a major part of Heather's passage to the colonies. He would make arrangements at Lancaster to bring Heather to the colonies. If she worked as an indentured servant in Philadelphia they could save enough money to pay the balance owed on her ship's passage. The eerie howls of a distant pack of wolves became integrated with the conflicting possibilities of his future, and an emotionally exhausted Angus settled alongside Schatto onto his bearskin and was quickly asleep.

Like heavy clouds, a patchy fog covered the meadow when Angus awoke, and as a light breeze moved the wispy haze back and forth across the large opening, Angus tried to spot the horses. He knew they could not have wandered far, but they were obscured from sight. He grabbed the deerskin bag with the blue stone and sounded the same whistle notes he had used the previous night, starting low then quickly increasing in frequency. He repeated the notes three times, while silently commanding, "Night Fog, here. Night Fog, here." Schatto's ears were pointed skyward as she studied Angus and his whistles. Angus recalled the Scottish sheepdogs that responded so obediently. With only whistles and arm movements, a shepherd could direct his dog to move sheep in a specific direction to a particular spot. Although he had no desire to train Schatto to herd sheep—no job for a pureblooded wolf—her ability to obey various whistle commands could prove useful.

A dim, ghostly form silently materialized from the fog as Night Fog responded to his whistle. As Angus began brushing her with one of the pinecones, the brown mare approached. Had she responded to the whistle or simply followed the gray? Quickly finishing Night Fog, Angus began brushing the brown mare. She stood patiently; skin quivering, as he worked the pinecone through her mane and over her sides.

Large clumps of winter-dulled hair were gently coaxed from the brown mare's coat by the bristly pinecone, revealing a shiny, chestnut-brown coat with a hint of red from the sun's low-angle morning rays. Eager to view the entirety of the mare's glistening summer coat, Angus continued brushing until no traces of the faded winter coat remained. Stepping back to admire both mares, he announced, "Glory be, what a handsome pair of horses I possess." An appropriate name for the brown mare had never occurred to Angus, but now he had an inspiration. "Your coat gleams like a buckeye fresh from its hull and regardless of any name you may have been given in the past, I hereby christen thee, Buckeye."

A search of the alder thicket revealed two rabbits caught in the snares, and Angus shortly had them roasting in the fire. Two sets of livers, hearts, and kidneys temporarily satisfied the pup's hunger, and she set out in search of another meadow vole while Angus monitored the cooking. As sunshine burned off the fog, Angus ate the backs and front legs of both rabbits, then wrapped his lunch of the large hind legs in grass and prepared the horses for the day's journey.

As usual, Angus let the reins of the gray mare hang down on the ground while he secured the pack baskets and tied the elk skin rope from Buckeye to the gray's saddle. As Night Fog moved her head from side to side, the reins began to swing and Schatto grabbed them in her mouth. Angus smiled as the pup pulled on the reins and the gray mare stood quietly, but eyed the pup intently. "A good animal trainer would convert this game into a useful command," thought Angus. With the blue stone in hand, Angus ordered, "Schatto, fetch Night Fog. Schatto, fetch Night Fog." Angus walked several yards away and repeated his command. Quickly the pup dropped the reins and started towards Angus. "Whoa," Angus commanded as he moved to the pup and placed the end of the reins in her mouth. She dropped them again, but when Angus repeated the act she held them firmly. He walked several yards away, and repeated the command. As the pup began moving in his direction while holding the reins, Angus could not help but smile. "Amazing," he said aloud. "Absolutely amazing!"

CHAPTER TWENTY
NEMACOLIN

THE NEXT DAY BEGAN uneventfully, but by mid-day Angus spotted a small river through the trees. It had to be the Youghiogheny, originating in the mountains of western Virginia and flowing northward through Maryland and Pennsylvania before entering the Monongahela. Angus sat atop his mount and gazed down at this body of water. Its size and direction of flow convinced him that it was indeed the last major stream they would pass before reaching the Potomac.

Running along the edge of the river was a long gravel bar and Angus decided to take a mid-day break. They were less than a day's travel from the Potomac. As the hobbled horses searched for grasses along the riverbank, Angus and Schatto ate their leftover rabbit and smoked venison. As he rested, Angus watched Schatto explore the gravel bar, where she picked up a forked object and begin chewing on it.

Curious to identify the object, Angus took occasion to call, "Fetch, fetch." He continued to rub the bag with the blue stone while calling, "Schatto, fetch." She was too engrossed in chewing the forked object to respond immediately, but on the second command she picked it up and carried it to Angus. The pup approached him but continued to hold her find, which Angus identified as the shed antler of a white-tailed deer. With the deerskin bag in hand, he commanded, "Drop, drop." Schatto dropped the antler and sat on her haunches as Angus examined a bony structure reminiscent of red deer antlers dropped on the mountainsides of Scotland. Antlers, even those of mature red deer stags, grew to an impressive size in less than one year, only to be shed during winter. It seemed such a waste of energy to grow antlers only to lose them.

To expand Schatto's training, Angus ordered her to stay while he carried the antler to the far end of the gravel bar. Angus concealed his actions as he pushed the antler into sand at the water's edge. Returning to the pup, he held the leather pouch and directed her, "Fetch, fetch." When the pup did not move, Angus moved forward two steps and pointed with his arm in the direction of the hidden antler as he repeated his command, "Fetch, fetch." This time Schatto took off running to the other end of the gravel bar and retrieved the half-buried antler. When she began chewing on one of the antler tines, Angus sternly called loudly, "Schatto, fetch, fetch." This time she returned the antler to him, and was rewarded with a small piece of smoked venison.

To continue the training, Angus again ordered her to stay, took the antler, and moved to the end of the gravel bar where he pretended to bury the antler at three different places before partially covering it with gravel. Schatto had been watching intently and seemed to anticipate this new game they were playing. She could barely contain herself as Angus returned to her side. At his command, "Fetch, fetch," the pup dashed for the antler and scurried back as fast as her short legs would carry her.

Watching her run, Angus was reminded that it would be several months before the pup's legs lengthened and strengthened enough to run with any speed. "Drop," he ordered, and Schatto squatted on her haunches waiting for the hide and seek game to continue. Angus buried the old antler slightly deeper each time until it was covered with two inches of gravel. Although she required several minutes to find the antler the last time, her nose detected the correct spot and she excitedly dug it out of the gravel.

Unbeknownst to Angus, the commotion of Hide-and-Seek had attracted the attention of an Indian on the opposite side of the river. Quietly slipping from tree to tree, the native stopped and peered curiously from behind a fallen sycamore. Angus had been so engrossed in training the Schatto that he forgot to scan the riverbank for danger. Even if he had been alert it was doubtful that he would have spotted the elusive Indian, hidden by the deep shadows. Sensing no danger from the strange white man clothed in deerskins, the Indian carefully studied his activities. He recognized the pup as a wolf and was amazed that such a wild animal would obey commands. Pups born in Indian villages were never trained and never became pets.

Expertly mimicking the call of a tufted titmouse, the muscular Indian signaled his companion to join him. In a few minutes a second Indian was peering out from behind the fallen sycamore, watching the strange game being played by white man and pup. After Angus had once again hidden the deer antler, and Schatto had once again retrieved it, the taller of the two Indians cautiously moved from behind the sycamore. Waiting until Angus had returned to the end of the gravel bar to bury the antler, the Indian took a few steps closer to the river.

Angus spotted the motion and crouched instantly, providing a smaller target than while upright. Although it appeared that the Indian was not carrying a weapon, Angus regretted that he did not have his own rifle. He could see it leaning against the log near the pup and likely the Indian also saw it. Were other Indians watching from the opposite shore? Should he start running towards the rifle? Should he run up over the riverbank and dive into the grassy vegetation? Should he attempt to talk to the Indian, hoping he only wanted to trade? Although the river was nearly twenty yards wide, Angus knew he would be an easy target for a skilled archer. How could he have let himself get into such a predicament, he wondered in agony.

As Angus pondered the situation, the Indian stepped to the water's edge with arms extended and hands held upright. At the same time, Angus spotted movement behind the sycamore. Concluding that this was a trap, Angus decided to make a dash for his rifle. Just as he was ready to spring from his crouch, the second Indian stepped into the open. Angus immediately relaxed when he noted it was a young boy, about the same size as Fritz, Katrina's twelve-year old brother. As the boy reached the water's edge, the two Indians began wading out into the water. The two slowly shuffled towards the middle, and at mid-point, with water waist-high on the young boy, Angus began walking in the direction of his rifle. His fears were partially allayed by the boy's presence, but he would feel much more secure with a rifle in his hands. When Angus was within twenty feet of his rifle, the taller Indian shouted, "Friend, friend, don't shoot." Still wary, Angus kneeled down on the gravel. Schatto had been watching the proceedings intently. What should she make of the people in the river or her master crouching on the gravel bar? She interpreted his crouching position as an invitation to join him and she immediately ran to crouch beside him.

The taller Indian continued to approach and yelled something that sounded like, "Nemacolin, Nemacolin," followed by, "Your name? Your name?"

The Scotsman answered, "Angus, Angus McCallander." As the men approached to within arm's length, they studied each other's face, while the boy and pup eyed each other intently. The boy had watched the pup's playful antics but was still apprehensive about its small, sharp teeth. Meanwhile, the pup remembered the Dunkard boys, Fritz and Jonathan, and their energizing romps. Gradually everyone relaxed, the Indian extended his arm forward, and Angus reciprocated. The two engaged in a cordial handshake. The Indian was two to three inches shorter than Angus, but his handshake was equally powerful. All men on the frontier respected a powerful handshake. A weak, feminine handshake connoted one who would not carry his share of the load.

Angus kneeled onto the gravel bar and motioned the boy to hold out his hand. To demonstrate his courage, the boy extended his open hand to the wolf pup. The open hand was an invitation for Schatto to inch forward and sniff until his curiosity was satisfied. When the pup's tongue began to lick his fingers the boy grinned with delight. Although Angus did not know if the Indians could speak English he suggested, "Scratch her head," and demonstrated for the boy. Without hesitation the boy began scratching and petting the pup. In no time, the two were romping on the gravel bar. Angus observed the other man staring intently at his rifle and remembered that few individuals on the frontier had seen such an attractive, ornate weapon. Most European muskets looked cumbersome, with ugly stocks and bulky barrels. In contrast, his muzzle-loader's elongated barrel was streamlined and the burnished maple stock embellished with fancy carvings seemed out-of-place on a weapon. The Indian would be even more impressed by the accuracy of the muzzle-loader, if he were to see a demonstration. Angus briefly considered shooting, but then promptly reconsidered. The less known about the superiority of his muzzle-loader over a musket, the less likely someone would try to steal it.

When both men were seated on the log, Angus asked, "Speak English?"

The Indian answered, "Yes," and explained that he had learned some of the language from the settlers at the Potowmack (as he pronounced it) where he regularly traded. Stating that he was a Delaware, he revealed that he lived in a cabin to the west, and he and his son were returning from a trip to the Wills Creek trading post. The two were camped a short distance upstream on the other side of the river and had been fishing when they spotted Angus.

Nemacolin was certain that Angus's deerskin clothing had been made by a Shawnee, so the Indian asked where he came from. Angus explained that he was a hunter, trapper, and trader and had lived a short time in the colonies after coming across the ocean from a place called Scotland. Nemacolin said he had never heard of Scotland and had never seen the ocean but had heard stories about the endless waters that sent huge waves crashing onto a sandy beach. He reckoned that someday he might follow the Potowmack River all the way to the endless waters called Atlantic.

Continuing, Angus confirmed that he had spent the winter with a tribe of Shawnee at the headwaters of the West Fork River, one of the major tributaries of the Monongahela. He described how he had floated a dugout canoe with hides and pelts to the Forks of the Ohio where he traded them to a Frenchman.

Angus wondered if he had misunderstood when the Indian told him his name was Nemacolin, and stated in a friendly manner, "Call me Angus. What should I call you?"

The Indian answered, "Nemacolin. And this is my son, Lonaconda."

Angus said, "According to Christopher Gist, the trail I followed is called the Nemacolin Trail." The Indian explained that he and Thomas Cresap of Wills Creek, had been hired by the Ohio Company to blaze the trail and clear it where possible, something that Angus already knew. Nemacolin claimed that he had made many trips between the Potowmack River and the Monongahela and was more familiar with the route than anyone else. He related that buffalo had created much of the route, so he flagged those stretches that were straightest and flattest.

Angus responded, "I'm proud to meet the person who marked the trail. It's the best trail I've traveled through the wilderness." Angus hesitated and then continued, "However, there's a large tree across the trail that you should remove as soon as possible."

Nemacolin said nothing, but studied Angus carefully. It appeared that his eyes were smiling, but the beard made it impossible to determine if his lips were smiling. After a few minutes of silence, the Indian responded, "I have axe. If you want tree removed you can use axe."

Angus let out a short laugh and answered, "On my return trip to the Monongahela, I'll clear it from the trail." The Indian grinned and nodded.

Although Nemacolin demonstrated an interest in Angus's muzzle-loader, it was obvious that he was fascinated with the wolf pup. He greatly admired the wolf packs of the Appalachians, especially the cooperation they displayed when hunting and rearing their young. He concluded that this trapper named Angus must have extraordinary skills or powers if he could train such a young pup to respond to his commands. Unable to restrain his curiosity he asked, "Where you get this pup?"

Angus recounted once again the story of the half-drowned pup.

Nemacolin responded, "Never have I seen or heard of a tame wolf. You have great skills as a teacher."

"I've raised and trained several hunting dogs, and training a wolf didn't seem too different," Angus said.

Angus asked Nemacolin what type of fish he usually caught, and the Delaware answered, "Brook trout." He described the colorful fish and noted that they provided the best eating of any fish present in the river. Because they had lost their only hooks, Nemacolin indicated their disappointment at having to end their fishing trip two days early. Angus remembered that he had swapped some deerskins for fishhooks, and considered giving the hooks to Nemacolin as a gift. He reminded himself, however, that he was a trader and should trade for something of value. He told the Delaware that he had some fishhooks in his pack basket and would get them.

Angus returned with five fishhooks and showed them to Nemacolin who nodded his head, took the hooks from Angus, and invited him to join them at their camp and go fishing with them.

The memories of many pleasant fishing trips on the rivers of the Scotland prompted Angus to accept the invitation. After rounding up his two horses, Angus lifted Schatto into her basket and asked Nemacolin if his son would like to ride across the river on Buckeye. Lonacona had never ridden a horse, but showed no fear and immediately said yes. Angus assisted the youngster, climbed into his own saddle, and the small party slowly crossed the river.

CHAPTER TWENTY-ONE
BROOK TROUT AND MORELS

THE INDIANS' CAMP CONSISTED of a small lean-to covered with wide strips of bark they had removed from a large tulip poplar. After unpacking the horses, Angus spread his bearskin at a fairly level site where he and Schatto would sleep. Nemacolin provided one of the extra horsehair fishing lines and long, limber saplings he and his son had brought with them, and in no time they had three fishing outfits rigged and ready to go. With a few hours of daylight remaining, Nemacolin predicted that they could catch enough brook trout for supper.

Angus had probably caught more and larger fish than Nemacolin, but he deferred to the Indian because a fisherman familiar with a particular river could almost always catch more fish than one who had never fished there. Nemacolin explained that the colorful trout usually concentrated in pools below small waterfalls, the sites where he and his son had lost their remaining hooks.

The three fishermen spread out along the riverbank, each concentrating on a separate small pool. An hour later they had twenty brook trout lying on the bank. The trout were considerably smaller than salmon, but Angus found trout more fun to fish because of their abundance.

Three pairs of capable hands soon had ten of the trout suspended on green branches over the fire. As they cooked, Angus described the size of salmon he had caught in the rivers across the ocean. Spreading his arms about three feet apart, he indicated that many salmon were nearly that long. Nemacolin said nothing, but spread his arms as wide as they would go, nearly six feet apart, and told about catching monsters called catfish in the Monongahela and

Potowmack rivers. Angus then told of huge fish called whales, which lived in the ocean near Scotland, that were longer than the giant trees in the Appalachians were tall. Nemacolin shook his head and politely claimed that all fishermen, regardless of where they were from, were inclined to lie a little. Angus smiled and agreed that he was probably right, while remembering one of his father's favorite sayings, "Every man's tale is good till another's told."

When the flesh of the smaller fish had turned an appealing pink, Angus and his two new friends stopped talking and began eating. Schatto sat patiently until Angus began feeding her pieces of trout neatly separated from the backbone. The pup swallowed the fish as rapidly as it was offered. Lonacona asked if he could also feed Schatto, but Angus declined.

He explained, "The danger of her being stolen will be reduced if she accepts food from no one else. However, you can help me train her. Lonacona, take one piece of fish and offer it to Schatto, so I can give her a lesson."

The boy did as Angus requested, and as Schatto moved to the offered food Angus sharply commanded, "No. No." Angus asked the boy to repeat the offer, and when the pup again started to take it from his hand, he again ordered, "No. No." This time Schatto drew back and sat at Angus's side with a puzzled look on her face. After Angus had taken a few more bites of his fish, he offered a bite to the pup, and although she hesitated, she did take the fish. Angus offered another, and this time she took it without hesitation.

As Nemacolin stripped the pink trout flesh from the backbone, Angus asked him to help repeat the lesson. The Delaware offered Schatto a piece of fish and she started towards his hand, but stopped immediately when Angus rebuked her. She hesitated only briefly before accepting the piece that Angus offered. Angus remembered his grandfather's dog-training rule, "Repeat and reward, repeat and reward." They repeated the lesson one final time, and Angus made a mental note to repeat the lesson with someone else, so Schatto would learn that she was to accept food only from her master. When they had eaten their fill, the other ten trout were set over the fire to be dried for the next day.

Nemacolin announced that he had something else to add to the meal. From a small basket he removed what Angus recognized as mushrooms, although they were different from any he had ever seen. Five to six inches tall, the caps of the yellowish-brown fungi were covered with deeply wrinkled grooves. Nemacolin called them morels, and declared they were the most delicious mushrooms in the forest. He sliced them lengthwise to remove any insects in the hollow stem and cap, then inserting a small branch through each of the halves, he suspended them over the fire and handed one of the uncooked pieces to Angus and urged him to eat it. He knew that some raw mushrooms were inedible, but assumed that the Indian could recognize poisonous mushrooms.

Nibbling off small bites, Angus ate the entire half and acknowledged that they were better than any raw mushroom he had eaten. Nemacolin explained that they often cooked the mushrooms in a pot, along with pieces of trout, but they had not brought a pot on this fishing trip. Nemacolin and his son removed two of the morel slices from the fire and urged Angus to do the same. The single tidbit was enough for Angus to agree that this was, without a doubt, the best mushroom he had ever eaten. Nemacolin had sliced fifteen mushrooms and put them in the fire, and in a few minutes all were eaten.

Angus asked, "Where did you get these delicacies?" and Nemacolin explained that they grew only in certain places and only at one time of the year. If Angus wished they would go out tomorrow morning and see if they could find some more.

Sitting around the campfire after supper, Angus asked Nemacolin about the Potomac. Would there be a trading post where he could get some cornmeal and salt?

Nemacolin answered, "It has a small trading post, and they usually keep a few barrels of cornmeal and salt. If you have something to trade you should be able to pick up some supplies." The Indian explained that he had just returned from the Potowmack where only one man was at the Wills Creek trading post. He continued, "Each trip to the Potowmack, I see many more settlers. Most follow the river to the rich bottomlands where they clear trees and build farms." Nemacolin stated that he was pleased when the trading post was first constructed, but now deer and elk were fewer in number.

The two planned their schedule for the next morning, and Angus announced he would check on his horses, and then retire. Shadows from the campfire flickered over the trunks of massive tulip poplars as Nemacolin and Lonacona crawled into their lean-to. Angus and Schatto crawled under their elk skin atop the soft bearskin. It had been another good day.

Deer meat and leftover trout provided the day's start before Nemacolin led the way around the hillside to a stand of white oaks. He demonstrated that morels often grew under oaks, and that they should find more at this spot. After a few minutes, Nemacolin spotted a small morel projecting up through the leaves and pointed it out to Angus. Lonacona and his father had barely spread out when Lonacona cried, "Here's one," and then, "Here's another." The two Indians found eight before Angus spotted his first. Obviously he needed more practice detecting the camouflaged mushrooms, so Angis moved up the hillside.

As Angus picked his second, he was surprised to see Schatto sniffing at another not far away, and remembered that the raw mushroom had a distinctive odor. After putting the morels into the small basket the Indian had given him, Angus kneeled beside the pup and quietly repeated, "Morel, morel, morel." Carefully turning his back to Nemacolin and Lonacona, Angus rubbed the blue stone and again uttered, "Find morels. Find morels." Angus moved around the hillside while the pup continued to sniff at every log and every tree trunk. Angus spotted a large morel, nearly eight inches tall, and urged Schatto to move in that direction. Three feet from the morel, the pup started to sniff more vigorously, and moved directly to the mushroom. Angus knelt beside her, chuckling to himself, picked the morel, and again rubbed the blue stone while repeating, "Find morels. Find morels."

An hour later, Angus, Nemacolin, and Lonacona rejoined and compared baskets. The Indians were surprised to see that Angus had collected nearly twice as many as they had. Nemacolin was obviously stymied with the results, and Angus realized he could not let the Indians think he was a better morel hunter than they were. He announced, "I found only a few of the morels, Schatto found most of them." This caused even more disbelief and a frown appeared on the Indians' faces. Angus knew that Schatto would have to demonstrate her morel-sniffing ability if feelings were to be smoothed. He asked Nemacolin to take them to another oak stand, ordered Schatto to "Heel," and the mushroom-hunting party headed higher up on the hillside.

Nemacolin had been coming to this particular spot for several years and was aware of several oak stands that were likely to have morels. As they entered the oak stand, Angus turned his back to the Indians, removed a morel from his basket with one hand while fingering the blue stone in his pouch, and commanded Schatto, "Find morels. Find morels." Before anyone had time to speak, she located one and looked back at the three. She located another, and then twelve more. The Indians were dumbfounded! Watching her locate and retrieve the old deer antler was an impressive feat, but seeing her sniff out morels was almost more than they could fathom. Nemacolin was speechless and could do no more than shake his head in disbelief.

As they returned to camp, it occurred to Nemacolin that even more amazing than Schatto's performance was Angus's ability to train her. Till now he had felt that few, if any, white men had outdoor skills to rival Indians. He wondered whether this frontiersman was equally talented in all outdoor skills. If so, friendship with such a man could be important some time in the future.

The morels were safely stored at the camp before the three picked up their fishing gear and headed for the river. Nemacolin led them to a new stretch of river, where the trout were just as hungry today as the day before. Thirty trout flopped around in their baskets as the fishermen returned to camp. Nemacolin proposed they dry enough to take with them, and Angus agreed that dried trout would make a tasty alternative to dried venison. Although their mid-day meal was identical to that of the previous evening, no one complained about eating two of the most delectable foods in the Appalachian forests.

While waiting for the remainder of the fish to dry, Nemacolin issued an invitation and detailed directions to his cabin. Angus disclosed he would go to the Wills Creek trading post and then on to Lancaster. Without going into details, he remarked that he would spend the summer with a gunsmith and would make a new muzzle-loader.

Angus failed to mention Heather, but he hoped a message from her was waiting at the gunsmith's in Lancaster. If not, he would send several more letters to Philadelphia and Scotland in an attempt to establish contact. He would also arrange with someone in Lancaster to bank his gold or ship it to Philadelphia.

Angus noticed a bow and a quiver full of arrows hanging in Nemacolin's lean-to. Angus asked if Nemacolin would be willing to trade for a couple arrows. The Delaware replied, "Of course, what do you have to trade?" Reaching into one of his pack baskets, Angus pulled out fishing hooks, an axe, a knife, and a fire-starting steel. After some friendly bartering, Angus agreed to trade ten fishing hooks and the axe for six arrows.

The arrows, with sharper points, straighter shafts, and better feather fletching, were higher quality than those he had retrieved from the dead Iroquois. Angus felt that he had missed all the gray squirrels because the arrows were poor quality. All hunters, however, looked for excuses for missed shots. While Nemacolin was getting the better part of the bargain, Angus had acquired much valuable knowledge from the Delaware and was banking goodwill for the future.

Now that the trading was over, Nemacolin asked Angus, "Why do you want arrows?" Angus had been hesitant about showing Nemacolin his bow and arrows because he did not want to explain where he got them. As Angus unwrapped the bow and arrows, Nemacolin studied them carefully but said nothing. Angus thought he could detect a hint of a frown on his brow. Wondering whether the Delaware could see they had been made by an Iroquois, he mentioned that he planned to use the bow for hunting and thus save his gunpowder. Holding one particular arrow at arm's length and sighting down its length, Nemacolin commented, "This arrow is crooked as a dog's hind leg. You couldn't hit the side of a wegiwa with it."

Angus inserted his new arrows in the quiver and with a friendly smile responded, "I'll use your arrows from now on, and will eat squirrel every meal."

Arising from the campfire, Angus gathered his horses and prepared for departure. He told Nemacolin that he was eager to reach the Potomac, but he would visit Nemacolin's cabin later that summer, on his way back to the Monongahela. With Schatto in her pack basket, Buckeye tied securely behind Night Fog, and the muzzle-loading rifle in his hand, Angus swung astride the gray mare. Nemacolin and Lonacona waved good-bye as Angus urged Night Fog away from the river along the trail named for the native he had just met.

The Delaware and his son returned to the campfire and began discussing Angus and his wolf pup. Nemacolin proclaimed, "I'm glad you're with me, my son, because no one would believe my stories of the wolf if you didn't tell them that you also saw it with your own eyes." Little did Angus know that he and his wolf pup were about to become legend throughout the central Appalachians.

The trail began to ascend shortly after crossing the Youghiogheny, and Angus reached the crest of the first of two mountains he must cross before descending to the Potomac. Early that afternoon Angus reached the highest mountain in the area, one that came to be called Big Savage. All the mountains ran from southwest to northeast, thus he crossed the ridges at an angle rather than directly across. Angus now left the horses at the edge of an opening, took Schatto, and climbed on foot to a boulder-strewn overlook. From that vantage point he could see two smaller ridges ahead, but both appeared to have breaches where streams had cut across, and in so doing created deep gaps.

Panoramic vistas were rare in the Monongahela region. Mountains were tree-covered and seldom were there openings through which Angus could view the smooth ridges blending one into the other, like storm waves on a large lake. The rugged splendor brought to mind one of his mother's favorite sayings, "These mountains are as easy to look at as a rainbow after an evening thunderstorm."

On the eastern slope of Big Savage Mountain, the trail followed small streams that cut through gaps in the mountains, and by late afternoon Angus reached the stream called Wills Creek. Nemacolin had described the stream as flowing directly into the Potowmack, after passing through a spot he termed the Narrows. As Angus followed the trail along Wills Creek, the steep hills on opposite sides of the creek began to crowd in tighter and tighter, until there was shoreline only on the trailside of the creek, and near-vertical cliff walls shut out all but the noonday sun. An hour later, however, a broad vista suddenly sprawled like a fan before Angus, and he realized he was looking at the Potomac River basin. Nemacolin had described water in the river near the mouth of Wills Creek as low enough to cross over to the trading post constructed by the Ohio Company.

The ever-wary Angus decided to spend the night on the north side of the Potomac where the town of Cumberland, Maryland, would eventually be built. He selected a spot off the trail at the base of one of the many high hills bordering Wills Creek, hobbled the horses, and set up camp. As darkness spread across the broad Potomac Valley, Angus and Schatto enjoyed each other's company and their evening meal. Angus amended his deerskin map, showing the locations of mountain ridges, gaps, and streams encountered that day.

A southerly breeze carried smoke up Wills Creek from the trading post, verifying the presence of people. Angus would cross early the next morning and spend the day getting to know the traders and the possibility of selling his furs and hides there the following year.

CHAPTER TWENTY-TWO
THE POTOMAC

─────────────────────

As the horses splashed across the Potomac from Maryland, Angus studied the small settlement on the Virginia side of the river. Blue smoke drifted out of the crude stone chimney built on one end of the log cabin, and a door facing the river stood open. A large open window flanked the door on both sides, addressing a heat buildup from a cooking fire inside. Two bark lean-tos were attached to the ends of the cabin. Four horses and two milk cows grazed in a clearing along the river. A small bark building was situated on the sloping hillside behind the cabin. Passing two beached canoes, Angus guided the horses up the southern bank of the Potomac towards the cabin. In customary greeting, he stopped the horses halfway to the building and called, "Hello, hello."

A short, stocky man appeared at the door and responded, "Come on up to my warehouse."

As Angus tied the horses to the porch railing, it became obvious that the Ohio Company had intended this trading post to be permanent. The warehouse was nearly three times as large as the temporary cabin the French had erected at the Forks of the Ohio, and the spaces between logs had been fully chinked with moss and mud to keep out cruel winter winds. Whereas the chimney on the French cabin had been constructed of mud and sticks, this one was solidly built of large stones. The wide front porch, which ran the complete length of the structure, was designed to protect both people and goods from the elements. The man on the porch announced, "I'm Edward Beatty. What's your name?"

The man was obviously English. Although Angus was relieved

to communicate easily with him, he harbored resentment towards most Englishmen. The cruel injustices inflicted on the Scottish Highlanders by the English were impossible to forget. The Scotsman answered, "Angus, Angus McCallander."

After exchanging handshakes, the two entered the log structure, and Angus was impressed with its internal design. One end was walled off to provide sleeping quarters and the opposite end, where the fireplace was located, was obviously the cooking and eating area. The central portion contained several long tables, while shelves along the back wall provided additional storage. Wooden barrels and several large crocks sat along one wall, and an endless array of pegs projected from the walls and rafters.

Edward explained, "This trading post doesn't amount to much now, but the Ohio Company plans to greatly expand the warehouse later this year. They also want to add a large residence, a stable, a meat house, cellars, and storage facilities for furs within the next couple years."

Angus then asked, "What trade goods do you have available? I need salt, cornmeal, and fishhooks. However, I have no furs left to trade."

Edward had been eyeing the fine muzzle-loader and asked Angus if he would be able to supply him with some fresh venison. He explained, "My partners took a load of furs down the Potomac, and I'm almost out of meat. I've been so busy repairing the warehouse that I haven't had time to hunt." He did not add that his own muskets were so inefficient that he had to stalk quite close to an animal to be certain of killing it. He had never seen a muzzle-loader like Angus,' but he thought it must be much more effective than a short-barreled musket. Edward went on to say that the small cabin behind the warehouse was a smokehouse, and Angus jumped at the chance to shoot a deer for trade.

As expected, questions arose about Schatto, who had followed him into the cabin and now sat obediently at his side. Though he would have preferred to guard the pup's identity, her wolf features were too obvious to hide. He had no compunction about lying, if the occasion dictated, but there was no real reason to hide Schatto's species. So once again the story was repeated.

Angus now inquired, "Where's a good place to hunt?" Edward suggested that Angus follow the Potomac River back upstream, where there were always deer and elk feeding on flat floodplains along either side of the river. Reluctant to leave his pack baskets and the hidden gold, Angus said he would take both horses and thus should be able to carry all the meat back in one trip. He suggested that Edward gather all the wood needed to smoke a deer and have it ready when he returned.

Placing Schatto in her basket, Angus mounted Night Fog and headed upstream, following the big bend in the river. Even though much of the floodplain bordering the Potomac was wooded, Angus passed through several small openings. Mid-day was one of the most difficult times to hunt deer, but Angus was confident.

After an hour of leisurely travel, during which time Angus passed several does with fawns, five velvet-antlered deer came into view. Though their antlers were not even half grown, they were adults. Quickly dismounting and tying Schatto to a tree, Angus began his stalk. Using trees to screen his outline, as he had done hundreds of times, he quickly approached to within shooting range of the small group. Carefully selecting the smallest antlered deer, which he reasoned would be the most tender, Angus held his rifle barrel against the side of a tulip poplar and gently squeezed the trigger. As expected, the deer collapsed on the ground while the others fled through the woods.

Quickly and efficiently, Angus skinned the deer, removed the backstraps, hams, and shoulders, wrapped them in the deer hide, and secured the bundle on Buckeye. With a bulging belly and a bloody muzzle, the pup was lifted into her basket and soon fell asleep as Angus guided the horses back to the Ohio Company warehouse. He would have brought the carcass back with him, so that Schatto could have the experience of chewing meat from the bones, but it was too bloody and messy to haul on the horses. The abandoned carcass would certainly not go to waste, and by the next day little would be left. If a bear or mountain lion found it they would eat all they could hold, then haul the remains away and bury them for the next day's meal. If foxes or bobcats found the carcass, however, they would race to remove what they could before the turkey vultures arrived. One vulture would be followed by a second, then a third, and in a few hours ten or twenty would be scavenging the carcass.

Warm weather dictated that the venison be quickly cut into strips and hung over the low fire in the smokehouse. Back at the cabin, Edward started a fire in the smokehouse and then fried some of the meat for their lunch. Meanwhile Angus hung the hams and shoulders in the dense hickory smoke to repel the flies, and efficiently sliced the backstraps into long, thin strips. By the time he had those strips hanging in the smoke, Edward had finished cooking the liver, and the two sat down to a relaxing meal on the porch of the cabin. Angus asked about travel on the river from Wills Creek to the Chesapeake Bay and Edward described it as being passable, but dangerous in several places. He said they preferred to haul their furs to the coast by horseback, to avoid upsetting a boat and losing the entire load of valuable cargo.

Taking little time to share stories, Edward and Angus finished their meal and hurried to the smokehouse. With two sharing the duties, it took only an hour to transform the two hams and two shoulders into narrow strips of bright red meat that would quickly turn dark reddish brown as the smoke and heat drove out most of the moisture. Comfortable with the Englishman's company, Angus decided to spend the night at the warehouse before continuing on to Lancaster.

That evening Edward detailed the history of the area, or at least as much as he knew. In the early 1700s a large Shawaneese (Shawnee) village, numbering more than a thousand Indians, was located along that section of the Potomac. The village, which was known as Shawaneese Oldtown, had been abandoned when the Indians were forced westward by the influx of early settlers. Wills Creek had been named for Chief Will, one of the few Shawnee to remain after his people moved westward.

Angus asked about Thomas Cresap, who according to Nemacolin had a cabin along the river. Edward replied that the Cresap cabin was located near the mouth of the South Branch of the Potomac; whereas their warehouse was located on the North Branch of the

Potomac. Because the North Branch entered rugged mountains about fifteen miles from Wills Creek, that particular arm of the Potomac offered little to a settler wanting to farm. In contrast, the South Branch flowed for nearly 100 miles through a broad valley. The fertile bottomlands along the South Branch had already attracted numerous settlers.

Angus mentioned his fifty acres, awarded by William Penn for fulfilling his indentured servitude, and expressed regret that he could not claim lands in Virginia. A light rain began falling while the Englishman and Scotsman sat on the porch exchanging information. As the mountains across the river faded from view Angus bid his host goodnight, and he and Schatto moved off the porch to the bark lean-to where they shared a bear hide. As rain blocked the usual night sounds, Angus noted that his arrival at the Potomac River marked successful passage through the most rugged portions of the Allegheny Mountains.

The lean-to faced east and the faint graying of the sky announced to Angus that it was time to rise and start another day. The rain had stopped, so Angus decided to reinforce some basic training. Ordering Schatto to stay, he picked up Night Fog's bridle and walked down to the riverbank where he turned and called, "Come, Schatto, come." Eagerly she leapt from the lean-to and ran full speed to his side. Angus dropped to one knee, rewarded her with a small piece of dried elk, and commanded, "Heel, Schatto, heel."

The two then worked their way along the riverbank to where the horses were grazing. After running his hands affectionately over the two mares, Angus removed their hobbles and attached the bridle to the gray. He placed the reins in the pup's mouth and slowly stepping away, ordered, "Schatto, bring Night Fog. Bring Night Fog." The wolf chewed lightly on the reins but made no effort to pull the gray mare. Angus fingered the blue stone and repeated the command and began walking towards the cabin. Schatto grasped the reins and followed Angus with the horse. Although the brown mare was not tied to the gray, she followed closely behind. In single file—Angus, Schatto, Night Fog, and Buckeye—paraded back to the cabin.

The Englishman emerged from the cabin and stared in disbelief as the quartet approached the cabin. While there were no obvious commands spoken, it was apparent that the three animals were responding in some way to Angus. Edward knew that a few, well-trained horses would follow a man, but to have a pup, only a few month's old, play such a key role was unlike anything he had ever seen or heard of. Noting the Englishman staring wide-eyed, Angus again hobbled the horses and, followed by Schatto, climbed the porch steps. The frontiersman nodded and smiled as he announced, "I'll eat a little of that deer venison we smoked yesterday and then head on downriver to the Cresap farm."

As the two men ate pieces of smoked backstrap and Schatto chewed on some of the leftover liver, Edward could no longer restrain his curiosity and asked, "How did you ever teach such a young pup to obey your commands?"

Angus casually answered, "I've trained many pups in my life, and this wolf is smarter than any of my dogs. She still has lots to learn, but I try to give her one short training session each day. Hopefully, by the time she's full grown she will understand all my commands." The answer did not satisfy Edward, but his life on the frontier had taught him not to pry too deeply into another person's life.

Angus guided Night Fog to the Potomac and the group retraced their path to end up once again on the north side of the river. Edward Beatty had informed Angus that a well-marked trail headed north to Raystown (later to be called Bedford), but he could pick up the Warrior's Trail at Shawaneese Oldtown and it would likewise take him to Raystown. Angus wanted to view the Cresap settlement located near Shawaneese Oldtown, so he reined Night Fog onto the well-marked trail headed east.

At the Wills Creek riverbank earlier that morning, Angus was astonished by thousands of birds flying towards the west and the south. The spectacular flights continued, and birds flew so low over the trail that Angus could easily distinguish the small head and neck, long pointed tail, elongated wings, and beautiful plumage. He had seen similar huge flocks the previous fall as he traveled from Lancaster to the Monongahela, and identified them as passenger pigeons. If there had been any doubt about their identity, the speed, grace, and maneuverability with which they flew would have confirmed his initial identification. Numbers steadily increased, and Angus estimated that tens of thousands passed overhead that morning along the Potomac.

Angus vividly remembered one especially vast flock of passenger pigeons from the previous fall. Like a strong wind disturbing the treetops, he had been alerted to their approach by the loud whisper of their wings. The sky darkened as if a heavy rain cloud were passing in front of the sun, and the huge flock of birds suddenly came into view. The dense mass continued flying overhead all that morning and halfway into the afternoon without even one small break. The passing flock was so wide that Angus could not see the outer edges. The huge flocks of waterfowl coursing over Delaware Bay and others migrating down the Susquehanna River were paltry compared to the one flock of passenger pigeons passing through central Pennsylvania on that day. He concluded that the sum of all the birds he had seen during his entire life, including those in both Scotland and America, would not equal that one flock of passenger pigeons.

Angus would have been amazed to learn that some flocks of passenger pigeons numbered in the billions, more than he or any human could comprehend. He would have been even more astonished to learn that the very last passenger pigeon on earth— one named Martha—would die in the Cincinnati Zoo in 1914.

CHAPTER TWENTY-THREE
THE PIGEON HARVEST

By MID-MORNING THE CRESAP settlement appeared, and Angus was surprised to see four log structures, in addition to one stone-and-log structure that resembled a small fort. As they neared a cabin, he spotted a boy playing with a dog near the front porch. Drawing Night Fog to an abrupt halt, Angus realized that a confrontation between the dog and Schatto was likely to occur. Schatto had been running alongside the horses, and Angus quickly dismounted and ordered her to sit.

Slowly moving closer to the boy and the dog, Angus concluded that the dog, although nearly twice the size of Schatto, was not yet an adult. Calling, "Hello, hello," Angus ordered the wolf pup to heel and she quickly responded. Fortunately, "heeling" was a natural behavior for members of a wolf pack that typically follow slightly behind their leader.

A tall, lanky man, sporting a thick black beard, came out of the cabin onto the porch. He called, "Come in, stranger." Upon hearing Angus call, the dog had stopped playing and stared curiously at the group coming up the trail. When Angus was within three horse-lengths, the young dog ran towards Schatto, stopping a body length away. Schatto nervously edged behind Angus and pressed tightly against his leg. Interpreting the young dog's actions as playful, rather than aggressive, Angus relaxed somewhat. The dog inched forward, touched Schatto's nose, and then begin running rapidly around Angus. After the second circle, Schatto began chasing the dog and it appeared that no fight would occur. However, a few minutes later the dog growled, jumped at the pup and nipped her on the rump.

Schatto immediately dropped onto the ground, rolled onto her back, and in so doing exposed her throat—the most vulnerable part of her body. Angus recognized her submissive posture and assumed that instinct had caused her to react as a wolf would to a dominant animal. Such behavior prevented fighting, yet still maintained the strong bond that was so essential to the social structure of a pack. The dog sniffed Schatto's neck, belly, and rear and then backed off. The submissive posture had prevented an attack, and in so doing prevented injury to both individuals.

Angus asked, "Are you Thomas Cresap?"

The man answered, "Yes, I am, and this is my son, Michael." He called into the cabin, and a woman and a skinny, blond-haired girl came onto the porch. Thomas said, "This is my wife, Hannah, and my daughter, Sarah."

Angus stepped onto the porch and introduced himself, "I'm Angus, Angus McCallander."

Thomas Cresap responded, "I met a trader named Robert Callander who said he was from Scotland. Are you related to him?"

Angus answered, "Not that I know of, but there are many Callanders and McCallanders in Scotland. Some spell their name with an 'a', and some with an 'e'. There is even one small town named Callander in central Scotland, east of Loch Loman."

Always curious about youngsters, and wanting to compare the Cresap children with the Dunkard children, Angus asked, "How old are your two children?"

Eva answered, "Michael is eleven and Sarah is thirteen." Hearing all the voices, Schatto and the dog came up on the porch and the wolf pup immediately began sniffing around the feet of the young girl. With pleasant memories of the German girl who had been so kind to her, Schatto expected the same treatment from this girl. In no time, Sarah was petting Schatto, and, much to the chagrin of her brother, she was the obvious favorite of the wolf pup.

Angus explained that he had come from Wills Creek, where he had spent the night at Edward Beatty's warehouse. He also mentioned meeting Chief Nemacolin, who suggested that Angus stop and visit with Thomas Cresap. Angus asked about the trail to Lancaster and was told to follow the Warrior's Path north to Raystown and then the Raystown Path east to the Susquehanna River. From there it was a short distance downstream to Lancaster. He should reach Raystown in one day, and the Susquehanna River in four to five days.

While sitting on the porch, Angus asked about the passenger pigeons flying over the river, and Tom Cresap acknowledged that a flock was nesting about two miles away. The birds crossing the river were the parent birds. Every morning the adults left the roost and spread out into the surrounding mountains in search of food, most preferably beechnuts. On their return to the roost area, called the "nesting," the adults fed the young squabs in the nests.

Tom explained, "For the first seven days of their lives the adults do not feed them beechnuts, but instead they feed them a substance called pigeon milk." Cresap was an amateur naturalist, who enjoyed sharing his knowledge and explained that the lining of the crop, that enlarged sac in the neck typically used to store food, sloughed off during the period the adults were brooding the young. The resultant thick, cheese-curd substance was pumped from the adult's throat into the young squab's mouth and constituted the only food they received during the first week of life. For the last seven days of the fourteen-day brood period their diet included seeds and small nuts.

Thomas Cresap described how some of the local Delaware Indians had discovered the near-by passenger pigeons nesting and for the past week had been hunting the birds—wood pidgeons they called them. Tom and his son, Michael, were going to the nesting that morning and Angus was welcome to come along. They would use horses to haul the harvested birds back to the Cresap settlement in pack baskets. Warning Angus that it was a messy job, Tom offered him a set of old, nearly worn-out clothes, including an old broad-brimmed hat. Angus could not imagine why he would need old clothes, since the deerskins he wore were already scratched, torn, and stained. However, he had learned not to question the actions of an experienced settler, and he readily accepted the offer. Angus did not need any more meat, but he did want to witness the nesting and learn how the Indians hunted this superabundant bird. He had never eaten a passenger pigeon but was always eager to try something new.

Because of the shooting and other activities associated with hunting the passenger pigeons, Angus had decided it would be best if he left Schatto at the Cresap settlement. Confident that the pup would cause no trouble, Angus asked Sarah if she would keep Schatto while he went on the hunt. As he had expected, she quickly agreed—pleased to show her brother that Angus considered her to be dependable. Instructing Angus on what to take, Thomas Cresap suggested, "I'll take my shotgun, but you won't need your rifle, since it would be of little use in collecting birds. All you need is a small axe, your horses, and the pack baskets."

With Angus, Thomas, and Michael each riding horses and each leading a packhorse carrying two pack baskets, they left the settlement and headed into the nearby mountains. As they rode, Tom told Angus that he had hunted passenger pigeons the previous fall, killing a hundred birds with one shot. A flock had flown so low over his cabin that he simply fired his shotgun into the middle of the mass and pigeons started falling out of the sky like leaves falling from a tree during an October windstorm. His family had feasted on grilled pigeon, fried pigeon, roasted pigeon, and smoked pigeon for several weeks.

As they moved up the hillside Angus began to notice pigeons landing in the trees overhead, and the first nests came into view. They were passing through oak woods, and Angus counted ten to twenty nests on the lower branches of every tree. Based on the flight paths of pigeons, he knew there were countless nests in the upper branches as well. Tom Cresap indicated that they were headed for a stand of hemlocks where the nests were more concentrated and closer to the ground. As they approached a small stream flowing down off the hillside, Angus spotted the stand of evergreens growing in the damp soil along the stream.

The hemlocks, like most conifers, had branches growing lower to the ground than oaks, tulip poplars, and black cherries. Several giant oaks lying on the ground blocked their route to the hemlock stand, and it was necessary for them to detour slightly. Cresap explained that the enormous weight of the roosting birds the previous fall had broken off many limbs and in some cases entire trees. He estimated that thousands of birds nested in each tree, either desiring or requiring the security provided by other birds.

As a plaintive chorus of coos drifted through the forest, Angus loudly repeated the Bible verse that his mother had read every spring in Scotland, "Flowers appear, the time of singing of birds arrives, and the voice of the turtle is heard in the land."

Thomas Cresap responded, "I know that verse quite well, my mother also used to read it to me. Many people think the reference to the voice of the turtle means a four-legged, hard-shelled reptile, but obviously you know it refers to turtle doves."

Nearing the hemlocks, Angus watched several Indians jabbing long poles into the lower branches. It was evident they were after the young in the nests rather than the adults. Tom said that the Indians did not kill adult birds because they feared they would not return in following years.

Angus knew right away why he had been urged to wear old clothes and a broad-brimmed hat. The forest floor was blanketed with pigeon dung, and the air was filled with falling squishy pigeon droppings. After tying the horses a short distance from the hemlock stand, Thomas Cresap showed Angus how to cut the longest, straightest sapling he could find. Because the mature hardwood forest contained few saplings, they were forced to find a natural blow-down area where sunlight had opened the forest floor and produced a thicket of tulip poplar saplings. With a few whacks of his axe, Angus soon brought down a sapling that was the thickness of his upper arm and nearly four times his height.

By watching the Indians, he saw there was little skill required. Anyone who could hold a long pole could collect pigeons! One of the women would jab her pole into the bottom of a pigeon nest, while a youngster would grab the young pigeon as it fell to the ground. After a quick and fatal twist of the neck, the squab was dropped into a basket. Angus was surprised to see some of the men shooting arrows into the nests and wondered if he should have brought his bow. On closer investigation, he saw that the arrows were blunted with leather and were intended to knock the squabs out of the nests rather than penetrate their bodies.

After moving some distance from the Indians, Angus and Thomas began poking the young squabs out of the nests while Michael retrieved them and loaded the pack baskets. The nests were flimsy affairs, constructed of a few twigs and small sticks lodged into the fork of a branch. Even though they were not woven into a solid bowl, like most bird nests, they were adequate to prevent the eggs from falling through. The nesting had been so synchronized that almost every nest held a single squab, but occasionally one contained a female incubating an egg. The hunters avoided these nests. Angus never found a nest with more than one squab and surmised that passenger pigeons rarely laid more than one egg.

Two hours later, each of their pack baskets was brimming over with squabs, so heavy that two men were required to load each basket onto a horse. Following the small brook, Thomas Cresap led the group down the hill to a site where the Delaware Indians had set up camp. Kettles were suspended over three fires, and seven more fires were being used to smoke squabs. When a basket was filled with squabs it was carried to the fires, the crop and entrails were removed from each bird, and the carcasses were either hung on branches over the smoky fire or dropped into kettles of boiling water.

Thomas explained that squabs were fatter and heavier than adults. As soon as they began to fly they would burn the stored body fat, and emerge as streamlined as the adults. The oil that was cooked out of the fat young squabs floated to the top of the boiling water, and the Indians used wooden dippers to transfer it from the kettles to smaller containers. Once cooled, the creamy substance partially solidified into a substance called squab butter, and was used for cooking. Angus also noticed some of the older women rubbing the butter onto their hands, faces, and feet, apparently as a softening agent.

Thomas Cresap stated that the nesting season typically lasted three to four weeks, and the Indians would remain at the site until squabs began to fly from the nests. Because the majority of the nests were high in the treetops, well out of reach of the prodding poles and even the arrows, the Indians would harvest an insignificant portion of nestlings. The adult pigeons would remain in the immediate area until all the squabs were capable fliers—a period of one to two weeks after brooding. Then the entire population formed one huge flock of nearly a million birds to crisscross the countryside in search of ripening fruits, berries, and nuts, often traveling hundreds of miles in a day. This particular flock might move south into Virginia or north into the massive black cherry forests of upper Pennsylvania.

Thomas, Angus, and Michael reached the Cresap settlement by early afternoon, and, after washing the squabs in the river, they immediately set fires in the smokehouse and under two large black kettles. Like the Delawares, they would smoke half of the squabs and boil the remainder to harvest the squab butter. Having none of the snow-white pig lard preferred for baking by cooks, Hannah Cresap and her young daughter would substitute squab butter for pies and cakes.

The cooking and smoking needed no further attention, so the disgustingly soiled hunters gathered a change of clothing and headed for the river. After wading into the water, all three removed their clothes and began scrubbing their bodies with sand to rid themselves of the day's accumulation of nasty pigeon droppings. The broad-rimmed hat provided by Thomas had kept Angus's head fairly clean, but gazing upward to locate nests resulted in countless droppings splattered onto his face and beard. Satisfied that he had finally removed most of the smelly dung, Angus began scrubbing his moccasins. At last he gave up trying to remove the dingy white stain, concluding that hours of walking in pigeon dung had stained them permanently. They were still wearable, but he would have to craft a new pair from one of his tanned elk skins.

Though the cooking and smoking operations were somewhat messy, they were not difficult, and by early evening a tired crew sat down to a supper of smoked squab and cornmeal mush fried in squab butter. Angus questioned whether smoked squab was as good as wild turkey grilled over an open campfire, but he agreed that it was a fine alternative to smoked venison. Hannah apologized for not having any dessert, but explained that they had run out of flour several months ago. It would be late summer before several barrels would arrive from eastern Pennsylvania.

Angus told Hannah about the pie with a crust of chestnut meal and acorn flour that he had eaten at the Dunkards, but did not tell that Katrina had baked it. Hannah commented, "Grinding chestnuts and acorns into meal is a lot of work, but Michael and Sarah are old enough to do most of the grinding." Although the two youngsters enjoyed pies and cakes as much as did the others, they immediately complained that they already had more chores than they could handle and did not need any more.

Michael added, "I'd rather eat chestnuts that have been roasted beneath hot coals. Those soft, sweet treats taste better than old dried-out chestnuts."

Sarah commented, "I prefer to simmer dried chestnuts with venison, and they are softened enough that anyone can eat them."

Angus asked Hannah, "Where is the rest of your family? Christopher Gist said you had five children."

The woman answered, "Our son Tom and oldest daughter, Elizabeth, are visiting friends who live along the South Branch. Our oldest son, Daniel, is hunting a panther up on the mountain west of here. That big cat killed one of our pigs night before last and Daniel took his old hound to track it down. Daniel has a small hunting cabin where he often stays and could be gone for a couple weeks. He spends so much time up there that we call it Dan's Mountain."

Angus and Schatto spent that night in one of the bark-covered storage buildings. In the morning, after getting directions from Thomas Cresap, they headed north along the Warrior's Path towards the settlement of Raystown. Tom had said it was about twenty-five miles, but was easy travel. Raystown was northeast of Wills Creek, and, because the mountains ran southwest to northeast, the trail followed the valley between the mountain ridges. Angus would have no mountains or rivers to cross, and it would be one of the easiest trails he would follow during his entire trip.

CHAPTER TWENTY-FOUR
NORTH TO RAYSTOWN

THE NORTHEAST TRAIL FROM the Potomac ran through a broad valley and was one of the most fulfilling segments since Angus left the Forks of the Ohio. On each side were rugged mountain ridges. The trail was indeed easy, threading over and around small rounded hills that lay nestled in the heavily forested valley. A mixture of oak, chestnut, tulip poplar, and black cherry trees blocked all but a scattering of sunlight that managed to reach the forest floor. The massive trees were over six feet in diameter but so widely spaced that they posed no barrier to travel. The valley's only stream meandered from one side to the other, providing drinking water for Angus and his animals, but was easily waded when they wanted to cross. To reach the Raystown settlement by late afternoon, Angus kept the horses moving at a steady pace. Schatto alternated running alongside the horses with resting in her basket atop Night Fog.

By late afternoon Angus detected the odor of wood smoke wafting through the trees, and a short distance beyond sat a cluster of five small log cabins. Thomas Cresap had described the Raystown settlement as a small trading post, with a stable and storage buildings, a residence, and a general-purpose building where travelers could spend the night during inclement weather. As he approached, Angus heard voices floating out from the largest of the cabins. Without announcing his presence, Angus climbed the porch steps and entered the cabin. With Schatto at his side and his muzzle-loader in hand, the self-assured woodsman made a lasting impression. Six men were inside, all dressed in woolen garb, revealing they had recently come from the colonies—none wore deerskin clothing. The one standing

246

behind a long table arranging a pile of blankets greeted him, "Hello stranger, come in."

Without speaking, Angus nodded his head and moved to a table loaded with trade goods. With a penetrating gaze directed in turn at each of the men, he carefully studied the features and clothing of each individual. The one arranging blankets was middle-aged and gave the appearance of having spent more time inside a cabin than in the forest. A second middle-aged man, smoking a corncob pipe, sat on a three-legged stool. A young man, probably a contemporary of Angus, had obviously done considerable physical labor, based on his worn clothing and well-tanned face. Two men sitting together along one wall wore British-style clothing, so torn, tattered, and stained that they must have arrived recently from Philadelphia, or another city along the eastern seaboard. The sixth man carried a British musket and stowed a long-bladed knife in his belt. Angus took him to be a hunter, but not really an experienced woodsman.

"Where do you hail from?" asked the man who had spoken first. It was the custom on the frontier to ask a man where he was from, but not usually acceptable to ask his name. If a person wanted to volunteer his name that was fine, and most usually did. Angus responded that he had come from Wills Creek on the Potomac and was headed for Lancaster. Following Angus's remarks the man stated, "My name is John Wray, and I'm in charge of this trading post." Pointing to the young man, he continued, "This is my assistant, Gerald. The man with the pipe is Garret Pendergrass."

The man Angus took to be a hunter spoke up, saying, "My name is Augustin."

Because the others had given their names Angus felt somewhat obliged to respond. "I'm Angus, Angus McCallander." Angus let his gaze wander to the two men sitting together along the wall, but they sat silently. They glanced at Schatto, but their attention was obviously directed at the muzzle-loader. Angus inquired, "Is there a shelter where I can spend the night? It looks like rain is on the way." The storekeeper motioned Angus out to the porch, and from there he pointed out a bark-covered lean-to where he would be protected from the weather.

The other men, including the two who had not spoken, came onto the porch and all sat down on rough-hewn benches. "Where exactly is the trail to Lancaster?" Angus asked.

Pointing to the eastern edge of the clearing, behind two of the log structures, the storekeeper answered, "Just look for the trees with axe blazes and you cannot miss it." Gerald, the youngest of the men, spotted the bow and quiver of arrows fastened behind the saddle on Night Fog and asked if Angus hunted with it. He seemed to be a likable sort and Angus responded in a congenial way that he had been trying unsuccessfully to shoot squirrels. He added that the only thing he had actually hit, other than some small targets, was a large, black timber rattlesnake that had lain across the trail.

The older of the two men who had not yet spoken, asked somewhat brusquely, "That sure looks like a wolf. Where did you get it?" Angus identified the man as English and, without much detail, replied that he had found it nearly drowned, at the edge of the river and decided to keep it because a rattlesnake had killed his previous dog.

Gerald interjected, "We killed a big rattlesnake near the stable yesterday. It was one of the biggest I ever saw, over seven feet long."

Casual conversation, involving the weather, hunting, settlers moving westward, and numerous other topics, continued for nearly two hours. Angus learned that the Raystown Trail was well marked and he should reach Lancaster in four days. He would cross three high ridges and several smaller hills, but nothing so rugged as those he had already traversed. With heavy clouds rolling in from the south, Angus announced that he would be leaving early the next morning and moved across the porch.

As Angus passed the two men who had not volunteered their names, Schatto began to growl. It was the first time Angus had heard her growl at someone, and he was puzzled by her actions. The men had made no motions and said nothing, but something disturbed Schatto. Was it possible she could sense the mistrust that Angus felt towards them, or did she somehow use her own special senses to evaluate them? Frowning quizzically, he reminded himself of the Highlander saying, "Avoid the English as you would the devil."

Ordering the pup to heel, Angus moved off the porch to the waiting horses.

The lean-to, used to store firewood the previous winter, was not large, but was sufficient to provide all the overhead shelter Angus needed. He moved the pack baskets, the saddle, and his bearskin and elk hides into the lean-to and freed the hobbled horses to graze near the woods. With lightning flashing like fireworks over the hills to the west and rain falling on the bark roof, Angus and Schatto ate a cold supper of elk and pigeon. A dim yellow light flickered from the trading post window, and Angus knew someone had lit a candle. No lights were visible at any of the other structures, and Angus went to sleep wondering where the six men were sleeping.

A steady rain fell throughout the night, and at the first sign of dawn Angus ate a breakfast identical to dinner. He saddled Night Fog, firmly secured the pack baskets on Buckeye, loaded Schatto into her basket, and led the horses over to the cabin with the trade goods. John Wray, Garret Pendergrass, and Gerald were sitting on the porch with cups in their hands, and both gave a friendly welcome. Angus thanked them for the use of the lean-to and told them he would probably return the following October, on his way back to the Monongahela. Curious, but reluctant to ask the whereabouts of the other men, Angus casually commented, "Bid farewell to Augustin and the other two men."

John Wray responded, "Augustin went on a two-day hunting trip and left long before daylight. The other two men announced last night that they would be leaving while it was still dark but did not say what direction they were headed." Without a word, Angus nodded his head and urged Night Fog towards the Raystown Trail. The last leg of his journey had begun. The north-south trail, though not nearly so well traveled as the Raystown Trail they were following, was quite distinct. Angus stopped the horses to study and assess the trail; seeing no fresh horse tracks he urged Night Fog eastward in the direction of the Susquehanna River. The clouds eventually moved out, the sky cleared, and the rain stopped completely. The forest floor was soon dappled with sunlight as Angus spotted a large tree blocking the trail some distance ahead.

"One more tree to detour around," he thought, "but this one should cause only a slight delay."

The tree was a huge tulip poplar, with few limbs along the clean, seven-foot-diameter trunk. Angus opined that it had died several years ago, and a winter storm had brought it crashing down. Its fall had torn down several nearby trees and, as a result, a large opening was dissected from the tree canopy. The treetop, with a few remaining dead branches, lay to the right and the splintered stump lay to the left. About ten horse lengths from the tree, Angus spotted a familiar object lying in the patch of sunlight near the trunk—a snake.

Stopping the horses, Angus dismounted, leaned his rifle against a nearby tree, gently pushed the pup down into her basket, and ordered, "Stay, Schatto, stay." With the quiver of arrows over his shoulder and the bow in his left hand, Angus slowly inched towards the snake. He could not pass up such an easy opportunity to obtain fresh meat for the pup. As he stalked closer Angus identified it as a rattlesnake, but he thought it looked a little strange.

When the snake did not coil, as was their usual custom, Angus moved around it to get a better look. A rifle shot suddenly shattered the quiet, and a bullet tore through his deerskin shirt and grazed his right side, just below the last rib. As he turned and darted for the nearest cover, a second shot exploded and he heard the rifle bullet thump into the trunk of the fallen poplar. Without hesitation, Angus dived into a shallow depression in front of the tree. He grew angry at being ambushed, and shouted loudly, "Stay, Schatto, stay."

The ambush had been hatched the previous evening. The two suspicious-looking men had been fascinated by the muzzle-loader, the horses, and whatever trade goods were hidden in the pack baskets. When Angus described how he killed the rattlesnake with an arrow, the idea flashed into the older man's head. As soon as they left the cabin that evening, the two agreed to ambush the trapper on the trail to the Susquehanna. They were experienced highway thieves who used diversion as the key element of an attack. Both had been arrested in England for robbery, and had been given the choice of going to prison for five years, or being sent to the colonies where they must work as indentured servants for five years. Workers were in great demand in the colonies, and the prisons in London were overflowing. If they completed their servitude they would be awarded a horse, a new set of clothing, an axe, and fifty acres in the Pennsylvania wilderness. Although they had no desire to work at manual labor for five years and no desire to be farmers, they would choose most any alternative to five years in prison, and therefore readily accepted the servitude option.

After two years of daylight-to-dark labor, loading and unloading ships at the docks near Philadelphia, however, the two men decided they had had enough. Having violated the terms of their parole, the violators knew they would be returned to a prison in England if caught, so they fled on foot to Lancaster where they stole horses and guns. With the French in control of the area near the Forks of the Ohio, they reasoned that if they could reach the Allegheny River they would be safe from arrest. Although they had conducted most of their crimes in the English countryside, they were not woodsmen. They were accustomed to stealing their food, not hunting for it. The trip from Lancaster had been a challenge.

The fallen tree supplied a perfect spot for their ambush. After hiding the horses down over the hill, they each selected a large tree on opposite sides of the trail. They waited patiently, as they had done so many times in the English countryside, until they heard the soft plodding of horses' hooves. The older man of the two, who thought he was the best marksman, agreed to shoot first, and if he did not bring Angus down, the other man would immediately shoot. Experience had taught them that they should always kill their victim, since a dead body was better than a live enemy. Luckily for Angus, the men had little practice with their stolen muskets.

Minutes later, a third shot kicked up dirt in front of the depression where Angus lay, and he squirmed backwards until his feet touched the tree trunk. He could go no further. He had spotted the flame bursting from the barrel of the musket and knew he would be exposed in the wide open if he tried to run from the depression. While peeking over the edge of the depression, Angus spotted one of the men skulking from tree to tree until he reached his partner. Leaving his loaded musket, he went for their horses. When Angus spotted him leading the horses up over the hill he raised his head a little too high and a fourth shot thudded into the ground near his face.

The older of the Englishmen led their two horses, one black and the other dun-colored, directly to Angus's two mares. His first act was to stuff an elk skin into the basket where Schatto hid, effectively trapping her inside. Concealed behind the horses, he quickly tied the reins of Night Fog to his own black, and the lead cord of Buckeye to his partner's dun. After tying his musket to the basket in which Schatto was entrapped, he picked up Angus's muzzle-loader and quickly mounted, while his partner, carrying his own musket, joined him.

Although Angus could not hear any words they spoke, it was evident that the older man, using arm signals, was giving directions to the younger. Angus watched helplessly as the men put the horses into a gallop and were soon out of sight, headed westward in the direction of Raystown.

Rage replaced fear as the adrenaline surged, and Angus bolted from the depression, chasing wildly after the two men. Once more he had been attacked by the enemy of all Highlanders—Englishmen. Angus settled into a slow, ground-covering run and once again his mind hearkened back to the moors. He knew he could not outrun the galloping horses, but he could outlast them. With his long legs covering strides of five feet, he scanned the trail in the distance, hoping to catch a glimpse of his two attackers. Hoof prints were so prominent in the rain-soaked ground that he did not need to concentrate on the trail. Instead, he focused on treacherous stones and tree limbs.

As Angus topped over a small knoll he caught a glimpse of a gray patch moving in the distance. It was Night Fog. Had she been brown or black he would never have spotted her from that distance. Angus ran a few more steps, slid behind a nearby tree trunk, and peered attentively at the men and horses. They had stopped, and after a brief arm signal, the man on the black horse signaled his partner to go south. They knew they could not return to the Raystown settlement with Angus's horses and muzzle-loader, so they had decided the previous night to detour around the settlement and meet on the trail to the Monongahela. From there they would head north to Montreal and resume the thievery they had mastered in England.

The silvery coat of the gray mare stood out prominently against the dark background of the forest, and Angus had no difficulty determining that the older man, riding the black and leading Night Fog, had turned north. As they faded into the gloom of the forest, Angus resumed his slow run. Though he knew their direction of travel, he faced a major dilemma. His gold was headed in one direction, while his muzzle-loader and wolf pup were headed in the opposite. He had worked so hard for the gold and had so desperately wanted to pay for Heather's passage to the colonies that losing the gold made his promise meaningless. Five years of planning to bring her to America and to settle in the wondrous Appalachian wilderness were fast disappearing to the south.

From visions of Heather beside a Highlands lake and cheerfully dancing to bagpipes to memories of Schatto retrieving a deer antler, digging out a meadow vole, and leading his gray mare, Angus was provoked into a blinding rage. However, that soon passed and he began to focus on his next steps. He could build another muzzle-loader, but he could never replace Schatto. Angus was only vaguely aware of the subconscious debate that was warring within, a debate that weighed a future with Heather on a farm near the Monongahela against a future with a wolf companion exploring the Appalachian wilderness. Had he been given hours or even days to weigh the benefits of each option, Angus might have made another decision. However, he was overcome by the wisdom of his grandfather, Harry McCallander, who advised that, in a quandary, a man's first decision was usually the correct one.

As he reached the trail where the Englishmen had separated, Angus stopped to study the hoof prints made by the horses. The leaf-covered ground revealed nothing distinctive about the tracks, so he would never be able to identify them in the future. With firm resolve, the pack leader, armed only with bow and arrows, instinctively took the trail to the north—in pursuit of a treasure more valuable than gold.

Resuming the ground-covering run, Angus once again directed his attention to the path and prayed, "O Laird, who created the soaring hawk and the raindrop glistening on the thistle leaf, show me the way." After a short distance the land flattened out, and hoof prints revealed that the Englishman had urged his horse into a gallop. Rather than running faster, Angus slowed somewhat. He could never keep pace with a galloping horse and would accomplish nothing by trying. He must exercise caution and restraint.

By mid-afternoon the trail became more treacherous, and the Englishman had slowed his horse to a walk. As the landscape became even more rugged, Angus forecast that the Englishman would stop before dark. He would probably move a short distance off the trail and set up camp, but with no campfire. Where the trail crossed a small stream, Angus stopped for a much-needed drink and began to formulate a plan. With eyes closed, Angus lay prone in a soft bed of dense green moss and repeated the familiar Scottish psalm, "Neath sun or moon, by day or night, I shalt not be afraid. I to the skies will lift my eyes. O whence shall come my aid?"

As the forest darkened and the trail ahead became difficult to discern, a revitalized Angus studied the hoof prints for one last time. The Englishman was still traveling at a steady walk, and Angus calculated that one hour of travel separated them. The Englishman would need at least thirty minutes to set up his campsite and hobble the horses, thus Angus would be about one-half hour behind the Englishman when complete darkness arrived. Without urgency, Angus continued his steady and committed trek northward.

When he could no longer make out even the giant trunks of trees, he was forced to feel his way through the forest. The terrain was sloping somewhat to the east and Angus deduced that the trail would follow the same basic contour. Slowly, but patiently, Angus eased forward, like a bat using sonar. He stumbled over branches, splashed through a small stream, and banged his shin so sharply on a small boulder that he had to muffle a cry of pain by pressing his forearm into his open mouth. His gasps and moans subsided as he continued. After approximately thirty minutes, he stopped and prepared to execute the next phase of his plan.

Sitting with his back to a tree trunk, Angus removed the blue stone from the pouch that hung around his neck. He tried to visualize the scene at the Englishman's camp. In a forest clearing with grassy vegetation, the horses would be hobbled. The Englishman would be seated at the base of a tree, and Schatto would be tied securely to a tree limb or to one of the saddles. The Englishman would have studied Angus's muzzle-loader with the last traces of daylight and would have hefted it several times to his shoulder, imagining himself the envy of all who saw him. He would be greatly respected for owning such a handsome weapon. He would begin to eat some of the smoked meat from the food bag affixed to Night Fog's saddle.

Angus's concerns primarily focused on Schatto. Had she been in her basket all day? Had she been given anything to eat or drink? Was she injured? There was no doubt in his mind that she was confused and frightened.

Concentrating his thoughts intently on the wolf pup, Angus began to softly caress the blue stone. As expected, the warmth flowed unfettered into his fingers. With trancelike concentration, Angus repeated the same silent message, time after time after time, "Schatto, howl. Schatto, howl, Schatto, howl. Schatto, howl." A slight breeze was blowing from the north and hopefully would carry sounds from the Englishman's camp in Angus's direction. Still mesmerized, with eyes closed, his ears strained to detect even the faintest of sounds, Angus searched almost desperately through the background of night sounds for a response. But he detected nothing. Maintaining his concentration, Angus continued to transmit his silent message, "Schatto, howl. Schatto, howl."

Through the calls of katydids and other forest insects, a feeble little howl floated through the forest—once, twice, three times. With tears of relief welling in his eyes, Angus abruptly ceased his commands. The captor would not tolerate her protests for long.

The waning moon would not rise until near midnight. In the meantime, he would slowly press on in the direction of the howls. Keeping downwind, so that the horses would not pick up his scent, Angus inched his way towards the Englishman's camp. Fearful of stumbling into the camp in the darkness, he stopped after advancing less than two hundred yards. He was tired and hungry, but wisely had refreshed his body with cool drinking water at several small streams. Now he longed for his bearskin pallet, but resorted to stretching out in the leaves where he eventually dozed off.

After a few hours of rest, Angus sat up and stared into the darkness. Waving his hand in front of him, he thought, "It's so dark I can't see my hand in front of my face." He had heard the saying in Scotland, in Ireland, and in the colonies, and figured someone had made a similar pronouncement every place on earth where man had set foot. He smiled as he fondly remembered one of his father's favorite comparisons, "It's darker than the insides of a dead dog."

To Angus, darkness was relative, and even on the darkest of nights the stars emitted enough ambient light that one could move safely through the Scottish Highlands. This dense forest, however, was different. As the moon rose above the eastern horizon, and slowly inched towards its zenith, Angus detected small rays of light seeping through the dense overhead canopy. The clouds had long since evaporated, and the combination of moonlight and starlight held promise for completing the next phase of his plan.

Once again Angus rubbed the blue stone, concentrating deeply on the pup, and repeated silently, "Schatto, howl. Schatto howl. Schatto howl." As the urgent message entered her still-growing brain, the wolf sat up on her haunches and responded—responded as if directed by the instincts passed from generation to generation of wolves.

As she began to once again yip and bark, the Englishman arose from Angus's bearskin, threw a large tree branch in her direction, and shouted, "Shut up, you worthless hound!" He and his partner had intended to haul the pup to Montreal and trade her to Indians for furs. They speculated she would not eat much and was tame enough to handle. Now, however, he concluded that she might be more trouble than she was worth. The wolf quieted, and her abductor resumed his sleep. He had at least four hours before the journey resumed.

Angus pinpointed the direction of the howls, and promptly proceeded towards his destination. It was essential that Angus approach close enough to confront his adversary before he broke camp the next morning. If he failed, all would be lost. His entire body was on highest alert. Straining his ears to detect any sounds that might reveal the precise location of the camp, Angus began to search for the one clue that would definitely reveal its location. Inch by inch, taking care not to step on a twig, he progressed with the greatest caution possible. His thick elk hide moccasins protected his feet from sharp twigs, rocks, and chestnut burrs, while his deerskin clothing made no sounds brushing against tree trunks.

It took two more hours of patient, but focused, searching for Angus to glimpse what he was looking for—a small gray spectral figure illuminated by the moonlight. Night Fog! Just as Angus predicted, the Englishman had camped at the edge of a natural opening so that the horses could graze. The opening in the forest canopy permitted moonlight and starlight to filter through to the ground and illuminate the gray coat of Night Fog.

Approaching as close as he dared, Angus sat down behind a smooth-barked tree, which he identified as a beech. When the first faint daylight filtered through the trees, the Englishman would be loaded and on his way. With only an hour to go before the first signs of daylight, Angus chose the best of the arrows that he had gotten from Nemacolin—one with extra long fletching and extra-sharp flint.

Time passed slowly, with few sounds other than an occasional snore from the Englishman. The stalker's night vision was optimal, as the first calls of songbirds signaled that dawn was approaching. With the earliest sign of stirring in the camp, Angus slowly and deliberately slipped the nock of his arrow into the bowstring and held the smooth wooden shaft against the center of the curved bow. With eyes closed, the better to concentrate his sense of hearing, Angus visualized the actions taking place less than thirty yards away. When it was obvious that the horses had been saddled and the baskets loaded, Angus cautiously peered out around the edge of the tree where he sat. With resurging anger he watched the Englishman grab the pup by the scruff of the neck, forcefully shove her into the bottom of her basket, and stuff an elk skin in on top of her. Like a shadow emerging from sunlight, Angus rose from his knees to a standing position and confidently readied the bow.

The Englishman held Angus's muzzle-loader in his right hand, slipped his left foot into the stirrup, and swung his right leg over the back of his horse as Angus stepped out from the tree's silhouette and quietly ordered, "Stop! Drop the rifle!" In one fluid motion, the Englishman turned his head to locate the source of the voice, swung the rifle to his shoulder, and pointed it in Angus's direction. Had he been carrying his short-barreled musket he might have gotten off a well-aimed shot, but the long-barreled muzzle-loader was an awkward substitute. The weapon that would have given him the advantage when fighting from a distance now restricted his movements. He did manage to jerk the trigger, but even before the bullet thudded harmlessly into the dirt, Nemacolin's arrow sliced through the man's buttock and shattered his hipbone. Screams of pain broke the thick silence of the forest. An expression of shock and agony covered the thief's contorted face, as the flint arrowhead entered its intended target.

Angus did not want to kill the Englishman, at least not before he learned where the two partners planned to rendezvous. He intended to disable the thief so that he could not escape. The muzzle-loader slipped slowly from his hands and fell onto the leaves as the bawling Englishman slumped over his saddle in agony. Angus had a second arrow notched into the bowstring, ready for shooting even before the heavy body thudded helplessly to the ground. As he dashed to his fallen adversary, Angus felt no apprehension of danger, confident his arrow had accomplished its mission. Angus stood over the vanquished abductor. As he squatted beside the grimacing, writhing Englishman lying awkwardly beside the black horse, the poor fellow grasped the offending arrow as blood soaked his woolen leggings.

As the maimed Englishman cursed the "bloody Scot," Angus ignored his anguish and removed the elk skin from Schatto's basket as he began talking to her. "Good girl, Schatto, good girl. Ye're a bonnie lass! It's all over now." After much petting, tail wagging, face licking, and head scratching, the two sat quietly at the base of a tree, with Schatto pressing tightly against her master's leg.

Approaching the wounded man, Angus asked, "Where will you be meeting your partner, English?"

With a snarl on his face, the man spat out through clenched teeth, "Pull out this arrow and I'll tell you."

Angus had no wish to get close enough to the man to grasp the arrow, even though he appeared harmless. "Nay English! You go first and then I'll take the arrow. And if you take too much time, I'll let the wolf start licking your wound." The two remained silent for several minutes, during which time the Englishman's woolen leggings became thoroughly soaked. The spurting continued, creating a bright red pool of blood in the leaves. The wolf pup, excited by the sight and smell of fresh blood, crouched nearby. Slowing sliding his hunting knife from the sheath, Angus held the imposing weapon with its bear jaw handle directly in front of the Englishman's face. Slowly and deliberately Angus moved behind the man, then quickly pushed the knife's sharp tip deep into his ear. As the wounded man shrieked in pain, Angus calmly restated his question. "Where's the meeting place, English?"

When no answer was given, Angus placed the knife tip in the other ear.

Now in excruciating pain, the man screamed, "Stop! I'll tell you."

As Angus waited patiently, he was alarmed to see all color vanish from the man's face. When the Englishman's head slumped awkwardly onto his chest, Angus grabbed him by the hair and yelled, "Where? Tell me where!" All signs of life drained from the Englishman, as Angus realized that his arrow had severed the major femoral artery that runs down the leg. The heavy leggings masked the fatal bleeding. Without remorse, Angus muttered, "Death's the cost of living, when ye're the Devil's own."

CHAPTER TWENTY-FIVE
THE MISSING GOLD

AFTER A LONG, DRAWN-OUT breakfast of smoked venison followed by a short nap in a sunny spot on the forest floor, Angus removed the powder horn, bullet pouch, hunting knife, and broad-brimmed hat from the dead Englishman and set about covering his body. He was not trying to hide it—from humans or scavengers—but even a dead Englishman deserved a semblance of a burial, so he placed the body in a natural depression and tossed limbs, rocks, and leaves atop until it was obscured.

After tying the Englishman's short-handled axe and musket to the saddle of the black horse, Angus secured the bow and arrow quiver behind his own saddle, and placed Schatto back into her basket. Angus scanned the campsite one last time, then mounted Night Fog and turned south to pursue the younger of the two Englishmen, the one with his brown mare and his hard-earned gold.

Angus returned to the point of the ambush where he located the tracks of the second thief, which he followed until early afternoon. The deep gloom of the forest brought a halt to the day's events, and forced them to camp along a small stream. At first light, Angus resumed his search for hoof prints. Leaving the hobbled horses, Angus and Schatto hunted on foot for any telltale signs their enemy might have left. By mid-day Angus admitted defeat, turned around, and headed back to the horses.

The younger Englishman now had almost two days' head start. It was highly unlikely that Angus could catch up to him and without tracks to follow, further pursuit seemed fruitless. Returning to the

Raystown trail, a frustrated Angus turned west back to the settlement he had left before the ambush from the Englishmen.

As he entered the clearing, Angus scanned the area hopefully for Buckeye. He was disappointed, but not surprised, to see neither his packhorse nor the Englishman's dun. Angus urged Night Fog to the cabin where John Wray and Gerald awaited. As he dismounted, the frowning storekeeper came out onto the front porch and silently studied the scene. Angus no longer had a brown mare with pack baskets but instead had a black horse bearing an empty saddle. "Had trouble, did you." he stated rather than asked.

Angus climbed the steps without expression and took a seat as Gerald joined them. Matter-of-factly he briefly explained that the two Englishman had ambushed him the morning he left the settlement and stolen his two horses. He had followed the one with his gray mare after they separated and managed to catch up with him. Noting simply that he had killed the older Englishman, he concluded, "I calculated they planned to separate and then meet up in a couple days. However, there's no way of knowing in what direction they planned their escape. I could hunt for days or even months and not find the second villain unless he stopped at a cabin or a settlement. He has enough food to last seven or eight days and is not likely to risk stopping where someone might recognize my brown mare with pack baskets."

The listeners could easily sense the white-hot anger that was festering inside those emotionless words. Not one of them would wish to cross this man when angered or wronged.

John Wray suggested, "He will probably get rid of your pack baskets for the very reasons you said—someone might identify them on your brown mare. He would have some explaining to do."

Angus then admitted he lost some gold, and reasoned that the Englishman would be unable to haul food, gold, and all the trade-goods without the pack baskets. Angus decided to omit the amount of gold he had carried, but he did detail the story of Heather, concluding his account by stating that the gold was promised to pay her ship's passage to the colonies.

Wray said, "Sorrow and ill weather often come uninvited. I'll send word, by way of future travelers, to Thomas Cresap, Edward Beatty, Christopher Gist, Nemacolin, and even the Forks of the Ohio, to be on the lookout for the thief."

Angus knew it would be a waste of time. There was no law on the Appalachian frontier to seek justice for this crime—none other than what the avenger might administer. Although Angus acknowledged he might never again see the gold, it was placating to know that widespread knowledge of its existence might make the Englishman himself a target and prevent him from harboring it. Angus would have any person on the frontier possess the gold, over the thieving Englishman. Ambivalence was overcome by passion.

In exchange for the saddle from the dead Englishman's horse, John Wray gave Angus two pack baskets, some venison and cornmeal, a cooking kettle, a couple fishhooks, and a handful of salt. Angus would keep the Englishman's horse, a young gelding somewhat larger than Night Fog. It would make an excellent substitute should he need another mount.

Because it was late afternoon, Angus opted to spend the night at the Raystown settlement and get an early start the next morning. The day had been rigorous, and he needed time to contemplate his options. As Angus, John Wray, and Gerald gathered for the evening meal, Augustin returned from his hunt. He joined them at the table and commented to Angus, "I thought you would be half way to Lancaster by now."

Angus repeated his story of the ambush while Augustin remained silent. After hearing all the details he said, "I was hunting northwest of here and around mid-morning spied a rider on a dun leading a brown packhorse. I was too far away to identify the man, and could not tell with certainty that the brown horse was yours."

Angus jerked upright in his seat and asked, "Which direction was he headed?"

"He came from the south and appeared to be swinging around towards the east. Most likely he was headed for the trail that runs north from Raystown to the Allegheny River."

Augustin added, "The last night they were here, the two Englishmen asked me if there were any cabins or shelters along the trail to the Allegheny. I told them about an old deserted one-room cabin located just off the trail about ten miles from here. It's possible that's where they planned to meet."

With renewed hope of recovering his gold, Angus bombarded Augustin with questions regarding the specific location of the cabin. He learned that it was built near where the trail crossed a small stream that flowed down out of the mountains. Augustin drew a rough sketch on a piece of deer hide, with landmarks to warn Angus when he was within one-half mile of the site. With firm conviction, Angus vowed to search the entire trail between Raystown and the Allegheny, if necessary. No one doubted his resolve or the outcome.

Following an early breakfast, Angus saddled Night Fog, loaded an anxious Schatto into her basket, tied the black horse's lead rope to his saddle, and exchanged farewells with the three men. Augustin offered to go with him, but Angus politely refused. He thanked the Swiss hunter for his kind offer and expressed confidence that he could find the cabin with the aid of his map.

After an hour of steady travel, Angus dismounted, placed Schatto on the ground, and continued northward while scanning everywhere for any signs of the Englishman's two horses. He spotted the tracks around mid-morning and a rush of adrenaline shot through his body. As expected, the tracks veered north, toward the cabin shown on the map. Angus warily followed the hoof prints until the cabin lay one-half mile beyond, out of earshot if the hobbled horses should whinny. Angus and Schatto continued their silent pursuit, and by mid-afternoon Angus detected the faint odor of wood smoke, blowing in his direction. Moving off the trail several hundred yards, the hunters began searching for the stream, found it within the hour, and followed it downstream towards the cabin. Schatto and her pack leader were on the prowl.

By late afternoon, Angus could see the old cabin in the distance. With heightened caution, he and Schatto stalked from tree to tree, edging within fifty yards of the cabin. Angus was relieved to see Buckeye and the Englishman's dun-colored horse grazing in a small clearing. Because the Englishman was nowhere in sight, Angus deduced that he was in the cabin, a dilapidated structure with one door and one window, both facing the stream. Angus cautiously crept through the woods until he had a clear view of the door and settled comfortably alongside a large sugar maple. While chewing on smoked venison, man and wolf relaxed for the first time that day. Although Schatto did not know what they were hunting, Angus's silent predatory behavior coupled with her instincts conveyed that they were on the prowl and excitement was soon to follow.

Two hours later the Englishman came out of the cabin, carrying his musket and a small kettle. With only a casual glance around the clearing he headed for the stream. As if in slow motion, Angus lifted his muzzle-loader into shooting position and settled the sights on the man's right shoulder. Although this man had tried to murder him, Angus's conscience stopped him from shooting the man in the back. And so, as the Englishman knelt to fill his kettle, Angus stepped from behind the tree and shouted, "Drop your musket and I won't shoot." The foolhardy man reacted instantly, dropping his kettle, whirling to face Angus, and hurriedly raising his musket to fire. As his lead ball slammed harmlessly into the large sugar maple where Angus stood, the Englishman turned to run. At the sight of powder exploding in the musket's firing pan, Angus responded. The front sights of his well-balanced muzzle-loader were already settled on the man's left shoulder and the blast of gunpowder followed. The fool managed only two steps before the bullet from the muzzle-loader plunged him face-first into the stream.

Angus prudently scanned the area for other humans, reloaded his rifle, called Schatto to heel, and moved cautiously to the stream. The musket lay at water's edge, and the man lay face down in red-stained water. Angus grasped an arm and dragged him onto shore while Schatto lapped the blood flowing from a hole in his shoulder. Blood frothing from the man's nose told Angus that the bullet had struck lungs after passing through the shoulder blade. The combination of swallowed water and punctured lungs was deadly, and the Englishman took two final gasps before his life ended.

Angus retrieved the Englishman's musket, powder horn, bullet bag, hunting knife, and broad-rimmed hat. The man's leather boots were nearly new, so a frugal Angus unlaced and yanked them off.

Leaving the body sprawled on the creek bank, Angus hurried to the cabin. There lay his bag of dried venison on a plank table in the middle of the room, and his stolen pack baskets rested against an inside wall. After moving the baskets out into the sunlight, he noted that the one holding his trade goods apparently had been emptied, contents examined, and repacked. His heart sank as he removed the tanned elk hides and decorated white deer hide from the other basket. The precious, hard-earned bag of gold was missing. Quickly returning to the cabin interior, he searched the entire structure, floor to ceiling, without success.

Once again, he scoured the pack baskets, emptying each one, but there was no gold. Puzzled and dejected, Angus sat down on an old stump and pondered the situation. The only logical conclusion was that the Englishman had hidden the gold. Why he hid it did not matter, but where he hid it certainly did. Angus calculated that the thief had reached the cabin the previous day and had spent one night. He would have discovered the gold shortly after reaching the log structure, and had plenty of time to hide it. If the bag of gold coins were buried at an easily identified nearby spot, Angus felt confident he would recover it.

With dusk fast approaching, Angus and Schatto retrieved Night Fog and the black gelding, and brought them to the cabin. Angus hobbled the four horses, built a small fire in the cabin's crude fireplace, and spread his bearskin onto the earthen floor. Clouds rolling in from the south convinced Angus to sleep inside. The search for gold would commence in the morning. Brooding somewhat over the gold, he thought to himself, "There never was a bad that couldn't be worse."

A thunderstorm rolled through the valley that night, but as the morning sun's rays slanted through the trees, only a few puffy white clouds were visible. Angus prefaced his search by asking himself questions. "Where would I have hidden the gold if I had stolen it? Would I choose a unique permanent landmark, one that could be easily located at any time? If I put it close to the stream, would floodwaters expose it? If I buried it, how would I find it later?" In response to his personal queries, Angus searched both sides of the stream for nearly a quarter mile in both directions. Next he searched both sides of the trail for an equal distance, hoping to find evidence of recent digging. He lifted rocks, rolled logs, and reached into hollow trees. By sunset he was spent and discouraged, but not yet ready to give up. He would resume the search the next day, and the next if necessary. That was his gold; he had endured much hardship in its quest, and by damn, he'd have it or know he'd given his best effort to regain it!

Angus moved upstream from the dead Englishman to fill his kettle with water that evening. He felt so compelled to find his gold that he had not taken time to bury the body. Now he was so disgusted with failing to find the gold that he had no stomach for burying the scoundrel. As Schatto sniffed at the dead stiff body and licked at the dried blood that had bubbled out of the nostrils, Angus commented bitterly, "I think I'll leave you here, English, and let the buzzards pick out your eyeballs."

The next morning Angus scoured the cabin interior—earthen floor, rafters, and inside the chimney. Inch-by-inch he examined the exterior of the cabin, with no success. For the remainder of the day, once more he searched along the stream and trail. The third day he examined less prominent areas, those with no recognizable landmarks. By the end of the fourth day he was exhausted, emotionally and physically. After spending one more night in the cabin, Angus saddled Night Fog, lashed the pack baskets onto Buckeye, and tied lead ropes to the Englishmen's two horses. As he mounted, Angus noted the Englishman's body along the creek bank. He dismounted and purposefully strode to the creek, rolled the body into the stream, and covered it partially with large rocks.

Hurrying back to the horses, Angus grabbed Night Fog's reins and headed south towards Raystown. Rather than riding, Angus walked the entire length of trail from the cabin to the spot where the tracks of the Englishman's horses first entered the trail. At that point, he mounted Night Fog, lifted Schatto into her basket, and resumed the trek southward. Angus contemplated whether he should tell the men at Raystown that he had not found the gold. If he did, they would certainly spend time searching and possibly tell others of its existence. He reached the settlement by late afternoon.

John Wray, Gerald, and Augustin were erecting a new cabin and stopped work immediately upon detecting Angus and his four horses emerging from the forest. As the party paused along the pile of logs, Augustin spoke, "I see you found the young Englishman."

Angus responded, "Aye, and that's the last time he'll rob a Scotsman. Shoot a thief when he's young, and he'll not steal when old." Angus provided all the essential details of shooting the Englishman, but made no mention of the gold and thankfully no one asked about it. To justify his extended absence, he added that he had explored the countryside for a couple days to search for beaver ponds. After the meal, Angus handed Augustin the young Englishman's musket, stating, "I want you to have this. Had ye not spotted him in the woods, I would never have found him."

Augustin examined the musket while smiling, and said, "Much thanks, I'll put it to good use."

CHAPTER TWENTY-SIX
THE CONESTOGA SETTLEMENT

AFTER RESTING ANOTHER NIGHT at the Raystown settlement, a discouraged Angus resumed his interrupted trip, traveling eastward to Lancaster. In the fertile valleys nestled within the Allegheny Mountains, Angus visited several settlers who had built cabins near the trail. He and Schatto were welcomed at each. Fine summer-like weather allowed Angus to reach the Susquehanna River in four days. He spent one night at the river settlement named Paxtant (the future Harrisburg) before following the Paxtant path south along the river's eastern bank to the settlement named Conestoga.

In Conestoga, the site of a former Indian village, Angus located the former friends of Johannes and Gisela. They seemed starved for news, and insisted he spend the night and tell them about the Dunkard farm. Several families from Conestoga were preparing to head west to the Monongahela and sought encouragement that the trip would not be a disaster. When it soon became evident that Angus knew more about the Monongahela region than anyone they had met, most of the Conestoga settlement was invited to a daylong meeting. Angus tried to answer the multitude of questions involving the unknowns they would face. He first warned them of the dangers, including his personal encounters with rattlesnakes, mountain lions, bears, wolves, flooded rivers, and life-threatening winter storms. He emphasized just as vividly, the fertile lands, the endless forests, the abundance of wild foods, and the unlimited numbers of wildlife available to feed and clothe a family.

He told them about John Wray at Raystown, Thomas Cresap near Shawaneese Oldtown, Edward Beatty at Wills Creek, Christopher

Gist near the Youghiogheny, and Nemacolin. But he also warned them about the thieves he had faced, and the dangers they posed.

He cautioned that some folks who ventured into the western frontier would probably die due to accidents or even starvation during the hard winters. However, he concluded that free land and unlimited opportunities awaited those hard-working families who dared travel into the Appalachians. He prepared rough maps, showing the major trails, rivers, mountains, cabins, settlements, and specific lands he thought would make productive farms. Knowledge, preparation, and caution would be their greatest allies.

The aspiring pioneers asked for a list of essential items they must take and questioned the use of wagons to haul their families and belongings westward. There was great disappointment when Angus explained that it would be impossible to use wagons on the rugged terrain and narrow trails they would be forced to follow. If they could not carry it on their backs or load it on a horse, they must leave it behind. This news brought more misgivings about the trip westward than any other hazard Angus described. All the adults present pictured in their own minds the items needed to make life bearable—tables, chairs, beds, and crocks; saws, plows, shovels, and rakes; chickens, cows, and pigs. How could they possibly load everything they needed on the backs of horses? Much soul-searching would take place before any final decision was reached to move to the Monongahela. Were free land and freedom from religious persecution worth the peril?

German immigrants—who would become the Pennsylvania Deutsch—had developed a wagon to haul farm products to market in Philadelphia. While roads had been built in that region, they were too often full of small boulders, fallen trees, and deep mud holes. The freight-hauling wagon was developed in Conestoga to carry heavy loads over long distances, and could endure poor road conditions. The four broad, sturdy, wooden wheels, five feet in diameter, raised the bed of the wagon high enough to pass safely over small boulders and through deep mud holes. The bed of the wagon, which at first glance appeared to be sagging in the middle from carrying heavy loads, was intentionally designed with upswept bow and stern.

The farmers had learned that boxes and baskets loaded with produce often slid around on the floor of regular, flat-bottom wagon beds. In contrast, a concave wagon bed kept boxes and baskets clustered in the middle, reducing spillage of their valuable contents. A cloth cover supported by gracefully curved wooden bows protected the baggage.

Recently arriving immigrants had used such wagons to haul their household goods, farm animals, and tools from Philadelphia to the Lancaster region. Several families vowed that they would not make the trip west if they could not take their wagons. As Angus departed the Conestoga settlement for Lancaster, realism replaced optimism for many who had dreamed of utopian life on the frontier.

On the western edge of Lancaster lived Henery Gumpf, the gunsmith who had taught Angus how to craft a muzzle-loading rifle. Angus arrived there by mid-afternoon and headed directly for the small building that served as Henery's workshop, eager to see his old friend and learn of news from Heather. He could hear hammering inside the building and figured Henery was working on another gun barrel. Angus knocked loudly on the open door and a loud, booming voice responded, "Come on in."

Once inside, Angus saw that little had changed. Two large worktables were the center of the gunsmith's efforts. Shelves and storage racks along each of the walls, along with baskets suspended from the ceiling, provided storage for the various tools, parts, and materials he needed. One of the large tables provided space for the actual woodworking. On it were mounted two vises, as well as saws, planes, knives, and files. Two finished gunstocks and several rough blanks for future gunstocks were visible. The second large table provided space for most of the metalworking, and already two octagonal barrels were clamped in vises for finishing work.

When Henery turned and recognized Angus, a broad smile spread across his face, and he immediately laid down his hammer. Moving quickly across the room to the front door, Henery grasped Angus's hand in a grip that spoke volumes about the strength of a gunsmith's hands.

Angus returned both the smile and the handshake and said, "Tis surely good to see you again."

Carefully studying the frontiersman's clothing and overall appearance, the gunsmith nodded and answered, "You sure are looking fit, and I'm ready for a break. Let's go outside and sit a spell. You can tell me all about your travels." Henery was staring intently at the horses when he spotted Schatto, which was tied to one of the porch posts. With a grin, he asked, "Where did you get that pup? It looks like a wolf."

Angus once again recounted his travels of the past nine months, including details of Schatto's arrival, the two ambushes and how he had been forced to kill his attackers. When finished he sadly reported, "I lost it all, Henery. I lost all the gold I worked so hard for."

Knowing there was nothing he could say that would make the situation any better, Henery offered, "Yes, you lost the gold, but you're still alive. You have four horses, some trade goods, and a wolf pup, plus you've learned how to survive in the Appalachian wilderness. You know more about the Monongahela region than any other white man, and your experiences will prove invaluable in the future."

Angus nodded his head as if in agreement, but said nothing.

Henery continued, "He who loses gold loses much. He who loses a friend loses more. He who loses faith loses all. You did not lose your wolf pup and you must not lose faith. You have a wonderful future ahead of you."

The conversation turned to weaponry. Of course, the gunsmith wanted to know how the muzzle-loader had functioned. Was it accurate enough for the type of hunting Angus had done? Was it powerful enough to bring down buffalo, elk, and bear? Was it dependable after being banged against rocks, dropped into water, and exposed to freezing weather? Did Angus have any problems carrying it for hours and days at a time, on foot and on horseback, over hundreds of wilderness miles?

Angus detailed every single shot he had taken with the muzzle-loader and concluded by telling Henery that his rifle had been a great success and widely coveted. Recalling how he had killed every animal he shot at, without crippling a single one, Angus said, "Without the muzzle-loader, I would not have survived my travels through the Appalachian wilderness." His account was the highest accolade he could have given his mentor.

Very proud, Henery told Angus to take his horses to the barn, while he informed his wife, Marianne, there would be one more person for supper that night. Angus gave his food bag, with the last of his smoked venison and passenger pigeons, to Henery and asked him to give it to Marianne. As Angus approached the house from the barn, a small girl with curly blonde hair came running to him. He kneeled down, caught her as she leaped into his arms, and announced, "Eva, you're as cute as a speckled pup."

As they hugged each other the four-year-old girl exclaimed, "Angus, Angus! I'm so glad to see you again. I did not think you were ever coming back to see me. You have been gone for years and years."

Angus feigned frustration as he replied, "I hurried the best I could, but a few problems slowed me down." Rising to his feet, he announced, "Eva, I have something to show you." Taking her hand, he led her to the barn and opened the door. The small girl's eyes rapidly adjusted to the shadows inside the barn, and then were affixed on Schatto.

"It's a puppy! You brought a puppy!" Schatto had never seen a child so small and was straining at her rope to greet her. Angus untied the pup and the two youngsters were soon running and chasing, and yelling and yipping around the barn floor. Angus let them play awhile then called them outside, and play continued in the yard until both were ready for a rest.

Henery had been watching from the cabin porch, and called, "Time to eat, Eva. You must wash your hands." Henery, Angus, Eva, and Schatto headed to the water trough. The three humans washed their hands, while the wolf drank water that spilled over the end of the trough. In the cabin, Marianne, who had been anxiously trying to prepare enough extra food, warmly greeted Angus. Angus had almost forgotten how much he enjoyed being around the Henery Gumpf family, and he truly hoped he could stay with them for the next month or two while he built a new rifle.

Following supper, Angus tried to answer the hundreds of questions asked by Marianne and Eva. Marianne was most interested in the people he had met, while Eva wanted to know about all the dangerous wild animals he had fought. Angus in turn wanted to know news from the colonies and England. When Marianne announced that it was Eva's bedtime, Angus asked if they had room for him to spend the night. Henery answered, "Of course, we would be hurt if you didn't. The lean-to at the end of the gun shop, where you slept last summer, is not too messy. You're welcome to sleep there or in the barn. Wherever you prefer."

As Angus rose to go to the lean-to, he could hold back his curiosity no longer and asked, "Did any letters come for me?"

Ten years older than Angus, Henery knew what his friend was waiting for. He dreaded having to disappoint the younger man. "Sorry, Angus, but nothing at all came while you were gone."

With unconcealed disappointment, Angus said goodnight and trudged out of the cabin. Why had no messages arrived? He had sent nearly twenty letters to Heather while he worked in Philadelphia and ten more during the time he worked in Lancaster. Certainly one of them had reached her. In one way he was relieved, since he had no gold to pay for her passage, but in another way he was extremely frustrated.

While Angus and Henery sat on the cabin porch drinking sassafras tea the next morning, the gunsmith carefully examined the muzzle-loader that Angus had carried through the wilderness for nearly nine months. He scrutinized all the scars and scratches resulting from the gun being dropped, banged against boulders, and clawed by animals. He assessed it carefully for signs of rust or weakness in the metal, and he checked to see if the barrel was still straight and firmly attached to the maple stock. Giving careful attention to the moving parts, he worked the flintlock, the trigger, and the ramrod. Everything was still functioning, and Angus convinced him that the weapon was as accurate as when it was new. Henery was openly gratified with the muzzle-loader, the first to be carried into the Appalachian wilderness.

They discussed the barrel length, the flintlock mechanism, the pan that held the gunpowder, and the caliber. Henery wanted to know if Angus would make any changes. Angus confirmed what

Henery believed—the gun was expertly designed and crafted. As the gun talk wrapped up, the German asked, "Angus, what are your plans for the summer?"

Relieved that he did not have to bring up the subject, Angus responded, "I'd like to work for you during the next two months and build a new rifle to carry when I return to the wilderness. I would expect no pay and would be willing to hunt for meat to pay for my keep. I haven't decided where I'll spend next winter, but most likely I'll trap and trade."

Henery nodded his head, and with a satisfied look on his face, answered, "We would be most pleased to have you spend two months with us. Stay as long as you like. I have orders for all the muzzle-loaders I can build. With your assistance, I can complete one or two more than I could have by myself." No further discussion was needed to finalize the informal agreement that typified the trust frontiersmen placed in one another.

Henery Gumpf had been a gunsmith in Germany, but had been tutored by Martin Meylin, a Swiss gunsmith who perfected the concept of cutting spiraling grooves inside a gun barrel to improve the accuracy and the distance a bullet could be fired. Although the tooled spirals—called "riefeln"—had been known in Europe for over two hundred years, the practice never became popular there, perhaps due to the expense of cutting the grooves.

After emigrating from Switzerland, Meylin found there were few gunsmiths in the colonies. Soon after landing in Philadelphia, he moved to Lancaster and began making rifles that resembled the German Jäeger. Those designs were slow to fire, had short range, and unpredictable accuracy. The huge, wooden butt on the stock, combined with over ten pounds of heft, made them clumsy to shoot. The barrels were smooth inside, firing either single lead bullets or a handful of small lead pellets. The only redeeming quality of the early muskets that Martin Meylin produced was the flintlock mechanism that ignited the black powder. Upon pulling the trigger, a piece of flint held in a lock sprang forward, struck a piece of steel, and produced a spark. The spark ignited black powder in a pan, which in turn ignited gunpowder inside the barrel. The resulting explosion forced the bullet through the gun barrel. The flintlock mechanism had been invented by the French in the 1600s, and was one of the most significant improvements in gun design ever to occur. When Meylin eventually supplemented his flintlocks with a rifled barrel, he had the optimum firearm.

Henery Gumpf enjoyed discussing muzzle-loaders with Angus. Always willing to share his knowledge, Henery detailed his tests with different types of spiral grooves inside the barrel and revealed he now had a rifle that would accurately hit a target at a distance of two hundred yards. Five spiral grooves running the length of the barrel forced the lead ball to spin when it was fired, thus stabilizing flight and improving accuracy. He offered to assist Angus in building a new muzzle-loader that would incorporate all of the new concepts he had been testing. Henery asked, "What caliber would be most useful for surviving along the frontier?"

Angus's head was spinning with all the possibilities. During his travels, he had given the question considerable thought, and decided that his new rifle would be a smaller caliber, perhaps forty instead of fifty. Although his original muzzle-loader brought down full-grown elk, buffalo, and black bear, he had used the gun primarily to shoot white-tailed deer, wild turkey, and yearling elk. A smaller caliber would require less powder and lead—scarce commodities in the wilderness. He also speculated that a smaller caliber would be more accurate, and accuracy was the most important attribute of any weapon. Even larger animals could be killed with the smaller bullet if it struck a vulnerable spot. Henery proposed that they build two or three rifles during the next couple of months and test the accuracy of each. Angus could then decide which one he wanted to carry with him.

Angus sought to create a rifle more accurate, lighter in weight, and more streamlined than his old one. Henery concurred they could reduce the bore and the overall diameter of the barrel, plus slim down the maple stock; in so doing the weight would decrease by one or two pounds. However, the length of the barrel—and thus the stock—could not be reduced, because every bit of the forty-eight inch length was critical for complete burning of the black powder.

Angus had in mind an especially fancy blank of curly maple with tiger striping to make the stock of his new rifle. He suggested to Henery that they attach brass mountings and include brass tubes to hold the ramrod. He had another suggestion that caught Henery by surprise. He suggested that they recess a patch box into the stock to hold the greased linen patches used to wrap around each bullet prior to ramming it down the barrel. Henery felt a bit flabbergasted that such an idea had never occurred to him, but readily agreed it would be a great improvement. Angus and Henery concurred that the muzzle-loading flintlock rifle would become the weapon of survival in the demanding conditions west of the Alleghenies.

CHAPTER TWENTY-SEVEN
SUMMER IN LANCASTER

THE NEXT MONTH PASSED quickly, as Angus and Henery concentrated all their energies working on new muzzle-loaders. Schatto and Eva played together, for hours at a time, and became bosom friends. The bond between Angus and Eva strengthened, and many evenings the little girl climbed onto his lap while he told stories of his wilderness adventures. His tales of wild animals, especially those involving fighting and blood, enthralled her, while he was captivated by her innocence and charm.

Although summer was not the best time to transport and preserve meat, Angus left the settlement one or two days each week to hunt. Not only did he harvest all the meat that the Gumpfs needed, but he also became the principal commercial hunter for the main butcher shop in Lancaster. No other hunter could so dependably supply deer, or turkey, or bear.

Angus traded surplus meat for gunpowder, lead bullets, axes, iron kettles, traps, salt, blankets, mirrors, and miscellaneous items the Indians wanted. He also traded for several sets of linen/woolen clothing and two broad-brimmed hats. Angus preferred clothing made of deerskin rather than wool to wear in the wilderness, but he conceded that a hat made of deerskin, raccoon, or rabbit fur did not provide the sun and rain protection afforded by a broad-brimmed woolen hat. Only during the worst of winter weather was a hat made of warm raccoon or rabbit fur desirable.

The daylong hunting trips in areas around Lancaster somewhat resembled the trek from the Forks of the Ohio. Angus rode his gray mare and led the black, now called Black Rock, and Schatto ran alongside. A hand signal prompted the pup to heel silently as he stalked close to deer, bear, or wild turkey. After the shot, Angus would lead the pup downwind of the fallen animal and then encourage her to hunt, by scent alone, until she saw it lying dead. She learned to follow a blood trail efficiently, never chasing wildly after an animal.

Trailing an animal by scent was natural and easily taught, but suppressing the urge to chase was a greater challenge. Natural instinct told her to run after prey animals as part of a pack. No wolf ever caught a meal by tracking stealthily. That strategy was used by mountain lions—stalk close and rush in for the kill. Wolves, however, chased and exhausted their prey until they were close enough to sever a hamstring or leap for the throat.

Angus found it relatively easy to teach positive commands such as "heel," "come," "stay," and "fetch." His repeat-and-reward strategy was effective. In contrast, it was extremely difficult to extinguish an undesirable action. Angus had reprimanded Schatto for digging in the Gumpf's yard unless she was digging for chipmunks or other small rodents. It was no doubt confusing to be rewarded for digging sometimes, then punished at other times.

Squelching Schatto's desire to chase large animals was even more difficult than suppressing her urge to dig around the Gumpf's house. Angus could reprimand her in the act of digging, but it was nearly impossible to scold her while she was chasing a bear or a deer. Only when she was on a long leash could he halt her pursuit before she raced out of sight. Yelling at an excited pup running headlong after its prey was useless. It was even less effective to scold and punish the pup after she returned from a wild chase that typically ended after she had lost the scent and returned for a reward.

As summer progressed, Schatto finally grasped what was expected of her, and she became a tracker/stalker. Angus's combination of muzzle-loader and wolf allowed him to haul in more meat than all the other Lancaster hunters combined.

One day in late August, when Angus brought a load of freshly killed elk meat to the Lancaster smoke house, the storekeeper announced, "A letter came for you today."

At the storekeeper's announcement, Angus nearly dropped the

elk's hindquarter he was lifting off his packhorse. His emotions were usually in check, but this sudden development caused his chest to tighten up. While experiencing difficulty breathing and speaking, Angus nodded his head and answered, "Thanks, I'll read it when I finish unloading the meat." Surely it was from Heather. Most of his relatives could not read or write, and he had received no letters from any of them while he was in Philadelphia or Lancaster. After washing his hands in a water trough, Angus retrieved the letter from the storekeeper and, somewhat grim-faced, mounted Night Fog. He would wait until returning to the Gumpf's cabin before opening the letter.

Angus unloaded the two horses, turned them loose in the pasture with the Gumpf's cattle, and then called Schatto into the barn. Taking a seat on a three-legged stool, Angus stared at the crumpled and stained letter. It had no return address, no date, and carried only the wording, "Angus McCallander, Henery Gumpf Cabin, Lancaster, Pennsylvania, American Colonies"—the exact wording that Angus had given in his letters to Heather.

After eight years, he had finally received a letter from Scotland. Angus had imagined an endless array of painful scenarios during his eight-year wait. Had Heather been injured or even killed in the fighting with the English? Was she still living in Scotland or had she fled to Ireland? Could she have agreed to an indentured servitude program and now be working in Philadelphia? Had the ship sunk while she was crossing the Atlantic? What if she had contracted some disease while working in the colonies and died?

Once again, it occurred to Angus that he was not meant to settle down on a patch of cleared land and live the life of a farmer. He was reminded of the Highlander saying, "Him that has a wife has a master." Admittedly, he had dedicated his life in America to obtaining enough gold to pay Heather's passage. Although he had lost all his gold, he could earn more in one or two winters of trapping and hunting.

Curiosity was like a poker burning into his hand, but he couldn't release the covert comfort of ignorance. When Henery interrupted his reverie by yelling that dinner was ready, Angus carefully opened the letter with the tip of his hunting knife and spread it over his knees. It was a simple and short message, but one that Angus could not fully process. The words were easily read, but their message was dumbfounding.

As Eva ran into the barn and firmly announced, "Angus, mother says that you better come to dinner right now, or it will get cold!" He rose and took Eva's hand. After dinner, Henery asked, "How did the hunt go today?"

Angus answered, "It went fine. I killed a nice yearling elk." Then with no further comments, he removed the letter from his pocket and announced, "I got a letter today." Marianne almost dropped the pewter plate she was carrying, immediately stopped clearing the table, and returned to her chair. Both she and Henery waited for Angus to say more. He had earlier told them all about Heather and his plans for bringing her to the colonies. Although they never expressed their doubts to Angus, they had decided that too many years had passed and she would never join Angus.

Without a word, or any expression that would reveal his feelings, Angus handed the letter across the table. Henery and his wife quickly read the six words, "I married your cousin Davitt. Heather."

With tears in her eyes, Marianne said, "Oh Angus, I am so sorry."

Henery sat silent, not knowing what to say, while Eva asked, "What does it say, mother? What does it say? Is she dead?"

With a sharp frown on her face, Marianne answered simply, "She is not coming."

With that one brief statement, she had summed it up very neatly, and Angus silently repeated it to himself, "She is not coming. She is not coming. She is … not coming." Slowly reaching for the letter, Angus said, "Perhaps I'll take Schatto for a walk down by the creek."

Jumping from her chair, Eva asked, "Can I go? Can I go?"

Her mother sharply answered, "No, Eva. We need to do some more work on your new dress."

Angus and Schatto meandered along Otter Creek until shadows had lengthened to their limits. Here, he came to the realization that his life would never be the same. While the day-to-day events of his life had not changed, his long-term goals certainly had. Suddenly, with one terse letter, all meaning and purpose were lost. He knew what he would be doing the rest of that summer and the following winter, but he did not know the purpose for doing it.

When Schatto let out a sharp yip and took off after a bounding cottontail, Angus shifted his thoughts. He smiled as Schatto closed in fast on the fleeing rabbit.

The rabbit, newly born that spring, had not yet attained the speed and elusive skills of an adult. Yet even this youngster was well equipped for escaping a predator in hot pursuit. Rapid twists and turns, alternated with sudden bursts of speed, enabled the rabbit to stay out of Schatto's reach. Schatto's recent diet of deer meat, corn meal, and milk from the Gumpf's cow had put several pounds on her body, while numerous hunting trips with Angus had strengthened her muscles. When the young cottontail made an error in judgment and ran headlong into a dense clump of sumac, Schatto leaped and clamped her jaws around its back. With fur flying and the rabbit squealing loudly, her grip snapped its back, and she carried its limp body proudly back to Angus. Angus took the rabbit from her jaws, congratulated the young wolf on her first kill of a mid-sized animal, and promptly returned the prize.

It occurred to him that for the near future Schatto would be the most prominent female in his life. As stars began to blink in the darkness overhead, Angus and Schatto headed back to the Gumpfs. Angus realized that he would never forget this day as long as he lived.

With darkness came the realization that his life had been defined by a series of events over extended periods of time—days, weeks, and years. The most notable events had cut into his life like a bolt of lightning cuts across a night sky. Gold had been the driving force behind all he had done or attempted to do during the past year, but now it seemed unimportant. He did not need gold to survive. He could trade furs or meat or sell his services for everything he needed.

Angus continued to build muzzle-loaders, but devoted increasingly more time training Schatto and Night Fog. The long, humid summer days provided at least two hours of daylight after the evening meal, and Angus made good use of them. Like many persons living outside Lancaster, Henery Gumpf had a small flock of sheep. Wool was a valuable commodity for frontier women to provide their families with woolen clothing. One Lancaster family used a Scottish border collie, a breed developed along the border of England and Scotland where large sheep herds were common. The Colonists all agreed that the Scottish sheep dog was the most amazing herding dog they had ever seen.

The longhaired dogs, using unsurpassed intelligence and natural instinct, had an inherent ability to move sheep where and when the dog, or the dog's owner, desired. By whistles or hand signals, the owner could direct his dog to move sheep from one pasture to another, into a barn, or into a small pen. At times, the dog moved slowly and deliberately with no barking, often coming to a crouching halt. At other times, with short bursts of energy, the dog darted after a wandering sheep.

The dog frequently established eye contact with an individual sheep, and in so doing thwarted its uncharted movements. Sheep appeared puzzled by this animal that did not attack wildly like most predators. As the choreographed dance between dog and sheep continued, it was obvious that the dog was somehow communicating with the sheep, controlling them by both mental and physical actions.

As a youngster, Angus had a sheep dog that he used to herd his clan's sheep. He enjoyed working with the dog, and was reminded of its prowess while staying with the Gumpf family in Lancaster. As he watched the Border collie perform, he wondered whether Schatto might be trained to herd animals. She had already mastered the process of fetching horses by circling behind them and nipping playfully at their heels.

On the way to Lancaster from the Monongahela, Angus had taught Schatto several whistle commands. When the whistles were reinforced with simple hand signals, she would follow his directions precisely. Angus spent several days sitting with Schatto at the edge of the pasture watching the Scottish sheep dog and its Lancaster owner handle the sheep. Schatto stared intently at the entire spectacle and made several attempts to join the dog, but Angus obliged her to sit quietly at his side. From pasture's edge, Angus and Schatto moved in behind the working sheep dog so the wolf would learn to associate the owner's whistles with the dog's responses. During every session, Angus talked quietly to Schatto while holding the blue stone.

Schatto's formal introduction to herding began when one of Henery Gumpf's half-grown lambs was released into a pasture by itself, while the rest of the small herd was held in a pen at one end of the pasture. Angus grasped the blue stone, untied the leash from Schatto's neck, and quietly explained what he wanted her to do. She ran towards the baffled animal and circled it, but stopped immediately when Angus whistled sharply. Crouching low to the ground, much like the Scottish sheepdog, she remained motionless. With an arm signal and a unique two-note whistle, Angus signaled her to move the lamb closer to the pen. After several errors, during which the lamb ran wildly around the perimeter of the pen, Schatto finally steered the sheep back to the rest of the herd. Angus smiled confidently, convinced that she could eventually learn to move sheep, or even cattle, at his command.

With practice, Schatto gradually learned the basics. The breakthrough came shortly after the Scottish sheepdog established its dominance by forcefully nipping the pup's throat two or three times. Initially, Schatto had tried to play with the sheepdog but was always ignored. The adult female sheep dog did not engage in frivolous play; her entire working life was devoted to herding sheep. Once Schatto accepted the submissive position, she instinctively began to imitate the adult dog's actions. When the two were paired to herd the sheep, Schatto remained somewhat behind the sheepdog, but mirrored her every move. By early September, Schatto was showing promise of herding animals as directed. Although Angus had no desire for her ever to herd sheep, he was convinced that every bit of discipline she mastered would make her a better hunter and companion.

Angus had yet to outline his specific destination for the coming winter, but he would trap and trade somewhere in western Pennsylvania. To do so he would need to be licensed as an Indian Trader. Accordingly, he petitioned the Lancaster County Court and, because of his experience in the Monongahela region and his winter spent with the Shawnee, was at once granted his license.

Every licensed Indian Trader was assigned a territory that typically included two Indian villages with which they were eligible to trade.

More than fifty Indian Traders had already been licensed to operate in western Pennsylvania, mostly in the Susquehanna and Allegheny watersheds. Since none were licensed to trade in the Monongahela watershed, the court was happy to assign Angus the entire Youghiogheny watershed, with its single Indian settlement, that of Queen Aliquippa. Christopher Gist had told him that several Indian families were scattered throughout the area, so he was hopeful that trading would be more lucrative than it appeared.

The Scottish families living in and around Lancaster had labored through a long, hot summer, and in September decided to stage a community festival to break the monotony. The Scots were eager to demonstrate their highland events to the Germans and invited them to participate. Summer harvests, including raspberries and blackberries, had been completed; numerous haystacks dotted the fields around Lancaster, while shocks of wheat and oats were scattered throughout other fields. The only major harvest remaining would target the hundreds of acres of life-sustaining corn growing around the settlement. Sometime in October, after the cornstalks had turned a golden tan, the entire community would join together for this harvest. It was essential that corn be completely dry before picking to prevent spoilage when stored in the wooden corn bins. Bright yellow ears of corn would be pulled by hand and thrown into the beds of horse-drawn wagons moving systematically up and down the long rows. Corn shocks, tied together in bundles of 50 to 100 fully leaved cornstalks, would be erected throughout the cornfields.

During the middle of winter, when the snow blanketed fields and obliterated animal forage, the life-sustaining shocks would be fed to the cattle. The stacks of nutritious hay were not plentiful enough to last the winter, but dried cornstalks—"fodder" as it was called—would prevent cattle from starving during the harsh Pennsylvania winters.

The women were busy preparing haggis, that traditional Scottish dish made by boiling a mixture of meats, grains, nuts, and spices inside a sheep's stomach. The men constructed a dance platform.

Accompanied by one bagpipe and two fiddles, dancers of all ages would perform their beloved Scottish flings and reels. Young girls in colorful kilts were the crowd favorite, but all who took their places on the wooden dance floor received loud approval. Angus also wore a colorful kilt, but not for dancing. Feats of strength and traditional games were his preferred activities.

It came as no surprise to anyone that Angus won every event he entered, including the sheath toss, hammer throw, and Clachneart—throwing a sixteen-pound stone. No one was jealous; most men set their sights on finishing second. While Angus excelled in all contests, his exploits were most amazing when he tossed the caber, a pole eight inches in diameter, nearly twelve feet in length, and weighing close to a hundred pounds. The caber was actually not tossed, rather heaved forward so that it would land on its end then flip over. The event began by standing the pole upright with its small end resting solidly on the ground. While balancing it upright against his shoulder, the contestant squatted down and, with interlaced fingers, firmly gripped the base of the pole. Maintaining superb balance, a man slowly lifted the pole off the ground, and when upright, deftly slipped his palms under the base of the caber. Continuing to carefully balance the heavy pole against his shoulder, the contestant began to slowly move forward, increasing his speed until he was almost running. To initiate the toss, he simultaneously stopped and squatted and then, with a tremendous effort and an explosive yell, his powerful leg muscles propelled the caber upward.

The heavy upper end of the pole—if balanced properly—assured that the caber would go forward, slowly arching over and landing on its big end. In a perfect toss the pole would continue to pivot, and the small end would rotate an additional one hundred eighty degrees, ending up pointing directly away from the man.

Most men had difficulty lifting the pole while maintaining its balance, and of the few who did both, none had the strength and skill necessary to flip the pole two hundred seventy degrees. Angus was the only person at the event who was able to complete the caber toss. Wearing nothing but a kilt, Angus was the focus of girls and women who attended solely to watch a true Scotsman demonstrate one of the greatest skills of strength and coordination they would ever witness.

Angus, with the eyes and ears of a hunter, was more attuned than others to events around them. Thus, he was the first to detect the disturbing bellows of a nearby bull. As he stood up to get a better view of the animal, others became aware of the unusual and alarming sound. The entire scene quickly materialized like a scary theatrical, and Marianne called out in fear, "The bull is headed for the girls!"

"The girls" turned out to be Eva and two others checking the peach trees that grew near the top of the hill. Only the week before, they found that the peaches were not yet ripe enough to pick. Everyone prized the sweet, juicy peaches, and the first peach pie of the summer was eagerly anticipated in all households. As the girls moved excitedly from tree to tree, in pursuit of fallen peaches, they paid no attention to the bovine bellowing.

The bull was itself an immigrant, one of the rugged Scottish breeds that thrived in the harsh climate of the Highlands. Solidly built, with thick, shaggy red hair, the bull was typically even-tempered and docile. There were times, however, when he became aggressive and charged anyone in the vicinity. The previous year he'd caught the owner with his horns, tossed him through the air, and then gored him with his massive head. Grinding his limp body into the soil, the bull had broken five of the man's ribs and his left arm. Fortunately for the man, several neighbors were able to drive off the bull. In Scotland the owner would have killed and butchered the dangerous beast. In America, however, cattle were too valuable to kill—even dangerous bulls. Without bulls there was no chance of increasing the size of cattle herds. Every family needed more cows to provide the vital and nutritious milk and cheese.

As the girls' mothers began screaming, Angus sprinted over to untie Schatto from the split-rail fence. Angus could see that the bull would reach the girls before any of the men could intervene, so calmly but urgently he cradled Schatto's head in one hand and with the other grasped the deerskin bag that held the blue stone. He stared deeply into her ice-blue eyes and commanded, "Herd the bull,

Schatto. Herd the bull." Like a cannon shot, Schatto exploded into action, leaping through the split-rail fence and racing up the hill like her own life was in jeopardy. Henery and another girl's father had crawled through the split-rail fence and began yelling as they ran like crazed men, but the wolf pup sped past them so fast that they paused in surprise. The amazed onlookers watched in anguish as Schatto quickly crossed the open pasture and approached the bull.

As the pup approached the bellowing bull, one of the women screamed, "The bull will kill it! The bull will kill the pup!" When the enraged bull spotted Schatto, it stopped and began pawing the earth. With head lowered and clods of sod flying over his back, the shaggy bull charged the pup. The people at the gathering could see the bull clearly, but Schatto was hidden in the dust thrown up by the bull. The small helpless girls, two of whom were crying and screaming, sensed the danger and were slinking behind the slim trunk of one of the peach trees. Only four inches in diameter, the tree trunk would not have deflected the bull's charge. As the spectacle continued to unfold, the bull stopped pawing, stopped bellowing, and stopped tossing its head.

The Scots and Germans stared in disbelief at Schatto moving back and forth on the uphill side of the bull. Incredibly, the massive animal began to retreat down the hill. With Schatto guiding and guarding, the bull eventually reached the fence where the Scots were gathering. The man who owned the bull quickly scaled the fence, opened the barn door, and hurried back. Angus signaled Schatto with whistles and arm commands and, as the hushed crowd watched, she maneuvered the bull into the barn. To everyone's delight, she sat on her haunches just outside the barn door and, with tongue hanging out, the panting pup turned and seemed to grin at the crowd.

Angus slipped through the fence, hurriedly closed the barn door, and called to Eva and the other girls to come down off the hill. As the near-tragedy ended, joy and immense relief replaced fear, and the crowd began wildly cheering and clapping. With Schatto heeling obediently at his left side, Angus returned to the crowd of onlookers. Man and wolf were immediately mobbed by grateful parents. Tearfully, Marianne and the other mothers hugged Angus.

Everyone was asking themselves if it was really possible for a thirty-pound pup to herd a thousand-pound, aggravated bull. They had seen it, but it still seemed incredible.

CHAPTER TWENTY-EIGHT
THE SHOOTING MATCH

SEPTEMBER WAS A BUSY month for farmers around Lancaster. The harvesting of various vegetable and fruit crops filled every daylight hour. The air hung heavy with the sweet smells. The last of the peaches, plums, and early apples were gathered, and the tempting aroma of pies seemed to encircle every house in the settlement. Flax had been harvested and stored in the barns to dry. The scutching process that produced the soft flax fibers used to weave linen cloth would be delayed until all other outdoor chores were completed. These community scutchings were an eagerly anticipated opportunity for neighbors to work socially, much like a barn raising.

Chestnuts, corn, pumpkins, and late apples would be gathered in October, but until they were ripe, a more pressing chore demanded their attention. The depleted stockpiles of firewood needed to be replenished. Although both food and firewood were essential to survival, many persons maintained they would prefer being warm to being well fed. Many Scots declared, "I would rather sit warmly before a fire and slowly starve to death, than sit at a table loaded with food and slowly freeze to death." Few had to make such a choice, although by winter's end most households were running low on both food and fuel.

The sound of crosscut saws and axes filled the daylight hours, as each family labored to store enough wood for cooking and heating—a pile equal in volume to their cabin. Trees that had been girdled in previous years stood dead and ready to harvest, simultaneously providing firewood while clearing land for crops.

As the long days of summer waned, Angus proudly assessed

the new rifle he would carry on his return trip to the wilderness. He had finally accumulated all the traps and trade goods he could haul on one packhorse. A second packhorse would be valuable, but of greater concern was finding enough forage to last the animals through a long, hard winter. When deep, heavy snow covered the ground it was nearly impossible for horses to dig down to the few dried grasses available.

Angus announced he would depart Lancaster by the end of October, after helping the Gumpfs fill their storage bins with corn, apples, and chestnuts. He pondered at length where to spend the winter, knowing he would need at least two weeks to reach his destination—wherever that might be. Furs, pelts, and hides would be prime by the end of November, after animals had shed their thin summer pelt and were decked with thick winter coats. So he wanted to be settled in his wintering home by the middle of November.

When November arrived, the last of the fall crops would have been gathered, and men of the settlement would begin the task of butchering. Most German families raised hogs, and they would slaughter two or three to make the tasty sausages and bratwurst they were so fond of. Few sheep and cattle would be butchered, because the wool and milk they provided were more important than the meat, especially since wild game was abundant.

Bears were even more abundant than were deer and elk, and they stored much more body fat than did non-hibernating animals. The settlers enjoyed venison, and each family consumed twenty to thirty deer every winter, but a bear was the most prized animal a hunter could bring home during November. Fortunately, bears were easy targets because they concentrated at sites where abundant acorns, beechnuts, or chestnuts had been produced. Those high-caloric nuts added several layers of fat prior to the bear entering hibernation.

The fat reserves so critical for a bear's survival were almost as important to the settlers. When pork fat was not available, bear lard was used in cooking; the fatty meat was used in making bear sausages. Meat of deer, elk, or buffalo lacked fat needed to make good sausage.

By December, cold cellars would be filled with crocks of bear sausage, each with a thick layer of rendered, white bear lard on top to prevent spoilage. Dozens of shoulders, haunches, and "hams" from bears, deer, and elk would be hanging in each smoke house. In the hunting scheme, bears had to be harvested prior to hibernation. Deer and elk, however, could be hunted throughout the winter. Whenever possible, it was also ideal to harvest the winter's supply of deer and elk during November and December, because the animals were fattest during those months.

Prior to the autumn hunting, every man in the settlement conditioned his firearms for serious shooting by repairing or replacing certain parts and sighting in the gun so that the lead bullet would always strike its intended mark. Consistent with the gun preparations each fall, shooting matches evolved in and around Lancaster. To test their guns, as well as their shooting skills, contests were held to determine who was the best shot.

Because long rifles (many called them muzzle-loaders) were more accurate and capable of shooting longer distances than muskets, separate contests were held for the two types of firearms. Lancaster was the first inland settlement of any size to become established in the colonies, and its location on the edge of the wilderness made it a logical place for advancements in building hunting rifles. Henery Gumpf was one of eleven gunsmiths who lived in and around Lancaster, and each was experimenting with different designs. Small changes in the trigger and flintlock mechanisms added to the gun's ease of firing, but changes in barrel rifling produced the greatest improvements in accuracy.

Angus had won the rifle contest the previous fall, but Henery told him that another gunsmith, Adam Deterer, reportedly had the most accurate long rifle ever made in Lancaster. Both Henery and Angus were eager to test their firearms against Deterer, and both felt they could outshoot him.

The shooting match formed the centerpiece of the October festival and was the culminating event before autumn was brought to a close. Musicians played, dancers performed their cultural dances, and cuisines of different countries were served throughout the day. Most Lancaster residents were of German descent, but other families had emigrated from Switzerland, Scotland, Ireland, and England. Although they had emigrated for a variety of reasons, all chose the American Colonies for the same basic tenet—freedom. For some it was freedom to follow their chosen religious or political beliefs; for some it was freedom to pursue a specific occupation; for others it was the freedom to start an entirely new life. Whatever the logic, each was bound in some way to his neighbor.

For the shooting contests, each shooter provided his own slab of wood that was leaned against a section of log. These rectangular slabs of white pine, measuring approximately ten inches by fifteen inches, were marked on one side with a readily visible "X" in the center and his initials carved on the opposite side. Each contestant got one shot at his target and after all had competed; the judges examined the slabs and selected the three whose bullets had come nearest to the center of the "X." The judges then spread the three slabs on a table and ranked them from first to third. With much ceremony, they turned them over, starting with the third-place winner, to reveal whose initials were carved into the back of the slab. The name was called out, followed by considerable applause. The second-place winner was announced, and finally the first-place winner. Competition ran high, and intense wagering heightened the overall interest.

The musket contest was held first, with shooters positioned fifty yards from their targets. Angus used the musket he had taken from the dead Englishman but managed to finish only fifth. Peter Roesser won the overall musket contest with a Swiss-made firearm he had modified in his own gunsmithery.

Contestants with muzzle-loading rifles were first positioned fifty yards from their targets. After all had fired at the targets, the slabs were retrieved. The slab of the third-place winner was turned over and the name, "Henery Gumpf," was announced. The slab of the second-place winner was turned over, and, with both pleasure and disappointment, Angus heard his name announced. While pleased that his shot had been the second best, he had expected to win. With deliberate hesitation, the judges turned over the winner's slab and announced the name, "Adam Deterer." Tales circulating through the settlement had been correct; Adam Deterer had indeed built a very accurate muzzle-loader.

With the targets now moved one hundred yards from the shooters, the second round of the muzzle-loader contest took place. When all contestants had shot and the slabs were returned to the judges, it was evident that several of the slabs, twice the size of those used at the fifty-yard range, had been completely missed. Many hunters did not have the strength and discipline necessary to hold a muzzle-loader steady while squeezing the trigger and waiting for the black powder to force the bullet out the end of the barrel.

Most of the shots that had struck a slab were widely scattered, with the exception of three. One had struck five inches from the "X," while the other two were both about three inches from the "X." After repeated measuring, the judges arranged the three slabs from third-place to first-place. The third-place slab was turned over, and the name was announced, "Henery Gumpf." The second-place slab was turned over, and Angus was pleased to hear the name, "Adam Deterer" announced. Angus had fired more than a hundred shots with his new rifle and was certain that he could hit his mark at almost any distance. The first-place slab was turned over, and, as expected, the Scotsman heard the judges announce, "Angus McCallander."

Because Angus and Adam Deterer had each won a round it was necessary for them to shoot at the two hundred yard range to determine the overall winner. The two men chose straws to determine the shooting order, and Angus chose the short straw. He would shoot last. White pine slabs, only slightly larger than those used at the one hundred yards, were positioned two hundred yards from the two shooters.

For his previous shots Angus had gauged the direction of the wind by tying a small turkey feather to the end of his ramrod. It was an unusually calm day, and Angus could detect no movement of the turkey feather. However, examination of the slabs had shown that his bullets fired at the fifty and one hundred-yard ranges had each struck slightly to the left of the "X." He deduced that there must be a slight breeze moving from right to left someplace between him and the target, and careful study did in fact reveal a slight movement of the grasses growing in the field. Confident his muzzle-loader did not shoot to the left, he decided to hold his sight slightly to the right of the "X."

The German gunsmith was slightly older and shorter than Angus. To his credit, he had built several dozen muzzle-loaders and had vastly more shooting experience than Angus. He exuded confidence, having been widely touted as the best shot in Lancaster. When Adam Deterer completed his shot, Angus stepped forward; applause for the German still echoing across the meadow. Angus was stronger than the German gunsmith and, more importantly, had the acumen to remain calm while shooting, slowing his heartbeat so that it did not interfere with his aim.

With feet spread wide to stabilize his body, Angus steadied the front end of the sleek muzzle-loader with his left hand while holding the curly maple stock firmly against his right cheek. His stance was that of a veteran marksman: left foot planted solidly under the long barrel, right foot braced below the right shoulder. The shiny brass plate at the butt end of the gunstock was pressed in place against his right shoulder as he sighted along the top of the barrel and locked first onto the "X," and then ever so slightly up and to the right. With a gentle squeeze of the trigger the flintlock was released and a spark ignited gunpowder in the pan. A loud boom announced that the black powder inside the barrel had exploded, and the five spiral grooves inside the barrel caused the perfectly round bullet to rotate like a vortex as it sped towards the slab of wood.

The two slabs were retrieved and placed on the table in front of the judges, and it was apparent to all nearby that one bullet had struck about six inches from the "X," while the bullet in the other slab was less than three inches. There was an indisputable winner. The judge held the two slabs high in the air for all to see, but kept his hand over the initials on the back to extend the suspense. After turning a complete circle so the entire crowd could examine each impact hole, he laid the slab of the second-place shooter on the table and with a loud-ringing voice announced, "The winner's initials are 'A' ... (long pause) ... 'M.'" A slow grin spread across Angus's face as he was congratulated by his very proud mentor and by a conciliatory Adam Deterer, and the gathered crowd cheered enthusiastically.

Henery was almost as proud as if he had won, because word would spread that a long rifle built in his shop had again won first place at the shooting match. Deterer was not all that disappointed in finishing second and told Angus sincerely, "You have yourself a mighty fine rifle."

After the festivities had ended, Angus, Henery, Marianne, and Eva followed the dirt road to the Gumpf farm. When they entered the yard, Eva asked, "Can I get Schatto?"

Angus answered, "Aye Lass. She's probably ready for a run. I need to clean my musket and muzzle-loader before hanging them in the barn." As Angus and Henery entered the gun shop to get their gun-cleaning supplies, Eva ran and unlatched the barn door.

Everyone suddenly stopped what they were doing when her high-pitched, girlish voice shrieked, "She's gone! Schatto is gone!" Angus was the first to reach the barn, and instantly saw that the deer hide leash, by which he had tied the wolf to a manger was missing. He had not taken her to the shooting match because of the noise and felt she would be safe in the barn for the few hours they were away. He'd left her tied inside the barn on several previous occasions, along with a bowl of water and a bone to chew.

The barn door had been latched, and if the leash had somehow come untied, Schatto still could not have gotten out of the building. Angus quickly checked for tracks in the dust outside the barn door and found an unfamiliar set of boot prints alongside an unfamiliar set of hoof prints. It was apparent that someone had arrived on horseback, entered the barn while they were at the shooting match, and had snatched Schatto. A distraught Angus asked Henery to spread the word throughout Lancaster that Schatto had been stolen and to ask if anyone had information regarding her whereabouts. Angus also requested that Henery and Marianne inquire about any strangers seen near their farm and whether anyone had suddenly left town.

Angus followed the hoof prints to the road where they turned west, out of town towards the Conestoga settlement, but after only a couple miles they were obliterated by the tracks of a small herd of cattle being moved to winter pasture. As the sun sank over the western hills so sank his heart, and Angus reluctantly turned back to the Gumpf farm.

One of the most satisfying days of his life had suddenly deteriorated into a rerun of the saddest. He had lost dogs before, but all had been adults; none had been so young as Schatto. He would not deny the overwhelming sense of loss he felt for an animal with such great promise. Angus sadly concluded, the more precious an object, the more likely it will be lost.

As Angus entered the Gumpf's compound, his eyes searched anxiously for a girl and wolf playing in the yard. But no pup was to be seen. The clanging of metal in the gun shop told Angus that Henery was working on a muzzle-loader. He hurried to the barn to see if Schatto had miraculously reappeared, and then opened the door to the gun shop.

Henery recognized the dejected look on his face and knew he had not found Schatto. In a comforting voice, he said, "No luck, huh?" Angus shook his head sideways and said nothing.

Taking a seat on a stool, Angus asked wearily, "Did you learn anything?"

Henery reported that no strangers had been seen around town, but one servant indentured to a shoe cobbler had not been seen since early morning. The young man had been of little help to the cobbler during the two months he was in town and did not enjoy repairing shoes. The cobbler had declared vehemently, "That boy is about as useless as teats on a boar hog." Henery remembered the same young man watching Angus train Schatto to herd sheep on several evenings. However, he cautioned Angus that nearly half of Lancaster had, at one time or another, come out to his farm to watch Schatto herd sheep. Henery added, "The boy had a black horse, but so do half the people in Lancaster."

Angus stated, "I remember that boy. He would do anything to avoid work. I'm positive I can identify him if we ever cross paths. His name is Charles. I'll find him and make him rue the day he touched my wolf."

CHAPTER TWENTY-NINE
THE SEARCH

ANGUS PACKED HIS SADDLEBAGS with enough food and supplies to last a week and, after cleaning his muzzle-loader and musket, he went to bed. Unable to sleep, Angus became fixated on recreating the theft. The kidnapper must have entered the barn, attached a long rawhide rope to the short leash that held the pup, dragged her out of the barn, mounted his horse, and pulled the protesting pup down the road. Schatto would have resisted, but would have been unable to escape. Tracks left in the dust indicated that she fought the choking rope, but finally succumbed to the pressure and walked behind the horse.

The thief probably had several hours head start before Eva noted Schatto's absence. He had most likely traveled until dark, covering five to ten miles, and camped off the road. Angus envisioned Schatto tied to a tree, probably given a few pieces of dried venison. However, because Angus had taught her to not accept food from another person she would have ignored the meat. After pulling frantically against the strong rawhide rope for several hours, she would have become exhausted, perhaps curled into a ball, and gone to sleep fitfully.

Angus bolted upright in bed. He realized for her to escape she must chew the rope that held her. If the thief were indeed the indentured shoe cobbler, he would have anticipated such a move and used the toughest rawhide rope he could find. But had he managed to loop the rawhide firmly around Schatto's neck without receiving a bloody bite? Many hours, or even days, of chewing would be required to bisect the tough rawhide. Her only escape lay in chewing through the short leash by which she had been tied in the barn—if it were still around her neck.

Removing the blue stone from the deerskin bag, a desperate Angus slowly caressed the magical gem between his rough fingers. As the warmth flowed, he closed his eyes and commanded, "Schatto, chew your leash. Chew your leash." Angus repeated the command for over an hour before falling asleep, exhausted from such intense concentration.

As dawn's faint illumination softened the darkness, Angus ended his long, tortured night. He gathered his hunting gear and padded softly through the damp grass to the Gumpf's cabin. The entire family was already sitting at the table; evidently they also were unable to sleep. With little conversation, Angus quickly ate the hearty breakfast of mush, eggs, and deer steak that Marianne had fried. Expressing his gratitude, he disclosed his plan to ride west toward the Conestoga settlement. From there he knew not where.

Only Eva had anything to say as Angus left the Gumpf's cabin that morning. She took hold of his great weathered hand, looked up at him sadly, and said, "Don't worry, Angus, Schatto will be alright. I prayed for her last night and I will pray for her every night when I go to bed. I sent angels to watch over her."

Touched beyond words, Angus gave her a prolonged hug, bid farewell with his eyes, mounted Night Fog, and followed the road to the point where he had lost the tracks the previous evening. Several small roads headed westward and Angus followed the one most traveled—the one to the Conestoga settlement. There had been nothing distinctive about the hoof prints left near the barn, and Angus deemed the search virtually hopeless. Convinced that he would never catch up with the thief, he nevertheless inquired at every cabin along the trail about anyone traveling westward.

At the Conestoga settlement, Angus rode directly to the home of Johannes' Dunkard friends. Briefly describing Schatto's theft, Angus asked if anyone had seen a man riding a black horse and leading a dog or wolf on a long rope. To emphasize the urgency of his search, Angus suggested that all nearby neighbors be immediately contacted. In less than an hour every family in Conestoga had been queried and all were eager to assist the Scotsman who had been so helpful in their preparations for settling in the Appalachians. The contacts were fruitless, except for one boy who had been fishing outside of town. He reported seeing a young man on a black horse, followed by what he thought was a gray dog. He caught only a brief glimpse of the man riding in the shadows at the edge of the forest along the Susquehanna River, north towards Paxtant. With no other leads, Angus concluded that he must pursue this one without delay.

It is said that hope springs eternal. So it was with a glimmer of renewed hope that Angus departed the Conestoga settlement and swiftly followed the trail bordering the Susquehanna. Pushing Night Fog to a rapid trot, Angus continually searched the trail for wolf tracks.

Self-recrimination invaded his thoughts, as he pondered what might have been done to prevent the theft. He asked, "Why did I train Schatto to interact with humans? I should have taught her to fear and avoid them all. Then she would not have allowed the thief to drag her out of the barn. I made her too friendly!" But in retrospect, Angus realized that had she not tolerated other humans, it would have been impossible for him to visit the Dunkards, the Gumpfs, or any other friends.

Campfires shared with the pup had provided countless opportunities to reflect on an exciting future that seemed so promising. Now, optimistic dreams were overwhelmed by pessimistic doubts. He grappled with the possibility he would never again see Schatto. Angus realized he could not dwell on her loss, or his life would be overwhelmed by remorse. Gradually he shoved the sadness that clouded the hours since her disappearance into the deep recesses of his mind and reminded himself how blessed he had been to have known her for the few months they were together. What he must do at this juncture was to gather his wits and apply every ounce of logic if there was to be any hope of recovering his wolf.

Angus spotted numerous horse tracks along the way, but none made by a wolf or large dog. Ghost-like tree trunks bordering the Susquehanna River became dim silhouettes as Angus stopped Night Fog and set up camp. With the hobbled gray mare grazing grasses along the riverbank, Angus slowly chewed enough dried jerky to satisfy his hunger. As a large woodpecker issued the day's last taps on a hollow tree, inky darkness replaced the pink glow in the western sky. A despondent Angus searched the horizon for evidence of a nearby campfire, breathing deeply to inhale any passing wafts of wood smoke and staring intently into the blanket of darkness for even a faint glimmer of flickering flames. But to no avail.

Remembering how he had encouraged Schatto to howl when stolen by the Englishman at Raystown, Angus issued the "howl" command, while rubbing the blue stone. Off and on for nearly an hour he pleaded for her to howl. Against the background of a gurgling river, and a cacophony of insect calls, he strained to detect the call of a wolf. Frogs and barred owls vocalized, but no wolves. If she had received his silent command, and subsequently howled, she must have been too far away to be heard.

After several hours, Angus concluded that the thief who stole Schatto would be asleep. Again rubbing the blue stone and concentrating fervently, he telepathically ordered her to chew her leash. She would be tired from walking or running all day, but she must not sleep. She must chew the leash until it separated. And she must do it before dawn. If the thief detected her chewing and realized that the rawhide was nearly severed he would take strong action.

Angus reached Paxtant the next day, but none of the settlers had seen a young man riding a black horse. Angus conducted five days of fruitless searching along the Susquehanna, and five nights of issuing the "howl" and "chew-leash" commands, before calling it quits. If Schatto were now an escapee, the chances of encountering her along the trail were very slim. With faint hopes that Henery might have some information, he turned Night Fog towards Lancaster.

Angus felt sure Schatto would make a beeline for the Gumpf farm at Lancaster—if she escaped. He concluded that she could eventually reach the Gumpf farm, using natural homing instincts. All dogs possess innate homing ability, but Schatto's inbred wolf traits would produce an enhanced ability to retrace her travels.

As he approached the Gumpf farm, Angus wantonly anticipated a wolf pup and a young girl playing in the yard, reminiscent of earlier, carefree summer days. What he saw, however, was an empty playground. Angus had dismounted and was dejectedly leading

Night Fog towards the barn when Eva came running breathlessly off the cabin porch. Halfway to Angus, she began screaming wildly, "She's back! She's back! Schatto is back!" Breathlessly, with sentences running together, she continued, "The angels did watch over her. I prayed every night for her to return and my prayers were answered; she was lying on the porch when we woke up this morning, all covered with mud, and dried blood all over her face and neck, she's in the barn, she won't eat. Oh Angus, I don't want her to die. You must take care of her. She will be so happy to see you."

Overwhelmed with relief and trepidation, Angus hurried to the barn. He jerked open the large wooden door, and there lay a very subdued Schatto on a pile of hay. She raised her head to meet his eyes, and the tip of her tail wagged feebly. But she did not run to him, and she did not even sit up. She was either too injured or too tired to respond. Angus knelt beside her, cradled her head in his hands, and lovingly hugged her as never before.

With tears running down his cheeks, Angus began a careful examination of Schatto's entire body. He grew alarmed to find the leather leash had tightened around her neck and was seriously restricting her breathing. With a quick slice of his hunting knife, Angus removed the deer hide leash, and Schatto's raspy breathing returned to normal. A large patch of hair was worn off her neck, exposing an ugly raw wound, apparently from being dragged behind the horse. As Eva reported, Schatto's coat was caked with mud, and her head and shoulders were coated with dried blood. Whether it came from an animal she had killed or the thief, Angus could not determine. The blood was certainly not hers. Although she had a small cut on her front leg she had licked it clean and there was no sign of infection.

Angus requested, "Eva, please go ask your mother for some food. A soft mix of cornbread, small pieces of venison, and cow's milk should do fine. Hurry!"

Quickly running to the barn door, Eva called back to Angus, "We must save Schatto! We cannot let her die!"

Eva returned in minutes and handed Angus a bowl containing a porridge mixture, which he held before Schatto. Slowly, but almost painfully, the pup lapped at the porridge. Surprisingly, she did not take large mouthfuls, as she would have normally. Her suffering was painfully obvious to her master. Speaking to her in a calm steady voice, Angus softly caressed her head while she continued to lap at the contents of the bowl. When her head dropped onto his leg, he knew she was done eating, and he lowered the bowl to the ground. Still speaking in a calm voice, he said to Eva, "We must let her sleep now. I'll stay here with Schatto and you go ask your mother if I can join you for supper."

Delighted to help, the small blonde-haired girl hurried out of the barn. Still holding Schatto's head on his leg, Angus continued to talk. "You're an amazing pup. How did you manage to make your way back to the Gumpf farm when you could barely breathe? You get better and we'll try to find the thief who did this to you. We'll give him a taste of being dragged behind a galloping horse with a tight rope around his neck."

Although Schatto's eyes had closed, the tip of her tail continued to wag. Placing her head gingerly in the soft hay, Angus rose to his feet, and said, "I'll leave the bowl here, and you can eat a little more when you wake up."

Angus could smell the pungent aroma of fried squash and onions when he climbed the porch steps, and knew that Marianne had prepared more than enough for the four of them. His relief masked his concern as Angus wearily lowered his tired, muscular frame into one of the rough-hewn chairs that lined the cabin porch. Henery joined him while Marianne and Eva finished supper. Angus briefly summarized his futile search for the man he assumed was the indentured shoe cobbler. He concluded, "I guess all is well that ends well. Now we must nurse Schatto back to health."

As the two friends sat quietly, both contemplating the recent events, Eva came onto the porch and announced with authority, "I hope your hands are washed. Supper is ready."

As all faced the bowls and platters holding stewed squash and onions, green beans, fried venison, and cornbread, Henery gave the blessing, "All of heaven and all of Lancaster celebrate Schatto's return. The mountains and hills will burst into song and all the trees of the forest will clap their hands. We are so grateful for you having returned her to us, Lord. May she fully recover from her dreadful experience, and join Angus in future journeys. Thank you for the bountiful meal you have set before us." He then quietly asked, "Eva, would you like to finish the prayer."

With head bowed, she responded, "Thank you, God, for bringing Schatto back to us. Make her better, so that she can run and jump, and chase rabbits and herd mean bulls, and go with Angus on his hunts. Amen."

"Amen, indeed," Angus thought.

By the next day Schatto was sitting, and by the third day she ventured outside the barn. A week later she was eating solid meat, running and jumping, and playing with Eva. There was little doubt that she would survive. With unlimited nourishing food, Schatto made a remarkable recovery. Angus stayed around Lancaster only long enough to help Henery complete his corn harvest.

On one frosty morning in late October, the trapper loaded the packhorse with his trade goods, bow and arrows, and musket, saddled Night Fog, and set a westward course towards the Monongahela. Schatto sensed action and followed his every step. He left his old muzzle-loader with Henery, because it was too awkward to haul through the mountains. Angus had refurbished it that summer, and asked Henery to sell it for him. Because Angus had used it to win the shooting match the previous year, the gunsmith told him it would be easy to find a hunter who would buy it. After hugging Eva and Marianne, and shaking hands with Henery, Angus proclaimed, "It's been a good summer!"

Henery countered, "It's been a good life!"

Angus nodded, mounted Night Fog, and with the impressively redesigned muzzle-loader resting across his lap departed the Lancaster settlement.

Angus had always preferred to travel alone, unencumbered by the conflicting interests of a companion and, more significantly, not having to share conversation. Silence and meditation hurt no man, he told himself; however, being solitary implied isolation from humans, not from canines. Regardless of the time and place, he now acknowledged he had always been more comfortable with a dog—or a wolf —at his side. It occurred to him that his best companions had four legs. Once again he had a four-legged companion running alongside his horse, and he deemed life was indeed good.

CHAPTER THIRTY
GREAT MEADOWS

ANGUS FOLLOWED THE SUSQUEHANNA northward to Paxtant, and veered west towards Raystown. Conditions were ideal for travel, with wildlife concentrated in forest stands and nuts falling like hail in a summer thunderstorm. Mast, the name settlers gave the nuts, was especially abundant that fall and Angus was staggered by the hundreds of black bears, thousands of gray squirrels, and millions of passenger pigeons feeding on the acorns, beechnuts, and chestnuts. He, himself, snacked on raw chestnuts while riding and supplemented his end-of-day meals with roasted chestnuts. The Shawnee had shown Angus how to place newly fallen chestnuts beneath hot coals, and thus make a soft, sweet treat. Dried chestnuts were equally versatile. During winter months they would be added to slowly simmering stewpots, softening adequately for even the youngest Shawnee to eat.

Angus stopped at the trading post in Raystown, described Schatto's theft, and asked John Wray if he had seen a young man riding a black horse. The storekeeper almost apologized while explaining that he had not seen anyone riding a black horse since mid-summer. He added, "You sure are having a run of tough luck. The two thieves ambush you, then someone steals your wolf pup. I guess there is always someone ready to steal rather than work for what they want." Angus nodded in agreement, but offered nothing else.

As Angus mounted Night Fog and prepared to move south to the Potomac, John Wray called, "Come again, you're not a ghost."

Angus backtracked the same trails between Raystown and the Monongahela that he had followed earlier that year. He spent one night with Thomas Cresap and the next with Edward Beatty along the Potomac before traveling north on the Nemacolin Trail. Both men vowed to watch for any suspicious individuals passing through the area, especially a young man named Charles. Angus reached Great Meadows late one afternoon and decided to spend the night at the edge of the natural grassland. Several deer and elk were grazing in the meadow and he was reminded of his camp at the site earlier that year—when he had a full bag of gold.

Forage for his horses was plentiful, and the wooded tree line surrounding the broad meadow provided a comfortable campsite. Angus hobbled the horses, released them to graze, and gathered enough fallen tree limbs for a small campfire. Under clear skies, frost was likely. The fire would feel good that evening and even better the next morning. As he and Schatto reclined on his bearskin near the campfire, countless sparkling stars created a polka-dotted palette in the clear night sky.

The autumn night turned gossamer as Angus snuggled deeper into his bearskin to escape the frosty air settling over the clearing. In his reverie, he was once again in Scotland, it was autumn, and he was sitting on a boulder-strewn hillside watching a small herd of red deer. One of the large stags was bugling, while Angus was mentally moving within shooting range. The bugling became louder and more frequent.

Suddenly Angus sat upright on his bearskin, his warm breath steaming in the brisk morning air. The bugling was not a dream. The normally silent mountains around Great Meadows resounded with the unmistakable piercing calls of bugling bull elk. The low-pitched bellows scaled upward eerily to high-pitched, distinct whistles. Each ascending flute-like note continued until the bull ran out of breath. The bugle then became a series of guttural grunts. Angus and Schatto were being treated to one of the most haunting, eerie sounds of the Appalachian wilderness.

The elk had shed their deep-reddish-brown summer coat and were gloriously cloaked in thicker winter covering. Heads, necks, and legs were a deep dark brown, their middle sections were a lighter brown, and a yellowish-white patch covered each of their rumps. By spring their predominantly brown coats would be bleached a light tan, thus giving rise to the Shawnee name "wapiti" (white deer).

The elk were grazers, attracted to the meadow by the abundance of grasses and sedges. They would feed in the meadow until deep winter snows made it impossible to reach the nutritious dried vegetation. Then they would be forced to move into the surrounding forest to feed on the woody browse provided by shrubs and young trees. As the sun topped the mountain range, the scene before Angus exploded in color. The grasses and sedges of the lush meadow projected vivid shades of browns and tans, while the framing forest was aflame with golden quaking aspens, red and yellow sugar maples, brown chestnut trees, scarlet oaks, and a scattering of green hemlocks. Angus was awestruck, for nothing like this could be witnessed in Scotland.

Along the western edge of Great Meadows stood a bull elk with a heavy dark mane, outstretched swollen neck, and immense antlers pointed backward, barely clearing the top of his shoulders. In addition to constant stomping, he frequently used his antlers as trowels to excavate and toss huge chunks of sod. As Angus watched the drama unfold, a second magnificent beast emerged from the surrounding forest and bugled in defiance. The rut, that period when the annual mating occurs, was in full swing. Earlier in September the bulls had rubbed their antlers against tree bark until the bloody velvet was shred off, and now the smooth, solid ivory-colored antlers gleamed in the early morning sunshine. The larger of the two combatants in the meadow had gathered a harem of eight cows and was now trying to defend them against the challenging newcomer.

The harem bull was noticeably larger than the challenger. The heavy rounded beams of the larger bull's antlers boasted sixteen points, in contrast to the challenger's ten points. As the smaller bull approached the harem bull, both lowered their antlers in preparation for a charge. The two bulls locked antlers, and initiated the pushing contest that would determine who controlled the harem. It must have been obvious to the smaller elk, as it was to Angus, that he was at a serious disadvantage. Seconds later, as he was being pushed backward, the smaller unscathed bull broke off the engagement and retreated into the woods. Angus was disappointed, because he enjoyed watching the bull-to-bull spectacles that were such a unique part of every autumn.

As the harem bull resumed his entertaining bugling, Angus reached a decision. Although his future was even foggier than it had been the previous year, Angus decided to lay claim to his 50 acres of land in the Great Meadows. Tomahawk rights, which were legally recognized throughout most of the Pennsylvania Colony, stipulated that a settler must deaden a few trees near a flowing spring, cut his name or initials in the bark of a living tree near the spring, and blaze trees at the corners of the fifty acres with three slashes, the sign of peace to the Indians. To establish permanent ownership, the settler was required to build a cabin and clear enough land to raise a crop.

Nothing about farming convinced Angus to become a farmer, but he decided that the Great Meadows had one advantage over any other site. It was natural grassland, and produced annual crops of hay essential to wintering horses or other livestock. He had seen first hand the exhaustive effort involved in cutting grasses and curing hay in barns or in pear-shaped stacks. Although it would still be necessary to cure and store hay if he spent a winter in the Great Meadows, horses could obtain many of the dried grasses on their own.

Angus spent three days at the Great Meadows, between the Youghiogheny and Monongahela Rivers, and he thoroughly explored and assessed the entire site. Much of the open area was too wet to produce good quality hay, so he carefully selected the driest part of the meadow for his fifty acres, approximately half meadow and half forest, including plentiful water from a large year-round spring and a small stream. The forested portion would provide logs to build a cabin, a barn, and enough firewood to heat his cabin. Angus blazed trees at the corners of his selected tract and cut his initials in a large beech at the large flowing spring. At the end of the trapping season he would return and begin work on the cabin.

With the establishment of his fifty acres, Angus decided to visit Nemacolin and his family who lived near the Monongahela River. Following the directions Nemacolin gave him when they had met earlier that summer, Angus readily found the small settlement. He followed the pungent drifts of hickory smoke to a clearing with two cabins, a barn, a smokehouse, and several bark lean-tos. Ever wary, Angus stopped just inside the forest edge, dismounted, and cautiously scanned every foot of the clearing and the structures. After ten minutes of scrutiny, he stepped into the clearing, lifted the muzzle-loader over his head with his right hand, and shouted, "Hello, in the cabin! Hello, in the cabin!"

The Scotsman's pronouncement prompted a woman and a boy to come to the door of the largest cabin, and a few minutes later a man exited the smokehouse. Angus recognized Nemacolin and Lonacona. Nemacolin in turn recognized Angus, and said, "Come on up!"

With the rifle in his right hand, the reins of Night Fog in his left, and Schatto heeling obediently, Angus slowly crossed the clearing to the buildings. He saw nothing suspicious as he approached the smokehouse and dropped the gray mare's reins to the ground. Night Fog immediately stopped, as she had been trained to do, and the packhorse did the same. Extending his right hand, Angus offered, "It's good to see you again, old friend." Although they had spent less than twenty-four hours together, Angus did consider the Indian to be a friend. They had fished together, hunted morels together, and shared a meal of brook trout and mushrooms around a wilderness campfire.

The Indian invited Angus into his cabin, where he introduced his wife, Kalmia, and then asked, "You remember my son, Lonacona?"

Angus responded, "Of course I remember him. I would never forget such a good fisherman." The boy smiled broadly, but said nothing.

After his brief visit with Angus and Schatto earlier that summer, Lonacona had talked continually about having a wolf pup of his own. He had elaborated to his mother how Schatto retrieved hidden items, obeyed numerous commands, and, most amazingly, found enough morels to fill a basket. Somewhat timidly Kalmia now asked, "I would like to see your wolf do some of the things that I heard about. Could you show me?"

Angus seized every opportunity to reinforce Schatto's instruction, and readily agreed. Lonacona asked if they could take her down to the nearby creek to see if she would retrieve hidden objects. He had been duly impressed with the way Schatto located hidden bones and then returned them to Angus. While Lonacona gathered some old deer bones, Angus took a few pieces of dried venison from the food bag tied to Night Fog's saddle.

Upon reaching the creek, Angus suggested that Lonacona hide one of the small deer bones at the end of the sand bar. The Indian boy partially buried a deer shoulder blade, while Schatto observed closely. Angus led the pup to the other end of the sandbar, gave an arm signal in the direction of the buried bone, and commanded, "Find the bone. Find the bone." Schatto immediately ran to the end of the sand bar, and after a few false searches, dug out the shoulder blade. Angus immediately shouted, "Fetch. Fetch the bone." After a slight hesitation, she grasped the wide, flat shoulder blade and carried it to Angus. Angus took the shoulder blade from the pup and immediately rewarded her with a piece of dried venison.

Lonacona wanted to repeat the test, and buried a leg bone at the edge of the sand bar. Angus took the pup to the opposite end and again commanded her to fetch. Lonacona had made three false holes, which he filled back in, before finally burying the leg bone. The boy had buried the bone so deep that little scent seeped through the wet sand, and it appeared Schatto would not find it. However, at Angus's urging she intensified the search and soon retrieved the hidden bone. Clenching it firmly in her mouth, she eagerly ran to Angus. When she sat obediently once again, he rewarded her with a piece of dried meat, verbal accolades, and stroking while he softly repeated, "Good girl. Good girl."

Angus kneeled in the sand beside Schatto, held her head in his hands, and commanded in a loud voice, "Bring Night Fog. Bring Night Fog." To the onlooker's surprise, the wolf pup ran up the hill to the buildings.

The horses were behind the barn, and when the pup disappeared from sight, Lonacona despaired, "She won't be back. I know she won't be back." No one else spoke a word. After what seemed to be an inordinate amount of time, Angus saw Schatto emerge from the back of the barn. As she moved farther around the side of the barn it was evident to all that the gray mare was following her docilely because in her mouth were the horse's reins! With great sighs of admiration, the Indian family smiled as the wolf led the gray mare directly to Angus.

After rewarding her with a piece of deer meat, and lovingly rubbing her head, ears, and belly Angus said, "That's one show completed, now let's finish the second."

Angus and the Indian family, followed by Schatto leading Night Fog, moved up the hill from the creek to the side of the barn. Angus had noticed an old milk cow grazing in the clearing behind the barn, and stated, "I'll have the pup drive the cow into your barn." Again kneeling beside the pup, Angus commanded, "Schatto, bring the cow to the barn." With arm signals and brief whistles, he indicated what he wanted her to do. Ears alternately raised and lowered, she quickly moved to the cow, then circled around behind her. At Angus's whistle the pup stopped and dropped flat onto the ground. At Angus's signal, the pup slowly but masterfully, urged the cow into the barn.

Angus spent that night with the Indian family, and took the occasion to discuss with Nemacolin the coming trapping season. Angus sought the Indian's opinion of the best places to trap and trade his furs. Should he return to the headwaters of the West Fork or follow another river? By all accounts, the headwaters of the river called LaCheathe were overflowing with beaver ponds, and a trapper could harvest hundreds of river otter, mink, and muskrat, as well as beaver. And although the lower stretches of the river were too dangerous to travel by canoe, he could load the valuable pelts onto his packhorse and follow ridge-top trails.

He told Nemacolin perhaps he would trap near the Youghiogheny or at the Forks of the Ohio. The French would certainly welcome him at the trading post, because they wanted to drive the English out of the fur trade. As he continued to pose the options to his friend, he awaited some type of omen or vision to guide him. Regardless of where he spent the trapping season, however, he planned to visit the Dunkards beforehand. He did not plan to spend the winter with them, but he did want to see Katrina.

Nemacolin listened intently before suggesting, "Why don't you spend the trapping season around the lower half of the Youghiogheny. Although there are several Indian families scattered throughout that region, none of them trap for beaver and otter. Also, many of them would prefer trading their deer hides to you rather than at the Turtle Creek or Wills Creek trading posts."

Angus enjoyed Kalmia's substantial breakfast, after which he saddled Night Fog, loaded the packhorse, and appointed Schatto to walk alongside Night Fog. He would require the pup to walk there until they moved a mile from Nemacolin's settlement, then she could run and hunt. As Angus prepared to mount, Lonacona ran up, gave him a sincere handshake, and said, "Angus, if you ever find another wolf pup, please give it to me. I really want one."

Remembering how strongly he had wanted a pup when he was a boy, Angus answered, "Aye, Laddie, I promise I'll look for another wolf pup, or at least a smart young dog, and if I find one I'll bring it to you." Then he placed a tender arm across the boy's shoulders and patted his arm reassuringly.

"Stop in and visit on your next trip," Nemacolin stated. "The road to a good friend's house is never long." Kalmia smiled and said to her husband, "It's too bad that all white men who travel the Appalachians are not like Angus."

Lonacona ran partway down the trail behind Angus, and with the sun shining brightly on his back, waved good-bye. As Angus urged Night Fog in the direction of the Youghiogheny, he heard the boy calling, "Come back Angus. Come back and bring me a wolf pup."

CHAPTER THIRTY-ONE
THE FRENCH

DURING THE NIGHT SPENT at Nemacolin's cabin Angus reached a decision regarding his travels for the next day—and perhaps for the coming winter. Because he was only one day's travel from the Christopher Gist Plantation, he would visit and inquire about opportunities to trap in the area.

As the sun climbed overhead, its passage marked by golden shafts of light penetrating the dense overhead tree canopy, Angus stopped the horses, dismounted, and gave Schatto the signal to hunt. She had been heeling alongside Night Fog and Angus knew she was tempted by a variety of enticing scents. Like a bird freed from its cage, she dashed off to one of the many giant sugar maples that grew in the area.

A gray squirrel skirted up the massive tree trunk and stopped at the first branch, where it agitatedly flicked its bushy tail and scolded Schatto who was peering intently at the rodent. Angus would have welcomed grilled squirrel for his next meal but concluded that the arrow would be permanently lost if he missed the target. He had decided to shoot only at those squirrels on the ground to minimize his arrow loss if he should miss. Reinforcing Schatto's previous training, Angus firmly repeated, "Squirrel, squirrel, squirrel."

The pedestrian remounted, beckoned to Schatto, and urged Night Fog up the trail. Schatto ran to catch up and for the next two hours followed the horses on foot. Squirrels and chipmunks were busily collecting acorns for the coming winter and provided endless entertainment for the pup. Although she would never catch one, she relentlessly pursued every one she spotted. Squirrels easily escaped by climbing trees, while chipmunks retreated into holes at the edges of rocks and logs. Schatto never seemed to tire of the game, and Angus never tired of watching her antics.

The air within the hardwood forest had warmed comfortably by mid-day and, as they approached a small stream, Angus halted the horses and dismounted to enjoy a meal of smoked venison. As man and wolf shared the deer meat, a strong refreshing breeze stirred the treetops. Many of the maple leaves whose petioles had dried when the leaves turned from green to reddish-yellow had detached and drifted to the forest floor. One landed on Schatto's back and she began a giddy game of jumping to catch the leaves that cascaded downward.

After crossing the Youghiogheny that afternoon, the trail began a slow ascent that would lead Angus to his evening destination. The sun was setting when a large clearing came into view, signaling that the Gist Plantation was ahead. Guiding the horses around a wide cornfield, Angus noticed that the ears had been harvested but the stiff brown cornstalks still stood erect. Apparently Christopher Gist had been too busy to cut and tie the stalks into shocks.

The open cabin door and a small plume of bluish smoke drifting from the chimney told him that someone was home. Stopping his horses a respectable distance from the cabin, Angus announced loudly, "Hello. Hello. Anyone home?"

A man emerged from the open cabin door, and Angus recognized him as Christopher Gist. Before he had time to give his name, Gist shouted a welcome, "Angus? Is that you, Angus McCallander?" Without responding, Angus waved his muzzle-loader high over his head and urged Night Fog towards the cabin.

Gist had moved down off the porch by the time Angus reached the cabin, and after a hearty handshake stated, "That wolf pup of yours sure has grown since I saw you last spring. She's more than doubled in size. You must be feeding her lots of deer meat."

With a slight smile, Angus answered, "Lots of deer meat and elk meat, plus plenty of milk from an old Jersey cow."

Obviously pleased at Angus's appearance, Gist announced, "Put your saddle and packs in the barn and turn your horses loose in the pasture. After you wash up at the water trough, come on in for supper. I have the ham of a young black bear hanging in the smokehouse and we'll fry some thick steaks for supper. I might even fix one steak just for the pup."

Following supper, the two men sat in front of the fireplace enjoying the blazing logs. Schatto, in typical fashion, stretched out on the earthen floor with her belly facing the fire. Angus detailed his ambush near Raystown by the two Englishmen. Describing his encounter with the younger thief who had taken Buckeye, Angus reiterated his belief that the gold was buried someplace near the stream where he had killed the Englishman.

Not wanting to appear too curious, Angus casually inquired about Gist's family. Christopher answered, "My sons Richard, Nathaniel, and Thomas took my wife, Sarah, to Winchester. Last winter was difficult for the women. We arrived too late the previous summer to clear adequate land for crops, and we ate nothing but wild game from December through April. This year hasn't been much better. One night last month, a herd of buffalo destroyed one of our cornfields, and the weather about ruined our gardens. Along with those setbacks, the French have sent out warnings that they plan to drive all settlers from the region. Most of the families who came with us last year have moved back east of the mountains.

John Frazier, who has a trading post on the Monongahela, has refused to leave, but figures this could be his last winter. The pacifist Quakers who dominate the Pennsylvania government have refused to take any action to protect settlers against the French. If the British government doesn't help, we face a dark future. However, this is beautiful country with great potential, and I'm not going to leave until they burn me out."

After an extended pause, Christopher Gist asked, "Where're you headed next, and where will you spend the winter?"

"I marked the corners of fifty acres in the Great Meadows to lay claim to that parcel," Angus replied. "I'm thinking seriously about building a small cabin in the meadow and using that as my base camp while I trap along several of the small streams that flow into the Youghiogheny. Many of them contain beaver dams, and I know I can trap quite a few beaver and otter from each of the small valleys."

Gist puffed on his corncob pipe for several minutes, and then proposed, "I have a load of work to do around here and could really use some help. My son, Nathaniel, was supposed to come help me, but he sent word last month that he'd broken his leg and would spend the winter in Winchester. Besides, the Ohio Company wants me to survey more of their lands near the Ohio and I'll need to make a couple trips. If you'll stay on and help me I'll let you use one of the other cabins, in addition to the smokehouse and the barn. You can graze your horses in the fenced meadow and feed them part of the hay and fodder when the snows get deep."

"What is it you need help with?," Angus asked.

"Cutting and stacking the remaining corn, cutting and hauling logs, building another cabin and a large storehouse, building fence, plus shooting enough elk and bear to fill my smokehouse. Also, someone needs to watch over this plantation while I'm away. I can draw you a map of most of the major streams that flow into this section of the Youghiogheny and indicate those areas having the biggest concentrations of beaver dams."

Gist carefully threw a piece of oak onto the fire and waited patiently for Angus to respond. Many frontiersmen typically paused five to ten minutes before responding to a question or a statement, following the popular adage, "Silence and thought hurt no man." Angus had already decided that he could not get a cabin built before the first snows whitened the mountaintops. Even though he could quickly build a bark lean-to, he did not want to spend many long winter nights with temperatures below freezing in an open shelter. Also, he needed a building to stretch, dry, and store the pelts he planned to harvest. Finally Angus spoke, "This is a mighty big decision. Let me study on it tonight and I'll let you know in the morning."

"That's fine," Gist replied. "You and Schatto can sleep here in front of the fire or you can sleep in my small cabin. It doesn't matter to me."

After a few minutes Angus answered, "If it's alright with you, I guess Schatto and I will sleep in your smaller cabin. That will give me a chance to think about using it this winter. I have two bear skins and we'll keep warm enough." With that, Angus rose from his chair, called Schatto, and as he strode out the door called, "See you in the morning."

While lying on his bearskins, with Schatto snuggled against his back, he once again weighed his options. He wanted to explore the country around the Allegheny and Ohio rivers, but realized that the French had probably trapped most of the area near the Forks of the Ohio, and they had certainly trapped the entire length of the Allegheny.

Gist explained that although the French had driven all English traders out of the region along the Allegheny, they would undoubtedly be eager to trade with Angus. Angus knew he would be welcomed by the Shawnee at the headwaters of the West Fork River and would certainly be welcomed by the Indian maiden named Sweetwater. He was equally sure the Dunkards would invite him to spend the winter with them. If he stayed with either the Shawnee or the Dunkards, however, it might appear that he was courting Sweetwater or Katrina.

He still had doubts about settling down and becoming a farmer and was not yet ready to make a commitment. Had he not recovered Schatto, he would have been more inclined towards such a future. Now that he had Schatto, it seemed that the next few years would be more enjoyable and rewarding if he continued his solitary life as a trader/trapper. However, before falling asleep a shy grin spread across his face as he contemplated the benefits of spending long, cold winter nights with Sweetwater or Katrina snuggling against his back—rather than Schatto.

By the next morning, Angus had reached a decision. He would spend the winter with Christopher Gist, trapping streams that flowed into the Youghiogheny. He might even have time to build a small log cabin in the Great Meadows. While eating a breakfast of venison and corn mush fried in a skillet over small flames within the fireplace, Angus informed Gist of his decision. From the positive response, it was apparent Christopher Gist needed more help than he had indicated. Angus was reminded of one of his grandfather's sayings, "A successful deal always benefits both sides." Perhaps both men would indeed benefit from their arrangement.

October was a marathon of preparation—forming corn shocks, cutting logs, repairing roof leaks, chinking cabin walls, and, the one chore that never ended, hauling firewood. Angus shot a yearling elk, and the sight of long strips of cured meat hanging in the smoke house satisfied his need for reserves. That elk meat would last until he returned from his first trapping excursion, and he would then shoot a couple bears before they entered hibernation.

Cold weather set in by the first of November and when ice formed in the water trough several nights in a row, Angus knew it was time to start trapping. Pelts of furbearers would soon be prime—the thick, dense, glossy stage when they were most valuable. Angus had decided to trap first those areas that were farthest removed from the Christopher Gist Plantation. Thus, when deep snows limited travel later in the season, he could trap nearby streams. Gist had drawn a rough map marking five mid-sized streams flowing into the Youghiogheny from the east. Those streams would one day be given the names Sewickley, Jacobs, Indian, Laurel Hill, and Casselman.

With pack baskets full of traps, scent baits, smoked elk, cornmeal, and a small bag of salt, Angus, Night Fog, Schatto, and the packhorse headed southeast towards the stream destined to become the Casselman River. Gist, who was not a trapper, described the many beaver ponds throughout the countryside and assured Angus that his biggest problem would be deciding which stream to trap.

Angus traveled all of one day, and as the sun approached its zenith on the second day he reached a mid-sized stream with several beaver lodges. After building a large bark lean-to, he set five traps in nearby beaver ponds, all underwater so that any animal captured would drown without a struggle. Returning to his temporary camp, Angus gathered firewood and cut flexible saplings to make a drying frame for each beaver pelt. The slender saplings were formed into round hoops, somewhat larger than the average beaver. After removing all flesh and fat, the hide from each trapped animal would be stretched taut with rawhide strips inside a hoop of saplings. When dried, the flattened pelt would be nearly round. A few hours over a smoky fire would eliminate any danger of flies laying eggs, even if the weather should turn warm.

A small fire built a few feet in front of the lean-to provided direct heat for man and wolf, as well as heat that radiated off the back of the bark structure. At ease with his surroundings, Angus once again expressed the Highlander prayer, "May you have walls for the wind, a roof for the rain, and a dog beside the fire."

A light snow fell that night as the two companions fell asleep anticipating their next day's bounty. Fatigued by the day's activities, Schatto awakened Angus several times with her jerking legs and quiet yips. After a satisfying breakfast of leftover elk and corn mush, Angus, with Schatto at heel, initiated a morning ritual of checking traps. Although the first trap was empty, the second, third, and fifth traps each held the targeted furbearer—a beaver. Because they were too heavy to easily carry back to camp, Angus skinned two as soon as he removed them from the water. Eagerly anticipating her usual reward of heart and liver, Schatto sat patiently while he sliced open the carcasses and fed her the bloody delicacies. Angus tied a long elk skin rope around the mid-section of the third beaver, which weighed over fifty pounds, and skidded it through the snow back to camp.

Angus skinned the third beaver, careful not to make any cuts in the middle of the round pelt, and skillfully butchered the carcass so that the tail, front legs, hind legs, lower back, and upper back with rib cage were ready for grilling. As the meat cooked over his campfire, Angus cut small slits around the edges of the beaver hides so that they could be laced into the round hoops. Schatto had chewed most of the meat from the head of the beaver by the time Angus finished stretching each pelt, and she was now anxious for more. Affectionately ruffling the fur on her neck, Angus observed, "Still hungry, I see. I reckon a growing pup is always hungry."

Angus continued to trap the beaver ponds in nearby streams and after ten days he had harvested twenty beaver and three river otter. Concerned that his packhorse could carry no more, he retrieved his traps, loaded his gear in pack baskets, secured the pelts on top of the pack baskets, and followed the Youghiogheny back to Gist's

Plantation. As he approached the cabin, Angus was surprised to see that no smoke drifted from the chimneys, even though the temperature was below freezing. When his shouts drew no response he knew that Gist was gone. He unloaded the two horses, stored his baskets and pelts inside the barn, and then took Schatto to the main cabin. A note lying on the rough-hewn table stated, "Went to Wills Creek to meet some men who need a guide. Will return to the Plantation in a few days. Take care of things until I get back."

Angus lightly smoked each of the pelts he had stretched, then hung them in the barn where they would be safe from scavengers. Although mice would probably chew on the edges of the hanging pelts, they would do no serious damage, and there was just no way to prevent mice from getting to them. In the following two days Angus felled a few more chestnut trees and hauled the larger branches to the cabin for firewood. Later that winter the logs would be cut into proper lengths for building another cabin.

On the evening of the third day, Angus was inside the cabin when he heard shouts from the edge of the woods. Moving onto the porch he spotted Gist and six other men approaching the barn. They unsaddled their horses, tied them in separate stalls, threw several pitchforks of hay to each, and then came to the cabin. Nodding to Angus as they entered, the men pulled off their heavy coats and hung them on wall pegs.

Christopher Gist announced, "Gentlemen, meet Angus McCallander. He's staying with me this winter while trapping beaver. Angus, this is Jacob Van Braam, Barnaby Curran, John McQuire, Henry Stewart, William Jenkins, and George Washington."

Angus had never met nor heard of any of the men, but they must be on some important mission if they needed Gist to guide them. As the men headed towards the fireplace they detected a low ominous growl and at the same time spotted Schatto sitting alertly in front of the flames. Angus had sternly ordered her to sit as the men entered the room and, as usual, she obeyed. Although the roaring fire threw considerable light into the cabin, the men could see only the imposing silhouette of the wolf. Each of them stopped short at the menacing growl, a warning that must be instantly heeded.

While Angus still thought of Schatto as a pup, the six men seeing her for the first time knew she was not. Weighing more than fifty pounds and standing nearly three feet tall at the shoulders, she was now the height and length of a full-grown wolf. The thick, silver-gray winter coat that had replaced her summer coat enhanced her appearance. Unlimited amounts of wild game meat had produced a strong healthy young wolf with a stout chest and finely chiseled head so characteristic of her breed. Although her weight would nearly double during the coming year, she appeared full-grown to those men facing her in the dimly lit cabin.

While their voices seemed friendly, Schatto viewed these men as intruders who did not belong in "her" cabin. Natural wolf instinct led her to protect her pack leader against any danger, real or perceived. These unfamiliar men had entered her territory and they must be regarded as a menace.

To some extent Angus enjoyed the confrontation. He studied the impressions on the men's faces—clearly illuminated by the fire— and realized that four of the six showed caution rather than fear. The other two, Van Braam and Washington, were clearly wary and guarded. Angus had become a student of the facial expressions and body positions of threatened individuals. He would have enjoyed more of the confrontation, but he knew that as Christopher Gist's guest he should make the visitors feel welcome.

The man named Barnaby Curran, dressed in well-worn buckskins, spoke quietly, "That sure looks like a wolf, and if it doesn't want me in here I'll be most happy to leave." The two men who had shown alarm moved backwards two steps towards the cabin door, and Angus noted that the one named Washington had dropped a hand to his belt knife.

Realizing that the game had gone far enough, Angus stepped to Schatto's side, placed a hand on her head, and softly uttered, "Good girl. Good girl." Turning to the men he announced, "You're right. This is a wolf. However, if you come as a friend you have nothing to fear. She has attacked a few humans, but has not yet killed one."

The man who had inched towards the door, the one named

George Washington, spoke a little nervously, "I thought all wolves were killers. I never heard of a tame one."

Angus responded, "I raised this wolf from a small pup, and it's as tame as any dog I ever owned. Take a seat and I'll introduce you." As each of the men pulled a chair up to the fire, Angus commanded Schatto to heel and walked slowly in front of the men. The wolf assertively sniffed at their boots and their pants, but ceased growling. Washington had chosen the chair farthest from Schatto and when she was sniffing his boots, Angus suggested, "Extend one hand directly in front of you with the palm facing upward. Schatto will decide whether you can be trusted."

Somewhat nervously, Washington slowly stretched his left hand forward until the wrist rested on his left knee. Curious as to her response, Angus subtly scratched Schatto's neck but said nothing. If the man expressed fear, even if not visible to the others, Angus was certain that Schatto would detect it. He had seen several men in Lancaster show fear, and Schatto had growled defiance at each. Angus had interpreted her actions as an attempt to show dominance over such timid individuals. Schatto continued sniffing Washington's hand and then with the haunting, penetrating gaze so characteristic of wolves, stared deeply into his eyes. After what seemed like several minutes, the wolf cautiously touched her tongue to the end of his longest finger and quickly withdrew it. When Angus noticed the tip of her tail wagging he knew there would be no further growling and he commented, "It appears that she's accepted you, but you'd do well not to try to pet her. She doesn't allow men to pet her until she's been around them for awhile."

After a meal of thick elk steaks, Angus learned more about the expedition that Gist was asked to guide. Governor Robert Dinwiddie of the Virginia Colony, upon learning that the French had built Fort Presque Isle on Lake Erie and Fort Le Boeuf south of the lake, appointed George Washington to lead an expedition and warn the French to withdraw from the region claimed by Virginia. Washington had left Winchester on the fifteenth of November and was joined by Gist and the other men at Wills Creek. From Gist's Plantation they would travel to John Frazier's Trading Post at the mouth of Turtle Creek on the Monongahela where two other men would join them. Governor Dinwiddie ordered them to travel to the Forks of the Ohio and up the Allegheny. Christopher Gist had been handpicked to guide the emissaries because his knowledge of the Allegheny region was unsurpassed and because of his employment by the Ohio Company—the financial group that had invested heavily in the settlement of the region.

As the men returned to their chairs before the fire, Washington said to Angus, "Sir, I heard that you floated a dugout canoe the entire length of the Monongahela, something no other white man, and probably no Indian, has ever done. Tell me about the headwaters of the Monongahela?"

After a long pause, Angus answered, "I spent the winter living with the Shawnee in the upper reaches of the West Fork of the Monongahela. Two large rivers flow into the Monongahela from the east. The river nearest the Forks of the Ohio is called La Cheathe, while the other is simply called the East Fork (later to be called Tygart). The Shawnee told me that both rivers flow out of the high mountains and many stretches are too dangerous to float a canoe. The land around the West Fork is not mountainous, but is much hillier than the country around here. Many sites are gently rolling and a few are almost flat. The soils appear to be rich and would make excellent farmland. The entire country is covered with beautiful stands of giant poplar, chestnut, maple, and oak. Beaver and river otter are common, while deer and elk are abundant wherever there are grassy areas. I saw several small herds of buffalo and enormous flocks of passenger pigeons. In addition, there are mountain lions and wolves. It's wild country, but beautiful. The Shawnee are quite happy there but have fears about settlers building cabins in the bottomlands."

Washington asked, "What about the French at the Forks of the Ohio?"

Angus continued, "They were eager to trade for my furs to prevent the English from getting them, and they paid me gold. They have built temporary buildings, but I got the impression they plan to build a permanent trading post."

The other five men remained silent as Washington quizzed Angus for nearly two hours about the Monongahela and the potential for settlement. Angus brought out the rough map he had burned onto the back of a deer hide, and Washington became quite excited when it was unrolled onto the table. He explained that he had done considerable surveying, and his first trip into the wilderness had been to determine the boundaries of Lord Fairfax's properties. Washington offered to buy the map, but Angus quickly answered that it was not for sale. However, after several minutes of congenial haggling they agreed on a price, and Angus told Washington he could pick it up after returning from the Allegheny. Angus was certain that his grandfather, who taught him to trade, would have approved of the deal. He had planned on making a new map anyway. There were several changes he wanted to make to clarify the locations of the many streams and rivers of the region. He could readily create an improved map on another deer hide during the long winter evenings he would be spending at Gist's cabin.

As they sat around the fire enjoying its dancing flames, Washington addressed Angus. "My grandfather spoke highly of the Highlands and I hope to visit them some day. I remember specifically one story I heard about Scotland. At the beginning of time, God was discussing the creation of the world with the angel Gabriel. Leaning back on his golden throne, he told of his plans for the land to someday be known as Scotland."

The Almighty declared, "I am going to give Scotland towering mountains and magnificent glens, resplendent with purple heather. Red deer will roam the countryside, golden eagles will soar in the skies, salmon will leap in the crystal clear rivers and lochs, and the surrounding seas will teem with fish. Agriculture will flourish and there will be a glorious joining of water with barley to form whiskey."

At that point, Gabriel interrupted and asked God if he wasn't being a wee bit too generous to the Scots.

With only a moment's hesitation, the Almighty replied, "It might appear to be so, but the splendor will forever be darkened by the presence of their neighbors to the south. Englishmen they will be called."

Grinning broadly, Angus chuckled as he responded, "Well-told, Sir. Well-told—and ever so true."

Angus concluded that Governor Dinwiddie must have great faith in the leadership abilities of Washington if he had sent him on such an important mission. Both he and Washington were in their early twenties. As the two men continued their conversation, they gained a genuine, mutual respect for one another. Washington recognized Angus as one of the most capable and knowledgeable woodsmen he had met, while Angus acknowledged that Washington had one of the most inquisitive and intellectual minds he had encountered. He exhibited the breeding and manners of a gentleman, along with the keen grasp of military arts and the politics of western expansion.

Before the men turned in for the night, Gist told Angus that he would be away for several weeks and hoped that Angus could take care of the place while he was gone. Angus readily accepted the assignment so that he could trap the nearby streams as originally planned. Even if he had to be gone for a few nights, Angus would leave enough feed to take care of the livestock. Gist casually told Angus, "If I don't return from this expedition you can spend the entire winter here." The terse statement gave Angus pause, and he silently prayed that he would never face such a possibility.

After a hearty breakfast of bear steaks, Gist, Washington, and the five other men loaded their packhorses in preparation for their journey north to the Forks of the Ohio. A heavy snow was falling, and Angus commented, "You picked a bad time of the year to make this expedition. Why didn't you go earlier in the fall when the weather was better?"

Washington explained, "Governor Dinwiddie just recently learned of the French forts south of Lake Erie, and quickly responded by arranging this expedition. He didn't want to wait until spring because informants reported that the French planned to build more forts on the Allegheny, possibly even at the Forks of the Ohio. So we have little choice about timing. We'll thank you for your blessings on our journey." With that, the group set out.

CHAPTER THIRTY-TWO
WINTER ALONG THE YOUGHIOGHENY

During the next three weeks Angus trapped many of the beaver ponds scattered along the streams located within a day's ride. By early December fifteen otter pelts and more than fifty beaver pelts hung in the barn. In addition, the hides of four deer and two elk were drying on the smokehouse wall. Christopher Gist had asked Angus to shoot a couple bears and smoke their hams and shoulders while he was gone. To avoid spoilage of the meat, Angus waited until December to start the bear hunts. Fatty bear meat, especially the huge hams, spoiled more easily than elk and venison. Angus learned from the Shawnee that bear sows entered hibernation much earlier in winter than males. Most years, all females were in hibernation by the end of November. In contrast, the boars often continued to feed until the middle of December. Veteran hunters throughout the world practiced the same frugality as Scotsman, shooting only males in order to maintain high numbers of game animals. Females were shot only if you wanted to reduce the numbers of animals in an area. Shooting females would be the same as eating your seed corn, a desperate act performed only when your survival depended upon it. As soon as the first snows fell in early November, Angus began scouting the nearby hillsides for bear tracks. By the end of November he had located several ridges where bears were attracted to concentrations of red oak acorns.

One evening during the second week of December, Angus pitched fodder in to the cows and horses. Snow, light as a whisper, began to fall—just what he had been waiting for. While sitting before the fire in Gist's cabin that night, Angus carefully laid his muzzle-loader, powder horn, lead bullets, and two extra-heavy, braided rawhide ropes beside the door. He spent several minutes honing a sharp edge on his skinning knife, then piled his cold-weather hunting clothes next to the bed. Schatto recognized such preparations and anticipated what was going to happen. She did not passively observe these proceedings, but trotted anxiously from Angus to the door. The wolf had no concept of time and was always ready to hunt. Frustrated, she reluctantly sprawled before the fire when Angus crawled into bed.

Sometime during the night the clouds moved away, revealing nearly three inches of snow covering the ground. Angus awoke, went out onto the porch with Schatto, and the two created yellow puddles in the snow. Angus and Schatto were invigorated by the ideal hunting conditions. Following bear tracks in the newly fallen snow would be as easy as picking ripe blackberries in the summer. After a substantial breakfast, Angus saddled Night Fog, secured a small pack basket behind the saddle, and eagerly swung up onto the mare's back. Schatto no longer rode in a basket, and kept pace with the horses regardless of distance traveled. Her stamina was surpassed only by her curiosity and enthusiasm for the hunt.

The silent, snow-covered woods were dazzling in the crisp, frigid morning air. An hour of slow travel and intense visual scans passed before Angus detected the first signs of bear. A fresh set of four-toed, human-like tracks crossed the trail, headed for a cove with abundant red oak acorns. Angus tied Night Fog to a tree, ordered Schatto to heel, and cautiously began his stalk. "Bear. Bear. Bear," the Scotsman uttered.

Stalking carefully from one gigantic tree trunk to another, Angus soon spotted a black form busily searching for acorns under the snow. Moving slowly downwind only when the bear's head was lowered, Angus halted within a hundred yards. At that distance he could deftly plant his rifle's heavy lead ball into the small spot behind the bear's shoulder to drop him instantly. If for some reason he missed the spot and the bear ran off, Schatto would cautiously track him until Angus could finish the kill.

Predictably, the bear dropped just after the explosion of

gunpowder. The hunter quickly reloaded his rifle, pulled two large pieces of dried jerky from his deerskin pouch, and took a comfortable seat beside one of the many large red oaks that dotted the hillside. Ordering Schatto to sit, Angus slowly bit off small pieces of the nearly blackened meat while Schatto downed hers in four quick gulps. The act of waiting patiently after an animal had been shot was one of the most difficult things for Schatto to accept. She knew that a meal of warm liver was forthcoming, but could not accept nor comprehend why they always sat and waited after the animal dropped. Even though Angus felt a little ridiculous conversing with an animal, he explained to her, "A wounded animal could escape if we approach too quickly, so we must wait to verify its demise. You will get your bloody liver soon enough."

Fifteen minutes later, Angus ordered Schatto to heel and the two cautiously approached the animal. A few jabs with the barrel of his muzzle-loader brought no reaction, so Angus leaned his gun against a nearby tree, removed his woolen hunting coat, rolled up the sleeves of his buckskin shirt, and began the messy gutting process. Shortly after, Schatto was happily biting off large chunks of bloody liver while Angus succeeded in pulling out the large mass of intestines. Once the four-hundred-pound boar was completely eviscerated, Angus cleaned the blood from his hands and arms with large clumps of snow. Within the hour, Night Fog was dragging the bear towards the Gist Plantation. Fortunately, the trip was mostly downhill and the smooth snow surface made the chore relatively easy.

Angus skinned the bear, hung it to cool, and prepared for another hunt. The results of the next day's hunt were similar to the first and by nightfall the hides of two large black bears were stretched on the barn wall, and two bear carcasses hung from a sturdy pole attached to the end of the barn.

Angus spent the next four days butchering. Several iron kettles, each big enough for Angus to sit inside, were filled with chunks of bear fat and suspended over small fires to produce the crocks of lard set aside for frying and baking. Hams and shoulders were rubbed with a layer of salt and hung in a wooden shed, where dense hickory smoke would flavor a favorite frontier food and prevent spoilage.

Slabs of side meat, also smoked, would be sliced and fried much like hog bacon. To sustain himself during butchering, Angus ate fried bear heart, fried bear liver, grilled bear ribs, and an assortment of other choice cuts. Just like pack members after a successful kill, Schatto shared in the feast, eating raw meat until her sides bulged.

Heavy snows piled up during the last two weeks in December, and Angus spent many days in front of the fire in Gist's cabin alternately scraping bear hides and stretching the few beaver and otter pelts he trapped from nearby streams. In addition, several hours each day were devoted to grinding acorns and chestnuts into meal using a solid hickory pole and a concave log like a mortar and pestle.

A cup of tea was always within reach when Angus was imprisoned in the cabin during severe weather. Like the Shawnee, he used herbal teas to compensate, in part, for the lack of fruits, berries, and vegetables. During the previous autumn, Angus had collected grapes, roots of sassafras, twigs of sweet birch and spicebush, and leaves of blackberry, goldenrod, and teaberry. Several baskets of dried bark, fruit, and leaves hung within easy reach from the cabin's rafters. In February, sap from maple and birch trees would be boiled with tips of spruce branches to produce a fermented drink that provided some of the vitamins missing from an all-meat diet.

When not engaged in physical labor, Angus sat before the fire reading and rereading a tattered and stained book that Washington had left. "Poor Richard, 1753," it was titled. The author was listed as R. Saunders, but Washington explained that the Almanac had actually been written by Benjamin Franklin, an influential Philadelphia businessman. As Angus studied the article that described how to secure houses from lightning, he vowed to tell Christopher Gist about the method so that his cabins and barns might be protected. Especially fascinating were the "sayings" that Angus reread until he had memorized almost every one. His favorites were, "When reason preaches, if you won't hear her, she'll box your ears," "Haste makes waste," "Anger is never without a reason, but seldom with a good one," and "Serving God is doing good to man, but praying is thought an easier service, and therefore more generally chosen." During the long dreary winter days that followed, Angus was surprised how frequently the Almanac sayings entered his thoughts.

Angus managed a few days of hunting when the weather permitted, and by the end of December he had dragged home a yearling elk and two large white-tailed deer. The smokehouse was nearly full, and the meat supply should last through winter. He planned to shoot at least one more deer or elk in January before the males began to drop their antlers or lost their fat accumulations, in case unexpected visitors dropped by for long periods.

Projects such as tanning bear hides and grinding acorns provided much time to think—possibly too much time. Angus's thoughts flitted from one topic to another, with his future front and center. Not that he actually worried, but he did weigh the consequences of every option he considered. He had never avoided physical labor, and often actually enjoyed it, but this extended stay at the Gist cabin reminded him of the dull, never-ending tasks necessary to maintain a farm.

Katrina, Sweetwater, and even Heather entered his thoughts nearly every day. He wondered what it would be like to spend the long winter days with a wife in a small cabin. If she talked too much it could be miserable. His father had often said, "The woman knows much who knows when to speak, but far more who knows when to hold her tongue." During other months he could spend the daylight hours hunting or working, and it would no doubt be enjoyable to spend a few hours each evening with a wife, eating a prepared meal, discussing the day's events, and sharing a warm bed. Regardless of his doubts, come spring, after the snows had melted and the flooded rivers had receded, he planned to make a trip to the Dunkards. He might even spend a couple weeks with them helping to fill their smokehouse and putting up another barn.

The Gist-Washington party returned from their Allegheny River trip the first week of January. Tired, bedraggled, frostbitten, and dejected, they stumbled wearily into the Gist camp late one afternoon. As they removed their heavy outerwear, the drained travelers explained to Angus that they had camped with the Delaware Indians at the mouth of the Youghiogheny until early that morning.

Washington used the occasion to visit with Queen Aliquippa. One of his assignments, in addition to confronting the French, was to secure commitments from the Indians of the region to back the English if fighting should occur. The men detailed their struggles over rugged trails, through deep snows and swollen rivers. They did reach Fort Venango and Fort Le Boeuf, where the French brusquely maintained that their forts were permanent and certainly would not be abandoned, despite English threats.

Gist detailed how they had obtained canoes from the Indians and attempted to float down the Allegheny to the Forks of the Ohio. He told Angus, "'Twas the most frightening canoe trip I've ever taken. I'll never venture on that river again. The rapids and huge boulders upset us several times, and we were lucky someone didn't drown."

Angus remembered how cold he had felt in spring after falling from his dugout canoe into the West Fork River and marveled that they had survived a soaking in the middle of winter. Washington's party spent two days at the Gist camp, during which time the men and their horses rested and recuperated from the strenuous trip. They ate heartily of bear, deer, and elk and steadfastly commended Angus on his hunting and butchering skills.

As they partook of his hunting success, Washington asked to examine Angus's rifle and took his time admiring and sizing up the weapon. Afterward the Virginian vowed to replace his unreliable musket before he made another trip into the wilderness. Angus responded that the best gunsmiths lived in Lancaster, and recommended Henery Gumpf.

Revived and resolute, Washington and the others left for Williamsburg. Angus and Christopher Gist settled into a daily routine that continued through January. In favorable weather, daylight hours were spent felling and hauling trees from the nearby forest. The two woodsmen amassed an impressive pile of logs to be used for buildings, and at the same time they cleared several acres of land destined for pasture or cropland. When a break in the harsh February weather offered good travel conditions, Gist set out to visit Ohio Company land at Redstone Creek. Angus replenished their smokehouse by shooting another deer, and thereafter made two more short trapping excursions.

One snowy day, as Angus used one of Gist's heavy workhorses to haul firewood from the nearby forest, he heard Schatto produce a series of low growls before he noticed her staring intently to the south. He followed her gaze and to his astonishment a large group of men, as many as forty, were emerging from the forest on horseback. The riders were followed by a long pack train of at least thirty horses. Angus's first reaction was to retreat into the forest, but shouts of greeting from the riders prompted him to do otherwise. This was the largest group of men he had seen in the area, and he figured they were headed for Frazier's Trading Post. But why were there so many men?

Urging the large draft horse down the hill, Angus ordered Schatto to heel and continued the task-at-hand. He had untied the ropes fastened around the log and ordered Schatto into the small cabin by the time the group of men reached the buildings. The packhorses carried saws, axes, and shovels, tools for building not trading. The leader, a man named Captain Trent, dismounted, and shouted, "Good day, sir." As he approached Angus standing outside the barn, he asked, "Is this the Christopher Gist plantation? Governor Dinwiddie has requested that Mr. Gist accompany us to the Forks of the Ohio and help select the site for a fort."

Angus replied, "Aye. But he's gone and won't return for a couple days. I'll give him your message when he returns." Trent said nothing, and after a brief pause Angus added, "You've terrible weather to be outdoors."

Shaking his head, Trent answered, "The Governor was warned that the French would begin building a fort when the snows melted, and he ordered us to have an English fort built before spring arrived. Given the choice, I would have waited. But the Governor gave orders, and as a paid soldier I must obey."

Seeing the misery in the eyes of the men, many who appeared to be boys, Angus offered the men some respite from the cold. "You're welcome to have a rest in the barn. If you've a cook to help, we'll make some hot broth to sustain your men. I've more than enough provisions to share some with you. You've a hard trip ahead."

After the men and horses were fed and rested, Angus pointed out where they would resume their journey. "Follow the main trail north-northwest and you can't miss the Forks. Three or four days should get you there."

The leader verbally expressed his thanks to Angus, and said Governor Dinwiddie would be told of his generosity. He blessed Angus on behalf of his men, several of whom saluted Angus as they formed ranks. In his mind, Trent was certain this man should be leading the construction of the British fort at the Forks. As he signaled the group forward, he casually remarked, "Take care of yourself out here in the wilderness, McCallander."

"Aye," Angus responded, "and you must be ever alert for danger—from man and beast. You'll be fortunate if you survive the French, the Indians, and the weather." Angus was well aware that their trip was fraught with danger and knew that he would not want to be building a fort in the middle of winter.

After the last of the pack train faded into the forest to the north, Angus threw some fodder to the horses and opened the cabin door for Schatto to exit. She quickly ran to the packed snow where the horses had walked and carefully examined each patch of urine-stained snow and every steaming pile of horse droppings. Finally satisfied, she joined Angus and the two returned to the main cabin. After feeding Schatto and tidying the cabin, he was relieved that the snow had stopped. Skillfully wielding the one-man crosscut saw and the broad axe, he reduced the log to sizes that he could maneuver into the fireplace.

Upon Gist's return a week later, Angus told him about the men who had passed the cabins and asked if he had seen them. Christopher explained that he had been surprised to encounter them on the trail but was pleased that Governor Dinwiddie was taking action to block the French presence in the region. As requested, he had accompanied them to the Forks and helped select the site for the fort. "Captain Trent plans first to cut enough trees to build permanent cabins, brutal winter weather dictating that they have adequate shelter and firewood to survive. Actual fort construction will not begin for another month."

While the mountains seemed to be void of living creatures during

February, there were actually many animals present. True, most birds had migrated hundreds and even thousands of miles south to escape the cold and dearth of food. Only a few birds, such as woodpeckers, chickadees, crows, and wild turkeys, were able to exploit the dregs of autumn and survive the ice and snow that dominated the landscape. Groundhogs, black bears, and other hibernating animals had disappeared from the forests in late fall. Other animals, such as mice, shrews, and weasels were active beneath the deep snow, but were seldom seen from above.

Tracks in the snow proved that many animals remained active even during the worst of winter. Braving the weather with their thickened coats of winter hair were the plant-eating rabbits and deer, and the down-laden grouse and turkey, typical prey for bobcats, wolves, and mountain lions. The latter predators were equally protected with heavy hides, underlain by fat layers to sustain them.

February in the Allegheny Mountains was a difficult time for wildlife that had not hibernated or migrated. It was especially difficult for the deer and elk. The nutritious acorns from October's bounty had been consumed by the end of December. The late summer grasses that had waved softly in the wind had been grazed to mere stubble, and what remained was now concealed under hard crusty snow.

By mid-winter, the haystacks and fodder shocks scattered throughout the Gist fields, intended for farm animals, were attracting deer and elk. Schatto was sent daily to drive unwanted wildlife from the fields. While the horses and cattle had become accustomed to her presence and barely raised their heads to acknowledge her appearance, the deer and elk fled wildly. With bounding leaps covering nearly ten feet, deer quickly bolted from the fields while elk relied more on an efficient ground-covering run.

The "Oft" command, which Angus issued to drive deer and elk from the haystacks, was one of Schatto's favorite. Angus began teaching Schatto the "Oft" command the previous autumn, when hunting wild turkey. Large flocks of fifty or more were common when the annual deluge of acorns and chestnuts blanketed the forest floor. Although Angus could usually get a decent shot at a feeding turkey, some times it was difficult to approach close enough for a good shot. On those days he utilized a technique he had learned from the Shawnee. After locating a flock, the Indians would rush wildly in their direction, widely scattering the individual birds. The birds would shortly return to the area in hopes of rejoining the other turkeys. The Indians then selected a hiding place and began imitating the "lost bird" call. Young birds were the most anxious to rejoin the flock and as a result, they were the first to respond to the Indians' call. The Shawnee were usually successful in luring naïve juveniles into shooting range.

Schatto had mastered the "Oft" command and appeared to delight in scattering turkeys. After the turkeys were scattered far and wide, Schatto would return to her pack leader and reluctantly plop down in the leaves to begin the frustrating wait for her next assignment. No doubt she wondered why Angus didn't allow her to stalk the birds as she did when hunting bears or elk. The wait between scattering turkeys and the successful shooting of a returning bird was too long for her to make the association between the two events.

As Schatto's instruction became more detailed Angus was pleased to note that the use of the blue stone was seldom necessary. The combination of his natural teaching skills and the wolf's intelligence made learning a new command relatively easy—especially commands related to hunting.

Stalking humans, however, was not so easily imparted. Angus had spent many days teaching the "Trail man" command, but unfortunately, they encountered too few humans for regular practice. However, with the assistance of Christopher Gist, a few nearby neighbors, and some visiting Indians, Angus was able to direct human-tracking exercises at irregular intervals during the winter months.

Gradually the wolf became proficient at following human scent and pinpointing their hiding location. Schatto would track within one hundred yards of the prey before she transitioned to a belly-crawl as if stalking deer, elk, or bear. Stalking was an innate hunting skill, rewarded ultimately by the kill and the hot, belly-filling meat after Angus shot the animal. Stalking humans involved no such reward, however, and without the reinforcement of a reward it was much more difficult to orchestrate.

Schatto had become adept at dispatching small and mid-sized wildlife such as rabbits, groundhogs, and raccoons. Still under a year old, she had also brought down three deer. When a firm crust formed on the snow, a lithe and lean Schatto was able to dash across the surface while the heavier ruminants broke through and labored to flee. As the deer scattered from the hayfield around Gist's cabin, Schatto pursued and made her first deer kill. Superbly designed to hunt, her long legs and large feet with calloused toe and heel pads enabled her to run faster than forty miles per hour and jump streams and other obstacles over fifteen feet wide. Overtaking the struggling deer, she sank her powerful canines into a hind leg, thereby knocking the prey off its feet. Thereafter, she locked her jaws around the deer's throat and death came quickly.

On other occasions, Angus spotted winter-weakened deer and gave the "Kill" command. Schatto pursued and brought down each animal, filling her belly with nearly fifteen pounds of deer flesh. Angus deemed it essential that she learn to kill enough prey to survive if she some day returned to the wild—an event he did not want to consider but thought possible.

The weariness of winter finally waned, and spring brought welcome relief. One sunny day in April while Angus and Christopher were notching the ends of logs to build a cabin, they were surprised to see a large group of men on horseback emerge from the forest to the north. As they approached, both Angus and Christopher recognized them as the group sent by Governor Dinwiddie to build a fort at the Forks of the Ohio. The numbers of both men and horses were noticeably smaller than two months earlier. Both men and horses had lost weight. Their clothing and gear were in serious disrepair. After initial greetings, the person in charge—Ensign Ward—dismounted and explained that they had nearly completed the small fort, which they named Fort Prince George, when the French attacked. Their leader, Captain Trent, was waiting for them at Wills Creek.

Greatly outnumbered and ill prepared for a major battle, the English soldiers immediately surrendered. The French had let them keep enough horses and supplies to reach Williamsburg but forced them to leave all their tools and the remaining horses. Before the

English soldiers departed, the French commander told them that he had orders to build a French fort at the site. He also sent word to Governor Dinwiddie that the French would continue to build forts along the Ohio, and the English should stay east of the mountains.

Gist offered the soldiers a place to rest and enough smoked meat to get them to Wills Creek, but could provide little else. The soldiers related stories of their hardships and news of the Ohio frontier. Theirs was not an easy assignment, but history-making perhaps. Unless they were caught by a late winter snowstorm Gist was certain they could safely cross over the mountains to Wills Creek. From there, they should experience only minor difficulties in following the Potomac River back to Williamsburg. Both Gist and Ensign Ward felt it was important that Governor Dinwiddie be informed as soon as possible. What steps he would take were unknown, but there was no doubt he would take strong action. All parties were somber as they contemplated that military conflict along the frontier was imminent.

CHAPTER THIRTY-THREE
FORT DUQUESNE

IN LATE APRIL, ANGUS decided it was time to take his hides and pelts to a trading post. Most of the goods he brought from Lancaster had been traded to the Indian families living around the lower Youghiogheny. Like the previous spring, Angus sought gold for his pelts, not trade goods. While at Frazier's Trading Post during his December trip with George Washington, Gist had mentioned that Angus would probably be bringing some furs to sell. Frazier had seemed more than eager to get the beaver pelts, because the Indians had very few to trade. Unfortunately, Frazier preferred to trade supplies for hides and pelts, and was unlikely to pay gold.

Angus had immediate plans for gold. It was essential in training Schatto to find buried coins. During the weeks of winter isolation, he had carefully formulated the training procedures for Schatto to detect the odor of gold. The repeat and reward training had worked well in the past, and he anticipated needing only a few exercises to teach Schatto this new skill. With the onset of spring, he would return to the small stream north of Raystown where he had killed the Englishman. Although days or weeks might be required, he was determined to find his stolen gold.

As Angus prepared to follow the trail north to Turtle Creek, Gist proposed that he continue on to the Forks of the Ohio after reaching Frazier's. Still employed by the Ohio Company, Christopher needed to assess French activities at the site. If Angus were to trade all his deer hides and just a few of his beaver pelts to John Frazier, then he could take the majority of his beaver and river otter pelts to the Forks to sell. If the French were building a fort at the site, as reported, there certainly would be people actively trading with the Indians. The French needed the natives on their side during any future conflicts and would raise the ante for hides and pelts to force out the English traders.

His packhorse and one of Gist's draft horses were loaded with hides and pelts as Angus set off for Frazier's Trading Post near the mouth of the Youghiogheny. Angus rode into Frazier's complex of rough-log buildings after two 14-hour days of travel. John Frazier seemed surprised to see Angus, but was eager to examine his pelts.

Angus was candid with Frazier, and explained that he was taking his beaver and river otter pelts to the Forks of the Ohio. If the French would not trade for gold he would return and trade them to Frazier for powder, lead bullets, and other needed supplies. Frazier realized he would be driven out once the French completed their fort at the Forks of the Ohio, and was eager to amass as many hides and pelts as possible before hauling them over the mountains to Philadelphia. He feared that upon return his trading post might be destroyed, or in the hands of a French trader.

By the next evening, the two had agreed on a trade for all of Angus's deer hides plus ten of the smaller beaver pelts. Frazier wanted all of the beaver and otter pelts but declined to pay gold for them.

The transfer of traded goods required another night at Frazier's Trading Post before Angus took leave for the Forks. Only one horse was needed to haul the remaining hides, so Angus left his other horse in Frazier's care until he returned. After a short trip down the Monongahela, Angus detected the sounds of pounding, sawing, and men yelling. Emerging into an opening, Angus saw the panorama unveiled. An extensive fort was being constructed on the sloping hillside above the Forks. Considerably larger than any other structure in the Appalachian Wilderness, it was clearly designed to be defended by the French.

Several workers watched Angus approach the nearly completed fort, but a lone rider posed no threat to such a large force. To avoid the same language problem he had faced previously at the Forks, Angus asked if anyone spoke English. Most men withdrew as Angus approached, obviously wary of Schatto. The same problem surfaced every place he visited, and he considered leaving Schatto tied to a tree in the woods before venturing into a settlement. Rejecting that option, he advanced through the construction. With the wolf heeling obediently at his left side, he finally was directed to one of the commanders who spoke English. Openly inquisitive about Angus and the English presence in the region, the Frenchman invited Angus to eat with him that night.

Angus discovered that Maurice, the trader he had dealt with the previous spring, had built a large cabin near the fort and was actively trading with the Indians and white trappers. The commander agreed to accompany Angus to the trader. With the commander serving as interpreter, Angus and Maurice soon reached a deal for all of his pelts. Maurice was eager to assure future trade and to establish good will with such a capable trapper, so he gave Angus a better price than he had the previous spring. As Angus counted the gold coins into a deerskin pouch, he wondered whether he could get them safely to Gist's Plantation. If he did, he had selected a large, hollow sycamore where he would secrete them until he could travel to Lancaster.

Three other French soldiers, each fluent in English, joined them for dinner that night. With pewter plates, metal forks, and a bottle of deep red wine to accompany the fried buffalo steaks, Angus was treated to the most formal dinner he had ever attended.

The meal was followed by three hours of congenial interrogation, during which time it was evident why Angus had been invited. The Frenchmen courteously inquired about his travels, the Monongahela region, the Indians, and most directly, the English. They asked pointedly, however, whether there were any forts along the Monongahela or Potomac, and how many English settlements existed between the Monongahela and the coastal cities. Noting that he was not English, based on his Scottish accent, a few inquiries were unabashedly aimed at determining his allegiance to the English. Angus sidestepped his disastrous battle against brutal Lord Cumberland at Culloden and his long-time resentment towards the English. Better to let them believe him neutral at this point, by expressing his desire to settle in a new land.

The following day Angus roamed freely around the gently sloping site above the junction of the two rivers where the fort was being constructed. It was to be called Fort Duquesne, in honor of the Marquis de Duquesne, recently named governor of New France (Canada). Angus carefully studied the design of the fort and weighed how it might be successfully attacked. Remembering his battles alongside Prince Charles, he looked for weaknesses in design or construction. He concluded that it would be foolish to attack the sides that faced the two rivers. The only possibility of success involved positioning cannons on the hill above the fort. However, that would be difficult because the French would stop any attempt to bring cannons in by boat. They would have to be brought cross-country, and Indian allies of the French would certainly inform them of any English troop movements.

With mixed emotions, Angus departed Fort Duquesne that afternoon. Natural Scottish contempt for the English clashed with his growing sympathy for the colonists. He faced the difficulty of separating his positive feelings for the American colonists from the negative ones he held towards England. Although they were English colonies in name, Angus viewed them as separate entities from the British Empire. Any troops sent to battle the French would most likely be English soldiers, not men living in the colonies. His packhorse load was lightened, but his spirits were not.

Angus arrived at Frazier's later that day, certain that John Frazier would be eager to hear about the progress on the fort and whether Angus had been successful in selling his furs. John Frazier knew the fort was being constructed, because on two occasions he had viewed the activities from the nearby forest. However, because of his known affiliation with the English he had not advanced close enough to be recognized or to scrutinize the layout. Angus therefore described the design and size of the fort and told Frazier that it could resist any attack, whether by English or Indians. Noticeably disturbed by the news, Frazier concluded that he would undeniably be forced to leave the region once the fort was completed. Only if the English succeeded in driving out the French could he remain.

George Washington had suggested that Angus stop in and pay his respects to Queen Aliquippa at her Indian settlement near the mouth of the Youghiogheny. When Angus left Frazier's Trading Post, he had outlined his plans to visit the Delaware Queen, hopefully arriving at mid-morning to avoid spending the night with the Indians. Leading the two packhorses and walking alongside Night Fog, Angus entered the camp with Schatto. Several surprised youngsters playing at the edge of a small stream had noted his arrival, and the barefooted harbingers quickly ran back to camp to announce the unexpected visitor. Before he reached the first bark wegiwa, Angus stopped and in passable Shawnee asked the nearest Indian where he might find Queen Aliquippa. Washington had reported that at least twenty families lived in the settlement, and while they were extremely friendly during his visit he recommended that Angus take gifts to the Queen to show his respect.

As Angus moved deliberately through camp, accompanied by a tall powerful Delaware, it seemed that every one of the residents was watching. While most Indians showed curiosity about the man and beast, the dogs showed obvious contempt. All were about half the size of Schatto but had the security of being in their own territory. For the first time in her life, Schatto faced a menacing threat. Neither Indians nor their dogs had ever been so close to a live wolf. While the size of Angus impressed them, they were utterly fascinated by the wolf. They'd heard rumors of a large, red-headed, man and his wolf, but none had believed them.

Most of the Indian dogs were barking insanely, but when one of the Indians shouted and threw a stone in their direction they slinked back behind one of the wegiwas. Angus carried his muzzle-loader in his right hand and led Night Fog with his left. Schatto was between him and Night Fog, positioned to avert direct encounters with the dogs. Flanked by horses and wolf, Angus became more imposing than a lone intruder. The largest dog in camp, a typical Indian dog with short dark-brown hair, did not bark but growled aggressively from beside one of the bark buildings. With the hair along its back standing erect and its lips curled back in a menacing snarl, Angus realized that it was more of a danger than any of the others. Under the circumstances, however, he could do little more than glance peripherally and stay on guard.

The Queen, much older than Angus had anticipated, came out of the bark dwelling and motioned Angus to approach. Her long black hair, showing considerable gray, was tied into a silken braid that draped like a satin rope over her left shoulder and hung nearly to her waist. A long cloth dress concealed her body shape, but she still had a relatively youthful figure. Faded and stained, the dress she wore was dark blue with white trim. Symbols of various designs had been sewn onto the sleeves for decoration, but other than the head of a mountain lion, none were recognizable.

With his attention focused on the Queen, Angus was unable to maintain eye contact with the growling dog. He was suddenly alerted to danger when he heard several Indian shouts and one scream. As soon as Angus turned his head to greet Queen Aliquippa, the dog charged. Intending to sink its canines into Schatto's neck or Angus's leg, the dog was only a muzzle-loader length away when Angus heard the attack. Before he could swing his rifle or draw his hunting knife he heard an enraged deep-throated growl erupt from Schatto. Her head had been slightly ahead of Angus's left leg, but in an instant she turned and lunged to counter the attacking dog. Schatto had killed groundhogs, raccoons, and deer, but she had never faced a veteran fighter as dangerous as the Indian dog. Although smaller than Schatto, the dog was much older and considerably more battle-experienced. It was the dominant dog, the alpha male, within the loosely formed pack of Indian dogs, and it feared nothing.

Instinctively throwing her shoulder into the charging dog, Schatto forced it to miss her. Although knocked off-balance, the snarling, salivating dog quickly regained its footing. But before it had the opportunity to renew the attack, Schatto took her advantage and made a powerful leap, clamping her jaws around the dog's neck. As the wolf's four long canines sank deeply into the dog's neck, Angus knew the fight was over. With a vicious toss, Schatto threw the limp body of the dog aside and returned to Angus. Angus ordered her to sit and, while gently patting her head, he said in a low voice, "Good girl. Good girl." She had proved to be more than equal to an untrained dog.

Everything had become still as a winter night in the Indian camp. It was surreal. No dogs barked. No Indians spoke. How valuable was such a dog to the Indians, Angus asked Queen Aliquippa with a questioning gaze. Frowning, she again motioned him to approach. In speaking range, Angus attempted to apologize for the incident. Searching desperately for the correct Shawnee words, he struggled to express his regrets. The Queen permitted him to continue for several minutes, then with a slight smile on her face said, "Not a big loss, we'll have the dog for supper."

He wanted to change the subject, however, and quickly moved to his pack baskets where he retrieved the gifts he had brought. As expected, the bright beads were obviously welcome, but Queen Aliquippa was more gratified with the packet of sewing needles, roll of bright blue cloth, and two iron kettles. Angus told her that his friend, George Washington, had suggested that he stop and visit, and related that Washington had arrived safely at the Gist Plantation. The two continued their talk for the rest of the morning, during which time Angus described his stay with the Shawnee the previous winter. Queen Aliquippa inquired about the location of the Shawnee village and whether they had any problems with enemies. Angus revealed that members of the Catawba tribe had attacked them when they lived along the Potomac, but they had enjoyed a trouble-free life along the West Fork.

After a mid-day meal of smoked turkey, Angus explained to the genial queen that he must leave now to arrive at Gist's Plantation the following day. Obviously disappointed, the charming lady urged him to stay and enjoy roast dog for dinner. Angus quickly, but politely, refused. He would not insult her by admitting there was no way he would eat dog meat. Every bite would make him think of Schatto, and even starvation would not compel him to eat his wolf companion. Angus told a disappointed Queen Aliquippa that he would visit her on his next trip to the Forks of the Ohio, and then exited her wegiwa.

As Angus, Schatto, Night Fog, and the packhorse moved through the crowd, a female voice called out, "Nice day, Canoe Man." Angus abruptly halted and slowly searched for the source of that voice. The vivid image of a nude Indian maiden standing erect on a downed sycamore at the edge of the Monongahela River brought a sly grin to his face. However, this time all the women were fully dressed, and he had no way of knowing which one had called out. He carefully studied each face, but realized that when he passed her in the dugout the previous summer he had not focused on her face. He smiled broadly as thought, "I could identify the lass if she didn't have any clothes on."

As he scanned the group, Angus detected several of the older women staring at a very attractive maiden standing in the rear of the crowd, and thought she could possibly be the river maiden. No other hints came from the crowd, and Angus reluctantly continued his departure from the Delaware camp. Next time he visited Queen Aliquippa's camp he would send advance notice and if the maiden wanted to present herself, she would have the opportunity to do so.

On the uneventful return trip, Angus was constantly alert for possible ambush. He returned to Gist's Plantation and surreptitiously hid his gold. Gist congratulated Angus for his successful trip, but voiced his overriding concerns about the construction of Fort Duquesne. The quiet and rewarding life he had enjoyed in the Appalachian wilderness could not last. The success of the Ohio Company was in doubt. It would be impossible to send settlers west of the Monongahela if the French established a strong presence in the region. Before eating their evening meal, Gist offered the blessing, then added, "May you live a long life, full of gladness and health, with a pocket full of gold as the least of your wealth."

CHAPTER THIRTY-FOUR
FORT NECESSITY

WHILE ANGUS WAS AT Fort Duquesne, Christopher Gist learned that George Washington and one hundred-fifty Virginia militia had been dispatched by Governor Dinwiddie to join Captain Trent at the Forks. Washington, now a Lieutenant Colonel, was charged with building a road from Wills Creek to the Monongahela for the purpose of expediting movements of men, goods, cannons, and ammunition.

When Washington learned that the French had captured the English fort and were constructing a fort of their own at the Forks of the Ohio, he realized the importance of completing his assignment. An attack on the French would certainly require cannons and considerable ammunition, and the only way to move artillery from Wills Creek to the Monongahela was by wagons. Thus it was that in April of 1754 the first mile of primitive road pushed into the Appalachian wilderness.

Angus had planned to visit the Dunkards in May. However, George Washington's arrival prompted Christopher Gist to ask Angus to assist with scouting French movements, posing a dilemma for the Scot. He had yet to decide whether to support the French or the English. Feeling an obligation to Christopher Gist, Angus agreed to delay his trip to the Dunkards. A major confrontation was imminent, Angus judged, so it would be better to wait until the battle was over before visiting Katrina and her family. At that time, he could summarize the latest developments on the frontier and advise them of future threats.

Following the Nemacolin trail most of the way, Washington pushed his road across the mountains and finally reached the Great

Meadows on May 24. To create a road capable of handling small wagons, trees were cut, logs were dragged, and small bridges were constructed. In some stretches, only a few miles were cleared in a day. Washington was fearful that a battle with the French could occur in the very near future, and therefore ordered his troops to build a log stockade in the Great Meadows. He surmised that a substantial structure within the open meadow could be effectively defended, and proclaimed to his men, "This is a charming field for an encounter."

In anticipation of Governor Dinwiddie's attack on Fort Duquesne, Washington pushed ahead with construction of the road to Gist's Plantation. Simultaneously, he directed English troops to complete the fort at Great Meadows. While his troops were busy building a road and a fort, Washington paid a visit to Gist's Plantation. He needed to evaluate the route for his road, but he was also eager to learn whether the Youghiogheny was navigable. Since it flowed into the Monongahela a short distance south of the Forks, it would be more efficient to move troops and cannons down the Youghiogheny than to build a wagon road across Laurel Mountain.

Washington had been advised that the Youghiogheny was clear, deep, and navigable. Gist refuted his information as totally incorrect; the river was narrow, with fast currents full of rocks and rapids. Washington convinced Angus to accompany him on an exploratory trip down the river, to judge for himself. "I want to get an early start in the morning," said the Virginian. "Nothing is more beautiful than the loveliness of the woods before sunrise."

Using a bark canoe that Washington bought from a local Indian, the two men set off down the river, departing from the ford at Great Crossing (currently covered by Youghiogheny Reservoir). Fortunately it was May and the water was relatively warm, because their canoe upset three times before they reached a high falls (currently Ohiopyle). That short escapade convinced Washington the idea of floating men and cannons downstream was totally impractical. With that avenue abandoned, Washington concluded that a road across the mountains was essential if they were to move troops and cannons downriver to the Forks via the Monongahela.

A large regiment of soldiers and several wagonloads of swivel guns and supplies arrived at Great Meadows the first week of June. The untimely death of Colonel Fry at Wills Creek relegated to Washington full command of the Virginia Regiment. Young Colonel Washington, at twenty-two years of age, found himself in charge of nearly three hundred men.

Although somewhat overwhelmed by the sudden development, Washington knew that he had one pressing mandate—to attack the French at Fort Duquesne and retake the Forks. True, the French numbered over one thousand, but Washington's hopes were buoyed when a company of more than a hundred regular English troops arrived from South Carolina. Unfortunately, Washington had been unable to convince any Indians to join his troops. The Colonel knew this was a major limitation and would greatly reduce his chances of defeating the French in any future battles.

Anticipating that the French and their Indian supporters were planning to attack his troops, on May 27 Washington asked Christopher Gist and Angus to scout the forests between Great Meadows and the Monongahela River. Late that same afternoon, while following one of the trails the French would likely use, the two men encountered an Indian chief, Tanacharisson, one of the few who had agreed to ally with the English in any battles against the French. The Seneca chief, given the name of Half-King by the English, revealed that a small party of French soldiers was hiding in a deep ravine along the side of Laurel Mountain. Quickly returning to Great Meadows, Gist and Angus relayed the information to Washington who promptly began formulating plans for an attack. He sent Gist to Williamsburg to inform Governor Dinwiddie of the imminent French invasion and to request additional troops.

Selecting forty of his best fighting men, Washington set out to locate the furtive French camp. To avoid detection, Washington and his troops traveled all night to reach their destination by daybreak the next morning. The English troops were strategically placed on the two sides of the ravine, with Half King's Indians guarding the opposite end to prevent escape. A brief fifteen-minute battle ensued, during which time Angus elected to remain several hundred yards behind the English troops and simply observe. Surprised and surrounded, the French suffered major casualties as a result of the first two volleys fired from English muskets. Of the thirty French soldiers, several died instantly while others suffered serious wounds. The hopelessness of their situation prompted the French commander to surrender.

As the firing ceased, Angus hurried forward to the edge of the ravine where he was able to observe surreptitiously the activities. While Washington and the French commander, Monsieur La Force, discussed terms of surrender, Angus feared that the Indians would not be satisfied with a peaceful surrender. Mumbling to himself, he said, "The Indians won't be happy with one or two scalps; they'll need more proof of their role in the battle."

Led by Half-King, the Indians began looting the French soldiers and scalping the dead. French muskets, powder horns, and bullet pouches were the first targets, followed by hats and jackets. Inching forward to a large boulder to witness the happenings, Angus was shocked to see Half-King and his warriors split the skulls of several helpless French soldiers sitting unarmed on the ground. Disgusted that Washington was unable, or unwilling, to stop the savage behavior, Angus began a stealthy retreat from the area. This was his first opportunity to observe Indian behavior in battle, and he had seen a belly-full.

Following a return to Gist's settlement, George Washington sent for Angus and urgently requested that he scout the trails near Fort Duquesne. Washington was certain the French would attack his troops in retaliation for the Laurel Mountain massacre. Traveling on foot to avoid detection, Angus and Schatto moved stealthily through the countryside south of the Forks. The French had Indian allies scouting the same area, so Angus spent considerable time visually scouring the countryside.

In front of Fort Duquesne several hundred canoes and other watercraft were moored along the riverbank, and Angus suspected that a large military campaign was set to begin. His suspicions were confirmed one day during the last week of June when he watched guns and ammunition being loaded into the canoes. The next morning canoes began moving up the Monongahela. He delayed only long enough to determine troop numbers, and then set out to report the discovery. Running at a ground-covering lope everywhere the terrain would permit, he reached George Washington in two days. Upon hearing Angus's report, the Colonel assembled his road-building troops and ordered them to return to Great Meadows and prepare for an attack. They had less than forty-eight hours to prepare.

As Angus provided Washington with details of the advancing force, Angus remarked, "It appears that a sturdy fort is surely a necessity now."

Washington thought about the comment for several minutes, and answered, "If we're going to build a fort it must have a name, and you have just given me that name, Sir. Fort Necessity it will be called!"

Washington attempted to convince Angus to join him at the fort, where his muzzle-loader would be much more effective than the inaccurate muskets carried by his troops. Angus resolutely declined, insisting that he did not want the French to know he had chosen to support the English. He further noted, "I think it prudent not to tell anyone about my assistance, or describe my contributions in any of your reports. A red-haired man and a large timber wolf are too easily spotted, and any further help would be impossible if the French learn of my cooperation with the English."

"If you can't join me at the fort, I'd be most indebted if you would scout the road between here and Great Meadows. I've received reports that suspicious Indians and Frenchmen were seen in the nearby woods, and I'm concerned about an ambush on the way back to my soldiers. The massacre of the French soldiers at Laurel Mountain will certainly bring retaliation. I'm waiting for Christopher Gist to bring me a report from near Redstone, but I cannot wait much longer."

Angus replied, "Aye, we can do that for you, because our presence in the woods will not be unusual. Wait an hour before you leave to give us time to search the area, and be very alert while approaching likely ambush sites."

Washington responded, "I can't wait that long. I must hurry back to Fort Necessity to supervise the digging of trenches, and besides, I may be more vulnerable to attack here than on the road." As they departed, Washington exclaimed, "I understand your decision not to join in a battle at the fort, but you must remember that you are no longer a Scotsman. You are now an American."

While Washington collected his belongings and prepared to return to Fort Necessity, Angus filled a deerskin bag with enough jerky to last five days and gathered his muzzle-loader, powder horn, and bullet pouch. As usual, his hunting knife and tomahawk were held securely on his belt. Calling Schatto, who had been patiently lying on the front porch, he dashed down the road towards Great Meadows.

In his mind, the potential sites for an ambush could be quickly narrowed to three locations. Each site was strategically adjacent to a stream crossing where Washington would be most vulnerable. The wind was blowing out of the east, prompting Angus to focus on the west side of the road leading from Gist's to Great Meadows. At a hundred yards off the road, Angus kneeled and gently grasped Schatto's head in his hands to get her attention. She had learned that behavior from her pack leader meant a deliberate command was to follow, and she responded by staring intently into his eyes. Quietly, but firmly, Angus commanded, "Man search. Man search."

To strengthen her grasp of the command, he removed one hand from her head and repeated the command several times while grasping the bag with the blue stone. The two stalkers employed their now-familiar hunting technique, moving in tandem soundlessly among the giant tree trunks. On those rare occasions when Schatto appeared to be distracted by animal scent, Angus stopped, kneeled to face her, and repeated the "Man search" command. Schatto sought to please her leader and became totally focused once again.

A thorough search revealed nothing suspicious at the first stream crossing, and they proceeded cautiously to the second. Minutes later and several hundred yards away, Schatto displayed the first hints of detecting human scent. As Angus scanned the terrain along this next crossing, he was analyzing the site to determine where men were likely in position for an ambush. As covertly as a serpent slithering through grass, he dropped to the ground and belly-crawled to a small knoll where he could peruse both a dense clump of willow shrubbery along the stream bank and a nearby blown-down tree.

The afternoon breeze suddenly picked up and Schatto immediately dropped to her belly and began to inch imperceptibly forward. As her stalk became ever more pronounced, Angus was convinced that one or more men were at the crossing. Only a hawk flying overhead could have detected the two stalkers as they crawled to the base of one of the huge tulip poplar trees that dominated the forest. With a guiding hand on Schatto's back, Angus carefully surveyed the area near the stream for any sign of human presence.

A nearly imperceptible movement at the edge of the willows betrayed one man, although Angus could not identify him as Indian or French. He continued scanning the area and there crouched behind a blown-down tree was a second, and almost definitely a third shrouded behind the tree trunk of a large sycamore. In all probability more assailants were hidden behind other trees.

Angus knew that Washington would be coming along at any minute, and he must waste no time. But what action should he take? He was nearly one hundred yards from the road and the same distance behind the men. By the time he circled around the men and back to the road it might be too late to intercept Washington. He could fire his rifle to warn Washington, but he did not want to reveal his presence to the men waiting in ambush. Even if he fired his rifle would Washington realize the type of danger? Another option that was quickly considered—and rejected—was to send Schatto to warn Washington. Angus had never sent Schatto to another person, so what command could he use? She was fully aware of the men hiding in ambush, and would be reluctant to abandon her "Man search."

The only other alternative was to attack. Assuming there were only three adversaries, Angus felt that he and Schatto could handily overpower them. The closest man was hiding behind the fallen tree, while the farthest was behind the sycamore. Although he could not clearly distinguish the body of the man in the willows, he was confident that he could shoot him with his muzzle-loader. The only unknown variable was whether Schatto would comprehend and obey a word combination he had never given.

Slipping back behind the tree trunk, Angus held Schatto's head in his hand, and ordered, "Kill man. Kill man." She tilted her head in a quizzical way as she stared at Angus, so he repeated the command three more times. If she did not comprehend and her attack was not a total surprise, she could be the victim.

Repeating the "kill" command for the last time, Angus uttered, "Aye, aye" while gently pushing her forward. Schatto must have processed the intent of the command, because she began a slow belly-dragging crawl towards the closest man, an Indian. The target was clearly visible to Angus, but Schatto did not identify his crouched outline as that of a man. His scent, however, pulled her toward him, just as surely as if she could see him.

Angus cautiously positioned himself so that he could steady his rifle barrel against the tree trunk, took aim at the man in the willows, and waited patiently as Schatto advanced. Closing the distance to forty yards, Schatto identified the Indian's outline and crouched even lower to the ground. Angus telepathically repeated the "Kill man" command several times. She would continue to crawl within ten yards, and then launch her attack. As soon as she struck her target he would take out the man hiding in the willows. The fate of the third man would depend on the outcome of the attacks on the other two.

Angus had an open view through the woods of the road approaching the stream crossing, and nervously glanced towards it to determine if Washington was near. As Schatto crept undetected in readiness to launch her attack, Angus caught a faint glimpse of the Virginian in the distance. He would shortly be less than a hundred yards from the stream, and an easy target for a muzzle-loader. Angus was confident, however, that the three men carried muskets, not muzzle-loaders, and would hold their fire until Washington was fifty yards away.

Schatto suddenly erupted from her crouch, like a rattlesnake striking its prey, and in two powerful bounds reached the Indian. The deep growl roaring from her throat terrified him, but before he could swing his musket in her direction, long canines sank deeply into his shoulder. Her attack caused him to drop his musket, and before he could draw his tomahawk she had knocked him to the ground. A loud scream from the Indian caused the man in the willows to turn and expose himself, and as he did Angus settled the muzzle-loader's sights on the man's chest and firmly squeezed the trigger. While the man in the willows crumpled to the ground, Angus hurriedly reloaded.

Schatto's powerful jaws, capable of breaking the leg bone of a deer, shattered the shrieking Indian's arm and then sank into his neck. Even though a violent shudder coursed through the Indian's body as he took his last breath, a tenacious Schatto continued her vicious attack. At the resounding explosion of the muzzle-loader, Washington quickly jumped off the road to gain protection from the closest tree trunk.

The opportunity to fire at Washington was lost, and now the third man stepped back to see what had happened to his two companions. Unable to glimpse either of them, he hesitated a moment too long. Angus was ready and lined the sights of his muzzle-loader on the man's chest. The exploding powder sent the deadly lead ball spiraling, and within seconds the third man was lying on the ground.

Angus could do nothing except wait and see if any other men waited in ambush. A startled Washington had clearly heard the two shots, but he could see no one, including Angus. As they waited anxiously for some indication of what to do next, Schatto ended her attack. Her victim was lifeless, and she proceeded to lick the blood that flowed from his deep wounds. After a wait of nearly ten minutes, Angus concluded there were no other ambushers, and firmly called, "Come, Schatto. Come." With the fight apparently ended, Angus pulled the wolf to his chest and held her tightly with one hand while caressing her majestic head with the other. To show her love for her pack leader, Schatto licked his face while wriggling with joy.

After waiting ten more minutes, during which time no man-made sounds broke the silence of the forest, Angus shouted, "George! George Washington!"

In response, he heard, "Angus? Is that you, Angus?"

With Schatto at heel, Angus cautiously moved through the forest towards Washington. A few minutes later Angus related the details of the encounter. Without elaborating, he stated, "Three men were waiting to ambush you. I shot two of them and Schatto killed the third." Washington appeared shaken and said nothing. A quick examination of the three men revealed that two were French and one was an Indian. There was no time to bury them without jeopardizing their safety, so Washington and Angus gathered their muskets and hurried down the road to Great Meadows.

At the sight of Great Meadows, Angus hastily bid Washington farewell. Washington firmly shook his hand, gave Schatto an affectionate pat on the head, and looked Angus in the eye as he declared, "I shall never forget what you did. You two saved my life."

Washington hurried on to Great Meadows where he inspected the digging of trenches and the strengthening of fort walls. Unfortunately, he never had the opportunity to complete a fort that could be successfully defended. A force of 600 French and 100 Indians took up positions in the woods around the fort on July 3.

The "charming field for an encounter," that Washington had chosen as the site of his fort, was not so favorable as he had first concluded. Heavy rains flooded the marshy ground and filled the trenches where Washington had planned to position his troops. With the French forces strategically situated behind trees around the open field, and their Indian allies hidden in the tall grasses and shrubs nearer the fort, fierce fighting was underway by midday.

Angus had secreted himself on a prominent overlook to the east of the fort, a vista through which all aspects of the battle were crystal clear. He was shocked to see that Fort Necessity sat prominently within the fifty-acre tract that he had previously claimed with tomahawk rights. He wondered, "Will my conflicts with the English never end? First they forced my family from our lands in Scotland, and now they have forced me from the land I claimed in America."

Far enough behind the French lines to avoid detection, Angus watched in misery as the fighting continued throughout the day. The partially completed fort was much too small to contain the English troops, forcing most to fight from water-filled trenches. His allegiance and passions were tested as the Indian allies of the French methodically killed all English horses and cows that were feeding around the fort.

Once again Angus suffered torn emotions. While he felt no loyalty to the French, the sight of English troops in their red uniforms evoked the suffering they had inflicted upon the Scottish. He reminded himself that Washington and most of the troops defending the fort were colonists and not English soldiers.

Unable to assess the losses suffered by either side, Angus was caught off guard when all firing stopped shortly before dark. In the evening twilight, made even dimmer by the falling rain, Angus beheld a meeting of English and French leaders outside the fort. It became apparent that a truce had been called. If so, it could only occur because the English were being soundly defeated. Had the French suffered major casualties, they would have quietly retreated into the surrounding forest as darkness fell. Angus wondered if Colonel Washington had survived the nearly constant rain of arrows and musket bullets that fell throughout the day.

Rains stopped during the night, and the next morning when Angus crawled from under his shelter beneath a fallen white oak, he was surprised to see English soldiers leaving the fort. While French soldiers looked on, the English followed the road southward to Wills Creek. Obviously the English had surrendered. Dozens of Indians were moving through the grasses and sedges along each of the trenches that surrounded the fort.

While Angus was too far away to see details, he noted that many of the Indians gradually amassed armloads of clothing and other items. Whether they were looting the dead or wounded English soldiers he could not determine. The scalping on Laurel Mountain was still vividly imprinted in his mind, and Angus did not want to see—or know—the details. He would learn later that thirty English were killed and seventy wounded. Only three French were killed.

Late that afternoon, after all the English had departed, Angus watched as the French pulled the English swivel guns out of the fort and hauled them towards the Monongahela. As dozens of hungry turkey vultures soared over the Great Meadows, fires began to appear throughout the fort. The bodies of horses and cows—and humans—would feed scavengers for many days.

As the blazes grew higher and dense smoke billowed into the sky, the inevitable was obvious—the French were burning the fort.

Angus recalled his mother proclaiming, "Even the longest day has an end."

July 4, 1754, ended with the English suffering a second grave setback at the hands of the French. Fort Prince George at the Forks of the Ohio was the first to be captured and burned, and now Fort Necessity at the Great Meadows was a casualty.

With Schatto at his side, Angus turned his moccasins in the direction of Gist's Plantation. He would retrieve Night Fog and head west to the Monongahela. After a visit with the Dunkards, and hopefully another of Katrina's pies, he would then embark on his next adventure. As he padded softly through the wilderness, his thoughts returned to the English and George Washington, the leader he now considered a friend. As he contemplated whether the Virginian had survived the battle, Angus pondered the man's destiny and weighed the meaning of the profound words that echoed tirelessly; "You are now an American."

EPILOGUE

A<small>S</small> A<small>NGUS</small> M<small>C</small>C<small>ALLANDER</small> <small>PONDERED</small> his immediate future, the relative calm that blanketed the Monongahela region was ending. The French had originally claimed the River Ohio and its tributaries (including the Allegheny and Monongahela) by virtue of its discovery by Sier de la Salle (La Salle). Because the Ohio River was a vital link between Montreal and Louisiana, another region the French claimed through discovery, their government was convinced that their future in America was in jeopardy. At the same time, the English realized that the western expansion of the American Colonies would be seriously restricted if the Ohio River Valley was governed by the French. Major conflict between the two European powers was imminent.

During the early 1700s, the French had extended their dominance westward along the St. Lawrence waterway from Montreal through Lake Ontario and on to Lake Erie. While forcing out the English traders, the French extended their claims to include the tributaries of the Ohio River. Defeat of the English at the Forks of the Ohio and at Fort Necessity in 1754 convinced all concerned that the struggles for the Ohio River country would be long and difficult. Thus began the French and Indian War.

All persons living in or traveling through the Allegheny and Monongahela regions would be directly affected by this war. Thousands would die and all would have their lives changed forever. Although the battle directly engaged the French and English, it would have a more direct impact on the Native American Indians who made their homes in the region. Both England and France acknowledged that they could not win the war without the aid of the Indians, and each began a vigorous campaign to enlist the aid of the strongest tribes.

In April 1755, General Braddock was ordered to lead his troops to Fort Cumberland (built earlier that year), then continue northwest to the Forks of the Ohio. The road to Fort Duquesne, which followed Nemacolin Trail, was widened and improved to within eight miles of the fort. However, before General Braddock and his troops reached the fort, a battle ensued. Thirteen hundred English soldiers were soundly defeated by six hundred French and Indians. Over two-thirds of the English soldiers were killed, and General Braddock died during the retreat. George Washington served under Braddock during this campaign and survived uninjured.

As a result of that battle and several others, the French gained control of the Allegheny and Monongahela region until 1758, when General John Forbes and his English regiment, including Colonel George Washington, attacked Fort Duquesne. Overwhelmed by legions of English, the French burned the fort, retreated, and abandoned their claim to the region. Numerous battles followed, some as far west as Detroit, until the war ended in 1763.

Conflicts in the Appalachians, however, accelerated during the remainder of the eighteenth century. Thousands of colonists and newly arrived Europeans, including settlers, explorers, hunters, trappers, and traders, were killed in confrontations with the Indians. While the invading Germans, Dutch, Swiss, Scots, and Irish were temporarily delayed in their attempts to settle the Appalachian region, the Indian cultures that had dominated the region for thousands of years were destroyed by the incursions of Europeans and their infectious diseases.

Along with the demise of the Indians, a similar fate would befall frontiersmen. Trailblazers such as Angus McCallander would be forced to move westward in an attempt to preserve their way of life; conceding that future travelers through the eastern forests would never again walk in the hoof prints of elk and buffalo; awaken to the howls of wolves and the screams of mountain lions; or view the tree tops buffeted by flocks of passenger pigeons too numerous to count. The vast and magnificent Appalachian wilderness eventually became settled, as we all know. But it would have taken much longer had it not been for men such as Washington and McCallander, and a wolf named Schatto.

CHRONOLOGY OF MAJOR EVENTS INVOLVING THE MONONGAHELA/POTOMAC REGION DURING THE EIGHTEENTH CENTURY

1681 Pennsylvania was granted to William Penn.

Early 1700s The large Shawaneese village (Shawnee Oldtown) present along the banks of the North Branch of the Potomac was abandoned.

1723/24 Jacques Cheathe, a French Huguenot from Quebec, was granted free rights to hunt/fish/trap/trade with the Cherokee Indian Elk Clan in northwestern Virginia. He constructed a temporary French trading post at mouth of Cheat River, close to Point Marion, PA.

1737 The name "Monongahela," meaning river of falling banks, first appeared on a map.

1740 Thomas Cresap erected a house, a small fortress, and a trading post at abandoned site of Shawnee Oldtown; presently Old Town, Maryland.

1742 The birth of a son (Michael) to Thomas Cresap was the first white child born in the area.

1748 The Ohio Company of Virginia was granted 200,000 acres by the British Crown, plus an additional 300,000 acres if they were successful in building a fort at the Forks of the Ohio (Allegheny and Monongahela rivers join to form Ohio) and in convincing at least 200 families to settle on their tract.

1750 The Ohio Company built a trading post along the south bank of the North Branch of the Potomac, opposite the mouth of Wills Creek, at present location of Cumberland, Maryland.

1751 The first "European" settlement was established in western Pennsylvania/Virginia. Wendell Brown and three sons came to Provance Bottom, between New Geneva and Masontown.

1751 The Ohio Company hired Thomas Cresap and Nemacolin to survey a route leading from Wills Creek to the Monongahela River.

1751/52 The French built Fort Presque Isle along Lake Erie and Fort Le Boeuf some miles south of Lake Erie.

1752 Christopher Gist's plantation was built between present location of Connellsville and Uniontown, Pennsylvania.

1752 The first families were sent westward by the Ohio Company.

1753 John Frazier's trading post was established at the junction of Turtle Creek and the Monongahela River.

1753 A sawmill was constructed at the Thomas Cresap settlement, greatly reducing time required to convert rough logs into boards.

1753 Governor Dinwiddie of Virginia sent an eight-man expedition under the command of George Washington to warn the French to withdraw from Fort Presque Isle and Fort Le Boeuf.

1753-54 The Ohio Company Trading Post complex at Wills Creek was enlarged to include a family residence, storage cellars, kitchen, stables, and a meat house.

1754 (January) Governor Dinwiddie sent a small group of Virginia soldiers to build a fort at the Forks of the Ohio, present site of Pittsburgh. This fort was alternately called Fort Prince George and Captain William Trent's Fort.

1754 (February) The French drove off the Colonists and expanded the English structures into a larger fort, called Fort Duquesne, at the Forks of the Ohio.

1754 (May/June) Lieutenant Colonel George Washington, with a regiment of Virginia frontiersmen, hastily constructed Fort Necessity at Great Meadows, southeast of Uniontown, Pennsylvania.

1754 (July) Six hundred French soldiers, aided by 100 Indians, attacked the British at Fort Necessity and forced them to surrender. After George Washington and the British troops left for Wills Creek, the French burned Fort Necessity. This was the start of the French and Indian War. The alliance of French military and Native Americans temporarily repelled the advance of English claims to land west of the Alleghenies.

1755 Fort Cumberland was constructed by the British government across the Potomac River from Wills Creek, at present site of Cumberland, Maryland.

1755 (July) Major General Edward Braddock and 1,300 troops marched towards Fort Duquesne, but they were attacked by a force of 600 French and Indians. Two-thirds of the British troops were killed or wounded, and General Braddock died during retreat.

1758 Fort Raystown was constructed at present site of Bedford, PA, and one year later was renamed Fort Bedford.

1758 General John Forbes marched against Fort Duquesne, but the French burned it prior to retreating. The Forks of the Ohio were now British territory.

1759-1761 Fort Pitt was constructed by British at the former site of Fort Duquesne at the Forks of the Ohio.

1763 French and Indian War ended with the destruction of French strongholds in North America.

CHARACTERS

THE FOLLOWING PERSONS are real-life individuals who lived at the time of the novel. All others mentioned in the novel are fictional.

Queen Alliquippa The matriarchal leader of a small band of Mohawks who lived along the Monongahela River, near the Forks of Ohio.

Jacob Van Braam A translator who accompanied George Washington when he warned the French along the Allegheny River to vacate the Ohio Valley.

Thomas Cresap A trader living at Oldtown, along the Potomac River.

Hannah Cresap The wife of Thomas Cresap.

Dan Cresap The son of Thomas Cresap.

Michael Cresap The son of Thomas Cresap and first non-Indian born west of the Appalachian Mountains.

Sarah Cresap The daughter of Thomas Cresap.

William Douglas Duke of Cumberland The English lord who led the English army to a victory over Prince Charles at the Battle of Culloden.

Barnaby Curran An explorer who accompanied George Washington when he warned the French along the Allegheny River to vacate the Ohio Valley.

Adam Deterer A gunsmith who built muzzle-loaders at Lancaster, PA.

Governor Dinwiddie The Governor of the Maryland Colony.

Samuel Eckerlin A trader who operated a trading post with James LeTorte along the Monongahela River, at the mouth of the Cheat River, the current site of Point Marion, PA.

Benjamin Franklin A politician, businessman, inventor, and author who lived in Philadelphia.

John Frazier A trader who operated a trading post along the Monongahela near the mouth of the Youghiogheny.

Christopher Gist A trader employed by the Ohio Company who lived in the vicinity of the Youghiogheny River, near current site of Uniontown, PA.

Nathaniel Gist The son of Christopher Gist.

Henery Gumpf A gunsmith who built muzzle-loaders at Lancaster, PA.

William Jenkins A frontiersman who accompanied George Washington when he warned the French along the Allegheny River to vacate the Ohio Valley.

Monsieur LaForce The French commander assigned to Fort Duquesne whose troops were defeated by George Washington during a surprise attack at Laurel Mountain, Pennsylvania.

James LeTorte A trader who operated a trading post with Samuel Eckerlin along the Monongahela River, at the mouth of the Cheat River, the current site of Point Marion, PA.

Lonacona The son of Nemacolin.

John McQuire A frontiersman who accompanied George Washington when he warned the French along the Allegheny River to vacate the Ohio Valley.

Martin Meylin A gunsmith who built muzzle-loaders at Lancaster, PA.

Nemacolin A Delaware Chief who assisted Thomas Cresap in establishing the trail between Wills Creek (Cumberland, Maryland) and the Monongahela River.

Garret Pendergrass A trapper in the Raystown area, current site of Bedford, PA.

Peter Roesser A gunsmith who built muzzle-loaders at Lancaster, PA.

Henry Stewart A frontiersman who accompanied George Washington when he warned the French along the Allegheny River to vacate the Ohio Valley.

Prince Charles Edward Stuart The son of King James VIII of Scotland, who battled the English to regain the throne of England for the Stuart dynasty. Also known as "Bonnie Prince Charlie."

Tanacharisson A Seneca chief, commonly referred to as "Half King," who sided with the British in French and Indian War.

Captain William Trent A soldier sent by Governor Dinwiddie to build a fort at the Forks of Ohio.

Ensign Edward Ward A soldier who accompanied Captain Trent in building a fort at the Forks of Ohio. He was in charge of troops when the French attacked and forced him to surrender.

George Washington A surveyor/soldier sent by Governor Dinwiddie to warn the French to abandon the Ohio Valley. Later was the Lieutenant General defeated by the French at the Battle of Fort Necessity.

John Wray A trader who lived at Raystown, current site of Bedford, PA.

ABOUT THE AUTHOR

DR. MICHAEL IS A NATIVE West Virginian. He was born on Plum Run, near Mannington and Farmington, attended elementary school at Shinnston, and graduated from Magnolia High School in New Martinsville. He received a B.S. degree in Biology from Marietta College, and M.S. and Ph.D. degrees in Wildlife Ecology from Texas A&M University. After teaching six years at Stephen F. Austin State University, in Nacogdoches, Texas, Dr. Michael returned to his beloved state and taught at West Virginia University from 1970 through 1997. Following retirement from West Virginia University he was awarded the title of Professor Emeritus in 1998. He became a part-time resident of Canaan Valley and conducted numerous studies on movements and behavior of snapping turtles in that unique ecosystem. That research formed the basis for his historical novel, *A Valley Called Canaan: 1885-2002*. His forty-five-year career as a wildlife biologist produced more than one hundred publications, both scientific and popular. Dr. Michael continues to be an active outdoorsman and researcher, concentrating most of his efforts on wildlife of the Appalachian Mountains.